Other Books by Luke Smitherd:

Full-Length Novels:
The Physics of the Dead
The Stone Man: The Stone Man, Book One
The Empty Men: The Stone Man, Book Two
The Stone Giant: The Stone Man, Book Three
A Head Full of Knives
Weird. Dark.
How To Be a Vigilante: A Diary
Kill Someone
You See The Monster

Novellas
The Man on Table Ten
Hold On Until Your Fingers Break
My Name Is Mister Grief
He Waits
Do Anything
The Man with All the Answers

For an up to date list of Luke Smitherd's other books, YouTube clips, his podcast, and to sign up for the Spam-Free Book Release Mailing List, visit
www.lukesmitherd.com

It's coming for you. You can't stop it, and you know it.

—David Goggins

The scariest moment is always just before you start.

—Stephen King

How did it feel when it came alive and took you?

—Royal Blood,
"Out of the Black"

Dedication:

For everyone that's come this far on the Stone journey.
There's at least one more part to come after this.

Reviewer Acknowledgements:

At the time of writing, the following people wrote a nice Amazon or Audible review of my recent novel You See the Monster. Thank you very, very much. only using the names you put on your reviews, as these will be ones you're happy to have associated with my work (I hope). In alphabetical order they are:

BSM, Wrensense., ALP, Aaron David Howard, Adam R., Alex Lancaster, Amalia Hopkins, Amy H. RN, Andy Holden, Andy P, Ang Wallis, Angie, Angie Hackett (Stormageddon), Anna Banana, Anon66, Anthony, Anthony Duscio, B. Jed Gilmore, B. Schmitt, B.H., Barbara Pfieffer, BarbaraC, Becky, Becky Hinchcliff, Bethany Smith, Bev Carmody, Big Daddy, BigOrangeDave, Blanchepadgett, Book Thief, BorisTheBlade, BranWick, C, C. Murphy, C. Peart, Calico Pete, Carl W., Carol, Carrotpipe, Cats, Charloola, Chris Nash, Chris Wells, Chrissy Derriso, Clara R. Arechiga, Craig, Crows, D. Marie, DC Fitzgerald, DWJ, David Plank, Davie R, Dean Owen, Deborah Lewis, DemonViewLLC, Denise Corlett, Devlin, DobieChuck, Don, Dozy, Mare, Drac1968, Dylan Roach, Eddie Clinton, Eire, Eivind, Eli Gassert, Empress Jenni, Equestrian, Faith, G. Parlee, Gary H., Ged Byrne, Gemma Chapman, Gloria C., Grace W., Greg James, Hatty B-R, Hepcat89, Humble & Honest, J. Nickey, JC, James Farler, Jameson Skaife, Jason Austin, Jason Goldsmid, Jason Herbert, Jess, Jfmdac, Jim, Jinny, Joe Eardley, Judy Mackie, Julie Blaskie, Justin, Justin M., K. Edwin Fritz, Katof9tails, Katrina, Katy Costello, Keely Mcgill, Kemo, KendallRN, Kenton, Kerry Mutter, Kia, Kimberly Garner, L. Bailey Humphries, Ladybug567Green, Laurie Davenport,Lawrence, Leigh-Ann, Lionel, Lisa, Lisaly, Lmiller, M. J. Mercer, Mariah H, Mark, Mark Norman, MarnaK, Mary J Burke, Maryann, Max D. Kimble, Me, Michael, Michael Whale, Mike, Milking Badger, MissSweet, Morgan B. Gainor, Mr. J. M. Young. Mr. P.J. Whittaker, Mrs A Z McCarthy, Mrs. Snaylor, NM, Neal Bailey, Neil, Nick C., Nicola Wilson, P.S. Stephenson, Pat Hannigan, Paul, Paul Ashworth, Paul Hopkinson, Peter Jersey, Peter McDade, Pomadour, Princess, QueenTulip, R. G, RCC, RJL, Rachel Jane, Rebecca M., Rebecca Stevens, Revtopsy, Rob Pomroy, Ryalls-Clephane, Ryan P., S I HYMAS, S. L. Madden, Sara, Sarah H, Scott, Shadowfire5371, Shannon, Sharon McLachlan, Shawn Chappell, Shelly Udomon, Shinyglasscat, Shoe Diva, Simon Haine, Stephani Meyer, Stephanie Simmons, Stephen, Steve Pentleton, Stu, Super Dark!, Swanbrod, Swebby, Tash, Terry H, TerryF, Theasophia, Thomas Ohrbom, Tom Whitaker, Tracey Mclean, Tracy Vasile, TripleD, Trish, Twixton, Virginia J, VoodooGold, W. H. Doernbach, W. Michael Mahoney, Wakana, Wayne Hall, Wendy Crisp, Wonderforest, Zobo, Zoe Mckechnie, author., Jamie Greenwood, and Steve Blencowe.

*If you asked for a Smithereen title, check out the list after the afterword to see yours (as well as the opening chapter from my other recent hit novel **YOU SEE THE MONSTER!**)*

The Stone Man: Book Three

The Stone Giant

By Luke Smitherd

What Just Happened:

The Empty Men Recap

✱✱✱

Five years have passed since the Third Arrival.

During that time the British government has revealed its weapon—the **Chisel**—which ministers claim can destroy the Stone Men. In a press announcement, it's admitted that a **Stone Man** had been held in captivity, but was destroyed on the first test fire of the device.

Maria Constance, a woman who suffered a miscarriage after the stress of both a close encounter with the original Stone Man during the First Arrival and a vision of **Patrick Marshall** (the Stone Man's first Target), returns to the UK after years in self-imposed European exile. After her traumatic experiences led to the collapse of her marriage, her growing terror of the Stone Men returning meant she could no longer stay in the UK. Now she's back for her mother's funeral. The timing couldn't be worse: Maria is on a beach on the south coast just in time to witness the beginning of the *Fourth* Arrival. A giant, spectral figure appears on the horizon before disappearing and appearing as a much smaller, white, ethereal figure on the shore. These figures begin to appear all around the country, seemingly smaller each time as they split and multiply. The media dubs them **The Empty Men**. Maria's attempts to flee the country prove fruitless as planes departing the UK crash for unknown reasons, and passengers on cross-channel ferries to Europe jump inexplicably over the vessels' sides. Maria is stranded. She visits her former sister-in-law, **Ruth**, who confesses that she also had visions during the first three Arrivals. When the Empty Men reach Ruth's home, Maria watches helplessly as one of them kills Ruth. The Empty Man then turns towards Maria, who discovers that, under great stress, she can somehow mentally hide herself from its lethal influence.

Meanwhile **Eric Hatton**, Stone conspiracy theorist and brother of **Theresa Pettifer** (one of the victims of the Stone Men during the first three Arrivals, along with her infant son **Aaron Pettifer**), is drawn to another Stone Sensitive person in the ruins of **Coventry**: an old homeless man called **Harry Regis**. The pair observe the appearance of an enormous Stone-like structure that they nickname **The Prism**. Many of Coventry's remaining inhabitants fall into a zombie-like trance, walking towards the Prism and becoming aggressive if approached. Soldiers from the now partially flattened **Ground Zero** building attempt to move them on; the scene becomes violent, and Eric takes a graze from a bullet in the crossfire. Eric and Harry dub these people the **Shufflers**, and can find no indication of why they're behaving this way. A transparent wall of energy emanates from the Prism and disappears over the horizon, killing everyone in its path . . . except Eric, Harry and the Shufflers. The energy fills the air above them, seeming to surround the city. The Shufflers prevent Eric from getting into the remains of the Ground Zero building for answers, so the pair depart for Harry's nearby stash of supplies and first aid. While Harry stitches Eric's wounded shoulder, Eric confesses he has recordings of interviews from a facility at the **Ladybower**

Reservoir in Sheffield. The voice on the recordings is a civilian volunteer named **Linda Wyken**, a woman who appears to have low-level **Stone Sensitivity**, who talks about her experiences of **Paul Winter**, a powerful kind of Stone battery who can boost the abilities of Stone Sensitives. She also talks about a woman called **Sophie Warrender**, a very high-level Stone Sensitive. Eric and Harry sleep, but are woken by a vision of a bright light. They follow their Stone instincts until they find the source: an impenetrable swirling, golden bubble in a squatter's apartment overlooking Ground Zero. Trapped inside it is a young woman, **Jenny Driver**. Along the way they meet **John Bates**, a man who claims to have gone out to where the wall of energy—the **Barrier**—ends, just outside of the city, forming a now-impassable wall. John carelessly touches Jenny's bubble and is immediately vaporised. Eric realises that he can influence the bubble and tries to free Jenny. With great effort, he wills a small hole in it but can do no more than that. The hole snaps shut, perfectly slicing off Eric's hand and cauterising his wrist. Eric experiences no pain but passes out in shock.

Maria, fleeing a solid wall of Empty Men, runs into a mother and son, and manages to hide them all from the oncoming Empty Men using her Stone abilities. The mother flees with her child and Maria feels them leave her circle of influence; her abilities have limits. Maria is rescued by a woman on a motorcycle, and the pair escape. The woman reveals herself to be Linda Wyken, and tells Maria she is heading for **Project Orobouros** at the Ladybower Reservoir. She believes that if anyone can help, they will be there. She also tells Maria that the Chisel is a lie, knowledge she gained from her time at the project; the reason the Stone Man is no longer in the possession of the government is because Paul Winter—the Stone Man's last Target, used as bait for his pursuer for the last five years—seemingly died, something that sends the Stone Men back to their point of origin.

Eric comes to. Harry tells him that he used to be an artist and that his ex-wife and child are in Europe. He gives Eric the key to his lockup, saying it's full of paintings that will be worth money after his death, and he makes Eric promise to give them to his daughter if he gets out of Coventry. From Jenny's apartment, they watch as the Prism seems to summon the Shufflers into it, devouring them in the process as it absorbs them into itself. The path now clear, Eric and Harry enter what's left of the Ground Zero building, where Eric retrieves a gun from a dead guard and a box full of papers marked with names. It appears to be some kind of census, listing everyone in the UK under five categories: **CROW, TIN, LION, GALE,** and **DIGGS**. They also come across two dead, multi-limbed creatures. Before they can investigate further, they are drawn outside by the sudden appearance of hundreds of Empty Men at Ground Zero. An Empty Man attacks Harry.

At Project Orobouros, Maria meets Paul Winter, who is very much alive and says he wants to take Maria's hand so that he can 'boost' her. The scientist there, one **Doctor Holbrooks**, believes Maria's abilities could be useful in turning the tide against the Empty Men. Paul begins the boost, and Maria has an ecstatic experience, receiving a vision of the entire country and a sense of her own raw power. The force of it is so powerful that the electronics in the room explode and Paul is knocked to the floor. The process didn't quite complete and they will need to rest before trying again, but there's no time—the Empty Men, seemingly drawn to the energy generated by Paul and Maria's interaction, have arrived at Project Orobouros. Fleeing for a helicopter, along with Project soldiers **Binley, Fletchamstead** and **Edgwick**, as well as an unnamed man that Paul seems to know, they are surrounded by Empty Men. In a Hail Mary move,

Paul tries to boost Maria again and this time the process completes. Not only does she effortlessly hide the group, she is also drawn to an energy signal from Coventry.

Eric hears Maria's voice in his head and begs her to save Harry. She does so, remotely hiding Harry from the influence of the Empty Man engulfing him, and then tells Eric to head to the military's fallback position, a base on the Isle of Skye. Her signal fades in Eric's mind; Maria has collapsed, unconscious. Eric watches as Empty Men from around the country pour into the walls of the Prism, sinking into its surface much like the Shufflers before them. The Prism begins to shake, crumbling the remains of the Ground Zero building and flattening everything within. It then begins to send out a protrusion, one that deposits a pale, semi-transparent humanoid figure into the former Millennium Place.

It is a newborn Stone Man. Armed only with a pistol and a sledgehammer, Eric and Harry approach it . . .

Prologue

***

You could have broken it. I think we have to count our blessings here.

No, goodness no. He couldn't say that to her, not right now; in fact, maybe he should just say nothing. He wouldn't be able to truly reach her for the rest of the day after all. Save the ra-ra until tomorrow.

His own memories of that feeling—of that worst kind of losing *because you hadn't really done anything wrong*—came creeping from the crevices in his mind, pieces of unfinished business that had been shoved or filed away rather than wrestled into submission and released.

His hands lightly strangled the steering wheel. It was just such a damned shame.

Trevor chanced a side-eyed glance at the passenger seat; he didn't want his daughter to know he was looking. She was staring out of the window, her phone held to her ear by her uncovered left hand. The bandage on her right was only there for a little extra support; that was the limb which had broken her fall. The bigger injury—the twisted-but-fortunately-not-torn ankle ligament—was out of sight in the footwell.

"No ... no, I know," Sophie said. Her monotone revealed nothing. Whatever Joe was saying on the other end of the line, Sophie wasn't listening. Trevor had a feeling Joe was giving the exact kind of platitudes Trevor had just talked himself out of. "Yeah," Sophie said. "Yeah, I know. I know." Joe was Sophie's closest training partner, even if he didn't compete. He couldn't come to support her today though; the UK qualifier for the Games in Wisconsin was smack in the middle of peak season for Joe's business. But he'd been texting and calling all day for updates and offering support, especially since Sophie's day had ended the way it had. "It happens," Sophie was saying quietly. "We've seen it happen. Had to be me sooner or later."

Sophie hadn't discovered CrossFit until her early thirties, still relatively young. *And those Warrender genes don't hurt*, Trevor thought, full of pride yet again on a day spent bursting with it ... then the memory of Sophie's pain lanced through him once more. *Ouch.*

A sneeze. A bloody *sneeze.* You couldn't train for that.

Helpfully arriving at exactly the wrong time, when in exactly the wrong position. Ninety-nine times out of a hundred she'd have continued without issue. Except this time was the freak show, the lightning strike, that perfect pisser of a confluence of biomechanical auto-responses all conspiring to make Sophie Warrender's right foot spasm perfectly incorrectly as it landed the eleventh of fifteen burpee box jumpovers.

They hadn't had a chance to talk about it much since it happened. Sophie—tall and blonde and (Trevor would daresay, but then he was of course biased) impressive, a lifelong athlete perhaps finally discovering her truest calling—had gone down with a brief, pained bark. She was immediately surrounded by her team, Trevor, and the event doctors. Sophie, ever the stoic, had gritted her teeth and taken Trevor's outstretched hand without looking as she listened silently to the doctors telling her what she already knew: her competition was over.

She'd prepared for this for a year, and Trevor had been there throughout, even if he didn't understand CrossFit at all. Tennis had always been his thing. He'd even turned briefly professional, as in played-in-a-few-majors good, if not quite elite enough to make a noise in the later stages. But if Sophie was into CrossFit, he would become the world's biggest CrossFit supporter; he went to every one of Sophie's contests and even helped coach her diet regime. "Trevor," Joe had once said, "when my Dad found out I was gay, he beat me with my own drumsticks. Can you imagine that? Two of the things you love most in all the world and one of them is using the other to play *Good Times Bad Times* on yer arse. You? You're always here, screaming your head off, cheering for the Ice Queen. You make me want to puke, old man." Trevor had laughed and not said in return what he was thinking: *she thinks I judge her if she doesn't win things, Joe. I don't know where that comes from. I've always given her my love so freely.* What he'd said was: "Gotta cheer for the Queen, right Joe?"

The Ice Queen. The affectionate nickname had to be accurate, because her separate social groups at the gym and the clinic both called her the same; she never even got upset when she had to put a pet down or deliver bad news to owners. She wasn't particularly alone in that, but apparently *all* of them had to break and shed a tear now and then. Never Sophie, never at work. *It's work*, she would complain to Trevor. *Of course I care. I just don't get why I'm supposed to be weird if I get on with things. It's not my fault if they're not professional.*

"Thanks," Sophie said into the phone. "Speak to you later." She hung up.

"Joe?" Trevor asked.

"Yeah, Joe. Good old Joe ..." She sighed and checked her phone. "Lotsa messages coming in. I guess everyone from the gym heard already."

"How are you feeling?" He knew the answer—winced in preparation to hear it—but asking was caring. She looked out of the window again, finally beginning to unleash her long hair from its tight pony tail.

"Actually, " she said, "... I'm okay."

"You are?"

"Mm."

"That's ... really good to hear, sweetheart," Trevor said, surprised. "Really good to hear. You were so quiet on the way to the car—"

"I was just ... you know. Processing." She turned to face him now with a gentle smile. "I'm okay. Really." He reached out a hand to her again, a gesture full of pride, and as she took it his fingers wrapped around hers and *squeezed* that pride into her. "I ... I think I'm *better* than okay, actually. I think ..." she grinned. "I think I'm delighted."

Her grin was infectious. Trevor returned it, happy but confused.

"Well then I am too," he chuckled. "But you have to fill me in on this one 'cos I'm dying to hear it."

"Did you see me up there?"

"I did."

"How did I look?"

Trevor saw it: Sophie the lithe but muscular specimen, not as built as some of the girls there but possessing a clear power, speed and technique in her movements. She'd clearly paid her dues.

"You looked *deadly*."

"Uh-huh. That's how I felt." She looked out the windscreen. "All I wanted was to feel—to know—that I really belonged there. And what I found was not only that I absolutely *did*, but that my numbers, for as long as they lasted as least, were contenders. Do you know how *that* makes me feel?"

"Delighted, I believe was the term Her Highness used," Trevor smiled.

"So I sneezed," Sophie said, chuckling. "Yeah, it ruined everything I've slaved at for a year. Okay. But you know what?" She raised a finger and held it up for Trevor, smiling. He loved this. He held up his finger, honouring the ritual.

"Why *no*, Sophie, what do I *need* to know?"

She winked.

"I'll tell you what you NEED to know." It was a term Sophie's former boss had used, one Sophie had jokingly brought home while she was still living with Trevor and Janet. Before Janet died. He often remembered those days as the happiest of his life, certainly since Sophie was little. "*Fuck* it," Sophie said. "That's what. I wasn't nervous, I performed great under pressure, the numbers were right up there with my best ... I *showed up*." She folded her arms and shrugged. "I didn't want it to end this way. But most importantly, I got what I wanted. So roll on next year. I'll be ready." She grinned, but then her brow furrowed at something in his expression, though she was still smiling. "What?"

"I. Am so. *Proud*. Of you."

"*Daaad ...*" She leaned over and kissed him on the cheek. "Thank you."

"Oh, no need to thank me, I'm just a silly old sod, what do I know ..."

"*Daaaaad ...*"

"No, no, I'm just gonna . . . turn the radio onto . . . Radio Four here . . ."

Both of them were grinning. He turned on the stereo. A political panel show was starting.

"Yep . . . this is it . . . this is the stuff for me . . . this is what gets me excited . . ."

"Dad!" Sophie laughed.

"Mm-hmm. Interesting . . . A discussion on Churchill's legacy . . . *fasc*inating . . . this is what really floats my old man boat . . ."

"Right, stop it, silly—"

The radio suddenly shrieked.

It wasn't the usual staccato digital breakup that happened on many a long drive. This was a long, drawn out, high-pitched needle scratch that *yelped* out of the radio, and then there was silence.

"Hmm," Trevor said, still smirking. "I guess even they couldn't stand to listen to—"

If Sophie hadn't been looking in the rearview mirror, she wouldn't have seen it; as it was, the road was also at an incline and so she had a long and clear view of the traffic behind them. It was a day of confluence, certainly; in this manner she saw the grey Audi A3 fifteen cars back suddenly jackknife sharply and collide with the Toyota to its right.

BANG. (Bang-bang . . . screech, bang.)

There had been no visible outside influence, no emerging *ploof* of dust and rubber to suggest a tyre had suddenly blown and caused the crash.

"Jesus!" Sophie gasped. "Did you see that? Ten seconds slower and we'd have been *in* that!"

She looked at her father for some comment, some dry observation. None came. He looked as if he was trying to remember if he'd left the gas on.

"Dad? Did you not see that?"

"Merrrrm."

". . . Dad?"

Trevor's eyes rolled up into their sockets. His hands fell limply off the steering wheel and into his lap.

"*Dad!*"

His body began to twitch. The car was already veering into the left-hand lane—

As Sophie lunged for the steering wheel her seatbelt snapped tight against her chest, keeping her in her seat. She still managed to correct the car's progress—"Dad! Dad!"—but her father was still having a stroke and they were still doing seventy.

"Dad! Hold on!"

Seventy, turn off the cruise control—

"Jesus!" She managed to thumb off the cruise control button, her hands shaking violently, and had the wherewithal to turn on the hazards; maybe that could clear them some space—

Let them know, let them know, you have to stop and he has to get help—

Trevor was twitching more and more in his seat and spittle was beginning to run out of the left side of his face where his head lolled sideways.

"Dad! Dad . . . it's . . ."

The car was only just starting to slow; the handbrake? No, still too fast! She couldn't reach the foot brake with her arm, the seatbelt was stopping her—

Frantic, her gaze snapped from her drooling father to the road through the windscreen, the edges of her vision starting to grey as she fumbled for the seatbelt catch. *What the hell is that, that's panic and we don't—*

She was aware of her hand involuntarily clenching into a fist—mercifully, she would later think, as a second more and that hand would have undone her seatbelt—and the way her stomach was curling inward as her legs tightened painfully of their own accord and lifted her knees towards her face, unbidden, before all sight of her father and the road ahead disappeared, replaced by darkness.

Darkness with a blurring, whirling mass at its centre.

She couldn't breathe.

Oh my God. We crashed. I'm dead. This is death.

Then the whirlwind clarified and became the face of a middle-aged man, one she didn't recognise.

A man with blond hair.

Who is . . . what . . .

She heard a car's horn blaring, the screech of tyres, and then a deafening bang. Even in the darkness, she felt a devastating force stun its way through the metal around her as the car turned, raised onto one side, and then nothing, as a different darkness took her.

***

"Sophie . . . *Warrender?*"

Christ, not now—

Chill out, she told herself, *they saved your life so don't start being a bitch just because you're being called away from the TV.* That said, not only were *everyone's* emotions all over the place—everyone in the country, not just those in the hospital waiting room—but she'd also had a near-death experience to add a little mustard onto what was already a nerve-shattering day.

"*Yes,* yes," she said, standing up. "That's me."

The pale-faced nurse, white even for a white woman and around Sophie's age, gave a weak smile. Perhaps the woman's skin wasn't normally that pallid; the faces of everyone else in the building, patients to staff, had a similar sheen. *And they're still working as hard as ever,* Sophie thought, her self-pity for her own injuries—now upgraded to a broken arm and a fractured collarbone, both down the left-hand side, maladies that *were* finally too much for her to disregard with positivity right now— reducing slightly. She'd thought she was tough, but compared to these folks . . .

"This way, please."

Sophie already knew her father was okay—she'd been told that when she'd come around herself—and had been stabilised. She gave a final glance at the TV on the wall as she left the seating area. None of the other silently-watching people present had even looked round when her name was called out. They stared at the screen, immobile and transfixed in horror, a room full of silent zombies held in the TV's thrall. She couldn't blame them.

"Your father's awake," the nurse said, confirming Sophie's assumption. "He's asking for you."

"Great," Sophie said, falling into step. "Does he know about . . . ?"

"*No,*" the nurse said, quietly but firmly. "No one on his ward does yet and visitors are under strict instructions to keep it that way for now, please. No excitement."

"Of course."

The nurse's eyes darted for a moment. Just before they reached the entrance to the ward, she added in a conspiratorial whisper, "I have to confess ... I am rather excited about it all myself, personally. I mean ... what *is* that thing?"

Sophie just nodded. Everyone in the country—everyone on the *planet*—was thinking the same thing right now.

The world had changed forever in the space of a few hours. The car crash had been just a symptom of that. *And we're so far away from Coventry*, she thought, *what does that mean for—*

"Mm," she said, not wanting to respond to the nurse's pointless question, thinking: *see if you feel that way tomorrow, Nursie. How* excited *will you be when that thing's still going and it's within fifty miles of this place?*

Sophie had been seeing the blond-haired man in her head all morning. She didn't feel excited at all. She was terrified, and the painkillers were only doing so much for her broken-and-reset bones.

They entered her father's ward. The air was clean but oppressive, just on the wrong side of warm. The ward TV had a piece of paper on it saying OUT OF ORDER. Drawn-back dividing curtains hung on rails between the beds. Even the usually-unsettling sight— grown men lying next to strangers with their dignity removed—couldn't dampen her delight when her father's hazy, smiling, and above all *living* eyes fell upon her.

"Dad ..."

Trevor weakly raised his arms and Sophie ran over for a careful hug, mindful of his fragile condition and her own damaged limbs.

"Not your day, sweetheart," he said.

"We didn't die. This is a brilliant day."

"Should have stayed at home the second I realised the fridge was buggered. It was a sign. We could have used up the meat. Had a barbecue. No car crashes at barbecues."

"Eating all that barbecued pork and ribs over the years probably led to you-know-what today ..."

Trevor scowled, waved her away.

"Please ..."

"Actually," the nurse piped up, looking at the doctor's notes, "your father's blood pressure, BMI etc ... all good. Still quite the athlete, Mr Warrender?"

Trevor's weak smile turned into a beam. Sophie smirked. Getting recognised was always a boost to her father's ego. She watched him shine.

"Especially when it proves my food-Nazi daughter wrong," he said. He stared at the nurse quizzically. "Did I coach you?"

"My sister. Lizzie Parr."

"Of course. Lizzie Parr. *Excellent* backhand. Textbook. Could have gone far. Gave it up for ... I want to say *architect?*"

"Graphic designer."

"Drawing, still drawing. That's good."

"I'll tell her I saw you," the nurse said, smiling. "The Doctor will be coming round shortly. I'll leave you two to it." She left, and Trevor looked at Sophie, suddenly serious.

"We didn't hurt anyone else," he said earnestly. "I asked when I woke up. Is that true?"

"Yes, yes it is." It was.

"Then why is everyone being so evasive?"

"... how do you mean?"

He shrugged, shook his head. *I'm a silly old man*, the gesture said.

"There's something wrong. I can feel it. I've been in hospitals enough to know this is different. Everyone's tense like there's been a terror attack or something. I keep seeing staff whispering."

"Hmm," Sophie said. "That's strange." She wasn't lying, at least. That observed behaviour *could* be described as strange.

"Do you know anything?"

Sophie believed in rules. She'd been told them and agreed with the reasons for them, and so responded without hesitation even if lying to her father was painful; she was a daddy's girl through and through.

"No. I can ask if you like, see if anyone knows anything?"

"No, no. Probably just me. I'd definitely feel better for a Fanta, though. I asked if I can have one and they said yes. I believe they're in the *vending machine . . .*"

Sophie theatrically rolled her eyes and stood.

"I'm going, I'm going . . ." It was a good performance, belying the unbelievable tension in her head and, more worryingly, her body. She hesitated for a moment, the question behind her lips: *did you see anything today, Dad? Like I did? Or was it really just what they're saying, an extremely lucky, minimally-damaging stroke?*

To ask it would be to give credence to his concerns.

Once she was outside the ward, she half-ran back to the waiting area. The previous silence had been replaced by a low-level murmuring; some people had even stood up. Something was about to happen? One glance at the screen confirmed it, even if it made her now ever-present headache that little bit worse. Just *looking* at it hurt her.

Onscreen, what the media were calling *the Stone Man* walked, alone.

It was approaching an oak tree.

No one seemed to know who had coined the name, but this one really named itself. It looked like a very big man and it appeared to be made of stone. No-brainer. In the few hours that the Stone Man had been walking, no one had yet dared to claim, really *state*, that it was alien in origin, but it had been implied. It had to be. Look at it. *Look at it!* It was terrifying and magnificent all at the same time. Slow and implacable, magic in concept but inarguably solid and real to see in motion. Her heart rate doubled just at the sight of it walking, but right now it looked like it was about to do the kind of thing she had, so far, only heard about: destroy.

Alien or not, the word the news kept using was *arrival*. That meant alien, didn't it? That an alien had *arrived*? The one question they didn't ask was the one Sophie, and no doubt everyone else, kept asking themselves: what if more of these things turn up? She'd missed all the onscreen urban destruction that it had left in its wake as it apparently made its way out of Coventry, of all places. Wherever it had originally *arrived*, the Stone Man was currently in a field somewhere, as shown by the continuing aerial shot from the Sky News helicopter.

What you really want to see, her mind whispered, *is how it smashes things up. And that tree is going to be perfect.*

It wasn't just animal eagerness that made her so thrilled to finally see the Stone Man go to work; thinking that way temporarily took away the intense fear (knowledge) that even from miles away this thing was somehow putting pictures in *her* brain—

Onscreen, the oak tree was very old and very big, embedded in the middle of a hedge dividing the current field and the next.

"He's going to hit it," an old black woman in a tracksuit and trainers said, suddenly stating the obvious and making the hypertense Sophie jump. She hadn't noticed the elderly lady, seated on one of the metal seats in the row to Sophie's right.

"No," an overweight white man in an ugly short-sleeved shirt said from the other side of the room. "They're about to do a thing. They're going to stop it."

"They're going to what?" Sophie blurted.

"They're going to stop it," the man repeated. "They just said. Watch."

"*Shh!*" someone else hissed.

Everyone fell silent. It wasn't just anticipation. They all knew: *the world will never be the same after this. It can't be.*

The Stone Man was still going to hit that tree; it was only about ten feet away and closing. Would it punch through the wood, exploding the mighty oak into thousands of splinters, or would it just push the thing out of the way? But wait, there were cables in the grass; now she'd seen one she could suddenly see them all, a little neat network of lines—

BOOM-BA-BA-BA—

Everyone gasped. The image became obscured for a moment as a combination of atomised mud, smoke, detonated blasting caps and explosives filled the air. The Stone Man had been lost at the centre of it. One or two people even cheered.

"No chance," a smartly-dressed young Asian man with a bandaged hand muttered. "No chance in hell."

Sophie watched the dense smoke. The Stone Man couldn't be seen.

Maybe it is *the smoke*, she thought. *Maybe all that smoke is exploded stone.*

The top of the oak tree, visible above the cloud, suddenly jerked violently to the left, paused . . . and then started to fall.

The aerial shot began to track away from the smoke as the Stone Man emerged out of the other side of the dust cloud. It was completely undamaged. Sophie's hand went to her mouth involuntarily and she let out a little moan.

They couldn't stop it.

What did that mean?

She didn't realise she was walking towards the TV, lost in thought, her arms limp at her sides. Her eyes locked on the ever-marching Stone Man. The question came again:

What does that mean?

Sophie didn't know. She waited, staring. The Stone Man filled her gaze.

No. Now it was filling her mind.

She felt cold. Her legs felt hollow. The room around her suddenly felt *thick*, as if the air had turned into custard. Breathing was laborious. What had they done to the air conditioning, it was like trying—

She looked around, to see if anyone else was reacting. They weren't, all of them still entranced by the impossible magic occurring onscreen. How could they *not* feel it? Her hand went to her chest and she took a step backwards, trying to slow her breathing. This was a panic attack. She had to breathe slowly. She stood there for a few minutes, breathing steadily until she understood that this *wasn't* a panic attack . . . but the air was still—

No. It wasn't the air. It was a creeping, searching presence.

An unseen something was filling the room, as tangible to Sophie as the people around her.

It's that thing, the realisation as clear and irrefutable as the knowledge of the ground she stood upon. *It's . . . here too somehow, doing something . . .*

What was it doing? She'd never felt anything like—

She looked in horror at the Stone Man onscreen. No, she *hadn't* ever felt anything like this before. But that's what *that thing* was feeling, and she was somehow . . . picking up on it?

That's how it sees us, she thought. *Like a blind bat seeing the world through sonar.*

Without knowing what she was doing—or *how* she knew it— she felt for the Stone Man with her mind.

After the first probing effort to know which was the right direction, the rest was instinctive, like the movement towards the surface after being submerged—

"Ah!"

Now everyone in the waiting area turned to look at Sophie, responding to her sudden cry, but Sophie didn't care in the least.

Something had pushed her back.

She suddenly felt exposed, observed from above and all around, even though she was inside a building with concrete walls and steel—

It began to creep into her. A presence, something searching, *analysing*, examining the lie of the land to find out where—

Get out, she thought. *Get out.*

She hid, burrowing back and away in her mind. The sensation lessened; whatever attention she had drawn to herself began to move quickly away, rapidly crossing the room and heading *through* all the other blissfully unaware observers who were already re-glued to the TV. She let out her breath, grabbing the back of a nearby chair for support with a badly shaking hand. It wasn't over, though.

What the fuck was that?

It wasn't fully gone; she knew that. She didn't dare move in case it came back for her. It was still nearby, searching. Moving away, though.

Towards—

She reached the realisation only a second before the shouting started and she saw doctors running towards her father's ward. Sophie began to run too. As she flew down the hallway and burst into the ward, she saw the chaos: two nurses struggling with her dad's limbs, the other patients sitting up in their beds, looking on with concern. His eyes were white and spittle was flying from his mouth. Before Sophie even reached the bed she confirmed the fear that clamped her heart; she could feel that alien presence on him, digging into him, moving the internal furniture around and inspecting it with a cold, detached gaze. *What do we have here?* Her dad's body and brain, fragile and damaged as they now were, couldn't take it.

"*Let us work!*" one of the nurses barked at Sophie, trying to hold her back, but that simply wasn't going to happen; they didn't understand what needed to be done and Sophie was very strong. Sophie didn't consciously understand what needed to be done either, but this was all suddenly as instinctive and natural as a flower moving towards the sun. Without a word, Sophie wrapped her good right arm around the waist of the nurse trying to hold her back and—crying out against the pain down her left-hand side as her injured body protested—bodily lifted the woman off the floor. Sophie's cry turned into a shriek as the pain peaked but she would not be stopped, turning away from the bed and gently placing the nurse back down on the linoleum tiles. The other nurse was so shocked that she stopped what she was doing and backed away from the bed. Sophie flung herself across her dad's trembling chest, instinct grappling with whatever new awareness she had of the world, leading her to reach out with her mind to her father's like a lifeguard lunging a float forward to a distressed swimmer.

Something in Sophie's head went *click*.

Suddenly her and her father's minds were a circuit.

Her newfound senses became even clearer and she knew that whatever had visited them was there, lurking right in the middle of Warrenders' shared energy.

Oh ... my ... God ...

Her father was dying. She couldn't see whatever was rummaging through him, but she could sense it; they could sense each other. Her dad's energy, too—good God, his energy, everything he was, *right there*—and as she flexed the muscles of her mind she discovered that she could be a wall.

She could be his bodyguard.

GET. OUT.

There was resistance to the thought, to that effort; the presence had great interest in her father. *Great* interest ... and wait, she felt that interest turn to her, wondering about *her*, she was apparently even more—

Sophie felt for the shape of the intrusion in her brain, desperate, and felt an edge ... and *pushed*.

There was a faint but palpable sense of its surprise—perhaps even its pain as it tried to cling on—and then it was gone. The room was suddenly full of nothing but people, beds and machines once more. She'd sent it away, *how the hell had she done that*—

But her father was still fitting—

Sophie jumped up and turned to the nurse she'd just moved, who was angry but not about to say anything, given how easily she'd been lifted.

"I'm really sorry," Sophie gasped, "please, please carry on, help him—"

Sophie allowed herself to be pushed aside as the nurses got back to work.

Her hands flew to her face as she saw she was too late.

She might have removed the influence, but the results of its handiwork were now in motion, her father's body locked up and spasming. This wasn't another stroke, and her father wasn't an epileptic; his ageing, well-used and stroke-impacted body simply hadn't been able to handle the arrival and departure of whatever had come to inspect him. Sophie did something she rarely did: she started to cry.

Even as her father's eyes continued to roll back in their sockets for the second time that day and his body arched viciously on the bed, Sophie felt something turn over in her brain and realised that her father was still there, inside her head.

Dad?

The circuit they'd somehow formed was still active.

And he was trying to tell her something.

. . . Dad?

(. . .)

DAD?!

(don't)

That was him. She wanted to scream, to tell him to hold on, that she loved him, but she could feel the connection dropping and she didn't dare say anything back in case it broke forever. She bit into her fingers as tears streamed down her cheeks. She had to listen.

(don't)

(let)   *(them)*

(see)   *(you)*

Then the connection dropped away, and Sophie's tears turned into a scream.

***

Part One

ERIC AND HARRY

Chapter One

The Beatdown

***

The Pale Stone Man stood silently—of course—before them as Eric and Harry strode towards it.

"Big bastard," Harry muttered. Eric had to agree.

The washed-out colour of the latest Arrival was in stark contrast to the darkness of the Prism behind it. This Stone Man may have been small in comparison to the massive structure that had only just birthed it, but Eric was awestruck nevertheless. To be in its physical presence was to sense its sheer magic; like being in the midst of a movie come to life. A horror movie, of course; as they drew closer, Eric's sense of dread began to grow.

It waited for them just outside the Prism-ruined remains of the Ground Zero fence, facing slightly away from their angle of approach and appearing as if it simply had other things on its mind. Eric couldn't tell if it was exhaustion—all of his recent exertions and injuries were finally catching up to him—or intimidation sapping his anger, the Pale Stone Man seeming to grow larger as the gap between them closed.

"Hold on, Harry." Eric said, stopping a few feet away from it and trying to regain his breath as he took in the monster from this new, closer vantage point.

He had initially thought the thing to be more translucent than it actually was. Its predecessors had been completely opaque, as opaque as the Prism, and from Jenny's apartment the Pale Stone Man had looked as if it might have even been made of bloodless flesh. From close range, however, it was clear to see that the texture of its surface, at least, *was* that of the Prism, albeit a different colour. He realised that he could see a little way inside it, and this was what had created the illusion of flesh. Only just visible, perhaps an inch or so beneath the surface, there was a criss-crossing network of ... cables? Wires? *Something*, a faint, complex and almost endless red-and-black spider web that ran throughout the torso and seemed to head off into each limb, where the minimal translucency of its 'skin' ended. Circuits? No, that didn't seem right, it couldn't be mechanical—

It's a central nervous system, his brain helpfully threw up. *If it's a machine, it's an organic one. It's been made from—*

He shook that thought out of his head, looking up at the Prism in horror, remembering how it had eaten the Shufflers. Mickey.

"Do you think," Harry began, his free hand—the one not holding the sledgehammer—pointing at the Pale Stone Man, "it's awa—*Eric!*" Eric was drawing the pistol he'd found inside Ground Zero out of its holster and raising it towards the Pale Stone Man's head. Harry darted across and grabbed Eric's wrist. "What are you doing!"

"Get off, Harry," Eric said quietly. "I'm shooting it in the head." Harry didn't let go, swaying slightly on the spot. Eric wondered how long it would take Harry to fully sober up.

"What the hell are you trying to do?" Harry yelled. "Wake it up? Piss it off?"

"It's not going anywhere!" Eric said. "Look at it!"

Harry did.

"What are you talking about?" he asked, confused.

"It's bent at the *waist*, Harry," Eric snapped, yanking his arm free and lowering the pistol.

"So?"

"They don't start walking until they straighten up, everyone knows that. They never start walking straightaway. Never. We've got hours, maybe even longer. The process varied in length but it *always* took at *least* several hours." The Pale Stone Man continued to stand there, impassive and unimpressed. Eric felt as if it was tormenting him with its silence, standing slouched and uninterested.

"Okay, but let's at least . . . let's . . ." Harry said, blinking as he trailed off. *You're not going to be much help in the planning stakes right now, Harry*, Eric thought, smelling the booze on Harry's breath.

"What else do you think we should do?"

"I just don't want to . . . set if off . . ." Harry muttered, looking everywhere but at Eric. The penny dropped.

"It's . . . it's alright to be scared, Harry," Eric said kindly, breathing out.

"I'm not," Harry snapped, straightening up . . . but then instantly deflated, grinning sheepishly. "Yeah, I'm terrified," he chuckled nervously. He wiped his forehead with the arm of his shabby suit. He glanced at the Pale Stone Man and chuckled again, trying to wash away his confession. "If you came home and found him in bed with your Mrs, you'd tuck him in, eh?" His anxious smiled died on his face.

"I'm going to shoot it," Eric said. "I don't see what other options we have. It looks weak, don't you think? Not fully baked? Maybe this will work. We can use the hammer if you like, but I think the gun is going to be the better option, don't you?"

Harry shuffled on the spot.

"Yeah," he said. "Okay." He looked up at Jenny's apartment building. "Do you think it's here to—"

"Yes," Eric said. "I do. That's why I want to shoot it."

"At least back up a bit," Harry said. "If it wakes up after you shoot it, I don't think you want to be within—"

"Okay," Eric said, fiddling with the gun's safety switch. "You might want to cover your ears."

"Now? You're just going to do it?"

"Yeah."

"It doesn't look like stone, does it? More like flesh."

"Yes."

Eric backed up about ten feet. He raised the gun and sighted down the barrel directly at the Pale Stone Man's head, trying to get his hand to stop shaking. He never used to be a great shot with his BB replica, but at this range he didn't think he could miss. He raised his left stump as an afterthought and braced his right forearm against it for stability, even as his stitched-up left shoulder protested. He briefly looked at the stump where his left hand used to be. A crazy thought occurred to him: did he need to be worried about infection? He'd had his hand amputated by an edge that, as far as he was aware, no one on earth had ever seen before and no one had ever analysed. Potentially there was alien bacteria in his skin. What could it be doing to him if there was? It looked clean, cauterised, and as healthy as a hand that wasn't there could reasonably be expected to look. It didn't even hurt. *But you'll never play the guitar again—*

No point whatsoever in thinking about that now; not only useless, but too unbearably painful. If his old life, his old job as a musician was dead before the Fourth Arrival, the corpse of it had now been burnt to ashes and hammered into dust.

Harry stood almost immediately behind Eric with his fingers in his ears.

"Do it," Harry said.

Eric's finger tightened on the trigger, but he didn't pull it. What was it he'd heard in movies? *Squeeze, don't pull.*

His knuckle whitened.

What are you waiting for?

He was scared. What if Harry was right and they just woke it up? What if—

He pulled the trigger.

The noise was deafening in the midst of the silent arena formerly known as Millennium Place. Eric's hearing immediately turned into a non-stop *eeeeee* sound, but he didn't care about that because *the Pale Stone Man was falling backwards*, the bullet lodged in its newly-minted head.

The shot hadn't been perfect; he'd been aiming right between where its eyes should have been, but the bullet had almost missed the thing's head completely. As it was, it had entered the bottom half of Pale Stone Man's face on the right-hand side. Its head had snapped up and back with the impact and toppled its weight over its heels, pitching it towards the earth. It didn't bend; limbs loose, its torso remained firmly locked in its semi-upright position, frozen like a store mannequin as it tumbled to the ground with a thud. The sensation of impact that reached Eric's feet through the concrete was lighter than he expected; he'd barely felt anything at all.

"Oh my God!" Harry screamed with glee, audible over the ringing in Eric's ears. *"Haaa!"* He began to slap repeatedly at Eric's arm. *"It worked!"* Harry shrieked. *"We killed it! We killed it!"*

Eric lowered the gun, breathless and shaking. He'd just done something even the combined might of the British Army had been unable to do. He'd put down a Stone Man. He'd damaged it, too; the bullet could be seen lodged in its translucent flesh at the bottom of a shallow hole. The impact crater wasn't deep, not that much more than the length of the bullet itself, but he'd broken the surface of its skin.

It wasn't normal Stone Man skin though, was it? The old ones didn't look like that—

No. He'd put down a Stone Man. *He'd put down a—*

"Yeeeeahhhh!" Eric yelled, turning round to face Harry, who grabbed his shoulders and shook him back and forth. Eric was so delighted he even blocked out the pain of Harry gripping him directly on his shallow and recently-stitched bullet wound. "We did it Harry! We did it!"

"I can't believe that shit worked!" Harry yelled, reaching into his jacket for the hip flask, and for once Eric was all for it. They'd managed the impossible.

"I can't either!" Eric gasped, feeling giddy. "I thought it would just bounce—*shit!*"

Both men jumped as a blast of arctic cold hit them, skittering grit and dust around their feet. Harry froze, one arm inside his jacket like Napoleon.

Neither of them moved.

Eric watched Harry's face, the *eeeeeee* still ringing away in his ears like an urgent, clamouring alert of imminent and terrible danger. Harry's eyes were fixed on a point behind Eric, low down.

A minute passed.

Maybe . . . maybe it was—

A bass note began to sound.

Harry clapped a hand to his mouth as the wind blew with greater force, unheard over the cacophonous noise and the ringing in Eric's battered ears. This wasn't the Horns. This was a new sound. Eric wanted to turn around, but he couldn't bring himself to see what he knew to be happening. He closed his eyes.

A win, he thought, trying to cling on to the last of his strength. *Please, please, let us have this win—*

He heard a scrape and felt the movement behind him vibrate through the ground. He opened his eyes and turned around.

"Eric—"

It was getting to its feet. It didn't use its arms to push itself up; it just bent upright at the waist and stood. The wind swirled and Harry cried out in pain against the cold. Both men began to back away, eyes locked on the Pale Stone Man.

"Shoot it again!" Harry yelled.

Eric did.

BANG.

The gunshot rang out once more just as the wind and the bone-rattling noise stopped. This time the bullet took the Pale Stone Man in the upper left chest and the creature toppled backwards to the ground just as before, the freshly-fired slug now a shallow implant inside the area where the creature's pectoral muscle should be. Again, the only sound in that concrete arena was the ringing in Eric's ears, accompanied now by Harry's laboured breathing. They both flinched, waiting for the noise and the ice-cold air to come again.

It didn't, but the Pale Stone Man began to rise all the same.

"AGAI—" Harry screamed, but Eric was already stepping forward and firing, teeth gritted. This time the shot was almost perfect as he'd reduced the distance between himself and his target, the bullet landing square in the centre of the Pale Stone Man's head. It hadn't made it all the way up to its feet this time either, blasting backwards onto the deck from its sitting-up position. Eric continued to walk towards it, feeling the veins standing out on his neck and forehead. "Kill it!" Harry yelled, but Eric wasn't listening.

"DIE!" Eric screamed, moving within five feet of the Pale Stone Man and pulling the trigger again. "DIE!" *BANG.* "DIE!" *BANG.* He was standing directly over it now, all three of the bullets entering its face and stopping almost immediately below the surface of its skin. Harry was babbling something but Eric wasn't listening to anything other than the thoughts that rioted inside its head—

Twelve bullets in the magazine, six more shots—

Newborn or not, don't touch it, you know what happens to people that touch them—

Theresa—

FUCK YOU, DIE—

He paused for a moment, chest heaving, and pulled the trigger again as the Pale Stone Man began to sit up once more. *THUD.*

Eric let out a half-moan, half-sob as the Pale Stone Man sat up yet again with the exact same amount of ease as before.

"*STAY DOWN!*" Eric screamed, and emptied the rest of the clip into the Pale Stone Man's head. The world became muffled to Eric's ears as they were overcome by the deafening sonic force assailing them, but not so much that Eric couldn't hear the gun's *click* as its slide finally locked back, chamber and magazine empty. Eric's own ragged breathing mingled with Harry's. Harry said something Eric couldn't hear.

"My ... my ears," Eric said. "They're ringing." Harry moved closer and whispered again.

"I said *get back*, Eric," Harry said quietly, and by the time he'd finished that short sentence the Pale Stone Man was already in the upright seated position. Eric holstered the pistol with a shaking hand and did as Harry asked without a word. "Do we run?" Harry asked.

"I don't know," Eric replied. He put his hand and his stump on his head.

The Pale Stone Man got back to its feet.

"Do we still have some time?" Harry gasped. "Before it starts—"

"I thought so, but this one ... I don't know—"

The Pale Stone Man took a single step forward.

Both men leapt back about a foot. The creature didn't take another immediately; Eric felt something in the ground and looked down to see the concrete around the Pale Stone Man's front foot was starting to crack. It was pressing more of its weight forward, leaning more and more into the step for some reason before taking a second. Again, the ground didn't crack at first, but then slowly began to do so as the Pale Stone Man seemed to put more and more weight into its foot. What was this business of leaning into the steps like that? Was it ... calibrating itself?

The Pale Stone Man began to walk.

Eric flinched, dropping into a half-squat as instinct prepared him to flee. Part of his brain was telling him exactly what Harry had said: he'd pissed it off, and the first person the Pale Stone Man would be coming for was him. It walked straight ahead though, and it was immediately clear that its path was going to carry it harmlessly in between Eric and Harry; even in the whirlwind of his fear, Eric marvelled at the way it looked in motion. No creases in the material of its body, the network of whatever it was that could be seen just underneath its skin remaining perfectly spaced apart, like cobwebs encased in some dull, washed-out amber. The word came to him again: *magic.* Its footsteps cracked the paving stones with each step, every one a heavy thud that seemed to vibrate in Eric's spine, the madness of it sending Eric's into a wild spiral:

How is that possible, it wasn't heavy enough a moment ago—

You saw the original stop itself from being picked up by helicopters like everyone else, XXXhis is nothing new—

He was suddenly delirious as the majesty of the Pale Stone Man passed by.

"*Look! Look!*" Harry yelled, pointing, but Eric didn't need to look. The thing's destination was clear. Its path was perfectly aligned with the St Joseph building.

Jenny.

But even the gun had been useless; the bullets to prove it were all wedged firmly yet utterly harmlessly inside the monster that was now bearing down on Jenny's building. And if that couldn't do anything—

Eric snapped out of his stunned funk as his drunk friend, clearly having already reached the same conclusion, charged up behind the disappearing Stone Man. Harry overhead-swung the sledgehammer with all his two-handed might, the weapon's heavy head meeting the Pale Stone Man's with a dull, fleshy *thud.*

Its gait faltered and it stumbled three extra steps, pitching forwards at the head before righting itself and continuing to walk.

Harry stared back at Eric, wide-eyed, staggering backwards a few steps himself. He looked strangely stunned, blinking.

"Do it again!" Eric screamed. Harry obliged, quickly and wheezily catching up with the Pale Stone Man and swinging the sledgehammer in a sideways arc this time, slamming into the right-hand side of the Pale Stone Man's head with staggering force, knocking it five feet sideways, and as it was regaining its gait Harry was already swinging the sledgehammer back the other way. *DUMPF—*

This time it couldn't correct its steps before it was knocked to the ground, landing face first with its arms by its sides.

"Yes Harry! Yes! Hit it again! Flatten it!"

But Harry had dropped the hammer and was whooping in deep breaths, his arms shaking wildly, face contorting as if he'd tasted something bitter.

"Feels . . . bad . . ." he said.

"What?" Eric yelled. "When you hit it?"

Harry nodded in wordless agreement, but was already bending to grab the sledgehammer as The Pale Stone Man began to fold backwards. It slid its chest along the floor as its rear raised up towards the sky, already beginning to stand, but Harry threw the sledgehammer up and over and down onto its head as if he were trying to ring the bell on a Test Your Strength machine. *Dumpf.* Its movements paused for the briefest moment, and then it continued to rise as Harry gritted his teeth and shook his head.

"Gah!" he cried, shaking off a convulsion.

"In the side! Hit it in the side—"

Harry hoofed in air and obliged, the blow knocking the Pale Stone Man sideways, flattening it to the ground again as Harry closed in, moaning loudly as he arced the hammer over and down. Harry's breathing came in shredded gulps but Eric couldn't take over. He had one hand. He couldn't swing it like—

Dumpf

—that.

Harry swung again, harder.

DUMPF.

The Pale Stone Man's head bounced a little.

Then . . . *it didn't move—*

Then it did—

Harry screamed as he brought the hammer round again.

DUMPF.

He didn't stop.

DUMPF. DUMPF. DUMPF.

"Take . . . take it . . ." Harry said, suddenly staggering backwards again and dropping the hammer, clutching at his chest. "It feels like . . . like I'm going to throw up. Take over a sec."

"Harry . . ." Eric breathed. The Pale Stone Man was still. It wasn't . . . getting up? "You . . . I think you . . ."

It started to move.

Eric darted over to where the hammer lay, snatching it up with his good hand and gripping it so hard his knuckles felt like they would burst through the skin. Adrenaline flooded his body and suddenly the hammer felt half as heavy. He bellowed and began to swing it one-handed as the Pale Stone Man recommenced its inexorable rise.

Chapter Two

The Very Movable Object Meets the Irresistible Force, and a Growing Concern

✳✳✳

Fifteen minutes later, Harry and Eric could barely stand.

Their clothes were soaked; Harry's suit jacket lay abandoned somewhere in the middle of Millennium Place, discarded and wet through, and Eric's T-shirt was stained front and back with sweat. The hammer felt as heavy as a car, and Eric could no longer physically raise it one-handed. He tried one more time, but his shoulder, bicep and forearm had gone from feeling full of fire, to broken glass, to flat out refusing to respond. The constant effort alone would have drained him—having to swing it one-handed not only due to his missing left hand but his stitched-up left shoulder—but Harry had been telling the truth; hitting the Pale Stone Man felt *bad*. It was as if some kind of sickening radiation was leaking out of it with every contact. Touching the Pale Stone Man with a pole, it seemed, might have protected you from becoming a babbling mess, but it didn't stop the awful nausea that came from physical contact with it; it seemed to travel up the sledgehammer's handle and right into Eric's bones, sapping his strength, and now Eric's already-drained tank was down to fumes. They'd given it everything they had, and now they had reached the entrance to the St Joseph building, battling the monster all the way.

All the while Eric had kept trying in his mind to contact Maria Constance; she'd saved them once, hadn't she? But there was nothing, not even the hint of a connection, only the endless void of his own thoughts. The sledgehammer's head currently rested against his foot, Eric's grip doing no more than keeping the hammer propped up. In vain he *willed* it into the air, but all that happened was it slipped out of his sweat-slicked grip.

The Pale Stone Man was rising to its feet once more. Each time it went down now, it took a little longer to rise ... but it *always* rose.

"Give ... give it to me," Harry said.

They couldn't meet each other's eyes.

Eric tried to pass him the hammer, but he couldn't get it off the ground.

"I can't," he said, cradling his arm. "I can't even ... grip ..." He suddenly spun on the spot and let out a bellow of frustration into the silent expanse of Coventry behind him. Above, the Barrier quietly churned. Harry staggered to the hammer and picked it up. He still had some strength in his arms, Eric could tell. Harry might have been older and generally fucked, but he two hands to bear the makeshift weapon's weight. His issue, though, was his breathing. Eric had thought the older man was going to keel over at several points, but he'd kept going. They both had.

Harry walked back to the rising Pale Stone Man and stood in front of it. He wobbled on his feet for a moment, coming frighteningly close to the visitor. Would it count if Harry's shoes touched it?

"Harry ... be careful," Eric said, blinking Harry back into focus. Harry ignored him and swung the hammer onto the Pale Stone Man's rising head. It fell to the ground once more and Harry suddenly retched violently, causing him to fall backwards and collide with the St Joseph building's metal and glass door. He dropped the hammer.

"Shit—"

"'M fine," Harry wheezed. He stood up.

Eric looked up at the windows of the building. Even in the grey daylight, the faint glow of the bubble that was Jenny's prison could be seen above them. It shone through the empty pane where the same sledgehammer Harry had just dropped had broken through the night before, swung in vain by a man called John Bates. It had bounced off the golden bubble, doing even less damage than the tiny amount Eric and Harry had managed to inflict on the Pale Stone Man.

John Bates had been trying to save Jenny too—

"Talk ... to her," Harry said.

"What?"

"You talked ..." Harry hacked up something foul and spat it out. "You talked to her before. Talk to her now," he said, as the Pale Stone Man began to rise—of course it did—once more.

Eric shook his head rapidly, staggering over and trying to snatch the sledgehammer from Harry. He gripped it and tried to lift it using his stump as an aid, but all that helped him do—as it had the last few times he'd tried it—was get the sledgehammer up to vaguely near his shoulder height.

"*Ggg—*" he hissed, straining with everything he had left in his poisoned body, and then something twisted sharply inside his exhausted and drained deltoid. It felt like barbed wire being dragged under the muscle. "*Fuck!*" he screeched, still trying to lift the hammer as all three heads of his shoulder muscle locked up against the motion ... but *yes*, he finally got the hammer up and over and down onto the Pale Stone Man's head.

It was pointless.

The force of the hammer's gentle blow wasn't even enough to slow their enemy's rise upwards; the sledgehammer simply bounced off ineffectively, narrowly missing Harry as it flew from Eric's weakened hand.

They couldn't even slow it down anymore.

Eric fell against the building's door, spent.

"Shit ... shit ..." Harry hissed, trying to get in air as the towering figure gradually rose to its full height in front of them. It blocked out the pale sun behind it, casting the two humans in shadow. Harry staggered towards the hammer and grabbed its handle, propping it up and using it like a walking stick to hold himself upright. He was only about five feet in front of the Pale Stone Man as it rose.

"You said ... if we survived the Barrier," he said, breathing hard and sounding broken inside, "then that means we're ... on the spectrum ... right?"

The Pale Stone Man was now fully upright.

Eric understood what Harry was planning to do at the same moment the Pale Stone Man began to walk.

"*Harry—*"

Harry began to charge towards it, his arms outstretched.

Eric lunged towards his friend and grabbed him from behind, falling onto him almost as a dead weight and wrapping his arms around Harry's waist, but the older man resisted, somehow staying up, Eric's attempted tackle weak and useless.

"*No—*"

The Pale Stone Man filled their vision, and the sound of its thundering footsteps cracking the concrete beneath them were like gunshots. Then it was upon them.

Harry stiffened as it hit him, and Eric couldn't yell his friend's name as the wind was blasted from his lungs, the pair of them knocked backwards by the Pale Stone Man's swinging arm. It hadn't been an intentional blow; they had simply been in the way. It felt as if someone had thrown a tightly-packed punchbag at them, the force of even a glancing hit from the creature enough to knock them both almost clear off the ground. Eric saw bright lights as Harry landed on top of him, the back of Eric's head careening off the concrete, but already Eric was scrambling up and out from under his friend even as the world became watery in his eyes. The ringing in his ears had abated a little now, but not much; his world was now adrenaline and instinct, more important than the information from his compromised vision and hearing.

"Harry, Harry—"

But Harry was clutching at his ribs and throwing up booze at the same time. Touching the Pale Stone Man may not have had the same effect as the original—or at least not on Stone Sensitives— but it was certainly even worse than touching it with a sledgehammer. Harry was pointing blindly at the stairs with his free hand; the other was holding his side tightly. Had Harry's ribs been cracked—

A deafening crash sounded, and Eric leapt to put himself between Harry and any flying glass from the doorway that the Pale Stone Man had just obliterated. It was heading for the stairs. Harry's hand found Eric's T-shirt and yanked at it, pulling Eric close, but Eric already knew.

"I'm going," he whispered, and looked for the sledgehammer as he watched the Pale Stone Man disappearing into the lobby of the building. He saw the fallen weapon lying near the doorway and hurried over to it, managing to pick it up but already knowing it was useless. He simply couldn't bring power to the swing anymore. All of those sickening, draining hits had taken everything he had.

Then why are you going in there?

Because . . . because . . .

She couldn't die alone. Not like—

The Pale Stone Man was reaching the bottom of the stairs. It didn't pause in its gait, stepping up easily. Eric almost felt surprised; he knew from his research that the Stone Man had displayed rudimentary problem-solving intelligence during the First Arrival. There had been claims of the Stone Man climbing the sheer wall by the Post Office Depot in Coventry during its first walk on earth, photographs of the impact marks of its round-tipped shovel 'hands' circulating as proof. As the Pale Stone Man scaled more steps though, Eric noticed that they weren't cracking as the concrete outside had. Even in the chaos, Eric's old instincts stirred:

How can it—

He couldn't take the same route as the Stone Man; he couldn't get past the it on the stairs. It would crush him against the wall. The other end of the hallway, there had to be a matching stairwell, he'd seen the sign earlier—

He glanced back at Harry outside who had made it to his feet using the doorframe and was waving at Eric to go, *go.* Eric did. He turned right and ran down the corridor, his limbs feeling like lead, the sound of the Pale Stone Man ascending the stairs becoming quieter. He was already wheezing like Harry by the time he reached the doorway at the other end of the hall. Was being this close to the Prism having an effect too? It had been all headaches and nausea since—

His mind was babbling at him, trying its absolute best to deny that another one of Eric's promises was about to be broken. As he burst out onto Jenny's floor, seeing the weak and grey sunlight leaking through the window at the other end, he paused and listened; he could hear the Pale Stone Man approaching. Then why wasn't he racing down the hallway to Jenny's apartment, using the precious time to . . . to . . .

Because had no idea what he could possibly say. They'd failed her.

Then at the very fucking least, he thought, *like you told Harry, she can't die alone—*

He suddenly felt completely detached from his aching, wheezing body as he broke into a hobbling run. He reached Jenny's door as the sounds of the Pale Stone Man's ascent on the stairs became louder still; it was nearly at her floor. As he opened Jenny's door it happened again; the golden glow of her bubble-like prison leaking out to him. It hit Eric's body and he winced. Being touched by any part of that awful thing was sickening.

Jenny was still there, of course, trapped within that awful light, but she was lying on the floor now, her ratty deckchair pushed to the bubble's edge. Eric stood in the doorway, unable to speak and knowing he had to. She hadn't looked up at the sound of the door opening.

"Jenny," he croaked, and then a deafening *BANG* came from the other end of the hallway outside. The Pale Stone Man was on their floor now. *"Jenny,"* Eric repeated, trying to hold down his panic, and rushed over to her, moving around to the window side of the bubble so he could see both Jenny and the now-ominous doorway.

Jenny wasn't home. Even with the bubble partially obscuring her from view, Eric could see that her eyes had rolled back in their sockets and her body was twitching lightly. He suddenly remembered her putting her hand against the bubble, squinting through it to see him, showing him—incredibly—compassion in the midst of her own terror. That woman was gone. A flicker fizzed around the surface of the bubble, so sharp and bright that Eric flinched away slightly, and then he saw it; the disgusting, turning light was alive in a way it hadn't been before. It looked—it *felt*—eager.

Did it know what was coming?

"Jenny!" Eric said as the footsteps of Jenny's approaching visitor became dark chimes of doom. "Can you hear—" He stopped. What was he doing? Did he want to wake her up for this? He froze. The Pale Stone Man's footsteps were an unstoppable death sentence. He was helpless to stop any of this from happening and he wanted to so badly, *he needed to.*

Get her out—

It was pointless, he knew, but he had to try. He had to do *something.* He slapped his good hand onto the bubble's surface once more, gritting his teeth against the pain in his remaining intact—but now injured—shoulder, and the loud but painless sizzling-bacon sound began again. Not so loud that it drowned out the thudding footsteps approaching outside. This time, when he tried to make the hole appear, the bubble responded in the opposite manner; this new, more violent tumbling of its surface became thicker, the light becoming more concentrated under his palm.

It was resisting him.

No—

He moved his hand. The concentrated light moved with it. What did it *know*?

Maria! He yet again thought in desperation, knowing it to be useless. *Maria Constance! Help me!*

Nothing.

Eric looked at the glowing bubble and was filled with helpless rage.

"Let. Her. Out!"

He couldn't open the hole as much as a millimetre.

"No!" he bellowed as Jenny's doorway exploded inwards and the Pale Stone Man strode into the apartment, not breaking its steady pace for even a moment. *"Get out!"* Eric screamed at it. *"Leave her alone!"* Then, even more pointlessly, *"She didn't do anything!"* On it came, crossing the distance between the entrance and Jenny's bubble in a few relaxed strides, seeming larger than ever inside that small space as it filled Eric's sight. He noticed with a strange horror that its head had angled downwards slightly— only a little—towards Jenny's unconscious form. *They never did that before.* Old instincts screamed inside his head, the thought not registering. He was squatting on the opposite side of the bubble to the creature; he remained there, looking up into its featureless face and trembling helplessly ... but he wouldn't back away.

It kept coming until it reached the bubble itself. Even then, it didn't stop; it stepped right inside it as if the bubble were made of nothing but regular, intangible light. Eric stopped breathing as part of his brain registered the fact his hand was touching something impossibly solid yet this being had stepped through it as if it were smoke.

The sizzling sound came again and quickly rose into a high-pitched noise that mixed with the ringing in Eric's own ears before the bubble suddenly exploded with a screeching roar.

The remaining windows of Jenny's apartment blew outwards, shattering into thousands of tiny pieces. Eric threw up his arms as he was knocked onto his backside, the shockwave rattling his skull. He tried to stand and couldn't. He could only take in the scene before him, rocking back and forth in a daze as he uselessly tried to find purchase.

Jenny was exposed, *free*, still lightly fitting on the floor. The Stone Giant had now—finally—stopped its accursed walking and stood motionless at Jenny's feet. If Eric could stand, regain his equilibrium, he could drag her away, get her out of there, figure out the next move—

Then his blinking and dazed eyes finally realised that couldn't be done.

The Pale Stone Man had stepped inside the bubble and directly *onto* Jenny's feet. They had now disappeared underneath the tips of the Stone Man's legs. A mixture of blood, bone and jellified flesh had sprayed outwards onto the floor as her feet burst, the meat of them flattened under the monster's stumps. Eric desperately searched Jenny's face for signs of awareness; mercifully, there were none as she continued to twitch and buck on the floor.

Her feet, he thought, as the sight took another irretrievable piece of Eric Hatton away.

Plumes of red mist begin to rise from underneath the Pale Stone Man's stumps and an awful, continuous *crackling* sound began to fill the room. It dimly reminded Eric of the sound of milk hitting a bowl of Rice Krispies.

The red mist wasn't mist, he realised. He had seen this before, at the Prism, when the Shufflers had—

His equilibrium returned.

Eric clambered to his feet, looking for something, anything to hit the monster with. There was nothing. The red mist—the vaporising chaff of Jenny—slowly started to form a thick cloud around the lower half of the Pale Stone Man, beginning to further obscure her from view, but not before Eric saw that her body was steadily sliding towards the creature. It was chewing her into itself, consuming her from the feet up, small jets of her blood occasionally pumping out around the Pale Stone Man's stumps. Without thinking, Eric darted around to the monster and thrust a forward kick at it with the little energy he had left, trying to push-strike it away with the heel of his boot. The impact did absolutely nothing but Eric felt like he had kicked a building, only managing to push himself away from the Pale Stone Man and sending a wash of nausea through his exhausted body as he collapsed onto his back.

Harry arrived at the ruined doorway, clutching at the sledgehammer with one hand and his ribs with the other.

"Oh sweet Jesus," he said quietly.

"Harry," Eric said, hearing the helpless pleading in his voice. His friend rushed over and went to raise the sledgehammer but then stopped as he saw—as the last, visible parts of Jenny began to disappear from view—what had happened to her. By now she was gone almost up to her waist and the floor beneath her swam with red, the accumulation of those small excess jets of blood forming a small lake. Harry looked up at the mountainous form of the Pale Stone Man, then back to what was left of Jenny.

"She's gone, Eric," he said, having to raise his voice over that terrible crunching, crackling noise. "Even if we could stop this . . . the blood loss . . ."

The sledgehammer clattered to the floor.

"Eric," Harry muttered, a new fear coming into his voice. Eric followed Harry's gaze.

The Pale Stone Man was pale no longer.

The translucency was gone; they couldn't see that network of lines under its skin anymore. Already it was appearing more Stone-like as its body became more and more opaque; but this was not the greyish-brown of the Stone Man or the Prism.

This Stone Man was turning a bright, garish red. And it was growing.

"We need to *go*," Harry whispered, picking up the sledgehammer and wincing as he did so. Eric looked at Jenny, or tried; he couldn't clearly see her face, obscured by the red vapour hanging in the air around her.

"We can't lea—" Eric began, but gave up halfway through the sentence. Jenny had already left. He took a staggering step backwards as a fresh wave of nausea hit them both, Harry swaying too, clutching at his injured side. Whatever was happening, it was getting worse.

"It's that thing," Harry yelled, the crackling now painfully loud. "We can't be here." Eric knew he was right but couldn't take his eyes off the now-solid-red Stone Man as its head continued towards the ceiling. It wasn't stopping; it looked like it was going to pass right through the— "It's gonna bring the ceiling down on us, Eric!" Harry yelled. "We have to *go!*" Eric could barely hear as the nausea continued to rise along with the Red Stone Man's head, whatever force was causing it to grow taller playing havoc with his central nervous system. The thought suddenly came to Eric:

there was an open window right there. They were six stories up. That would do it, wouldn't it?

Listen to this world you're in. Look at what you're up against.

He looked at the window. Turned towards it, even. Took a few steps.

"Eric!"

He whipped back around in time to see the Red Stone Man's head crash through the ceiling. Its body was wider now too, thicker all over. Both men backed up as plaster and dust rained down in a seemingly endless waterfall of detritus; the hole in the ceiling began to crack outwards. The Red Stone Man kept going, half of its head gone from sight. What was it now, twelve feet tall? And it was still going. Harry grabbed at Eric's arm.

"The whole ceiling's going to come in!"

It was. Eric nodded and let Harry drag him towards the door, neither of them turning away from the monster in their midst. He couldn't look down at Jenny, didn't want to see.

The crackling continued.

"The rucksack!" Harry shouted, dashing to retrieve the bag from the floor. While he did, Eric looked where Jenny had been lying.

Her body was now gone, a pool of already congealed-to-jelly blood on the floor as the only sign she had ever been there. The remaining red vapour was beginning to lower, the cloud slowly spreading outwards and downwards. Eric and Harry covered their mouths as they backed into the apartment's entrance for safety; the ceiling really could come down at any minute as the Red Stone Man continued to rise. It was embedded up to its shoulders and still going, but the torrent of falling plaster and wood was now reducing to a trickle. Amazingly, the rest of the ceiling held. The thing had to be at least fifteen feet tall now, maybe higher. If the Stone Men had been big, this was enormous. It looked like a—

"It's a giant," Harry whispered, awestruck, staring from where they now stood outside the doorway.

"Yeah," Eric said, but he wasn't looking at the red colossus anymore. His eyes were on that patch of blood. He blinked, blinked again. Then a slap struck him, cracking him across the face. He whirled around, looking for whatever new horror had arrived, before realising the slap had come from Harry. His friend's eyes held Eric's apologetically.

"Stay with me, I need you!" he said firmly, raising his voice as a loud creaking noise emanated from the abused ceiling. "We deal with that shit later! *What are we going to do?*"

"We didn't save her, Harry—"

"*Later!*"

Harry was right. Jenny, his missing hand ... he pushed all of it to the other side of a flimsy wall for now, letting rational thought take over. That was better. As long as they kept moving—

"Uh ... we, uh ..." He looked at the Stone Giant as it continued to grow, obscured now by a torrent of falling plaster. If it was still going at the rate it started ... how big must it be now? There was a *crunch* from lower down. Was that the apartment's floor?

Harry put a hand to his head.

"*Jesus ...*" he said. Eric felt it too; it was getting worse. Something was filling the room, he realised; the air between the walls seemed to be pressing in on them, *no*, pressing *outwards* from the Stone Giant. Whatever it was radiating was increasing rapidly now, a presence, an aura—

"Power," Harry breathed, staring at the legs and lower torso of the enormous, growing red figure before him. "It's just ..."

Harry's whole body stiffened.

"*Hup,*" he said, and his fingers clenched into fists. They spasmed in and out for a moment, and Eric thought Harry was finally having that stroke.

"Harry? Harry!"

Then it stopped. Harry blinked for a moment, looking around himself without moving his head, frozen to the spot, re-establishing where he was.

Harry had just gone somewhere, that much was clear.

"We have to go," he whispered, and Eric realised that Harry was trying not to be heard. "Now. We have to go *now.*"

Eric was dumbfounded. The rumours were true. *Stone Sight.* It was real, and it had just happened to Harry.

"You saw what *it* saw," Eric said. "You just connected to it!"

"Let's go!" Harry hissed, already backing into the hallway as the crunching and crumbling noises from the apartment swelled to a crescendo.

"You said you'd had visions before but you never said about—"

"We can't be here!" Harry hissed, suddenly looking furious. "That thing is nothing like—*you can feel it.*"

Eric absolutely could. If being bathed in the bubble's light had felt like radiation, being in the presence of the Stone Giant felt like standing by the main reactor at Chernobyl. The thing *oozed* power. The room was filled with it and Eric half-expected to see the paint peeling back on the walls—

WHOOF.

A tsunami of rubble fell to the floor of the apartment with an enormous crash, tumbling from the huge but now-unfilled hole in the ceiling.

The Stone Giant had vanished.

No Horns, no cold snap. It had simply left. Harry jumped in surprise, then yelled in angry pain as he clutched at his chest and damaged ribs.

"Holy *shit!*"

"Where's it gone?" Eric asked stupidly, even as relief flooded his system. He hadn't fully expected it to wake up and come for them, but there was always that chance ... then he saw the red stain on the floor once more. "Doesn't matter right now, we ... we stick to the plan," he said. "You've ... got the rucksack?"

"Yeah."

"Then we take Jenny's ca—" Not *Jenny's* car anymore. "We take the Honda."

"Still have the keys?"

"In my pocket. We drive out to the A45, where John said the edge of the big barrier was."

"What if we can't—"

"We see if I can open it," Eric said, cutting the question off, "or we figure a way out. We get to the Isle of Skye."

"What?"

Of course. Harry didn't know. He hadn't heard Maria Constance in his head while she'd saved them.

"I'll tell you on the way. There's help there, Harry."

"How do you know?"

"Because they talked to me. They were in my head. They saved *you.*"

"What?"

He couldn't explain it now. It was just too much.

"Please ... just trust me on this, okay? I'll tell you in the car. I promise."

Harry opened his mouth to complain, then just shook his head, looking at the red stain on the floor now too.

"Okay," Harry said, his voice heavy. "Let's go."

A memory snapped Eric's eyes open.

"The box!" The only thing they'd managed to get out of Ground Zero. They'd left it in the middle of Millennium Place!

Already back on the job, he thought bitterly, his ears continuing to ring in the silence.

"It's heavy," Harry said, shrugging. "It won't have blown away—"

(Whoof)

The sound had come from far away, but they'd both heard it. The implication was immediate and awful in Eric's mind.

"Nonononono," he babbled, beginning to rush into the apartment to look out of the window.

"The floor—" Harry began.

"It's *fine!*" Eric yelled, but he was running along the outside edge of the room just in case. Even so, he had to see.

He saw.

"Oh ..." After a moment, Harry joined him at the window, wincing and wheezing with every movement. "Gimme the bag Harry, gimme the bag." He was asking because he wanted the binoculars, but they weren't necessary. Even at this distance, the bright red shape stood out in dramatic contrast to the greyness of Millennium Place around it.

The Stone Giant had already returned to the Prism.

"It can't do that," Harry breathed. "They can't be that fast, they can't just teleport like that, they always *walk*—"

"They always disappeared when they went home," Eric said wearily as he frantically fished in the rucksack for the binoculars anyway. Some part of him needed to confirm it beyond doubt, a tiny piece that couldn't accept the truth. "Back to the point of origin. They returned to a certain point, just as they always *arrived* at a certain point. Anywhere else, they walked. Being recalled is different—"

"But it hasn't gone home!" Harry cried. "It's right *there*—"

"Yeah," Eric said, finally pulling the binoculars free and crossing back to the window. "Back at its point of origin. Like I said."

"But . . ." Harry trailed off as it sank in. "The Prism," he said. "The point of origin has been brought here."

"Yeah . . ." Eric sighed darkly, looking through the binoculars now. There the Stone Giant stood, right where it had been born, huge and indomitable. Based on what Eric knew of the Prism, he guessed its completed height had to be around fifteen feet tall.

"But the Arrivals in the past," Harry said, almost whining. "They were months apart, *months*, when they disappeared—"

"They were," Eric said, lowering the binoculars. "And it was five years between the Third Arrival and the Prism showing up. Were they making plans all that time? Or did it just take that long for the Prism to get here?" He looked at Harry, who was still staring at the Stone Giant.

"You mean, wherever they came from," Harry murmured, "or where they were going back to . . . you think it was so far away that all of the time in between the Arrivals was just . . . what, travel time?" Eric scowled darkly and jabbed a finger at the Stone Giant, a red marker in the distance.

"We've just seen it reach its Target, do what it came to do, and then vanish, like before," Eric said. "Then it's instantly reappeared right there back at home base. What do you think?"

"But why would it need to go back to the Prism?" Harry asked. Eric considered it.

"I don't know," he said, feeling something he hadn't felt for over five years: the sensation of not *wanting* to know. "I just want us to get out of here. There's a woman on the Isle of Skye. She can help us. If there's any way we're going to get payback..." *Payback* wasn't right but he couldn't say what he really thought:

The only way I can atone.

The sound of their breathing mingled with the gentle, cold breeze coming through the apartment's broken window.

"This woman spoke to me in my head, Harry," Eric said quietly. "Maria Constance. She can obviously do Stone-related stuff, same way I could with the bubble, but she's on some other level. She hid you from the Empty Man, saved you." He waited to see how Harry would react, but his friend was simply watching and nodding. "She told me she was going to the Isle of Skye, and that I should go there."

"Why?"

"I don't know. But if she can do stuff like that without even physically being here—if she's that powerful—and we don't have any other options right now, I'd say that trying to get there is our best bet."

"If we can get out of Coventry."

"If we can get out of Coventry, yes," Eric said. "Not being sarcastic, but... do you have any other suggestions?"

Harry slowly shook his head... then stopped.

"The wind is blowing harder," he said quietly, just as Eric felt a colder blast of air rushing in through the broken window; it then turned into an arctic blast. *"Aaaaah!"* Just before he dropped the binoculars and wrapped his arms around himself, Eric saw it; a rippling in the air around the Stone Giant that looked like a heat haze. It was travelling from the Stone Giant to the Prism.

It's communicating with it—

The air got even colder. The Horns sounded.

"Get down!" Eric hissed, and they did, dropping below the windowpane so they were out of the immediate jet of ice-cold air that had now become too much to bear.

"What's it doing? What fucking now?" Harry yelled ... and then it stopped.

Something was different. Both men could feel it even before they stood up; they knew it because it was familiar.

Something else was arriving.

Oh God. Oh, please.

Eric picked up the binoculars as he rose and slowly turned to the window. Again, he didn't think that the binoculars would be needed, but he wanted them.

"Oh ..." Harry said, witnessing the movement below, "... oh, Jesus."

Something wasn't arriving.

Something was returning.

They were slowly emerging from the Prism, being pushed out of it. It was different to the emergence of the Pale Stone Man; that had looked like a birth, like a foetus emerging fresh and glistening from its amniotic sac, slowly tearing free. This was easy, simple, like a disembarking, which was exactly what was happening. Six holes had appeared in the Prism and the passengers weren't *walking* out of the Prism; they were gliding slowly out as if on a moving walkway, standing upright and stationary on whatever surface was emerging from the Prism to deliver them.

The six Blue Stone Men had returned. The Fourth Arrival had begun in earnest.

And Eric and Harry were trapped inside a dead city with all of them.

"Let's ... let's ..."

For a moment, neither man could move.

THE STONE GIANT

***

Chapter Three:

Worse than the DTs, and Eric and Harry Arrive at the Great Barrier

***

"That was an awful, awful way to die," Harry said.

They hadn't spoken since they'd set off out of the city in Jenny's Honda. Harry was driving; there might have been plenty of alcohol still in his system, but what they'd just witnessed in Coventry was enough to sober anyone up. Plus, as far as they knew, they were the only—or two of the very few—people left in the city.

On top of that, Harry had two hands.

"It was," Eric replied. "I hope . . . I hope she was as unaware of what was happening as she looked." He was staring out of the window, watching the green spaces either side of the A45 out of Coventry moving past, leaving the city centre behind them. It had been a while since he'd ridden inside a car. He looked out of the window and remembered the drives to gigs, to work . . . to Theresa's house to see her and Aaron. He watched the divider ticking past them on their right and could believe that the world was still normal. Harry gave a pained grunt. They'd taped his damaged ribs as best they could with what they had and re-dressed Eric's shoulder stitches. Harry said he was fine and had insisted on driving, and Eric had a newfound respect for his friend. Harry was a tough son of a bitch.

Unlike you.

Had they been just a few more swings of the sledgehammer away from putting the pre-Stone Giant down for good? They *had* been slowing it a little. He looked at his intact arm, resting inside a makeshift sling. It was a good job they'd taken the first aid kit from his stash, and not just for the sling; the painkillers had reduced the broken-glass feeling in his hammer-swinging shoulder to a dull, heavy throb. One hand gone, the top of his left shoulder skimmed by a bullet and patched up, the right shoulder now temporarily taken out of commission, and his ears were still ringing like a *bastard*.

More excuses.

"Tell me about this woman," Harry said. "The one in your head." Eric did, glad to think about something other than Jenny's unspeakable death and the madness that was preparing to begin all over again back at Ground Zero. Even all the way out here, they were both faintly aware of the existence of the Stone Giant, radiating its power through the Barrier that turned in the sky, speaking silently to its small army of Blues.

All of them hell-bent on adding to their ranks.

When Eric was done talking, Harry simply said, "Okay. Better try and get to her then." After a moment, he added, "Need to tell her thanks, too."

"Now you tell me something," Eric said. "You saw through that thing's ..." He went to say *eyes* and stopped. The Stone Men didn't have eyes. "You saw what it saw?"

"Yeah."

"Had that happened before?"

"No." Harry grunted again and shifted in his seat, twisting gingerly at the waist. "Never been that close to one before, though."

"What do you think that means?"

Harry considered the question, scratching at his cheek for a moment.

"I've no idea," he said eventually.

"Did you feel anything physically?"

"No." He grimaced again. "Feel like shit now, though."

"Your ribs?"

"No," Harry said again, cricking his neck. "Still nauseous. Those rations in your stash were all good, right?"

"Totally." That was strange. The nausea that had washed out of the Stone Giant's presence had faded now in Eric; it was still affecting Harry? He'd updated all of the food supplies in his stashes every six months, too. He and Harry had just forced down some tuna and crackers; not the most appetising meal at the best of times, and certainly not after watching what had just happened to Jenny. "Is it your stomach?"

"It'll pass, it'll pass," Harry said dismissively. Silence reigned. Eric tried the radio again; every time he'd tried, he picked up nothing, and this was no different. He clicked it off and closed his eyes.

"You did your best," Harry said quietly.

"You too," Eric said immediately. He paused. "We *did*, right?"

Harry raised his eyebrows.

"I don't say shit I don't mean." He winced again. "Everything hurts." Eric noticed small beads of sweat on Harry's forehead, and it wasn't hot in the car. Harry's jacket had been collected from Millennium Place and thrown on the back seat, along with the sledgehammer and Eric's now-empty gun with its shoulder holster. Eric fished in the bag for the water and handed it to Harry, who took it gratefully.

"The Shufflers, Harry," Eric said, shaking his head, and then covered his eyes with his hand as the image returned to him: all the mindless, previously-normal folks, pressing against the Prism as they were chewed away to nothing. "The Prism had so much control over them that they kept walking right into that thing, even when it was eating them. And the Barrier didn't burst them like the soldiers at Ground Zero either, so the Shufflers were Stone Sensitive too. But *we're* Stone Sensitive, Harry. So why did they get drawn into it and not us?"

"Why could I see through the Stone Giant's ... sight?" Harry asked. "Why could you open a hole in that bubble? Like I said before: different levels. Shufflers *could* be affected that way, so they were. They were meat for it. Fuel." He sighed heavily. "Same as Jenny was for that half-baked Stone Man. Right?" Eric said nothing, remembering the picture he'd imagined in Jenny's apartment; the government assassin's bullets ricocheting off Jenny's golden prison, failing to kill her before the Stone Men could take her. She was special, and so the Stone Men had found a way to make it so nothing could stop them harvesting—

Harvesting. He nearly threw up. Harry jerked his thumb over his shoulder at the other item on the back seat: the Ground Zero box they'd collected from Millennium Place.

"That list proves it, I think," Harry said. "Nearly everyone on there is CROW. That has to be all the regular Joes. The other ones ... they have to be the other levels. The top brass figured it out."

It made sense. Eric hadn't been able to bring himself to go through the box when they'd first left, but already his obsession was creeping back; soon he would be poring over it, searching for answers ... but now he was less interested in the government that had taken his sister to the Stone Men themselves. Even so, the box was a lead, information. Maybe it would help them figure things out.

"You know that tape you have?" Harry asked. "That woman being interviewed by the government types? Linda, I think?"

"Yes?" Eric asked, surprised at this change of subject.

"She talked about hearing a noise, right? She latched onto some signal and got cut off from it?"

"She did."

Harry paused for a moment, sighed.

"We've made a lot of contact with those things," he said eventually. "Following a signal ourselves to find Jenny, then me getting extremely up close and personal with those white things too—until, according to you, this *Maria* woman stepped in—and then the being in the room with that Stone Giant ..." He shifted uncomfortably in the driving seat. "You think they, you know ... saw you and me too?" His eyes darted skywards. *"Them?"*

It wasn't a pleasant thought ... but then car finally rounded the long curve just outside of Meriden and Eric saw something ahead.

"Maybe," Harry was saying, lost in thought and not watching the road, made complacent by the endless stretch of empty concrete. "that Linda was just a low-level person. Like if she was on that list in the box—"

"Harry!" Eric yelled, scaring the older man out of his mind, who jumped in his seat, yelling out in pain as he stamped on the brake and the car began to skid.

"Faaaaaaaaaaaaaa—" Harry hissed, grabbing his ribs as the car finally came to a stop, the sledgehammer, box, and gun

banging into the backs of their seats once the car halted. *"Fuck me, fuck me—"*

"Harry I'm sorry," Eric said, patting his friend on the shoulder with his stump but not taking his eyes off the road ahead. What he'd seen was still a long way off, and his cry to Harry hadn't been a warning. It had been a bark of surprise.

In the distance, shimmering like an impossible heat haze on that grey, cool September day, was the edge of the Barrier.

Its moving surface was bright and clear here, even far away. How had John Bates described it, that poor unfortunate blowhard who'd blown himself up by touching the bubble at Jenny's apartment? *Like a waterfall but thinner than a waterfall could ever be.* Eric could see, even at range, that John's description was at least half right. The Barrier did look like a waterfall. Now that the car was stopped, its engine stalled, Eric and Harry could hear the noise. Not the blast of the Horns, or the rush of oncoming wind, but a roaring of voices.

On the other side of the Barrier was a mass of people, held back by a blockade of three military vehicles, some army personnel, and some red-and-white striped wooden sawhorses that the crowd pressed up against. Everyone there was looking at Eric and Harry's—*Jenny's*—car. The crowd was losing its collective mind, jumping up and down and pointing. Away to the right was some sort of tent, white, with cables running out of it to a generator nearby. Two people emerged as the crowd bellowed, smartly-dressed civilian types. Scientists, surely. Overhead, circling low, was a military-looking helicopter.

"Well," Harry grunted.

"People, Harry," Eric gasped, wide-eyed. "They must be—" He understood it then. The people couldn't get in. Here, *Eric and Harry* were the ones with the answers, at least in the crowd's eyes. His hope began to turn into a slowly sinking sensation. "Are you okay?" he asked Harry.

"Yeah," Harry said quietly. "Just my ribs . . . and I'm so *dizzy*."

Eric's worry deepened.

Maybe it would be okay. Maybe he *could* open this Barrier. Maybe he could get Harry out, get them both out . . . but as his eyes followed the watery, silver-grey, semi-transparent churn of the distant Barrier up into the sky, he thought of what a bubble a fraction of its size had done to his hand, and hopeful thoughts seemed very far away.

Are you angry? he asked himself.

He was.

"Let's drive up there, Harry."

***

The noise was deafening as they stepped out of the car—the Barrier had no effect on sound travelling between them and the outside world, then—but turned to a worried, murmuring babble as the crowd took in the sight of the two survivors from Coventry. Eric knew what they must look like; dirty, bloodied, bruised and scratched, their clothes still damp from the sweat. One of them was wearing a sling and missing a hand, for crying out loud. Eric gingerly moved his right arm out of the sling; it'd had a little rest and the painkillers were going to work, so he thought it could stay out for now. He was excited to see human beings—help, potentially, even if it was on the other side of the Barrier—but when he saw them and heard the noise, his breath caught. *People.* Frantic people. Crowds had been his bread and butter back in his musician days. Now he found himself recoiling. Living in a dead city will do that to a person—

He felt something.

What was that? Something coming off the Barrier, now they were this close? An energy? He braced immediately, expecting the nausea that had led them from Kasbah to Jenny's apartment, but it didn't come. So what was this now?

He sighed heavily as he trudged towards the Barrier. The answer would come eventually, he knew, although he was finding that the answers he'd craved for so long only seemed to bring horror as they arrived.

The people fell almost silent as he and Harry walked closer. One of the soldiers broke from the pack and headed over the edge of the Barrier to greet them, and Eric opened his mouth to yell a warning, but the soldier held up a hand. "I know," he called to Eric as he walked over. "I won't touch it." Of course the soldier knew; Eric saw the dried, crunchy blood smears over the road on their side of the Barrier. People had come up and touched it, then, presumably before the military set up their blockade. The crowd was much further back than the soldiers; the grunts at the Barrier's very edge were clearly there as a last resort. Eric could see reporters and cameras in the scrum; oh shit, was he on TV? He didn't want that at all. "Are there others?" the soldier called as he and Harry came within a few feet of the Barrier.

"Not with us," Harry said, and then groaned slightly and gave a brief shudder.

"Harry," Eric muttered, "do you wanna sit down?" Harry scowled and shook his head . . . and then his eye fell on the grassy embankment at the roadside.

"Gonna lie down, yeah," he said, staggering a step backwards. "I don't feel good at all." He stopped and looked at Eric. "You got all this, right?" he asked, gesturing towards the crowd and the Barrier. He was sweating hard now.

"Yeah," Eric said, put a hand on his friend's shoulder. Harry was shivering. "Is it the nausea?"

"Just ... I feel so bloody tense," he said. "Stomach turning over and over. Feels like ... like stage fright or something."

Eric froze.

Don't say anything, he thought. *Talk to the soldiers and see what your next move is. See if you can get him out.*

"Okay Harry," he said, patting Harry's shoulder. "Okay. You've had a hell of day. Go and lie down in the car actually, that'll be better. Run the AC, and I'll speak to this guy and come back with the news."

"Got it," Harry said, turning away. Eric watched him go. *Just talk to the soldier,* he thought.

But, of course, there was something he had to try first.

***

The Barrier really *did* look like a waterfall up close, but that term didn't do it justice. It was thin, as John Bates had said, which in itself wasn't too unusual—Eric had seen similar artificial waterfalls in fancy hotels and casinos—but he'd never seen one that flowed *sideways,* with rivulets and different currents that turned and swirled. He didn't see all that right now, though; his eyes were closed and he was concentrating for all he was worth.

"*Guh!*" he gasped, nearly collapsing onto the Barrier, before spinning on the spot and clenching his one good fist at the sky, red-faced, teeth gritted, grunting at the pain in his "good" shoulder.

He couldn't even begin to open a hole in the Barrier. He couldn't even seem to truly *connect* mentally with it, let alone affect it. While he hadn't touched the Barrier yet—he didn't know if it could kill him now it was solid, as it was clearly a larger concentration of energy than the bubble had been—his mind had hooked up to Jenny's bubble before he even touched it, and no such connection was happening here.

It wasn't just that, though. There was something coming off it ... wasn't there?

He couldn't say for sure. The sensation had been so brief and so faint that it might only have been exhaustion kicking in, or it might really have been some awful new mischief from the Stone Men, but he'd been dimly aware of ... faint streams? *Threads* of something coming from the Barrier? Or maybe transmitting through it?

Or just the blown mind of an exhausted, injured and traumatised man? Either way, he was getting nowhere, and couldn't risk actually touching the Barrier in an attempt to clarify further. If he did and ended up being burst by the now-solid Barrier, then Harry was definitely doomed.

The solider that had approached—the one Eric had told to wait a second—watched in amazement. The two presumed-scientists had joined him now, standing nearby. The crowd's noise had returned and increased to a frenzy, all of them—reporters, of course, included—barking questions from a hundred feet away as soldiers held them back.

"What were you doing?" the soldier asked him.

"Nothing," Eric snapped. "Nothing. Trying to open it, doesn't matter, can't do it, *fuck*—" He looked up into the taller—and older—man's face. "Has anyone else found a way out?" he pleaded. "Have you heard anything? I have to get my friend out of here. *We* have to get out of here—"

"Okay, okay, let's stay calm," one of the scientists said, stepping forward. She was a short, young-looking woman with dark hair tied up in a bun. Her male colleague was fiddling with a military radio, clearly dealing with an inconsistent signal. "We're going to help you, okay? We're going to do our best." Her features were only slightly distorted by the silvery-grey tumble of the Barrier.

"Did anyone else get out?" Eric insisted.

"Sir, hold on," she said. "We know very little here and this isn't the only checkpoint around the city, we have other people that might be able to help." She held out her hand for her colleague's radio. "Let me try to talk to them, okay? It might take a minute or two, though."

"... yeah. Alright, yeah." Eric dropped his shoulders, unclenched his hands.

"My superiors," the soldier added, "are going to want to talk to you too, give me a moment ..." He turned away, speaking quietly into his radio.

"Who?" Eric asked, suddenly calm. "Who will want to ... ?" The soldier ignored him and carried on talking into his radio. *"Hey."* The soldier turned around, red-faced himself; he looked scared to death being that close to the Barrier. "Who are your superiors?"

"What?"

"Who do you answer—" He shook his head, frustrated and eager. "I want to talk to the person in charge."

"Yes, that's what I'm—"

"Brigadier Straub," Eric hissed, a feeling of deep satisfaction penetrating his fear.

"I don't know who that—"

"Get me Brigadier Straub," Eric said. "If you don't know her, someone else will, and if she isn't here, *get* her here. I'll talk to her and no one else."

***

Chapter Four

An Unexpected Meeting, Eric's Dilemma, and a Growing Problem

***

About twenty minutes later, Eric watched through the Honda's windscreen as the chopper flew in low, coming down to land somewhere out of sight behind the nearby bank of trees. Five minutes after that, the distant crowd was parting like the red sea as one of the vehicles that had been dispatched to collect the passengers slowly returned through their midst, the soldiers briefly opening up the sawhorse blockade to let it through.

Eric had returned to the car to wait, frustrated, and was sitting in the driver's seat. Harry was seated next to him and looking far worse now, shaking and holding himself. His responses had been reduced to single syllables. Eric sighed and thought about the last time he saw Straub; she'd come to see him when he was in prison for affray after kicking off at Theresa's local police station for answers. The tone of her visit had ostensibly been one of a courtesy call; if so, it was confusing how her approach of offering nothing but an endless stream of lies was meant to reduce his grieving. Eric revisited the conversation now in his mind, but not to reinforce the grounds for payback, as he certainly would have in the past. He was trying to refamiliarize himself with that fucking alien poker face Straub used. He couldn't let it make him blow up at her here. He had to keep cool. The objective was to help Harry.

"Harry?"

"Yeh," Harry whispered from the opposite seat, his eyes closed, his breathing laboured.

"I said she's here. The Brigadier. I'm going to go talk to her, okay?" He couldn't believe what he was saying. Once, he would have given everything he had for this.

"No," Harry mumbled, sounding as if he were talking in his sleep. "Can't go out . . . got to be . . . inside . . ."

Oh, Jesus, Harry.

"You can stay here. It's going to be alright mate," Eric said softly. "Leave it with me." He opened the car door and Harry shot bolt upright in his seat, looking around. "It's okay," Eric soothed, his heart breaking again. He didn't know how there was any of it left. "I'm just getting out, I'm going to close the door again right now. Okay?" He quickly stepped out and closed the car door behind him. Through the window he watched Harry shiver and lie back in his seat, pulling his jacket up and over his head.

Eric covered his mouth and turned away, heading back up the road to where Straub stood patiently waiting on the other side of the Barrier.

"Mr Hatton," Straub said, her face . . . pitying? He hadn't expected that. She was in full field uniform. As he drew closer he noticed how much she'd aged. Whatever they'd been up to for the last five years, be it at the supposed base in Sheffield or in some other clandestine spook location, it had taken a toll on her.

Good.

"Come over here," Eric said to her quietly, walking away from where the rest of the soldiers stood. "I want to talk to you in private." Straub followed, waving the now slightly-larger cluster of scientists back. A long way behind her, the crowd was yelling again, knowing that someone of significance had arrived to talk to the survivors.

"Are you hurt—" she began, and then noticed his hand. "Good God, did that happen in there?"

"Yes," he said, holding up the stump. "Want to know *how?* Happy to tell you. Just answer some of *my* questions first."

His heart raced as, *yes*, there was the poker face in return. It felt good to see it this time. *That's right, Brigadier.*

"I see," she sighed eventually. "I can't say I blame you," she said. She looked back at the car. "A friend of yours? Someone you knew before this?"

"Can you get us out of here?" Eric said, ignoring the question.

"Not yet. We're running every kind of analysis we can but—"

"Then you tell me—you finally tell me—what happens," Eric said, stepping as close to the Barrier as he dared. "Tell me what happens when the Stone Men—the *normal* Stone Men—take the people they select. No lies, no runaround. The truth. The *truth.*" He was doing his best to stay calm but ever since he'd seen Straub's SUV come through the crowd the rage had been rising. Even so, he'd enjoyed the change in Straub's fucking face when he said the words *normal Stone Men.*

"Mr Hatton," Straub said gently, "with nothing but total respect ... I don't think now is the time to be discussing your sister—"

"This has nothing to do with Theresa you fucking bitch," Eric spat. So much for staying calm. The venom was instant when she'd spoken Theresa's name. "Keep her name out of your lying fucking mou—" He breathed in sharply, and wiped his face. Straub's expression didn't change. "Give me a second," he said.

"I'm sorry," she said, and for a crazy moment he thought Straub was finally apologising to him for— "I didn't mean to upset you."

"*Listen,*" Eric hissed. "I'm asking you what happens because ... because I think ... I think my friend ... Harry ..." Eric said, suddenly beginning to cry and hating himself for doing it in front of *this* person, of all people. He looked at the sky, unable to keep it together and talk to Straub. *Not Harry too. I can't take any more. I just can't.* "I think Harry is about to be selected by the Stone Men, Straub. Is *being* selected. He's displaying all the symptoms of the Quarry Response. And we ..." He let out a sob and then belted himself across the jaw with his stump, hard enough to knock himself sideways.

"*Mr Hatton,* please don't—"

"*And we can't get out of here,*" Eric sniffed, grimacing as he held his jaw with his good hand. "And they're back, they're fucking *back,* and we ... we were right by ... and Harry's nauseous and becoming anxious ... and he's, he's Stone Sensitive ..." He stared at her, pleading. "Tell me what happens."

Straub nodded calmly, considering her response.

"You're sure he's Stone Sensitive?" she asked.

"Yes. He survived the Barrier expanding, he had visions—"

"Mm," Straub said, and then looked at the ground for a moment, thinking. "Very well," she eventually said, putting her hands behind her back and looking up at Eric. She almost looked sad. "I'll answer your question and leave mine for a moment—I have many of them, as I'm sure you understand—except for one. It's pertinent to the one you just asked me: the Stone Men are back? They're here? In Coventry?"

"Yes."

"Are they at Ground Zero? By the anomaly?"

"The Prism? The big Stone building? Yes."

"I see. And your friend didn't manifest any symptoms before they Arrived?"

"No, not like this . . . but then they never Arrived like this."

"How do you mean?"

"Later," Eric snapped, glowering through red, wet eyes. "Why are *you* asking about how they Arrived?"

"Because ordinarily the Quarry Response manifests *before* Arrival, often several days before, in fact," Straub said. She sighed again. "I don't wish to upset you again, but . . . that was the case with your sister too, correct?"

Eric bristled.

"*. . . yes.*"

"So it would unusual, if your friend does have the Quarry Response, that it wouldn't come until after they Arrive. When did it start?"

"Within the last hour."

"Mm. That's very fast," Straub said, almost to herself. "The rules are changing since the anomaly arrived, it seems, and dramatically so. Mr Hatton, if your friend is manifesting the Quarry Response—and if he is, soon there will be no room for doubt—then you need to . . ." She took a deep breath. "You wanted the truth, and I'm very sorry to tell you this , Eric. You need to kill him as quickly and painlessly as possible. I know it's the last thing you wanted to hear."

Eric blinked. Straub just stared at him with that fucking *look* on her face.

He burst out laughing, a mad belly laugh that rang out across the empty dual carriageway and doubled him up at the waist.

"You *what?*" he gasped, standing up straight. "Have you lost your mind—"

"Mr Hatton," Straub said, holding up a hand, and Eric's lunatic laughter died in his throat because now she *did* look sad, and the sight of Straub's shell cracking was sobering indeed. "I truly am sorry. Do you have any weapons, I know there will be some back at the Ground Zero facility but I don't know how you'd—"

"Stop," Eric said, backing up a little in horror. "Please."

"Mr Hatton, I know this is extremely difficult to hear but you *must* listen," she said. "If you don't, what will happen to your friend will be so much worse. Do you understand?"

"No!"

Straub closed her eyes, her lips tightly pressed together. *She actually closed her eyes*, Eric thought madly.

"He will descend into a state of greater and greater anxiety, paranoia, and overwhelming nausea," she said slowly. "Soon he won't be able to move from the surrounding area, pinned in place by the Stone Men's remote energy fields." *Oh, it's gone way beyond that now Brigadier*, Eric thought crazily, *and I've got the stump to prove it.* "Now, I am telling you this next part," Straub continued, "so that you have the courage to help him avoid it: if you don't kill him first, he will die in unbearable pain. The Stone Man will come, and it will burrow into his spine. Harry will be conscious for all of this. The Stone Man will then remove a segment of his spine from his body. It will *harvest* him, Eric," she said, her hands coming up into little pincer shapes. "Believe me. I've seen it. I've been in war zones, and I have never seen a more painful death."

Eric felt as if his brain had been struck with a metal baseball bat. What she was saying could not be true. It simply couldn't . . . but what horrified him the most was that of all the theories on the forums, all the discussions, all the evidence, *none* of it had said anything about this. Straub was telling the truth.

"Why . . ." he muttered, "why . . . do they . . ."

"They make more of themselves," Straub said quietly. "They remove the segment of spine and use it to make more Stone Men. *Eric*, listen to me." She pointed a finger towards Jenny's car, and Harry inside. He was hidden under his coat, his wrapped torso rocking back and forth in the seat, head shaking. "You have to do this incredibly difficult thing for your friend to spare him the most intense suffering. And, more importantly from my perspective, to stop any more of those things being made who will then *do it to somebody else*. Do you understand?"

"But . . . that's not what the Stone Giant . . ." he began.

He stared at the car.

The gun, he thought. *You wasted all of your bullets on the Pale Stone Man.*

He caught his thoughts, realised what he was doing. Then all of the blood suddenly drained out of his face as a terrible understanding hit him. He turned back to Straub, terrified of the answer she might give to his question.

"You said you'd seen this," he said coldly. "You'd seen them *do* this."

"Yes."

"They did this to *Theresa*."

Straub continued to poker-stare.

"If you," Eric said, raising a shaking finger, "want to know *anything* … about what's happened in here … you'll tell me. *Now.*"

And if Straub paused just an extra heartbeat too long before she answered, her eyes finally looking away—moving up and to the right—before she responded, Eric was too hyped-up to notice.

"We executed her, Eric," Straub said. Her face was like a frozen lake, smooth and cold and concealing all the depths beneath. "We spared her from an agonising death and stopped her body being used to create more Stone Men. She was lost in the Quarry Response and knew nothing about what happened to her. It was quick and painless."

Eric staggered backwards, his hands over his mouth.

"And . . . Aaron . . ."

"Theresa had gone mad from the Quarry Response, Eric. She had smothered your nephew before we got there. She believed she was sparing him a far worse death. She was right. She saved her son. And this is *very* important: her doing that was how we eventually discovered that if a Target died before a Stone Man reached them—if we spared them that painful death—then that Stone Man went home. The destruction could be cut short. So many lives were saved this way. Aaron's death . . . it meant something. I hope that is of some comfort to you."

But Eric was looking the car again. Dazed, he raised his hand and his stump in front of his face, staring at them, and wondering how the fucking hell it had ever come to anything like this.

He finally had his answers about Theresa and Aaron. All he felt was numbness, and right now that was good. He wanted to scream at Straub about letting the media smear Theresa's name after her death while the other were hailed as heroes . . . but he just didn't have it anymore.

"Eric." Straub was saying his name, drawing him slowly out of his cloud. "Time is against us. I wish we had—"

"What's the list all about?"

He'd said it so quietly Straub had barely heard him.

"What?"

"The list," Eric intoned, looking down at the floor. "We found boxes in Ground Zero, ones you were trying to get out—"

"You were in there?" Straub asked in surprise. "What happened? Were the—"

"—trying to destroy your precious fucking secrets," Eric muttered, ignoring her. "Or transport them, or whatever. But we got one—"

"You got into Ground Zero?"

"Yep..."

Straub stepped forward, suddenly intense and moving so quickly that it startled Eric a little.

"This is *very important*, Eric," Straub said, wide-eyed. Once, such a display of emotion from Straub would have filled Eric with vicious delight, getting under her ice-cold skin and finding out she was warm-blooded after all. Right now he felt nothing at all for her. "Very important. Did you see any . . ." She looked back at the crowd briefly, even though they were far too distant and making too much noise to hear her. "Did you see the creatures in there? Were they mobile? Did the Arrival trigger them?"

Now Eric felt something; Straub's expression and her voice were scaring Eric to death.

Straub looked terrified.

She had to be talking about the two dead creatures. The ones he and Harry had found in the glass room at Ground Zero. Straub was spilling *all* the beans today.

"The things with all the legs?"

"Yes, yes—"

"They were dead, Straub," Eric told her, watching her face. Straub breathed out heavily, her composure falling back onto her, in front of her, like a steel portcullis. "Dead as the building itself, I might add." Eric's own composure was starting to creep back now: Work Mode, ever reliable, compartmentalising away. It had to, or Harry would be doomed.

"What?"

"It's gone. The whole building collapsed. Those things are buried in there, along with all your boxes, except the one we have in the car there. Lotta people on CROW. Not so much in all the others. So that says to me it's a list of all the different Stone levels the people are on. Right?"

"What does that have to do with your—"

"Then you *tell me*," Eric said, pointing at her again, "what it's all about. What the list is. Where were Theresa and Aaron on there? I bet you don't know where Harry was off the top of your head, but you'd know where *their* names were, correct? You'd had their bodies after all, you'd have taken ..." He couldn't finish the sentence. The next word was *samples.* "If you can't get us out, then tell me about the list so I can at least try to—"

"Will you actually tell me what's been going on in there if I do, Eric?" she asked him. "We have Stone Sensitive volunteers that are still on our books, but no one that can 'see' inside the Barrier—"

"I'll tell you everything," Eric said, "and believe me, it's a lot, and it's all bad news." He considered this a moment. "Not all, actually," he said. "There's a woman, she spoke to me in my head, and she's going to the—" He caught himself. He mustn't give anything away for free. "Answer my question: where were Theresa and Aaron on your list, and what *is* the fucking list."

"Do you give me your word?"

"What? Of course. Why wouldn't I? Don't you think I want to help stop these things?"

Straub shrugged.

"You're holding information to ransom and you have an understandable hatred of me," Straub said. "I believe you to be an honourable man, Mr Hatton, but I also believe that your judgement may be compromised right now."

Holding information to ransom? He was, he realised.

"I give you my word."

Straub hesitated for a moment.

"Did you get your immune booster for the Panama Flu?" Straub asked.

"Are you seriously asking me that?" Eric scoffed.

"In this case, the conspiracy theorists were correct; there *was* no Panama Flu. It was a screen to collate a genetic database of the British public. We called it the *Kindness Protocol*. We were given unprecedented resources and secret international collaboration; it would normally have taken years longer to process all of the genetic information. The plan was to know at a glance who all the potential Targets would be in the event of a Fourth Arrival, which would speed the up the process of the *Goodnight Protocol*: contacting them beforehand and prepping them to be evacuated and put into a comatose state the second any Stone Men arrived. We knew, thanks to the success with *Dispensatori*, our original test subject, that it could work; we could stop any Arrivals as soon as they started, and there was even serious talk of having a Stone Draft to force people in LION and above to volunteer. With the people we did have—and being able to work with them and the remaining Stone Man while we had it—we discovered more and more about the different divisions between the brackets: CROW, TIN, LION, GALE and DIGGS. A person's particular type of genetic propensity for Stone Sensitivity determined which bracket they were in . . . but by the time all the data was compiled the brackets mattered a hell of a lot less. The waters had been muddied by what we'd discovered with the volunteers who worked with the Stone Man; as everyone now knows, we had it in our possession. Different factors turned out to affect a person's bracket: antidepressants, addictions, medication, amount of meditation hours, even childhood trauma. We found ourselves talking about things like *epigenetics*, if you can believe that—"

"What did they mean," Eric asked quietly. "The different brackets."

Straub nodded and held up a finger.

"CROW," she said. "Ordinary human. No significant Stone Sensitivity and would never be a Target for the Stone Men." She counted off a second finger. "TIN. Target. May experience visions and a level of connectedness to either the Stone Man or its overseers. Minor levels of ability." Part of Eric couldn't believe it: Straub was singing like a canary but somehow he couldn't seem to take it in. *Harry*, his brain hissed at him.

But what could he do? Other than the unthinkable.

"LION," Straub was saying. "Can identify the Targets that the Stone Men are pursuing and lead us to them—"

"Which bracket could see what the Stone Men see?"

"Would you like me to explain this, or do you want to do it as a Q and A? I'm not being sarcastic."

"Harry saw what the Stone Giant saw," Eric said quietly, ignoring her. Straub hesitated in what looked like surprise, hearing the word *Giant* ... but of course, only for the briefest of moments.

"Then Harry is GALE," she sighed solemnly. "I was getting to that. The bracket that some would say is the 'top' level, depending on your point of view. Technically, the very top *genetic* level, at least, is DIGGS, the most genetically abundant, although these people are few and far between and don't seem to be able to do very much. Practically useless. No, GALE people are *much* more interesting—"

"Was Andy Pointer GALE, then?"

Straub hesitated again.

"Yes," she said. "He could, as we call it, *flash in* to the Stone Man's vision—all the GALE people could, although he was the best at it—"

"DIGGS couldn't do anything? At all?"

"At best, they'd experienced some vision during the Arrivals," Straub said. "No unique abilities, nothing. You'd think their genetic stock made them ideal Targets, but checking the DNA of their remains told us that no DIGGS people were harvested during the first three Arrivals. Maybe the Stone Men could only identify people as general Targets, not their specific levels."

A horrible thought occurred to Eric.

"The name *Jenny Drewett*," he said. "It'll be on the List somewhere."

"How do you—"

"Check the List."

Straub turned and called to the female scientist who was still standing a little way off, looking anxious to be asked into the conversation.

"Willenhall?" she said. As the scientist hurried over, Straub turned back to Eric. "Mind telling me why that name is important?" she asked him.

"Jenny's part of what's happened in Coventry," Eric snapped, "just check it and I'll tell you in a minute." Eric glanced briefly at Harry's coat-hidden form in the car.

How could he even do it, if it came down to it?

With the sledgehammer?

"Do you know the name *Jenny Drewett?*" Straub asked Willenhall.

"Yes," the scientist said, looking concerned. "She's on DIGGS."

Eric swore quietly.

"Thought she was," Straub muttered, to Eric's surprise. "We'll have to check age and place of work to get a rough confirmation, but..."

"How do you know that?" Eric asked, confused.

"The DIGGS list is short," Straub said. "I know all of those names. Eric..." she began, her tone careful. "What happened to Jenny Drewett? Who is she?"

Eric's hands were shaking a little.

"I think I know what the DIGGS people are for," he said. He paused briefly, the horror of Jenny's final moments spiking behind his eyes once more. He took a deep breath. "Here's what's happened in Coventry."

Eric began to tell her. After a minute or two, he noticed Straub make a near-imperceptible gesture towards Willenhall, who began taking notes. Eric just kept talking. All the while, he kept glancing back at his friend seated inside Jenny's Honda.

Harry, hidden inside a stranger's car, shivering under his dirty jacket.

***

Eric finished talking.

The only sounds on the A45 by then were those of the breeze and the murmur of the nearby crowd. Straub stood with her arms folded across her chest. Willenhall was the first of the three of them to speak.

"That's possibly one mystery solved then, Brigadier," she said quietly.

"Go on," Straub said. Eric opened his mouth before realising she was talking to the scientist.

"DIGGS," Willenhall said. "Sounds like their purpose was to be a catalyst. For transforming newborns into . . . well. Stone adults."

"As in helping a Stone caterpillar turn into a Stone butterfly?" Straub said, turning to Willenhall. "It was apparently so weak beforehand that a middle-aged alcoholic could knock it down with a sledgehammer. What was that then, the pupus stage?"

"*Pupal* stage," Willenhall politely corrected, "and logically, it's very possible, yes. Even in our natural world, there are creatures that need outside influence to—"

"Why wouldn't they go for DIGGS-level people the first time?" Eric interrupted. "With the bubbles they could have—" He stopped, already having reached a conclusion: in the first three Arrivals, the Stone Men didn't have the Prism. If that had been a tool to make the bubbles, it made sense that they could potentially use the it to be more *accurate* too. "Where's Harry Regis on the list?" Eric asked softly. He didn't ask about Theresa and Aaron. They were already gone.

"There's only one Harry Regis listed as Stone Sensitive," Willenhall said, "and he's on GALE."

"And where am I?"

"Did you receive your immune booster as part of the Panama Flu program?"

". . . no."

Willenhall politely shrugged as if to say *well there you go.*

"But by the looks of what you've been able to do," she continued, "if you haven't flashed into a Stone Man when you

were standing next to it, and you're alive, I'd say you're on LION—
"

"Do you think you could have broken the bubble around Jenny if you'd used the gun?" Straub suddenly interrupted. Eric was stunned. He hadn't even thought about it. He'd emptied the clip into the Pale Stone Man without thinking of using it on the bubble. Straub scowled, seemingly at herself. "Excuse my directness, I didn't mean that as an admonishment. I'm checking: there was no give whatsoever when you struck it with the sledgehammer, correct?"

"None . . ." Eric had told himself there had been no way to get Jenny out—

"Then our previous option for sending the Stone Men away just got taken off the table," Straub said grimly, "at least for preventing DIGGS people from getting harvested."

"Or unless regular Targets are put inside more of these bubbles," Willenhall said.

"Mm."

Straub paused, as if considering her next words very carefully. "Eric," she said softly, "I'm going to head to the Isle of Skye now myself."

"What? How do I—"

"I'm going to leave Willenhall here with you in case you have questions or need help with any developments," Straub continued, holding up a hand, "but if this Maria Constance is on her way there with my people then she'll be going to our other research facility; our communications have been extremely difficult since the anomaly's Arrival, but we got word of a departure from Ladybower. I believe what you're saying about your experience with her is true and it needs investigating . . . and me leaving to potentially meet with her offers far greater hope for your friend than me talking here with you. Don't you agree?" He had to, but he couldn't admit it to her. "This *is* hope, Eric; I've never heard of anyone mentally communicating messages long-distance like that, not in any of the Arrivals. So please: don't give up. I can't guarantee you'll be able to get hold of me if you need to; our radios are becoming more and more useless, but I think this is too important to not see to personally. But I have to ask you something." Eric waited without responding. "Do you trust me now?"

"No." The answer was given gently but without hesitation.

"Alright," Straub said. "That's your choice and I respect it. But if you can trust me on anything at all, do trust what I said: if your friend is being Targeted, you will be doing him a great disservice if you don't end his life before a Stone Man gets here. *Believe me on that.* Please." She held his gaze. "If you do get out of Coventry somehow and make it to the Isle of Skye, I'll see you there." She sighed heavily. "You have some major challenges ahead of you, Eric. I hope you succeed. I really do." She gestured to Eric's missing hand. "And I think, by the sounds of what you were able to do, we could even use your help. Please," she said, taking a step back from the barrier, "get there." She nodded at Willenhall. "Doctor."

"Ma'am," Willenhall said. "Good luck."

"Thank you."

Straub turned and walked away. Eric watched her leave, his ears ringing mercilessly, while Willenhall stood awkwardly nearby. The distant crowd's hubbub began again in earnest as Straub was escorted back to her ride.

"When did you last sleep, Eric?" Willenhall asked.

"Give me a second," Eric muttered before turning and heading back to the car. As he drew closer to the vehicle he could see Harry still rocking in his seat, hidden by his jacket. Its material was pulled taut, clutched in Harry's fists. Faint gibbering sounds came from the other side of the glass. Eric's hand went to his mouth as he let out a little moan of his own.

He tried to tell himself it might not be the Quarry Response. But what else *could* it be? Stress, a mental breakdown? That was possible, given what they'd been through on so little sleep, as well as Harry's drinking. They were stuck inside Coventry with seven Stone Men. Was it not conceivable—even *very* conceivable—that Harry was having a breakdown? The logic was pretty convincing, but Eric's eyes still flitted to the sledgehammer now lying in the rear footwell.

His shoulder was screwed, and he only had one hand. Would he even be able to get enough power into the swing to—

He realised what he was thinking and thrust the idea away. Eric lightly tapped on the glass.

Harry let out a cry and jumped violently in his seat.

"Harry, it's okay," Eric said softly, "it's me, I just want to talk to you and make sure you're okay." Harry didn't respond, instead recommencing his rocking, perhaps a little faster, and with even more rapid-fire babble. Eric ran a hand through his hair. If he broke now, he knew, it'd be the end of both of them. He'd fall apart and Harry would die. Eric's hand found the handle of the car door. "I'm going to open the door—"

He popped it open very gently and slowly. The second the rubber seal between door and frame squeaked apart, Harry screamed and leapt across to the opposite seat, coat flying up, and began scrabbling at the other door's interior panel with his fingers like a dog pawing to be let out. "Okay, okay!" Eric let the door go. "Hey, it can stay closed Harry, don't—" Harry's fingers found the door release catch and he burst from the car, a frantic greyhound released from its trap. Eric watched in dismay as his friend ran across the abandoned road, moaning and gibbering, coat pulled over his head, and leapt over the roadside barrier, diving into the ditch beneath the hedgerow that lined the dual carriageway. Eric watched, then put his hands to his temples and closed his eyes.

It could be a breakdown, he thought. *It could be a breakdown.*

There was only one thing left to try.

He sat down in the passenger seat himself, put his right arm back in its sling, sighed heavily, closed his eyes, and recommenced trying to call Maria.

***

An hour or so later Eric was out of the Honda and pacing back and forth as he tried fruitlessly to reach her. He'd had to; he'd kept falling asleep in the front seat. He'd checked on Harry a few times but doing so had been pointless, and Eric's headache was getting worse and worse. In fact . . .

A rush of cold shot up his back.

Oh God.

It had to happen, of course it did. The Stone Men were going to wake soon, and that meant—

Eric felt his body land on the concrete but felt no pain, not even in his stitched-up shoulder. He was in the darkness, the vision coming up fast, his body feeling like it belonged to someone else as it locked up, the swirl of faces beginning in front of Eric's eyes.

He caught a glimpse of one particular face in the tumble. Brief, but enough.

No, no, no—

With his last remaining shred of mental fortitude he tried to push *away* from the vision for once rather than trying to see what it was; to his amazement, he half-managed it, feeling himself return to his body even as his sight continued to switch between the concrete of a Midlands road and the impossible magic of the Stone Men's signal. Using the side of the car to pull himself up, trying to keep his focus on the physical world around him, Eric made it to his feet. He spun around so his back was against the car, getting his drunk-feeling bearings, and his eyes fell upon the Barrier and Willenhall's concerned face.

After what he'd just seen, he had to take the chance.

Eric began to stagger forward, swaying left and right as the sight of Willenhall and the Barrier switched places constantly with the tumbling chaos in the projector screen of his mind. He was walking through the world as if it were an old, strobing cinematograph. The swirling Barrier didn't help with his disorientation as he came within feet of it; for a moment he thought he couldn't go any further and nearly blacked out, suddenly careening ten feet to the left and beginning to succumb to the vision once more, but dammit, *Harry*—

He straightened up, blinked, and dived forward. Willenhall was yelling something to him and her words became a scream as Eric's hand and stump came up and the scientist understood the risk he was about to take.

"Eric, *stop!* You don't know what will happen with this one—"

He fell face-first against the Barrier and as he did so the sight of the road—Willenhall, the crowd in the distance, the soldiers, the hedges and the concrete—all of it went away and stayed away.

He didn't burst. He was alive. Part one of his last-ditch gamble had paid off; now he would see if the second did, too.

After all, Maria had spoken to him through the Stone Men's circuit, hadn't she? If this thing wasn't connected to it too, then he didn't know what the hell else could be. He saw nothing at all, though. Only quiet. It was . . . nice. The faces of his vision were still there, rolling in his head, but now that he was connected to the Barrier he found he could compartmentalise them away. It was easy.

There, again! They *had* been there for just a moment—seen out of the corner of his mental eye, hanging there like the shadowy after-image seen behind closed eyelids after looking at a bright light—and Eric thought he'd been right earlier. Streams? Threads? Whatever they were, he'd glimpsed them again, but what was staying now—growing louder, clearer—were the sounds. They were coming in very faintly; a metallic screeching, heard like radio static from five rooms away. Was that sound coming *from* the threads? Was that what the threads were carrying, then? If he couldn't see them, he could certainly hear them, albeit faintly. But it was just . . . noise.

Then he could see something again, but not the threads.

Lights.

He was looking down at a vast but dim shape far below him. He couldn't see it clearly; was that dark outline the whole country? Yes, and he knew now that the big light right in the centre was the Barrier, and far away from it a tiny light was blinking into existence. Eric recognised it by feel, not by sight; after all, he'd made extremely personal contact with one. It was a bubble, being switched on. Imprisoning some poor, doomed soul. Away to the west, another lit up.

The penny dropped. There would be at least six more of these, seven if the Stone Giant walked too, and one of them—

Trying to suppress his panic, Eric reached out in the darkness, feeling his way. He could remember what Maria's voice had felt like in his head, the sensation of its presence burned into his brain, and if he could find her—

Stay calm, he thought. *You can do this—*

But there was something else beneath it all. That distant, metallic screaming that he could hear, carried along those almost-invisible threads perhaps. He began to understand that it wasn't just static. It was information.

The Stone Men—or their leaders—were talking to one another, and Eric could hear it.

The most insane part was that Eric realised he could understand some of it.

Oh . . . my . . . God . . .

He couldn't directly translate it, but he could get a vague sense of what they were telling one another. Something was . . . building up, right on the verge of happening? The faces in the back of his mind were growing larger, more forceful, and soon he might not be able to keep them locked in their compartment while he worked; the Stone Men were about to set off; was this *build-up* the preparation to do that? No, he didn't think that was it. Whatever they were talking about was larger—

Harry—

Why the hell couldn't he find Maria? She had been a beacon before, he couldn't understand why—

There.

He had her. But she was muffled . . . and moving fast. Of course she was; if she was heading to Skye and being transported by the military, then she was probably flying, but smothered like that? Was she wrapped up? Being kidnapped?

He could feel the quiet of her mind. She was asleep, then. She'd expended so much; the exhaustion was clear. She'd saved Harry before, and surely others too.

But he needed her to save Harry again.

Maria.

Nothing.

MARIA. It's Eric. You saved me and Harry in Coventry. I need you again. We *need you.*

...Eric...?

He had her! She sounded as if she were dazed, dreamlike ... had he actually woken her up yet? She still felt asleep—

Yes! Yes, it's me!

...how...

I'm on the outskirts of Coventry, I'm touching the big energy Barrier thing and I think it's—

That didn't matter.

Maria, they're back! The Stone Men are back!

Silence. Was she all the way back under? She clearly wasn't awake then—

...Stone Men...

They're at Ground Zero, Eric said, *they're back and there's a big one, a, a big red one, and either they or the others where they're from are talking to each other, they're doing something, but Maria, they're going to start walking again and I think they're going to come and take my friend! I need you to save him like you did before!*

There was silence. He could feel her trying to get her body to wake up, to comprehend what he was saying, her fear of—

He suddenly knew how to wake her. It was brutal, but Harry's life was on the line.

Can you see Coventry, Maria? Can you see it like you saw us before?

...yes...

Go there now. Go and see what's there.

... 'kay...

He felt her move away for a moment. All the while that horrible, metallic screeching grew louder; Eric understood snatches of it, they were talking about ... a next ... *life?* No, not life, a stage, a phase ... and the faces continued to tumble in the back of his mind, slowing as the screeching's volume increased, and Eric was rocked sideways as they came to an awful and undeniable selection of seven, slow and clear as they cycled in the darkness. The Targets had been selected, and finalised.

Among them, unmistakable now, was Harry's face.

As Eric spun away from the Barrier to see Harry, ignoring Willenhall's questions, he felt the sparking burst of Maria's terror jolt through his body as she remotely saw the seven Stone Men standing at Ground Zero. His stump unintentionally left the Barrier's swirling transparent surface and he had time to hear Maria's terrified awakening scream of **Eri—** before the connection broke. He gasped and went to slap his stump back onto the solid wall of light, but just as he did he glanced to the ditch where Harry lay, out of sight, as the A45 came back into view.

Eric could already see the beginnings of a glow emanating from down in the earth.

He turned and broke for the ditch with only moments to spare, he knew, limbs flailing as he stumbled towards it; Maria might not be able to do anything if Harry's bubble was allowed to close over him, and it would in seconds. Jenny had said hers had started low on the floor, her Quarry Response so strong that she was frightened to get out from inside it. Maria or no Maria, he had to move Harry first. The thought came to him as he ran: *a bubble for even the regular Targets now, then; the Prism doing it? The Stone Giant?* The glow from Harry's emerging bubble wasn't golden, like Jenny's; this was a dull grey, not dissimilar to the larger Barrier. He moved as fast as he could, closing the thirty feet or so between himself and the ditch, but it was like trying to run in a nightmare; his body, still thrumming with the Barrier-muted effects of the vision, was only just coming back to itself, and wasn't responding as it should. What should have been a dash of a few seconds stretched out maddeningly as he hobble-ran like a mannequin coming clumsily to life. As he plunged towards that awful dull glow, watching the grim light rise higher, he understood the truth.

He wasn't going to make it.

Pop.

The bubble completed.

"No!" Eric screamed, closing the last few feet of distance between himself and the bubble in the ditch. He fell onto its surface, not caring if it killed him, and it *sizzled* like Jenny's had, only at a lower pitch. Through its dirty, swirling silver surface he saw Harry's twitching body, curled up in a foetal position in the dirt and slowly beginning to still its terrified-mouse movements. Like Jenny, the Quarry Response was abating, but there wasn't time to analyse that. Eric yanked his intact arm out of the sling and slapped his hand onto the bubble, pouring his mind into it.

Open.

The bubble shifted a fraction, the protesting, hissing sound becoming louder as a tiny hole opened in its surface, but this time he had even less strength.

OPEN.

The hole stopped growing.

OPEN YOU FUCKER, OPEN. PLEASE!

The hole slowly began to close against Eric's cries until it sealed over as if it had never been, vanishing back into the bubble's endlessly churning surface.

Maria—

He flailed his way back to the Barrier and slapped his hands onto it.

"Eric, what's hap—"

Willenhall's face and words disappeared as Eric entered the larger circuit once more. This time Maria was easy to find; she was awake and alert, shining before him. But if he could see her—

Maria!

Wait, he's back, shut up, he heard her barking to someone; it sounded slightly more distant, as if she were talking aloud to someone present with her physical voice rather than her mind, for when she spoke next he could hear it was directly to him, her words as clear as winter rain: ***Eric, I tried to hide you, where are you, what's happening?***

Harry, Eric told her, *he's, they've, the Stone Men are back and there's a new one, a Stone Giant and, and the Prism, the big building thing, I think the giant one used it to put Harry under this bubble thing, like the big Barrier around Coventry only much smaller, can you see him? Can you?*

There was a pause.

Yes, just, looking through that thing around the city is hard, it's so dense, but . . . yes . . . There was another pause. **Eric . . . I can't free him.**

What?

I . . . I . . .

Eric felt her shift in his head.

I can't open either of them. The big one or the little one! I don't think I can control those things. Eric . . . she paused again.

I'm so sorry. You have to understand, when you woke me up, I could feel them searching. All the faces were being chosen and ... Eric ... some of the faces were ours, here, and I could hide us. But I only have so much. Do you understand?

He did. Oh sweet heavens above, he did.

No ... you have to help Harry ... please ...

Eric, you said you were in trouble and we were talking and ... I only had enough left in me, enough time, *to, to hide one more person. I ... it all happened so quickly ...*

Eric heard the mental equivalent of a deep breath.

I hid you, Eric.

A shiver ran down Eric's back—they'd nearly chosen him—but that meant Harry ...

Try now. Try hiding him.

Silence.

I can't do it, Eric. I don't ... I don't have enough. And you have to listen to me.

Eric stood in the dim light of the circuit's vision of the country below him. There were now five lights around the shape that was Britain. One more, he knew, was being obscured by the glowing light around Coventry. The screeching was so *loud* now, and he could make out more of it, but all he could think about was Harry. A selfish thought struck him, and he hated himself even more, if that were possible, the great fucking *failure* that he was: when Harry was gone, he would be all alone inside the Barrier.

The ... Stone Men ... Her voice in Eric's head trembled as she took a moment to compose herself. *The new one. The really big one. I can't clearly see what's happening, but I can feel it ... doing something. It's not just preparing to walk, I think. It's talking to the big building thing, the Prism you called it. The energy, all of it, it's so* busy. *Something is about to—*

Y-yes . . . I can hear them talking about—

You can hear them talking?

Yes, *dammit,* Eric interrupted, desperate, *but . . . Harry,* he added dumbly, sounding like a lost child. *You can't—*

I'm so sorry, Eric.

But—

His body alerted him, splitting his consciousness between whatever plane he was on with Maria and the long stretch of concrete outside of Coventry. His hand and his stump were feeling something physical.

The Barrier was vibrating under his hands.

He looked through it at Willenhall's face. She looked confused, not afraid. She couldn't feel it then? That chaotic, metallic screaming in his head was intensifying and the concept it was communicating came through to him loud and clear, like a bell:

NOW, it said.

Then the rest came, and Eric understood what they were about to do, and for a moment he was so horrified that he couldn't speak.

"Get away," Eric said to Willenhall. The words were a croak. Then again, louder: "Get away! Now!" He looked at the crowd behind their own smaller wooden sawhorse barriers in the distance.

"You're all going to die!" Eric screamed. *"You have to run!"* Willenhall, to her credit, paused for only a moment, before turning and running away up the A45 as fast as she could, dropping her radio and pen in her haste. The soldiers closest to the Barrier looked to one another in confusion and then turned to watch Willenhall disappearing. Eric, scared out of his mind, plunged back into the darkness and found Maria again.

Are you flying?

Yes, what's hap—

Land! LAND! LAND RIGHT NOW—

The air around Eric moved heavily, followed by the sound of a rapid, wet, but staccato tattoo.

Whoof.

Popopopopopopopopopopopopopopopopop—

One moment, Eric was looking at some soldiers, some military vehicles, and a crowd of people and reporters further up the road. The next, there was a terrible, ripping, rapid-repeat bursting sound like the world's largest pan of popcorn, and then all of the people were gone, replaced by a red fog that hung in the air.

Far away down the road, he had the briefest glimpse of the Barrier shooting over the horizon at incalculable speed before its ugly light seemed to blend into the sky. Immediately in front of him, the clothes and weapons of soldiers lay on the floor, with the all-too-familiar coating of congealed blood. A little farther away, Willenhall's coat lay on the ground in a similar state. The clothes of the crowd formed a small sea of fabric, with the last of the remains of the people that once filled them now slowly drifting to earth like a crimson early-morning dew.

There was a rushing sound away to his right, and then a deafening bang. He spun round, prepared for some new atrocity, but as he saw the thick plumes of black smoke rising he understood what had happened: the Barrier had taken out the pilot of the military helicopter that had been circling overhead. Now there was silence, save for the faint buffeting of the wind in his ears, and Eric was alone on the empty road.

No. Not alone.

He spun once more on his heels; Harry's bubble hadn't moved or expanded. It sat there over the ditch, its ugly, dirty-silver surface spinning like eddying, poisoned water. Eric walked—not ran—towards it. As he came close enough, he could see that Harry was now sitting up inside the bubble, lucid, the Quarry Response abated. Eric squatted down and rested his forearms on Harry's new prison.

"Hi, Harry," he said.

"Hello mate," Harry said quietly. He had pulled out his hip flask and was unscrewing the lid; he paused for a moment, trying to think of something more to say. Then he gave up, shook his head, and took a long pull, eyes screwed tightly shut.

Part TWO

ANDY AND PAUL

Chapter Five

Andy at the End, Paul's Long Days

***

Andy Pointer.
The Larson Hotel, Birmingham.
Five Years Ago.
The Third Arrival.

"And that's the big surprise for me in all of this," Andy said. He didn't even bother to wipe the free-flowing tears from his face now, although he was glad his voice wasn't choking up. He paused before continuing, staring at the red light shining out of the Dictaphone's black plastic casing. "When it really counts, some people can just do what needs to be done ... but it turns out I'm one of them." He paused again; could he admit the next part? Then he realised it was of no concern. Soon he would be past caring about anything. "And I've been a coward all my life," he said. The damning words seemed to echo off the walls of the hotel penthouse.

His thumb hovered over the record button; one press and his last words would be complete.

"Who knew?" he said, sniffing. "I've always—" He didn't know how to finish the sentence and didn't really have anything else to say; this was just more stalling. "No," he said. "Doing it again. I'm going."

Then end the recording, he thought. The red light shone back at him, taunting him. *I dare you*, it said, *because when this ends, you do too—*

"... Bye." He stopped the recording. The red light went off. *"Fuck!"*

He drew his arm back to throw the gadget across the room ... but realised that would damage the memory card inside, ruining not only the hours and hours of audio he'd recorded here at the beginning of the Third Arrival, but his earlier, on-the-scene recordings from the First. As drunk as he was—he'd emptied the minibar—he managed to restrain himself and instead lightly tossed the Dictaphone onto the bed. He put his head in his hands and sobbed, rocking back and forth and feeling justifiably sorry for himself.

You deserve this, he thought. *You and Paul, you hunted those people down—*

But they'd saved lives, hadn't they? They'd made the difficult decisions. Paul might not see it that way, but Andy did.

Didn't hurt to make a little money on the side thought did it, eh?

For once his self-response was honest, blunt, and—to him—irrefutable.

No, he thought. *It didn't. And I'm paying the maximum price for it, so on balance, fuck off.*

On the TV, the cluster of Stone Men stood in the pointlessly water-filled enclosure of Ground Zero, waiting to be off. Andy felt an odd mix of relief and jealousy; they would be someone else's responsibility now, and *that* individual would be the most important person in the world. Not Andy. How did he feel about—

Stop stalling.

He stood and crossed to the penthouse TV. It looked heavy. Heavy enough to break the glass in the window. He hobbled around to the back of the set, his legs threatening to give way, and bent down to remove the plug from the wall.

There was a knock at the door.

Andy briefly considered not answering it. What would be the point? But it might be housekeeping and they might let themselves in—

"No thank you," he called, trying to sound normal. Dammit, had that broken the spell? Could he still go through with—

You can, something solid inside him replied. *You know you can. You don't have to doubt yourself anymore.*

"Can I talk to you, Andy?"

Straub.

It was *Straub.*

Andy was so shocked that he remained frozen.

Brigadier fucking Straub?!

How the hell did she know where he was? He stayed silent, hoping she'd go away.

"I'm not going to go away Andy," she said. Damn. She really was good. "I'm not going to stop you either. I just want to talk to you."

"We . . . we already talked," Andy called, still bent at the waist and holding the TV's power cord. "What's this about?"

Perhaps Straub wasn't taking any chances? Maybe that wouldn't be so bad after all. He'd turned down her earlier telephone offer of 'help' with what he had to do, but maybe that was a mistake?

"I'm still going to do it," he said, dropping the cable, but making sure to back out of the firing line of the doorway. "You don't need to be here ..." He struggled to remember her name. She'd told him on the phone when they'd last spoken. ". . . Laura."

"I believe you," she said. "I honestly do. Can you open the door please? I don't want to shout about this. I just want a few minutes of your time. You definitely want to hear it."

It's kind of precious right now, Laura, Andy thought bitterly. He crossed to the door. *You definitely want to hear it*, she'd said. Maybe they'd come up with a way to—

No. No way. He flattened himself against the wall by the doorframe, using his dressing gown to wipe the saltwater from his cheeks, and chanced a quick glance through the spyhole.

Straub stood by herself in the hallway. She was wearing civilian clothes, a smart black suit and a white blouse. She looked strangely taller, and then Andy mentally kicked himself; street clothes probably meant seeing her in heels for the first time. He was so taken aback by the sight of Civilian Straub that his hand went to the latch without thinking and opened it. Straub smiled faintly when she saw him. Andy didn't smile back. He quickly stuck his head out into the hallway and looked down it; no other people there.

"Where's the goon squad?" Andy asked.

"There are two APVs in the car park," Straub said. "But I thought it best I just come and knock first. What would be the point of armed men anyway? Threaten to kill you if you didn't listen? Or rush you and you then jump out of the window?"

"What's with the getup?"

"I'm hardly going to come in here in field uniform, Andy. I do sometimes need to keep a low profile, you know."

He didn't step back to let her in.

"How'd you find me? My phones were all off."

"You should have paid cash at the desk, Andy." *Andy* now. Not *Mister Pointer.*

"Jesus. Fucking idiot."

Straub shrugged. *You said it,* the gesture said. She looked at his red face.

"Are you alright?" she asked. Andy screwed his face up. "Okay," she said. "Silly question." She paused and took a breath. "Andy . . ." Straub sighed, "I don't want to get your hopes up, but it might be extremely lucky that we caught you in time. We've come up with an idea."

Andy didn't dare to even breathe.

"It's a theory and nothing more," she continued, "but it has to be worth a try. But if this doesn't work, the end result has to be the same. We couldn't let you go off by yourself again afterwards. We'd have to take care of . . . the deed. It wouldn't hurt. Winter's gone AWOL, you see, and we can't get hold of him. We don't know if he's going to go through with it, so we couldn't risk you doing the same. Not again."

He faintly registered the news in his mind—Paul had gone AWOL—but the previous news was vastly more important. *There was a chance.*

"Brigadier—Laura—I need you . . . to be clear," Andy said carefully. The hallway swam behind her, the colours of the wallpaper becoming too bright. "Wait. Come inside." He stepped back and Straub crossed the threshold. There wasn't much point; the entire top floor belonged to the Penthouse suite, and there would be no one listening nearby. He closed the door behind her and actually gripped Straub gently by the shoulders. She let him, looking up into his pleading eyes. "Tell me what you're saying," he said.

"I will, Andy," she said calmly. "We want to try inducing you into a coma."

Andy blinked.

"We have an escort standing by, as I say," Straub said, "and we can have you prepped and ready to go within thirty minutes. We want to see if the reduction in brain wave activity is sufficient to simulate death in the Stone Men's eyes, therefore sending home whichever Stone Man is pursuing you. From the little we know about them, it appears that their connection to their Targets is mental, as well as detecting the Targets' genes. It has to be worth a try. Plus, if it works and you survive, you could be an asset down the line, even if you remain cut off as you currently are. You and the others would be invaluable for research."

Andy swallowed hard. A sensation began to flood through him, as if he were clawing his way out from under six feet of earth. He slumped sideways slightly against the door as his legs gave way. Straub was still talking. "The Stone Men will start walking any minute now," she said, "but they will still take hours to get out of Coventry. That's damage that, given the potentially enormous benefits of this attempt, we can afford to risk. It gives us time to try this and see what happens—"

Andy collapsed against her, bawling. He didn't even try to hide it. Straub felt still and hard against him; there was no physical give in her. He didn't even know what he expected her to do, but to his amazement, he felt one of her hands patting him on the back.

"There are no guarantees here, Andy," she said quietly. "You have to understand that."

"I know, I know," he said, but already his desperate mind was turning *chance* into *fact*. He straightened and wiped his eyes with his sleeve, feeling lightheaded. "You have to tell Pau—" *Paul,* he thought. "You said Paul hasn't checked in?"

"No." Something in her eyes made Andy pause.

"You *are* going to tell him, right?"

"If the coma trick works immediately with you? Yes."

"And if it doesn't?"

"If it doesn't work immediately, then no," Straub said, that impenetrable poker face locked down once more. "Time and collateral damage are massive factors; this *is* a gamble, Andy. We're prepared to put one person under—you—and give it time to hopefully work, and any damage inflicted by the Stone Man in the meantime will be all be worth it if it turns out to be an effective way of protecting our assets. Our *Stone Sensitives* if you will." She sighed again. "But we can't afford to gamble *twice.*"

This was the same woman that had just been comforting him? A mere pat on the back, perhaps, but for Straub that must be the equivalent of washing Andy's feet.

"If you'd found Paul first," Andy asked slowly, "you would have done this with him instead?"

"Yes, Andy."

"And what would you have told him if you hadn't gotten hold of me yet?"

"We would have told him that you killed yourself, Andy. We wouldn't want him to consider the possibility of not going through with it. Do you understand? How important it would be that he does his duty? If I didn't know exactly where you were and, being blunt, couldn't have you acquired immediately if needed, then I wouldn't be telling you the truth either." There were only two options, Andy realised, feeling that earth start to close over him once more. The coma plan, or a bullet. "Plus," Straub added, "there's a growing consensus amongst our analysts that, if there's a mental connection to the Stone Men, it might go both ways; what might they know that we know as a result? What if the coma plan works but there was even a chance of them knowing, from what *Paul* knows, that their Targets weren't really dead? We couldn't risk that."

"And if this works quickly enough with me ... is there a chance you might try it with Paul?"

Straub just stared back at him.

"You'd best get properly dressed," she said, finally. "Did you wear any kind of covering on your way in, sunglasses, a hat perhaps—"

Andy blinked.

"Uh, yeah," he babbled, "Both, but ..." He had to push it, for Paul's sake. "Can I refuse to do this unless you try it with Paul too? He's ... he's my friend." It didn't sound heroic, but at least he'd said it.

"That's not much of a bluff, Andy," Straub said. "You're not exactly in a strong negotiating position, given the circumstances. But I will give you my word of this much: *if* it works quickly with you, then we'll try it with Paul too. Now, please hurry. Put some clothes on, and let's go."

Let's go, she'd said. Andy looked at the bed and the spray of empty minibar bottles. He looked at the TV, and the window it had been about to pass through.

He had been prepared to die in this room. Now, suddenly, he was leaving.

"Alright," he said. "I'll get dressed."

***

White walls. A steady beeping of a—

—heart monitor—

His eyes opened slowly.

—alive—

He was alive, he was fucking *alive* ... wait. Wait. He'd already ... woken up once, hadn't he ... ? He'd gone back to sleep again, but naturally, normally, for maybe ... a day? Two? Everything was hazy. He took in the room. It was a private hospital room somewhere. He tried to lift his arms, but they wouldn't move properly. He couldn't even seem to straighten them—

—atrophy—

He'd been in a coma. They'd reminded him of that. And *yes,* that was it, his muscles had atrophied, his joints tightened, and he would be fine, but he'd need rehab to stretch—

—ALIVE—

They'd told him that.

The plan had worked. How long had he been ... no, they hadn't told him that yet, which meant it was obviously a long time—

"Mr Pointer?" Someone was in the room with him. Andy tried to focus on them but his eyes weren't working properly, washed with the harsh glow of the strip lighting above that was bouncing off white walls. He heard the quick rustling of paper; someone had been sitting reading something, waiting for—"Hold on Mr Pointer," a youngish woman's voice said eagerly, sounding in her thirties. "Let me get someone, I'll be right back—"

But Andy didn't care. He was crying and feeling no shame for it, only a kind of embarrassed wonder at the situation. Why did he deserve to live? He closed his eyes again as the tears ran ... and he realised that he could still see. That was strange; his eyes were closed now. Was he dreaming? He was still so hazy ... no, he could definitely see something.

He'd thought he was in a hospital bed, but now he realised he was wrong.

He was actually inside a large hangar, and in front of him was some sort of big metal caravan on wheels.

He was following it for some reason, which meant somebody must have been pushing his bed—

Pain flooded his skull and he began to scream as he realised that this vision was not his own, and what that meant.

But you were cut off, how is this—

He knew the answer immediately, the same way he would feel that an oven was on if he stood close by. This wasn't some grand, nationwide connection that he could be snipped out of by the Stone powers that be; this was *impossible* for him to miss.

He was right next to it. Somehow, the Stone Man was nearby.

That means it's still here, it's still fucking here—

Before, his disconnect from the signal to the Targets had been like being disconnected from the radio signal of a broadcast, but that didn't matter here. His connection to the Stone Man himself—for this was the original, Caementum, that much was clear—was in his bones, his DNA. They couldn't cut him off from *this*. No radio signal was needed at this range; he was right outside the stadium and there was no way he couldn't hear the rock concert.

It's not here for you.

That was obvious. The Stone Man's quarry was inside that cabin. It was pulling Andy forward, so much so that he couldn't help but be drawn—

"Poll," Andy croaked, his friend's name rasping strangely from his lips, and just before the sight of the strange hangar disappeared and the clinical white walls of his hospital room came back into focus, he sensed something else about the Stone Man itself, that something was different—

Then the bigger realisation truly hit him.

PAUL IS ALIVE TOO—

The tears turned into amazed, hysterical laughter; part joy, part madness.

How the flying fuck had they both pulled this off?

The door opened and Straub entered quietly, followed by two people in civilian dress that Andy didn't recognise and, of course, David, Straub's head spook. To Andy's amazement, David was actually smiling at him. Andy supposed David must have heard that Straub had only just caught Andy before he did the deed. *If that's what it takes to get in your good books, Davey Boy*, Andy thought crazily, getting a fresh set of the giggles, *I'll stay in your Twat Book, thank you.*

"Strobb," Andy croaked, knowing how insane he must look, tear streaked and cackling.

"Try not to talk, Mr Pointer," one of the civilian types said. A doctor, perhaps. "You've had a long sleep. Just blink twice for yes and three times for no, okay?"

"Stone Man," Andy gasped, his eyes on Straub. "Here."

Straub and David exchanged a surprised look.

"Okay," she said. "Yes."

"Paul," Andy said. "Inside . . . thing."

"Oh my God," Straub said, a rare slip indeed. She immediately snapped back into form. "Well there goes at least one need-to-know restriction . . ."

"Something . . . wrong with it," Andy gasped.

Shocked silence.

"How do you mean, Andy?" David said carefully, sounding tense and stepping forward. "There's something wrong with the Stone Man?" Straub gently put her hand on David's arm, but Andy was already answering.

"Mm." It sank into him then. It wasn't over. He'd hoped that if he'd been put to sleep he'd wake up in a world where the Stone Men could at least be someone else's problem. But here he was, still at the heart of it—

He twitched on the bed. They'd woken him up. Why would they risk that if something important hadn't—

"We'll have questions about that later, Andy, but they can wait for now," Straub said. "Do you remember when we spoke before?"

"Nn."

"Okay. Just remember this: the Blue that was pursuing you went home. It took quite a few hours for it to get the message—we nearly gave up—but eventually it stopped walking. It then stuck around for a short while, and then it disappeared. *The plan worked*, Mr Pointer." Andy let out a shivering breath. "There have been no more Arrivals since then, either," Straub continued. "If yours comes back now you're awake, we can put you back under, as we know it works. But . . . well, we need you now, and we think waking you up is a calculated risk. We'll explain how Paul made it and what's been going on with him and Caementum, but for now just know that you don't have to worry. No hunting Targets. That's done. We only want you to help us connect with it, a little like before." She stepped forward and put a hand on his shoulder. "You're going to be kept safe. Alright?"

Safe . . . but trapped again.

"How l'ng . . . sleep?" Andy asked.

"You don't remember us telling you?"

He tried.

"...no."

"You've been under for two and a half years, Andy," David said quietly. Once, Andy knew, David would have said it with eager malice. Now the man almost sounded sorry.

"Can see ... Poll?"

"No," Straub said. "Not yet, anyway. Same rules apply as before; need to know basis only. We don't know what knowledge the Stone Men can pick up from him. Plus, if there's anything we've learned here at the Project, it's that Stone Sensitives need to be at a good level of physical fitness before they can be involved. You have a few months of physical therapy before we can get you in there. Eventually, you'll see him. But he has to stay in the dark for now."

Project? Andy tried to sit up.

"Best not to try and move right now, Mr Pointer," the doctor said.

"Lorra—" Andy began, but Straub winced a little.

"It's Brigadier Straub," she said gently. "We're on a military base, and I'm at work. Okay?"

"...where?"

"Sheffield."

Fucking hell, Andy thought. *I can't get away from this place.*

***

Paul.
Project Orobouros.
Six Months Later.

Paul heard the cabin's visitor alert sound.

It didn't exactly rouse Paul from his thoughts as he didn't really think that much anymore, but it did at least interrupt his staring at the switched-off TV. What time was it? He didn't know. He just knew how much everything in him *ached.*

He had to give Straub and her people credit where it was due: they generally tried to be as accommodating as possible. The alert was a good example of that. They'd installed it at his request after his first year in the cabin; he'd asked if they could always allow at least ten minutes' notice before coming to see him. He assumed that the soothing, slowly-fading-in tone of the alert had been designed to trigger as little anxiety as possible.

He moved the unused Xbox controller off his lap. He couldn't know, but he was convinced that there must be a newer version of the video game system out by now. He had never been a gamer in his old life, but the machine had become a pillar of his daily routine, at least until recently. They brought him new (old?) games on request. He yawned, dimly baffled yet again by just how tired he seemed to feel all the time. He'd never exercised this much in his life, and even if he'd slacked off a lot lately—it was so hard to find the willpower now—he was eating well. That was easy. They did look after him—and he'd even been offered study materials. He'd thought about learning something that might be useful if he ever got out of there, but then decided against it; to do so would be to keep confronting the fact that he was probably going to be in there for the rest of his life. The thought had an almost physical effect, like being stabbed. Paul knew that as long as the Right Honourable Gentleman was around it was very unlikely that he would ever be able to leave.

All signs seemed to point to it being around for a very long time.

Paul had decided to learn to play the guitar.

He got to his feet, letting out a long *oof* of effort, and crossed the short distance to the window. These days the suspension on the cabin—what was this, the Mark 6 now? 7?—was so good that the windows barely even vibrated with the cabin's movement. He could see the smaller-but-still-hulking shape of the companion cabin as it made its slow, trundling way across the hangar. Its rooflight switched from a rhythmic flashing to a steady always-on. This meant it had synced with Paul's own cabin—which apparently had its own, matching light—and manual control could be ceded to the companion cabin's self-docking procedure. He'd been amazed the first time he'd seen it, but now they told him there were production cars already being made that would soon be on public roads, driving themselves. The human-driven motor car—perhaps the most significant embodiment of his generation's way of life before the internet generation turned up—would soon be on its way out. Piece by piece the world he knew was becoming obsolete. Didn't it make sense that he should also?

Soon, his cabin would be turning. Then, of course, he'd be able to see—

Don't look at it.

He had that particular thought ten or twenty times a day. He managed to listen to it only half of the time now. He was getting better. Naturally they'd assigned him a very fine shrink indeed. Said shrink had been emphatic about Paul's need to accept the Right Honourable Gentleman's presence. *Think of it less as "don't* look at it", the shrink had said, *and more as "I don't need to check on it". See the difference? It's neither good or bad. It just* is.

Easy for her to say. In his early days in the cabin Paul had thought he might eventually get used to the Right Honourable Gentleman's steady pursuit. That never happened. The boffins had wondered if this was something to do with its ability to induce the Quarry Response. Paul had experienced it himself, after all; perhaps it wasn't possible for him to lose it altogether?

He still couldn't stop looking at it, though.

In the past he could always catch a quick glimpse of it as the cabin turned, but the larger windows on the latest model made that glimpse even easier, unless he had visitors. The companion cabin's docked presence blocked all outside vision, but right now there was still time to spot the Right Honourable Gentleman before the docking procedure completed. He knew the timings of the endless dance between cabin and pursuer on an almost instinctive level now, the way someone is aware of the motion of the elevator they're riding.

And . . . now.

More than three years of chasing him and that thing hadn't slowed down as much a nanosecond. Meanwhile, Paul felt strung out. He knew that was a side effect of depression, but he looked at his relentless, silent and ever-fresh pursuer and couldn't help but feel a stab of envy; Paul's body felt like it was winding down a little more every day.

Was that even a bad thing?

The Stone Man followed.

Paul watched while the seconds passed, as inexorable as Caementum himself. The Stone Man didn't have eyes, but whenever he saw it Paul felt as if the thing were gazing into his soul.

Then the Stone Man was gone from sight and the window was full of the gunmetal grey of the companion cabin.

Paul moved to the bed and sat on the edge of it to wait. A few seconds later there was a gentle clunk as the walkway slotted home, and then the doorbell rang.

"Come in," Paul said. Of course, there wasn't a door handle on the inside. There was a *t-chak* sound, the metal door swung open, and three people stepped in. One of them was the standard armed military escort they always supplied for visitors. The second was, as expected, Dr Holbrooks. The other, to Paul's surprise, was Brigadier Straub.

A second surprise came with the Brigadier's appearance: Paul was pleased to see her.

"Goodness me," Paul said, the smile on his face feeling unfamiliar. "Fancy ..." The mild witticism died on his lips. What had he been going to say? *Fancy seeing you here? Do you come here often?* He would have said any of the above once upon a time. Now he'd lost his train of thought halfway through the sentence. "I'm surprised to see you," he said, finally. He was still smiling though. Straub smiled back. Unlike everyone else at the Project these days, Holbrooks was in civilian-workplace dress, wearing a white collared shirt and trousers. Straub wore the same non-military looking 'uniform' as the other grunts, but hers was the only polo shirt without any markings or pips at all.

"Hello, Paul," Straub said warmly, or warmly by Straub's inscrutable standards. "It's good to see you."

"Likewise." She may have been his captor, but she'd also saved his life, as far as Paul was concerned. If it wasn't for Straub allowing him the resources of the British Army, the Right Honourable Gentleman would have removed some of Paul's spine and part of his brain stem (from just above the C1 vertebra to the

T5, naturally). He may have resented the place, but the cabin wasn't a prison to Paul.

The cabin was a priest hole.

"What's up, Doc?" Paul said, nodding at Holbrooks, who returned the gesture. The terrible joke was automatic, started by a man Paul no longer remembered yet still made every time Holbrooks put in an appearance.

"I'm well thank you, Mr Winter." If Straub was businesslike, Holbrooks went about his work like a focused whirlwind of intensity. He was kind, but not a man for small talk. Paul saw him at least once a month and the meetings were always brief. Paul had long since given up on asking questions; it hurt far too much when the rare answers he *did* get turned out to be wrong, revealed as indescribably painful messages of false hope: a potential development in the use of soundwaves as a weapon (this had turned out to be an error in the test results analysis); a possible weakening in the integrity of the invisible barrier the Stone Man used to keep its Quarry in place. They tested it a few times a year now and Paul always found doing so to be an absolute bastard. The edge of that unseen energy field, intangible to anyone but Paul—Paul's actual, personal prison—was, of course, situated just outside the hangar that had been specially constructed inside its circumference. The logistics of avoiding the Right Honourable Gentleman during the journey to and from his Barrier weren't that hard to overcome in a practical sense, certainly no more than the challenge of keeping the Stone Man hidden from outside eyes as they did so. The mental toll it took was another matter entirely.

Paul discovered that he did not like to leave the cabin at all.

The sense of exposure—of the Right Honourable Gentleman being only a few feet away with no cabin for protection (even though the cabin might as well have been made of tissue paper)—was too much to bear. The stupid thing was that they took him over in the companion cabin—a vessel every bit as un-Stoneproof as his usual home and built along identical lines—and he *still* experienced panic attacks. They didn't want to drug him up too much to help suppress his anxiety because, they said, they were always too worried about altering his brain chemistry in any significant, semi-permanent way. What if they did something to him—the lynchpin here—and the Stone Man went haywire?

The Barrier was always, of course, as strong as ever.

"How are you feeling, Paul?" Straub asked. They'd last spoken maybe two months before.

"Mustn't grumble," Paul said with a shrug, even though the action hurt. "Intact spine, everything's fine. Spine partially gone?"

"Something's wrong," Straub finished for him, her tone that of an eye-roll . . . but was that the edge of a smirk around her lips? He was surprised she remembered his line. He pointed a finger-gun at her and fired it lazily.

'That's the one," he said, and gestured to the armchairs nearby. By now, the cabin was the size of the average bungalow. They'd even added a separate bedroom above the main living area. The pair sat, but Paul hesitated. "Tea? Coffee? I still even have some IPA left from my birthday." He was allowed a little booze now and then; any potential alterations to his brain chemistry as a result would be minor and brief, he'd argued, and he'd been a drinker before any of the Arrivals.

"I'm touched," Straub said, meaning it. "Thank you. But no, I'm fine thanks."

"Nothing for me, thank you," Holbrooks added.

"Okay. How are you, Brigadier?" He actually wanted to know. "Doing okay?" Now it was Straub's turn to shrug.

"I'm fine Paul, thank you. Husband has the 'flu so I have two full-time jobs right now, but I'm doing well. Another five years and I can move to Europe. France, most likely." It was a third surprise inside the space of five minutes.

"Retirement? You?"

"Oh, yes," Straub said sincerely. "Can't wait. I've always loved this job, but since the Arrivals there have been so many elements that are ..." She shrugged. Whenever Straub let out rare information about her life, Paul never had a response. He often wondered if this was how Andy had felt when talking to people.

"I can imagine," Paul said simply. "So what's this about? When I saw the companion coming over, I thought you would be an unscheduled civilian to do the shake-hands-n'-boost with. Both of you here together, though ... I'm assuming this is something important?" Holbrooks looked at Straub, who gestured *the floor is yours* in response.

"Well, we don't know about important yet," Holbrooks began, leaning forward, "but interesting, certainly." The man had always looked wiry but Paul noticed that Holbrooks was looking *thin*. It wasn't surprising; the rumour was that Holbrooks' predecessor, Dr Boldfield, had tapped out of the job because it was simply too intense. "We're bringing someone in today who we'd like you to touch. And then, if we get a good response, we'd like them to do a little work with you in the cabin. Today, if you're both up to it afterwards."

If they were both up to it? Paul hadn't told Holbrooks how tired he'd been feeling.

"What kind of work?"

Holbrooks gave Paul a rare but reluctant smile.

"Mr Winter , you know ..."

"Well, won't it be bloody obvious what the work is once we start doing it?"

"Probably. But that can come when and if it comes. In the meantime, we have to be aware of . . ."

The apologetic shrug. The Caeterus.

Whatever force had sent the Stone Men. The pronunciation varied from boffin to boffin, some using the soft C and others using the hard, like the first time Paul had first heard it a few years ago. *I wonder what they're cooking up for us next* had been the old Paul's response. It got a laugh out of one of the three people present and that had been it. Always a tough crowd in the cabin, always. They'd explained the name was Latin, he'd asked what it meant, and when they told him he didn't think it very funny anymore.

It meant *Other*, or *the Rest*. Paul thought those far more appropriate-sounding names.

Whatever Holbrooks' crew called them, history told that the Caeterus eventually knew when people were connected to their processes, so much so that the Caeterus seemingly severed that connection; as they'd done with Andy, Paul, and all of the people who had ever become connected to the Stone Men's feeds.

But could that feed also run in the opposite direction? What if it had only been severed one way?

Andy Pointer had seen the Stone Man's visual feed, looked through its 'eyes', after all. So what if the Caeterus could through their Quarries' eyes, knew of what they—of what Paul—knew? That meant, wherever possible, keeping Paul in the dark. Even Paul agreed with it, as frustrating as it often was.

"Yes, yes," Paul said, irritated. "Okay. Why did this need both of you to tell me?"

"I haven't spoken to you myself in a while," Straub said. "Today's work is going to be a little different, and I wanted to touch base with you. Last time we spoke, you were . . ." She held his gaze, not finishing the sentence to avoid embarrassing him in front of Holbrooks. Paul appreciated the gesture. It had just been Straub and an escort present to witness his first real meltdown a few months ago. In retrospect, he was surprised it had taken so long to actually happen.

It was because he'd finally run the numbers. What started as a bored maths doodle ended in a hysterical call to the main hub and a demand to see Straub immediately.

It had been 4 a.m.

While a sleepy Straub had watched he'd paced the cabin's gently rumbling floor, wearing nothing but a T-shirt and a pair of boxers, clutching paper and a pencil.

"Andy always said it wasn't an invasion," he'd babbled. "The Stone Men take their target, extract the body part, split it and create two new Stone Men. And that's way too slow to be an invasion since the population would grow, so the harvest would always be relatively small compared with that. Right?"

Straub nodded wearily.

"But look. Look!" He yanked the paper open and held it up for her to see. "Here! First Arrival: one Stone Man creates two more. Right? We now have three. Second Arrival: three stone men create two more each; okay, one failed in reality because one of the Targets was killed before they could be harvested, but let's just go with their ideal Stone fucking model here."

He paused for a moment, remembering just how that particular Target died: an infant killed by his mother, Theresa Pettifer, the other Target in the equation, driven to madness by the Quarry Response. "So," he continued, "we would now have six *new* Stone Men, making a total of nine. Third Arrival: each of the nine Stone Men—if we hadn't had our Hunters tracking Targets down to remove them from the board—would each make two more. Now we're at twenty-seven of them. Imagine a Fourth Arrival happens: 27 x 3 = 81. The number of Stone Men, in their ideal scenario, trebles each visit. *If those things come back—*"

"Paul," Straub said, holding up a hand. Later, Paul would realise that he didn't remember when Straub had started using his first name. There had been a time when it would have felt unusual. When had that transition happened? He still didn't know her first name, but it didn't matter. Brigadier felt like a nickname. "You know we don't believe that will happen, she'd said. Keeping Caementum here—"

"He's the *lynchpin*, yes, and I'll come to that," Paul breathed, not breaking stride. His back was covered in sweat. "If they come back, by the end of the *Tenth* Arrival there will be 3 x 3 x 3 x 3 x 3 x 3 x 3 x 3 x 3 Stone Men. That's 59,049 of the bastards. Still pretty small compared to the population of the UK, perhaps—let's put aside the fact that so many of them walking would probably flatten all of our infrastructure—but how about after just five more Arrivals?" He shoved the paper back into her face, close enough for Straub's armed escort to bristle, but Straub waved the soldier down. Paul jabbed a finger at the hastily scrawled number on the paper.

"Arrival Fifteen," he said. "14.3 *million* Stone Men."

He stared at Straub, waiting for a facial reaction that he knew wouldn't come. "That's a big chunk," he said. "Arrival Eighteen? 387 million Stone Men. We've run out of British people." He paused, swallowed, blinked a few times, then tapped the last number on his page with the pencil. "Arrival Twenty . . ." His voice choked for a moment. "Arrival Twenty wipes out half the world's population."

"Don't you think we already knew this, Paul?" Straub sighed, shifting in her seat, folding her arms. "I can see you're very upset, but when I get an urgent call in the middle of the night I'm expecting—"

"I know you do, I know you do, I know you do," he babbled, resuming his pacing once more. "What I wanted to tell you ... what I needed to tell you ..."

What had his point been again? He couldn't remember. His head felt as if it was being inflated from the inside. His hands were shaking. And outside, that fucking thing was—

"I wanted to tell you that I understand ... what I'm stopping from happening. Why I need to be here. It's important, it's the most important thing in the world—"

"Yes," Straub said. "Yes it is, Paul."

He stood there for a moment, feeling the veins popping in his forehead and neck. "Right. But what if ... what *if* ..."

He knew she knew where this was going. She'd have read his therapy notes. But he had to tell her, tell someone significant, and without Andy the only person who could possibly understand him was Brigadier Straub.

"What if we're not making any difference at all?" he said. "What if this pause would have happened anyway? What if they only do three visits *anyway?*"

"There's another possibility," Straub said. "You know what that is, don't you?" He did. The other possibility as to why there hadn't been another Arrival: that there was simply never going to be any more Arrivals.

"On top of that, Straub continued, "you know we don't think those numbers would work that way. We don't think they can just take *anyone*; there might only be a handful of viable Targets in the whole country. But none of this is anything new. What is this really about, Paul?"

He couldn't tell her. The dream had woken him, and he couldn't admit it, even though the clues would be in his notes. The faces. The ones he and Andy had—

"You said it yourself," Straub said softly. "This is the most important work in the world. You're living in a prison so it can happen—"

"And saving my own fucking skin," he'd said.

"—and it doesn't matter if the Project is keeping a Fourth Arrival from happening or not," Straub continued, "not in terms of you and what you have or haven't done. Keeping Caementum in pursuit of you means the research we're doing here can continue. Does that not make you understand how valuable you are?" She stood suddenly and crossed the short distance to him. "You have nothing to redeem, Paul. Nothing."

"You don't understand," he said quietly, his voice cracking. The victims rotated in his dreams. Sometimes it was Patrick that he saw. Sometimes it was Henry. Sometimes it was Theresa Pettifer, seen from afar from the back of a truck at the peak of the Third Arrival.

"I can't even . . ." he began, amazed he was about to admit it aloud for the first time. "I wish I could end it. But I have to . . . t-to stay here . . ."

The sound of the slap rang through the cabin. It didn't hurt—Paul was still a big, big man then, and Straub was very small—but it shocked him.

"Listen to me," she said. "There are so many things left to try, Paul, I promise. A lot of research. Hold on and we will get you out of here. And if you need to take a more cynical view of it in order to believe me: in the eyes of the top brass, it's not about you. It's about learning more about *that*." She pointed towards the wall. Paul knew what she meant. "We learn how to stop it, and you can go home. We achieve our objective and your freedom is only a very happy side effect for us both. So *hang on*."

It was easy for her to say. She didn't feel the weight of it. Whether or not the Caementum-as-Lynchpin Theory was correct, it all added up to the same thing: he was essential. Paul was the lynchpin of the *human* side of the project.

That's what you deserve, he'd thought, *and here you are*.

And now—a few months removed from that frantic early morning discussion—here he still was, sitting with Holbrooks and Straub and about to hear whatever their latest plan turned out to be.

"That was then," Paul said curtly, then turned to Holbrooks. "And I'm fine now. When are we doing it? This *different work* you're talking about?"

Holbrooks and Straub exchanged a glance.

"The volunteer is actually waiting in the companion cabin right now," Holbrooks said. "We thought we'd have them ready in case you were. If you need a little time, that's fine too—"

"I'm ready," Paul said quickly. He cracked his neck and stood, managing to hide the sway in his stance. Was he actually ready? He wouldn't be any less tired tomorrow. He couldn't ask for a coffee or a Red Bull now; boosting someone always temporarily jolted his central nervous system up to the maximum. Adding caffeine and taurine on top would probably kill him.

"Good," said Straub.

"I'll give you a few minutes to get ready," Holbrooks said, "And then we'll bring Mr Baker in."

Mr Baker. It was the kind of name that, in the past, would have been an open goal for a pointless pun. Now Paul lazily fumbled around in his brain for a moment and gave up.

"No problem," he said.

Chapter Six

The Amazing Mister Baker

✱✱✱

Andy sat and waited in Straub's office at the Project, calmly drinking his tea.

She was late; very unlike her. It struck him how, in his former life, waiting an unspecified amount of time like this—especially without a phone, as he wasn't allowed one on base—would have driven him crazy. One of the benefits of the daily meditation sessions—which felt like a treat in comparison to the months of daily post-coma physical therapy he'd had to endure—was that he'd learned to be a lot more patient.

He had to be. He was, to all intents and purposes, a prisoner, even though the word was never used. It still beat being dead, and he owed these people his life. One surprising thing he'd found at Project Ouroboros was a sense of purpose, and that, it turned out, made a great deal of life worth living. He even wondered sometimes if he was happy, but a happy prisoner was still a prisoner.

He was *important* here, though. Jesus Christ, that meant something. The only person more important than him on base was inside a metal cabin on wheels. They'd tried to find people better, of course; not out of any kind of spite, but just because why wouldn't they?

But they hadn't. No one could flash in like Andy could.

His job was to try and make the other Stone volunteers better, but as the saying goes—and as Andy would always sigh to himself as yet another disciple failed to manage flashing into Caementum more than once in a session—you can't teach that. He smiled to himself as he leaned back in the chair on the opposite side of Straub's desk, but that judgmental voice spoke up.

That's your failure as a teacher, it reminded him. *Not really something to be smug about.*

True. But it was also tough being number one.

When they'd first woken him up, it was like going back into a nightmare. But the Blue that had been pursuing him before he went to sleep had never come back. Eventually, he began to almost fully believe it never would, and nowadays this felt like the first job he'd ever ... enjoyed? Could he really say that? That might be the antidepressants talking, but Andy was never sure if they actually did anything.

He hardly ever thought about the Targets he'd hunted down.

He adjusted his baseball cap as he swayed the chair on its back legs. He never went anywhere on base without it, or his sunglasses—the ones that he always wore in the common areas—that were currently hanging from the neck of his T-shirt. Straub had insisted on both. Andy's face was too well-known, and Straub wanted the volunteers to know as little as possible.

Straub. He had an important question for her today, so much so that he couldn't stop his left leg from jiggling.

The door opened.

"Hello, Mr Pointer," Straub said. Andy had long since given up trying to get her to call him by his first name again. She didn't apologise for being late.

"Morning," he replied, smiling.

"A good mood, I see," Straub said, sitting down. "Good. I saw your report from the latest intake. I can't say I share your positivity."

Ouch.

"Well ... Jesus," Andy shrugged. "It's their first week. Sometimes it takes a while for them to show anything special. Remember Lansdown? He was nearly shipped out before he produced the goods *big* time." Straub just stared at him. "Hey," he added, his brow furrowing. "You're not blaming me for this, are you? I didn't pick 'em."

"No, I'm not," Straub said eventually. "But I'm concerned about these notes in your assessment."

"Holbrooks' notes?" *You should ask everyone else here for their notes on him*, Andy nearly said, but didn't. There was gossip going around about how the man chose to cope, but Holbrooks had always been alright with Andy. He didn't want to cause trouble for the doctor.

Straub opened a file on the desktop PC in front of her.

"Your recent level of vision," she said. "When you flash into Caementum. You reported ..." She checked the notes. *"Decreased clarity and sense of presence."* She gave Andy a dead-eyed stare. "I told you to tell me personally about anything like that. If you're having issues, how do you expect to be able to tell others—"

"I'd been sick, remember?" Andy said, throwing his hands up and rolling his eyes. "Food poisoning, from canteen food as well, I might add. You said it yourself: good fitness levels required for this. I nearly didn't say anything about it for that reason as I knew bloody Holbrooks would make a big deal out of it. I'll be fine next time."

"And you've noticed no further deterioration with Caementum?"

"Wouldn't I have put it in the report if I had?"

"You just told me that you're prepared to edit your findings, Mr Pointer, so I'm asking you for clarity."

Andy folded his arms, shaking his head.

"Nothing dramatic, no." He sighed and looked out the window, taking in the green flowing lines of the hills around the Ladybower Reservoir. "The day you woke me up and I felt that something was wrong with it . . . you know what it reminded me of?"

"Enlighten me."

". . . actually, no. It's something from a kids' book," he said, waving her away. "And you never struck me as the type to indulge in fantastical thinking. I picture you reading *The Art of War* in pre-school and forming political allegiances in the playground. Not really one for the *Oz* books."

Straub raised her eyebrows . . . and then shrugged.

"I was always more of an Enid Blyton girl."

"Tik-Tok the Machine Man," Andy said, still staring out of the window. "He's in *Ozma of Oz*, I think that's his book." He smiled, remembering. "He's clockwork, you see, and when they find him he's alone in this cave, just standing there, not moving. All of his functions run on clockwork; thinking, talking, walking, all that. He has all these different keys on his body to wind the different parts up. So they wind up his Thinking Key first, and he doesn't do anything, and they realise well of course, he's just standing there thinking. So then they wind up his Talking key, and then he can talk, and he tells them about how he ended up there. And then they wind up his Moving key I think, and they're off to the races, and he joins them on their journey." He turned back to the Brigadier and put his coffee on the table. "Great stuff, man. I loved it. But the thing is, all the while, he'll suddenly run out of something, like in the middle of a fight he'll suddenly stop, boom, because his Moving Key wound down. Or he'll stop in the middle of a sentence because his Talking Key wound down. So they have to keep him constantly wound up."

"I see where you're going with this."

"Yes," Andy said. "What's keeping Caementum wound up?"

"We know the Stone Men don't obey all the natural laws as we know them. Energy and consumption—"

"It's been following Paul for three years, Brigadier. And I'm saying that if the reason my flashed-in vision isn't as clear *wasn't* because I ate government food and had the three-bob bits for a week, then yes, perhaps Caementum is deteriorating, to use your word . . . and that brings me to one of the things I wanted to talk to you about."

"Go on."

"I can feel Paul," he said, leaning forward. "When I connect to that thing. You know that."

"Yes."

"I can feel it's connection to him. And that feels wrong, too. *Paul* feels wrong."

He paused, giving Straub a moment to jump in. She waited a second too long.

"And you didn't put this in your report, either?" she asked.

"I notice you don't look even a little bit surprised," Andy countered, not answering the question. "It's him, isn't it?"

"What is?"

"Paul is the thing keeping the Stone Man wound up. He's always been a booster. A *battery*. And Caementum is running out of juice."

Straub steepled her fingers and put them to her lips. She didn't answer.

"I want to see him," Andy said, tensing up. It had been two months since his last denial, but he'd come here today fully intending to push it. "I think he's sick and I want to see him."

"We ... have a similar theory to yours, Mr Pointer," Straub said carefully. "We have, of course, been tracking the speed of Caementum's path behind Mr Winter's cabin. The Stone Man is now seven per cent slower than it was when it first came here."

Andy's jaw fell open. It was the first time there had ever been any sign of weakness in any of the Stone Men.

"It's not a lot," Straub said, "And Paul says that his Barrier is still in place as much as ever. He says he can feel it, but we do intend to take him out of the hangar at some point soon to double check its integrity. It's been a while since we last did that."

"You plan on getting him away from Caementum if the Barrier is weakened?" Andy asked. He realised that he hadn't had the usual straight *no* to his request of seeing Paul.

"Goodness, no," Straub said, scowling. It was a surprising show of emotion that told Andy that she absolutely meant it. "Even a Stone Man at seven per cent reduced capacity is still a force unlike any other on this earth. We couldn't risk it getting out of our control and, being blunt, being able to use Winter as a carrot here is a blessing that I thank the heavens for every day I'm at this project. Not to mention his ability to boost the volunteers. But ... we do think something has gone wrong with Caementum, yes." She pointed at Andy. "I knew this conversation was coming. Need-to-know is still need-to-know, and *I* think you now need to know what *we* think here. Holbrooks thinks it's to do with Paul's unique nature as a battery. Genetically, yes, he's on the spectrum—"

"Is the List finished?" Andy asked, but Straub ignored him and continued.

"—but his past head trauma has, as you know, seemed to make him somehow unique. The Stone Men didn't seem to expect that he could boost humans; it would make sense, therefore, that they didn't expect him to be a battery for Caementum. Perhaps Caementum was meant to eventually wind down, to use your metaphor."

"Wait," Andy asked, sitting up. "So what do you think happens to Paul when they drain the battery?"

That careful pause again.

"How do you mean?"

"Oh, come on. Credit me with some intelligence. Does Paul know?"

"He's reported some physical ailments."

"You're not going to tell him about the seven per cent?" Andy felt his blood beginning to rise. It had been a while. "Are you kidding me?"

"We are," Straub said, holding up a hand. "Mr Pointer, you have to understand: Mr Winter's mental health is extremely precarious. He's been confined to a cabin for three years, pursued relentlessly by a creature whose only goal is to kill him in a most unpleasant manner, a method that the pair of you were unfortunate enough to witness first-hand." Andy winced at the reminder; something cold and eager ran down his—blessedly intact—spine, almost like a direct message from the Stone Masters themselves, breaking through the carefully-built walls in his memory. *Don't get too comfortable*, it said. *We can always come back. You don't know anything about us.* "We aren't keeping this a secret to exploit him," Straub said, holding up her hands. "Remember, Mr Winter has a remarkable amount of remorse. As much as he has struggled with his imprisonment, evaluations tell us that he has come to see it as some sort of penance. He wants to help. If we discover definitively that the Stone Man is affecting his health ... we're not sure how Mr Winter would respond to that right now."

"But you're still letting him boost people," Andy replied. "That could be draining him too." Straub didn't respond. "Don't you think the seven per cent thing might give him hope?"

"We'll tell him when the psych team determines that the time is right. But we *will* tell him."

"Let me see him."

"Not yet."

Andy sat bolt upright ... and then shook his head, laughing and letting the steam out. This was a dance. Straub was doing her job. He would go crazy if he got angry at every injustice. He had to see the funny side, or he would never ... get out?

What would he even do if he did?

He still had all his big-time money, at least. Before he'd been put under, he'd been very clear in telling Straub that he *absolutely* withdrew his pre-hey-there-may-be-a-way-out instructions to donate all his money to the Coventry Refugee Fund.

He'd still sent them ten per cent of it though. They'd been blown away. He was still a good guy. Still a good guy for sure.

"Come on, Brigadier. *Laura*," he chuckled bitterly, chancing the use of her name as it was only the two of them in the room. Straub raised an eyebrow but said nothing. "I thought we were friends. Hook a brother up."

"I don't have work friends, Mr Pointer," she said, smiling coldly. "I only have colleagues. Personal rule."

"Oh, come on." He was smiling but surprised to feel mildly hurt.

"So, all that said," Straub continued briskly, "it's fortunate that we were meeting today as I've just had confirmation from Mahal over in Strachan Group this morning. There's someone we want you to work with."

"Nothing new there, why would—"

"This ... this is something new, we think," she said, smiling more warmly now. "We've not seen anything quite like this before."

"A new bracket on the List?"

"Actually, quite possibly, yes," Straub said. "We think we may find more out as the List is further compiled, but that's still a good year or two away. It isn't necessarily a hierarchical list, either. Lot of processing still to be done, but regardless: this individual is proving to be quite resourceful."

"What were they like before Paul boosted them?"

"They haven't even met yet."

Now it was Andy's turn to raise an eyebrow.

"Well, now."

"Quite." She picked up the phone on her desk. "Send—"

"A second, if I may, Brigadier?"

"One moment, please," Straub said into the mouthpiece, and replaced the receiver back in its cradle. "Yes, Mr Pointer?"

"I wanted to ask about holiday time," he said quietly, trying to meet Straub's megawatt stare. "I've been working hard here, and everyone else gets leave except me. I'd like a week off. Just a week. What do you say? I can wear an ankle tag if you're worried, like when you let me walk up in the hills. I don't even need to go to a hotel or leave the country. I can just rent a holiday cottage somewhere, one with a pool, and that'd be great. My mental health is important, and all that. What do you say?"

"I'll review that with the team at some point," Straub said, "and we'll come back to you."

"When?"

"It's hard to say for certain," Straub said, her face as inscrutable as ever. "It wouldn't just be me and the other staff here discussing it; the top brass would have to be involved, and I don't know when I can get them all together. But it'll be reviewed in due course."

"Brigadier," Andy said, keeping his cool. "You said that two months ago."

"Like I say, Andy," Brigadier said, her voice leaden. "There are a lot of people involved in a decision like this."

Silence. Andy felt his chest constrict a little.

"Look, you *know* I like working here," he tried. "I just . . . I get these . . . I just want to feel normal for a few days, and then I can come right back. It's not even a big deal. You could approve it, right?"

"We'll see," she said, and then picked up the receiver again. Andy stared at her, shocked and dismissed. "Send Mr Baker in, please," she said.

"Brigadier—Andy began, but then the door on the opposite side of Straub's office was opening. He sat up, flustered and straightening his Project Ouroboros polo shirt. However the exchange with Straub may have gone, he took a surprising amount of pride in wearing the uniform, in his on-site reputation. He'd never been part of something so much bigger than him; nothing earthly, anyway.

Will you still want to wear it, he asked himself, *when another six months go by and still they won't let you leave even for a week?*

A small, dark haired, dark-skinned man entered the room and walked towards Andy, making an unnerving amount of eye contact.

"Hello," he said, extending a hand. His voice was soft and high-pitched. Andy got to his feet, feeling strangely rattled by the newcomer. He was the top dog here, yet he suddenly felt like he needed to be on his toes, and it wasn't just the usual pre-Stone-handshake jitters. Shaking hands with other Stone Sensitives always came with a mild jolt, even if they were nothing compared to his first handshake with Paul. Andy forced himself to meet the newcomer's dark eyes confidently, smiling as he thrust his hand into theirs. He heard Straub say *this is Carl Baker* as he braced himself for a jolt that never came.

Instead, it felt like his hand kept going all the way into Carl's arm.

Carl's eyes never left Andy's, seeming to see all the way into Andy's mind as they merged. Andy couldn't breathe. What the fuck was this? He'd never had experienced anything like it. He felt like he'd fall over but then discovered that he couldn't feel his body. He was just a mind.

No. Two minds.

—(Hello   Andy)—

"Holy shit," Andy heard someone say out loud, realising it was himself. Carl Baker just continued to stare at him, that strange half-smile on his face.

"Can you hear me, Andy?" Straub said.

"Yes . . ."

"Are you alright? Do you need a moment?"

He did, but he wasn't going to let them know that . . . unless Carl already read his—

He didn't want Carl to—

Stay out, he thought.

Pop.

Like that, he felt the wall come up in his mind, willing a blockade between them into existence. They were still connected, but—

—(very   good)—

Carl's smile was a little larger.

"Thanks," Andy gasped. *No,* he thought, *that's not good enough.* He had to show he could also—

—How—

—he sent back. Now Carl full-on grinned, looking delighted. Then he let Andy go . . . but he did it mentally before he released the physical handshake.

The room came back into focus, and Andy stumbled back more than he wanted to.

"That's . . ." There was no point playing it down. "That's impressive."

Carl smiled, nodded, and that was that.

"Carl came back from America this summer," Straub said, sounding pleased. "He'd been working at Google. Dream job, right Carl?"

"Yes," Carl said quietly.

"Came back home to see his parents, shook hands with the wrong person, and couldn't keep it quiet anymore."

"You couldn't . . ." Andy coughed, straightened up. "You couldn't do that before any of the Arrivals?" It was a stupid question, but he had to say something. None of the Stone

Sensitives had any gifts unless a Stone Man was here or on their way here.

"No," Carl said, still smiling.

"It seems," Straub said, standing and crossing to Carl, "for people like Mr Baker here at least—if there are more like him— that proximity is a factor, i.e. being on UK soil when Caementum and his ilk are here. Naturally, we'd like you both to work together."

Andy was surprised to feel excited—

"Has he ever flashed in?" He realised he was addressing Straub. "Sorry, Carl, I mean have you—"

"No, I haven't."

"Like I said, Mr Pointer," Straub said, "different-but-not-necessarily-hierarchical brackets. We think Mr Baker is the missing piece. If he can connect to Stone Sensitives like that, perhaps he can finally help us communicate with Caementum."

Carl—not Andy—was going to be the one to finally talk to it? Andy's excitement vanished.

"Well—"

"We think—we hope—Mr Baker can be the bridge between you and Mr Winter," Straub said, reading Andy like a book, "and Caementum. The only catch is that, as always, Paul can't know that you are involved, Andy, for reasons you already understand. Carl has demonstrated that he can keep mental knowledge from people inside the chain of connection." *I just did that myself*, Andy wanted to say, *no big deal*. "You aren't allowed to try and communicate with Paul once you are all in-circuit," Straub finished.

"You really think the Stone Masters would still care if I—"

"The what?" Straub asked. "The Stone Masters?"

"Have I not used that in front of you before?" Andy asked, feeling silly. "It's . . . just what I always sort of called them,"

"Hmm. Yes," Straub said, after a moment. "I suppose that's rather appropriate actually, but Caeterus is the official term now."

". . . okay."

"Even if we can't communicate with them," Straub said, "this could make flashing in easier for the others in your bracket, Andy. Are you ready?"

"What, now?"

"Yes."

"I'm supposed to have meditation at one." Why was he stalling? This was a potentially huge breakthrough.

He had to admit it: he was frightened.

What if it worked and the Stone Man talked back?

"Your class is cancelled for today," Straub said briskly. "Andy, you will remain in the companion cabin, and Carl will be in the main cabin with Paul." This was a double hit; Andy never liked being out on the hangar floor at the best of times, and *Carl* got to see Paul? "Mr Pointer?"

He hadn't responded, he realised.

"Yes," he said, trying to fake enthusiasm. "No time . . . like the present . . ."

Was that a smirk from Straub?

"Good," she said. "We'll get you prepared for the communication techniques we want you to use. They're extremely basic, so that will only take a few minutes." She clapped her hands together, once, a rare gesture of enthusiasm. Andy knew she was extremely excited; Straub clapping her hands was the equivalent of the average person streaking naked onto the pitch at Wembley Stadium.

"Does Carl ..." Andy paused, reluctant to ask the question in front of Baker as he knew Straub wouldn't like it ... but fuck her. If this man didn't know the risks, then he needed to. "Does Carl know what he might be letting himself in for? Getting on the inside with them, as it were?" Straub's face stiffened, but Carl spoke first in his quiet, high voice.

"I know the risks," he said. "And no one has done this before. And yes, it might be very bad for me." He seemed almost robotic. Was he super-Asperger's, then? Most of the volunteers were on the spectrum—Andy included, of course—but this guy ,,, "But I want to try," Carl continued. "I feel like an astronaut." He didn't smile, and Andy didn't think Carl was joking.

"Okay," Andy said.

"Good," Straub said, "if that's all clear ..."

She stood and gestured towards the door.

"Are you ready to talk to the Stone Man?

***

Andy was in two places at once.

His body was inside the companion cabin.

His mind was inside the Stone Man.

He had never, ever flashed in like this.

Energy radiated out all around him, from him—no, from the *Stone Man*, he reminded himself—way out past the walls of the hangar, through Paul's cabin in front of him—no, in front of the *Stone Man*—and all that power broadcasting out of him of it felt endless; if he picked out any one silvery, ethereal thread of it, he knew he could ride along it to the very furthest reaches of—

Pop.

He was back in the companion cabin, seated on a cushion on the floor of its completely bare interior. The only people with him were Straub and her military escorts, standing only a few feet away.

Dammit, he'd lost it—

—(Dak, da-da-dak dak)—

Andy heard Carl inside his head—Baker's own body seated inside the other cabin, Paul's cabin, alongside the man himself— and closed his eyes. He could do this. He reached around in the emptiness, felt for the much, much thinner thread from Carl, and responded:

—Dak Dak—

Pop.

With that brief rhythmic back and forth, they had calibrated, and Andy was back in. His body's mouth gasped with amazement. They were doing it.

With Carl involved, he could flash in at will, instantly.

The sensation of Paul nearby was indescribable; it was as if Paul were his only focus, reason for being—

No. Not yours. The Stone Man's. Get it together.

His mind spun and he tried to focus, to remember the very basic plan, but this was so much of a fucking rush that even that was next to impossible.

You don't know how long you can do this, he thought. *Or what this is doing to Paul.*

***

Paul sat on the edge of his bed, breathing hard and trying to calm down as he watched the back of Carl Baker's head. Carl's boosting was complete. It had been the most physically impactful he'd ever experienced.

That had been thirty minutes ago, and he still hadn't managed to slow his heart rate. How could he? The air inside the cabin—to Paul, at least—was crackling with electricity. To his right, Holbrooks and two members of his team were busily checking the readouts of his and Carl's vitals. If they could feel the thickness in the atmosphere, they didn't show it.

Carl Baker—that small, dark, quiet and very intense young man—hadn't said anything to Paul other than to give his name. Baker's eyes had stayed on the cabin's window until the moment of boosting, watching for a glimpse of the Stone Man. Holbrooks had given Baker the usual spiel, asked if Baker understood, and after receiving a single "yes", had hooked them up to their electrodes and asked them to clasp hands.

The next thing knew he was coming to on the bed, attended by Holbrooks and his orderlies. He'd looked around for Carl and saw his new companion sitting on a high stool by the cabin's window, looking out.

Jesus, Paul had thought.

Everything inside him had been thrumming since that moment; he felt like a drunk waiting for his buzz to subside, yet wrapped up, cocooned in energy. Something important was happening in the cabin; a connection had been made between him and Carl, one that—*yes*—was still there. Fragile, but there, and of a different nature to the one he'd had with Andy.

"Carl," Carl's high-pitched voice muttered yet again, and Paul looked up from where he sat on the bed. *Carl* was one of only two things the little man kept repeating. After a pause, the other followed: "Dak, da-da-dak dak." Paul recognised the rhythm of it; it was the old *shave and-a-haircut: two pence* beat, without the *two pence* on the end. Carl didn't repeat these things in any kind of order; sometimes it would be nothing but his name for a few minutes. Every now and then he would give a little shudder, and Holbrooks would bolt upright, and Carl would wave him away without a word, shaking his head sharply.

Paul could feel Carl concentrating away inside his head. When Carl shuddered, Paul shuddered. It wasn't like the contagious effect of a yawn. It was simultaneous, like there was an invisible cable that ran directly from Paul's brain to Carl's. Paul wanted to ask what the hell was going on, but that would require talking. Besides, while the *how* might have been a mystery, the *what* was obvious. Whatever was different about Carl, the purpose of his visit was clear.

They were trying to communicate with the Stone Man.

All Paul could do was sway lightly on the spot in stunned amazement. The Stone Men had cut off Paul's ability to sense the countrywide network of Stone Sensitives years ago, yet here he was inside some kind of entirely different circuit. Who was this strange little man who—

Lincoln, England. Cats, Esmerelda and Fivel. Hiking on the—

Paul's head twitched. He glanced at Holbrooks. They hadn't noticed. He looked at the back of Carl's head. No movement.

Those words had come from Carl.

Pieces of Carl. It was self-evident; not because they were things that Paul didn't know, but by their nature, the same way someone could taste the difference between fish and lamb without knowing what they were.

"Winter, heart rate—"

"I'm fine," Paul snapped, finding the words in his desperation to not be disturbed as he felt along the invisible thread linking him to Carl and knowing he shouldn't be doing so but *oh my God*, he couldn't help it. The electricity in him, around him, crackled and spat—

Archery class. Graham Crackers, the first time in Florida—

Paul didn't care about the knowledge itself, only the ability to reach it, to marvel at the process of unpacking it. The room around him began to disappear and Paul's vision was swallowed by light as he travelled along the thread. He hadn't even reached the other end when he felt something hidden.

There was a blockade in Carl's mind.

Carl had ... mental walls up? Something Paul wasn't supposed to—

(No, Paul)—(Not that)

That was Carl.

"Buh," Paul said aloud. Then he was being pushed gently out along the thread and back into his body. Carl was removing him, firmly but kindly. "Buh ..."

"Winter?" That was Holbrooks. Paul just blinked. That had been ... that had been ... "Winter," Holbrooks repeated. Paul just looked at Holbrooks, unable to even give the thumbs-up. Holbrooks quickly crossed to Paul and shone a light in his eyes. "Blink twice if you can continue." Paul did, not wanting this to stop. "Okay. Vitals are good. Mr Winter, you're doing very well. Just a little longer. Mr Baker—" Carl's thumb went up. He didn't even turn around.

"Dak, da-da-dak dak."

Holbrooks returned to his station. Minutes passed. The thread between Paul and Carl remained, still fragile, but there. It called to Paul, daring him to travel along it once more, but he'd been caught snooping once and he was beginning to feel shaky. He was running out of energy; there was no spare juice for any mental field trips. If he got to do this again—surely he would—he'd ask for a meal immediately before. He needed the calories to go longer. Or maybe he was just so much weaker now?

The lights from the hangar ceiling outside passed over Carl as the vehicle turned, a sped-up sunset that framed the little man in silhouette.

Oh Jesus, Paul thought as he watched in awe. *We're going to do it. We're going to talk to Caementum. If this kid can't do it, no one can.*

What in God's name would it tell them?

And then:

We could ask it to stop. We could ask it to leave me alone.

"Carl," Carl said ... and then slowly straightened up in his seat. Everyone else in the room froze.

Oh... Paul thought. *Oh my God...*

***

Andy's brain buzzed with desperate questions, marvelling at the way Carl had joined them to—or perhaps created—the thread between themselves and the Stone Man.

It felt ... wait, what was that other sense, that of ... wastage? Seeping away?

No time, Andy told himself, *what if it shuts you down? Focus on the plan.*

He was to 'say' to the Stone Man the first part of the same calibration rhythm that he and Carl were using, and then see if

Caementum finished or repeated it. Basic, basic, basic, and now the connection between him and Carl felt solid, it was time.

He opened the minds-eye version of his mouth ... and then Carl spoke to it first.

—*(Dak, da-da-dak dak)*—

Hey! That was Andy's job! His! And wait, how could Carl even do that? He couldn't flash in, so how could he—*fuck it*, that didn't matter, the little bastard—

He caught himself; even by his own standards, that was petulance on a dramatic level. Why was he reacting like—

It didn't matter right now. The vision was becoming murkier, his connection to the Stone Man fading. A sensation of blind panic gripped him, which in his rational mind would have made no sense, but in that moment all he knew was that he *had* to be back inside the Stone Man.

—Listen—Carl—

"Carl! CARL!!" he screamed out loud, but that cut the fragile connection between them and put him back in the companion cabin again.

"Andy," Straub said calmly as Andy desperately tried to get back in. He *needed* it, his own body and world seeming weak and insignificant by comparison. The rush—

"Dak, da-da—" he began to say to Carl, then realised he was speaking aloud.

—Dak, da-da—

He immediately bounced back into the companion cabin again.

Carl was keeping him out?!

"Fucker!"

"Andy!"

Worse, he could feel Carl still connected to him . . . *oh my God.* Carl was using him. Using Andy's ability.

Carl had felt what was in there, and he wanted it all for himself. Had Carl flashed inside? Carl could do that? No, Carl couldn't, but *Andy* could, and Carl was somehow—

—(Carl)—(Carl)—

He could hear the bastard trying to talk to it, to introduce himself. Andy's rage became incandescent. If Carl had been with Andy in the companion cabin and not inside Paul's, Andy would have strangled the little man.

"Get me out of here!" Andy barked at Straub, standing up. "I won't let him do this!"

"Do what? He's talking to it?"

"He's trying to, yes! He's—"

"He's using the protocol?" Straub said eagerly, deadly serious. "The rhythm and his name?"

"Yes!"

"And he's flashed into it? It's working?"

"I . . . I think so . . ." The penny dropped. Andy thrust a finger at the companion cabin's wall, pointing at Paul's cabin outside where Carl sat. "Take me back to my quarters! He's using my . . ." One look at her face told him everything. "You can't let him do this, Laura," he said. He was pleading. "He's . . ." Andy desperately switched tactics. "It's not safe. The feeling in there . . . it's drawn him in. He's pushed me out and that tells you he's losing it. We need to . . . we have to . . . regroup . . ." Straub stepped forward and touched his arm.

"I'm sorry, Mr Pointer," she said quietly, but firmly. "If it's working, we're not going to interrupt it." Andy's mouth worked silently, wanting to scream *this is my body and my mind he's using* ... but his rage was dissipating as the memory of the rush was already fading. All he'd wanted was to stay flashed in like that. He'd never felt that connection ... but perhaps he'd also had a very, very close miss. The energy flowing out of the Stone Man had been so tempting, the urge to follow it and see where it went—

"Something *is* wrong with it," Andy said suddenly, breathing hard. "Whatever it was broadcasting back home, I could feel that, but there was also this sense of it just flowing away. Maybe it's the strain of keeping Paul's barrier up, or being so close to such a fucked-up Target as Paul, but even so ... Brigadier, that much power ... even if it's on its way out, the thing's still packing some serious heat."

"That's good intel Andy, that's good," Straub said.

"It genuinely isn't safe though," Andy said, and now he meant it. "I need to talk to Carl, I need to warn him."

"Is it safe for you, though?" Straub asked. "Your reaction then—"

"I know, I know," Andy babbled, feeling time slip away. He didn't know what would happen to Carl if he followed those outward-flowing and oh-so-tempting threads. "But I think I need to reach him before it washes him away. We might lose him! Don't worry. I won't reconnect to the Stone Man, I don't think there's room for two in there—"

"Do it."

Andy rushed back to the cushion, sat, closing his eyes, and found the thread between him and Carl once more. Baker was drawing from whatever Andy had, but there was no time to ponder that.

—Carl talk to me—

No answer.

—(Carl)—

Carl wasn't addressing Andy. He was still trying to talk to the Stone Man.

"He's ignoring me," Andy said, opening his eyes and trying to stay calm, not thinking about Carl helping himself to whatever gifts Andy had and wielding them. "Radio Holbrooks and ask if they could just grab him and—"

—(Carl)—

Andy jolted as he felt something come down the thread. Feedback?

Feedback from something big.

"What happened? Straub barked.

"Shit—"

Andy tried to claw his way back along the thread to reach Carl but he felt the little man shove him back in place once more.

—It's not safe, Carl—You have to stop—

He tried to see what Carl was seeing, what he was feeling, but Carl firmly held Andy in place, talking all the while

—(Carl)—(Carl)—(Carl)—

The word repeated along the thread like an addict begging for a fix.

"Straub, something's happening—"

There was an intensity in the voice in Andy's head, a shakiness that hadn't been there before. *What was Carl seeing—*

***

"Carl," Carl said aloud, more emphatically, the volume enough for his voice to reverberate off the walls of Paul's cabin. "Ca—*Carl.*"

Paul could feel the electricity surging from the smaller man but it was second hand; he didn't know what Carl knew, didn't see what Carl saw, but Paul *felt* the response.

"Dak, da-da—" Carl froze again. "Carl." Carl's hands flew to the edges of his seat, gripping it tightly. Paul twitched sharply.

"Mr Baker—"

"Levels still good, sir—"

"Carl, are you—"

"They . . ." Carl said, breathlessly. "*I see them.*"

No one spoke.

Paul lunged with his mind for the invisible thread, desperate to see too, but it began to feel slack in his mind, a tightrope loosening on one end.

"Holbrooks—" Paul gasped.

"Spike, Sir, spike—"

"*They're endless,*" Carl breathed.

***

"You need to get him out of this hangar right now!" Andy yelled, but then something came down the thread that slammed into him and bent him over double. He couldn't see what Carl saw, but the palpable awe from him was devastating and *something else*: Andy saw that something had crumbled in Carl's mind, a mental blockade now destroyed in shock.

Andy knew it because he became aware of *another* thread, one previously hidden.

For the briefest of moments, he felt Paul's eyes on him.

Then Carl's presence spiked sharply too, and his thread snapped.

***

All of the electricity that Paul could feel, all of Carl's presence, vanished. The little man became completely limp and tumbled backwards from the stool without even trying to break his fall, his skull hitting the ground first, hard. It was a tumble that would certainly have concussed him, if not for the fact that Carl was already dead. Paul knew it before Carl had even fallen.

"Companion cabin!" Holbrooks barked into his headset, calling for medical transport as his underlings dived for the crash cart. Paul slumped backwards onto the bed, gasping, his strings cut, but the thread was already retracting back into his mind like a tape measure—

Wham, the thick coating of Carl's consciousness that the thread had retained slapped into Paul like a club made of thought.

"Buh, buh, buh—"

It flooded into him, and Paul, unnoticed in the chaos around Carl, began to convulse.

—nopacmangameforchristmaskissinglisaholl
owayIdontunderstandallthefussabout—

"Buh, buh, buh—"

The rush of Carl's mind didn't stop:

—scaredofhorsespleasedontmakemeridetheh
orseeventhoughitspretty—

Then the little walled-off section that Carl had kept hidden transferred into Paul too, the knowledge he had so carefully kept secret, and suddenly Paul was very present indeed as he glimpsed something, *learned* something, just before the last of the thread detached for good.

That can't be true, that can't be true, he thought wildly, *that can't be true,* Caeterus *or not—*

"Winter!' he heard Holbrooks bark, finally spotting Paul's predicament. "Get him stabilised!" He felt the hands of Holbrooks' two underlings on him and immediately lashed out a weak arm. He gripped the back of one of their necks and yanked their face as close as he could, forcing his eyes to focus.

"Strufff," Paul hissed, then gasped and tried again. "Strrrraub. Straub. Get me Straub."

"Mr Winter, you need to—"

"Tell her I know," he said. Holbrooks turned around to look at him, amazed, and Paul repeated the line for the Doctor's sake.

"Tell her *I know.*"

***

"Ah," Andy said, toppling gently backwards from the cushion onto the floor. "Ah." Straub's people rushed over to help him up, but he was already turning hazily to Straub, the knowledge as certain as anything could be in this world of Stone madness.

"Carl's . . . dead," he said.

Even as Straub snatched up the radio and began to yell into it, the thought in Andy's brain was instant.

Holy fucking shit. That could have been me.

***

Paul paced as the companion cabin docked for the second time that day. The electricity from Carl—along with the more vivid elements of the young man's memories—had faded over the last few hours, but Paul had a nervous energy all of his own. What he'd learned from Carl couldn't possibly be true ... and yet he knew it somehow was. Paul wasn't hugely amazed anymore by the fact he'd gleaned things from the young man's mind—he'd already experienced more than enough crazy psychic phenomena since the First Arrival—but startling news was still startling news.

The doorbell rang.

"Yes," Paul said, tersely. The metal door opened, and Straub stood there, armed escort in tow. "I'm not angry," Paul said quickly. "I know how you did it, simulated his death. The thread told me, right at the end. I just want to see him for myself, immediately."

"I know you're not angry, Paul," she said. "You're a smart man. I know you understand about the Caeterus and why we have to keep things on a need to know basis."

"Then bloody come in and let's talk."

Straub hesitated, then sighed.

"He's here with me," she said, looking genuinely annoyed. She sighed, shaking her head irritably. "I'm not one for this kind of behaviour, as you well know ... but he wanted to make a bloody entrance and I've promised that he could when the day finally arrived, *even if the circumstances today are awful ...*" she said, directing this last part over her shoulder to someone behind her, out of sight inside the companion cabin. "I keep my word, Paul," she finished.

Paul stopped pacing and smiled. Of *course* the idiot wanted to make an entrance.

"He's in the companion cabin? Now?" Paul asked, the grin spreading. He didn't care about Carl. Carl was a stranger, memories or not, and an actual miracle was about to happen before Paul's eyes. "Right now? Is he okay?" Straub shuffled awkwardly on her feet. Paul was amazed. Of all the things to finally rattle Straub, it turned out her weakness was theatrics. She scowled and spoke over her shoulder again.

"Are you coming out? Can we get this done? A man died today. I think this is highly inappropriate."

"Well, Jesus," said a petulant and familiar voice, coming closer. "Thanks. You just killed the moment." The speaker was moving closer.

"Don't push it," Straub said, her voice icy cold, "just come in. I have things to do."

A man in a baseball cap and sunglasses pushed past her, composing himself as he entered the cabin, red-faced. He was clearly irritated because whatever he'd planned had been spoiled, and was trying to get himself back under control. He also wore the polo shirt uniform that the soldiers wore, with a unique symbol on his upper arm. He looked in better shape than when Paul had last seen him, and although that wasn't saying much, Paul thought the man looked absolutely fantastic. Joyful tears sprang to Paul's eyes, and as his visitor saw them, he removed his shades and hat, his own anger visibly vanishing into a watery, happy grin.

"The rumours of my rumour," said Andy Pointer, gasping with emotion as he saw his old friend's joy, "have been greatly—" He realised he'd messed up the line. "Ah fuck—"

Andy didn't get to complete his sentence as Paul bowled him over in an embrace, the bigger but weakened man's legs finally giving way. The two men fell to the floor, laughing and crying.

"I've give you two a few minutes," Straub said, unable to suppress a smile herself. "When you're done, we have a lot to cover."

***

"You look like shit," Andy said, grinning from ear to ear as he clapped Paul on the shoulder and wiped the tears from his own face. Once they'd finally stood up from rolling around on the floor they'd been talking for about twenty minutes straight.

"I feel like it," Paul replied, grinning equally stupidly. Neither man had acknowledged the death of Carl Baker. Baker was a volunteer, and he'd known the risks; this was a death that they were both comfortable with. This was a death, for once, that was not their fault.

"Gentlemen," Straub said, now that Paul and Andy had finished embracing, crying, and filling each other in. "We didn't expect to be doing any of this right now, but the truth came out, so . . . here we are."

Andy wasn't listening as Straub filled Paul in about the reasons for keeping Andy's survival a secret. He was both delighted and horrified to see Paul. He'd made a joke out of it, but Paul wasn't just a shadow of his former self. He was a wisp. The man had lost far too much weight; his eyes looked haunted, staring out from sunken sockets.

"I can't promise to give you all the answers, Mr Winter, for reasons you know," Straub said, "but if you have any questions about all this, I'll try to answer them." It was only the three of them inside Paul's cabin now. The interior was nicer than Andy had expected. Luxurious, even. They hadn't been kidding about caring for Paul's mental health. You had to look after your thoroughbred.

Paul sniffed, smiled at Andy again and patted his friend's leg, taking Andy in as if checking his friend was still really there. Then Paul turned to Straub.

"Am I dying?" he asked her.

Jesus, Andy thought.

"That . . . wasn't the kind of question I meant," she said.

"I think I am, Brigadier," Paul said, a shake in his voice. "I really do. And I feel even worse after . . . that. So please—"

"You feel worse after that?" Andy asked. It was half genuine concern, half self-preservation. "Like worse for connecting?"

"Yes," Paul said, a weary smirk creeping onto his face. "I think Carl used some of me up to do what he just did. It's alright. I don't think he meant to. I felt it happen while we were doing it, I felt something stream out of me. I'm . . . less than I was this morning." He turned to Straub. "That's what's doing it, isn't it? Boosting all these people."

"Yes, it is," Straub said, without hesitation. Andy searched her face and could see no trace of the half-lie there. He waited for her to elaborate on the seven per cent reduction in the Stone Man's speed, their theory that Paul was the battery keeping it going. She didn't. Then her eyes found Andy's, telling him what to do. Anger flared . . . but Andy kept his mouth shut. He trusted Straub, as foolish as that may be, and more importantly, where could Paul go? Even if the Stone Man was draining him all the time, what did it benefit him to know? "We don't know if you're dying, Paul, but yes, your overall fitness, blood pressure, metabolic rate etc . . . they're becoming considerably worse, and we know you've been sticking to your diet and fitness plans."

Andy hesitated—even now, he hesitated—then reached out and put a hand on his friend's shoulder.

"We'll figure it out mate," he said. "Carl won't be the last—" He heard himself and stopped talking.

"Just like old times," Paul said. Andy's face fell. "Hey, I'm joking, I'm joking," he said kindly. "And I haven't done that for a while either. It's so good to see you, man, this is unbelievable."

"You obviously can't leave here, Paul," Straub interrupted, using his first name. "But I have been authorised to offer you something." Both men looked at her. "You don't have to keep boosting new volunteers, Paul. This isn't an entirely altruistic offer; if boosting people is . . . damaging you, then we don't want anything to hasten the Stone Man's departure, if you understand me."

"Bloody hell," Paul said, shaking his head. "That's some world-class talking around the issue, Brigadier."

"Indeed. If it looks like it's continuing to cause significant issues with your body chemistry, then we would stop the boosting anyway. Keeping Caementum locked in pursuit is the number one priority at this project, research is second. But we've decided to give you a choice now. As always, your mental health is very important to us. Do you want to keep working with the volunteers?"

"Yes," Paul said, without hesitation.

"You don't have to," Andy chipped in, surprised at Paul's quick reply.

"Even if it means another Carl Baker situation?" Straub asked, ignoring Andy.

"Will they be told of the risks?" Paul asked. Straub bristled a little. "I can tell them myself, Brigadier," he said. "From what I experienced today, I know I could tell them in our minds when we're connected. You wouldn't even hear it."

"They'll be told."

"Then yes, I definitely want to keep working with them."

"Really?" Andy asked.

"Yeah. For the same reason I'm not demanding that they put me in a coma and send the Right Honourable Gentleman home."

Haven't you been punished enough, Andy wanted to ask, but Paul's haunted eyes gave him his answer.

"What about you, Mr Pointer?"

Andy's jaw dropped.

"You're asking me if I want to leave?"

"No," Straub said, far too quickly. "My apologies, I should have been clearer. Are you comfortable trying to communicate with Caementum again, should the opportunity arise? From what I saw today, Mr Baker did you a favour. He took over ... and you saw what happened. Do you want to risk that? And understand that any future Carl Bakers will be taking that risk too?"

Andy hesitated, still thinking about Straub's super-quick *no.* Paul was looking at him.

"No judgement, mate," Paul said.

"I'll keep doing it," Andy said. Later, he would wonder if his answer would have been the same if Paul wasn't there, but in that moment, he meant it. Straub nodded. Andy glanced out of the window as the cabin turned; outside, the Stone Man continued its endless pursuit. *Maybe not so endless,* Andy reminded himself.

"Very well," Straub said. "Mr Winter, would you like Mr Pointer to stay for a while? I think we can allow a special dispensation for some extra alcohol, given the circumstances." Paul's forehead relaxed and his shoulders dropped; Andy could see the concept land in his brain. Paul was going to have a drink with an actual friend like a regular person. Andy was dimly aware of the fact that they were having a celebration-esque catch up while Carl's body was still cooling on a slab somewhere in the Project, and knew Paul was aware of that too, but at the same time—

"Jesus Christ," Paul said, fresh tears coming to his eyes. "Jesus Christ, that would be wonderful."

Chapter Seven

Long Distance Connections, Holbrooks Unloads, and Changes to the Itinerary

*****

Andy.
Somewhere above Scotland.
Now.

"Is it alright for her to be out this long?" Andy asked, raising his voice to be heard. He didn't just have the helicopter's droning blades to contend with; they had all inserted pieces of Linda's tissues into their ears to help with the noise. "Is it safe?"

He meant Maria. He hadn't spoken since they'd taken off from the Project, lost in dark thoughts, but his concern for this new, mysteriously powerful woman had grown the longer she'd been out.

Back at the Project she'd saved all eight of the passengers in this helicopter from the Empty Men that had surrounded them, a wall of awful whiteness closing in, encircling their group; who knew what would have happened if Paul hadn't fully boosted her in time? Then she'd collapsed and Andy had been relieved to know she was still alive, but to see her unconscious for this long reminded him of—

"She's fine," Holbrooks said briskly, having to raise his thin, shell-shocked voice to be heard over the only-slightly-muffled roar of the rotary blades. Andy watched as Dr Holbrooks finished setting the unconscious Maria's broken fingers, snapped cleanly in two by Paul's unintentionally crushing grip during the completion of her boosting. "She's just asleep. That's ... that's probably for the best right now. And she isn't your concern." He suddenly shot Paul a strange glance, then looked away quickly.

"Doctor? You okay?" Andy asked Holbrooks, surprised, but the doctor just scowled and shook his head before moving away to sit against the helicopter's metal wall. Holbrooks hadn't made real eye contact with anyone since take-off, Andy noticed, staring at the gunmetal floor that lay between them and the Scottish landscape below. Were the man's hands shaking? Paul looked at Andy and shrugged. *Bugger him*, the gesture said. Andy agreed. He didn't have the energy to deal with Holbrooks' trauma response right now either. Instead, he watched Maria's slow, steady breathing. She was laid out on the helicopter floor, a jacket under her head for comfort. Andy turned his head slowly to take in the rest of the band of escapees from the fallen Project Ouroboros, spread out around the chopper's cargo section. Paul was opposite Andy, with Linda seated immediately to his right, her arm stretched out to uselessly rub the unconscious Maria's foot. Edgwick's bulky form sat against the opposite wall, the fingers of one hand interlaced into the netting hanging from the machine's walls, the other repeatedly rubbing at his bright ginger moustache as he stared off into nothing. Andy wondered what he was thinking. Edgwick was a ranked officer. The man would have seen a lot of action in his time, surely? So what did he make of the impossible chaos and madness that had been the last twenty-four hours at the Ladybower Reservoir? Of being face to face with a wall of Empty Men, no less? The other military men on board—the hulking Private Fletchamstead and the considerably smaller Private Binley—were seated up front in the pilot's section.

The *helicopter's* pilot's section. Andy didn't like helicopters. Hadn't since the day Straub had given the order for the Permutatio Protocol to be triggered.

That's putting it mildly, an ugly voice in his head told him. *Ever since the* black helicopter—

He cut the sentence off immediately in his mind, fearing it would become a crowbar between the floorboards of his memories. He'd become good at keeping thoughts of the *Black Helicopter* buried.

Their flight continued.

"Are *you* okay, Andy?" Paul asked him, gently.

"Yeah," Andy said quickly. "Fine." He hoped Paul would drop it there.

"I think we've all had a rough day," Linda said kindly, and Andy forced a smile, but he caught Paul's sympathetic eye as he did so. He nodded quickly for Paul's benefit. *It's okay.* It wasn't Linda's fault; she didn't know what Paul's *are you okay* had been referring to.

"*Ha,*" Holbrooks slurred. *What the hell was that supposed to mean*, Andy wondered. Holbrooks lifted his head and Andy drew a breath at the sight of him. The man was pale as a sheet. The reason why was obvious; Dr Holbrooks had seen the Empty Men up close, twice, in less than twenty-four hours, and he wasn't a soldier. Was this PTSD, perhaps? And when had Holbrooks last slept? Andy didn't think the man had been to bed for at least forty-eight hours, perhaps longer. Certainly not since the latest

Arrival started. Holbrooks had been one of the most dedicated employees at the Project, a champion of Stone research to a fault. There had been rumours at the Project a while back, that coincided with Holbrooks going on a sudden and unannounced three weeks of leave, destination undisclosed. Word on the base had been that Holbrooks, in the depths of Stone research-related mania, had been abusing amphetamines in order to work around the clock, and had been forced to take time off. Andy could relate. He knew what it was to be dedicated to the Project beyond reason, even if he'd come out the other side of it some time ago. Had the Doctor, during the madness of the last few days, fallen back on old habits? Edgwick's was furrowed; the big soldier had noticed the doctor's face too.

"Craig," Edgwick said, using Holbrooks' first name for the first time within earshot of Andy. "When did you last eat?" Holbrooks looked back down.

"We didn't have a clue," Holbrooks said quietly, ignoring the question, his head swaying. "We spent all that time preparing for the wrong thing. It was a waste of time. A total waste of time."

Andy wanted to say *you couldn't know* but thought better of it. Holbrooks, traumatised by his terrifying ordeal—an experience likely made infinitely worse by a mix of sleep deprivation and stimulants—seemed to be spiralling badly now that he'd carried out his last immediate task, namely fixing Maria's fingers. When they got to the Chisel, Andy would make sure the medical team there—

Holbrooks' head snapped up.

"Did you *feel* them?" he asked Paul. The tone was there again: accusatory, suspicious. Andy wasn't worried about Holbrooks as a physical threat to his friend, however—even in his current slimmer form, Paul was bigger than the Doctor—he was more concerned about Holbrooks' well-being. He knew Craig Holbrooks to be a good man.

Plus, he knew who Holbrooks was referring to. *What* he was referring to.

"Yes," Paul replied quietly.

Holbrooks' eyes stared through Paul, clearly seeing *them* again. The wall of white becoming larger in his mind as they drew in around him.

"Of *course* you did," he said, as if to himself, "The connections with those things go both ways after all, don't they?" His eyes narrowed. Holbrooks was . . . suspicious? *What?*

"Holbrooks," Andy said carefully. "Ease down a bit, okay?"

"Breathe, Craig," Edgwick said, his tone soft. "*Doctor.* Head back and breathe." Holbrooks gave a shivering little nod and put his head back against the metal wall. Silence returned to the cargo hold, aside from the noise of the blades. Andy glanced at the cockpit; Binley and the enormous but always silent Fletchamstead remained unconcerned by Holbrooks' minor outburst, staring out into the grey sky ahead.

"Why are we going to the Isle of Skye?" Linda asked.

"The Chisel's the fallback position," Edgwick said. "If Project Ouroboros was ever compromised, that's where we go. I think it's fair to say the Project was compromised today. If you'd arrived thirty minutes later than you did, we'd have already left, so count yourself lucky."

"Lucky for *you*, then," Linda told Edgwick, raising her eyebrows, "that we got there when we did, then, or maybe you wouldn't have left at all." Edgwick's steely gaze held Linda's for a second. Then he shrugged.

"Ah, fair point," he sniffed, pinching the bridge of his nose. He looked tired. "Fair point," he repeated, and nodded at the sleeping

Maria. "I think we might indeed have been in trouble if you hadn't." It was clear he was referring to more than just the people inside the helicopter when he said *we*.

"I hate to break it to you, but I think we're still in trouble, buddy," Linda said, but she was smiling now. "And our best shot won't wake up."

"Best shot?" Andy said, offended. from the opposite end of the cargo hold. "What am I, some kind of arsehole?"

"Should I answer that?" Edgwick asked Andy.

"Says the TIN man," Andy sniffed; it was a petulant comeback, but he didn't care. Then he saw Paul smirking.

"Tin man . . . ?" Linda began, but now Paul was chuckling.

"If there's one way to bring you to life, Andy," he said, "it's by bruising your ego."

Andy bristled some more . . . but then let out a hiss that was almost a laugh, shaking his head, and waved Edgwick away.

"So . . . the Chisel," Linda said quickly. "It really was the name for another base? So why bother with the fake press conference, that fake Chisel device they had at the Ground Zero conference?"

"The official documents had leaked, as had the name," Edgwick said. "What better way to keep people in the dark than to tell them that the incorrect thing they already believe is true?" Andy noticed that Holbrooks' left hand was inside the right hand side of his jacket, moving slowly. Was the man stroking his own chest?

"Are you two friends?" Paul asked Linda, nodding at Maria.

"We only met today," Linda said, reddening slightly. "We came to the project together."

"Were you a volunteer before then, is that how you knew about it?" Andy asked. "I thought I recognised you from around."

"Yes, I was, but ... I think I recognise *you*, actually. I don't think I saw you at the Project though ... where do I know you from?"

A smile slowly crept onto Andy's face as he felt old, forgotten instincts kick in.

"Oh, well, you might know me from TV, back in the day," Andy said, swelling a little. "I was quite notorious, in fact, for a little while—" He stopped as he noticed Paul covering his face to stop himself laughing. Andy was embarrassed. He hadn't talked like that in a while. "So, uh, Maria here," Andy said quickly, addressing Paul. "She has to be at least LION, right? How else could she have done what she did back there?"

"Yeah," Paul said. "She's LION, Andy, but she's, you know ... " He suddenly sounded cautious, the smirk leaving his face. "... a Watchmaker type. Like, uh, Carl Baker was."

"You mean like *Sophie* was," Andy said quickly.

"D'you mean Sophie Warrender?" Linda asked, brightening. "The volunteer from the Project?" Andy felt cold. He noticed Paul gently touching Linda's shoulder, but in her excitement she missed the hint and carried right on talking. "She was moved straight into the higher groups. She have been the codename we always heard mentioned, *Dispensatori*, right?"

"No," Andy said. "That's me."

On the opposite wall, Holbrooks made a quiet scoffing sound. Andy noticed the doctor's hand again, still strangely inside his jacket. Wait, *was* he stroking himself?

"Oh, right," Linda said. "Was she still at the Project? Is she on one of the other helicopters?"

"No ..." Andy said quietly, avoiding Paul eyes. "She died."

"Oh," Linda said again. "Can I ... can I ask—"

She broke off and, for a split second, Andy wondered why everyone was leaning sideways—*how did they know to do that all at the same time*—before he noticed a long-forgotten tingling in his nose, scalp and neck. Pulse suddenly racing, he tried to speak but not only did his jaw not respond—it was, in fact, clamping down as hard as possible—but one look at Paul told Andy all he needed to know. Then his limbs locked out from his seated position and his tightening, spasming body juddered sideways onto the deck. His head hit the metal floor, but it didn't hurt. He heard some of the others fall, and then found himself looking into the staring eyes of Edgwick, the soldier, a Stone Sensitive too, lost in a fit of his own.

There was only one possible cause for them fitting right now. The moment he'd been dreading ever since the Empty Men showed up.

He waited, lying in awkward, floor level, wide-twitching-eye contact with Edgwick until, as he expected, the soldier's face disappeared. Someone else's would follow . . .

But there were no faces.

First, there was light.

Then—*oh no*—something else—

Then the helicopter's cargo hold came back, showing Edgwick beginning to blink movement back into his shoulders before Andy understood his own limbs were back under his control.

"—*appening? What's happening? What are you seeing, what are they doing? Are they coming here, are they coming to us?! Ah!*"

That was . . . Holbrooks? He sounded as if the hounds of hell were after him.

"Andy. . ." Paul gasped. "Did you see . . ."

"No," Andy gasped back as Paul checked on Linda, who was holding her head and stomach and looking pale but seemed otherwise fine, only lightly affected by the vision. *"No Targets, but Paul . . . I saw . . ."*

"What was it?" Holbrooks barked. The doctor's knees were drawn up to his chest and his hitching breath wasn't slowing.

"It's . . . alright, doctor," Linda tried. "They're can't get to us here, we're in the air—"

"What *happened* there—" Holbrooks yelled, ignoring her, but Andy cut him off, his voice now returned.

"Shut up a second, doctor," Andy hissed, pinching the bridge of his nose. "Paul, did you see it you get the vision—"

"No, no vision," Paul breathed, shaking his head and rubbing his eyes. "No faces. No one." His hands moved down to his mouth, muffling his next words: *"Thnk Gdd . . ."*

"The *light,*" Andy said, moving hurriedly over to Paul on his hands and knees. "You see that?"

"Yes," Paul said. "It was like a . . ."

"Like a circle, a ball—"

"Yeah."

"Well what the fuck was *that?*"

"You saw something?" Linda asked Paul, grabbing his arm. "Wait, are you—"

"I'm fine," Paul said quickly.

"Of *course* he is," Holbrooks snapped, actually beginning to wag a finger at Paul, squinting. "You were connected to that thing for *years.*" The doctor's face was bright red now; it looked as if this latest remote-but-still-close encounter had tipped him even further over the edge. Paul thought Holbrooks would be beyond reason for a short while. "And we didn't know if those signals went both ways, did we?" Holbrooks continued. "Or what *else* those signals might be capable of doing to a person?"

"Shut up a second Holbrooks!" Andy snapped. "Paul, I saw more than the light though."

"But you and I are cut off from the wider signals—" Paul began ... but then he looked at Maria's sleeping face, clearly thinking the same as Andy. Had boosting Maria somehow plugged Paul back into the Stone system, and by default Andy, the other half of Paul's circuit? What did that mean now that—

"I saw a light too, like a bubble," Edgwick rasped.

"*Paul*," Andy insisted, ignoring Edgwick. His voice was a croak, struggling to admit what he'd seen, past trauma catching the words in its claw. "I saw—" He couldn't say it. "I saw ... Coventry. Understand?"

The fear on Paul's face told Andy that he understood; his response told Andy that he wanted to deny it.

"You just mean, around the light or whatever, right? You saw the city like, like, from afar—"

"*No,*" Andy hissed, closing his eyes in fear and frustration. He had to say it, admit what was happening. "I flashed into *it* again, like before." He felt like Marley's ghost, a spectre bringing the gravest of warnings. "I was ... I saw what *it* saw," he said, shuddering as he relived it. "I was coming out of something. I was coming out of *stone*. It was like I was being ..." He couldn't say the next word: *born*. Andy put his hands into his hair, tightened them into fists, and then confirmed the worst case scenario; the one that had haunted both of their dreams.

"It's a new one," Andy said quietly. "A new Stone Man is here."

No one spoke.

"Paul—" Andy began, but Paul held up a hand.

"What do we do, Paul—" Andy began,

"Can you give me a few minutes please bud?" he said quietly. "I gotta . . . just let me sit for a minute. Then we can discuss. Okay?"

For once, Andy managed to read the room, even off the back of the news they'd all just learned . . . and the idea that was forming in his head. Paul needed a moment.

"Yes," he said. "Yes. Let's all take . . . yes."

"Thanks, Andy." Paul breathed out and waited for his heartbeat to slow down. No one spoke for a good fifteen minutes until Andy finally felt like he couldn't keep his idea in any more.

"I think we need to try and wake Maria up," he said.

"Yeah," Paul said. "I think—"

Everyone jumped as Holbrooks suddenly became alert, getting up quickly and scuttling over to Maria.

"*No,*" he hissed, glaring. "We've tried, and we don't know what we're dealing with. Short of an adrenaline shot, which we don't have, she's *out.*" The whites of the doctor's wide eyes were bloodshot. "*Why* are you so determined to wake her up?"

"What the fuck is wrong with you, Holbrooks?" Andy cried. "What's with all these comments?" Holbrooks stared back at him, saying nothing. "We told you what just happened in Coventry, they're *back!* That woman," he said, jabbing a finger in Maria's direction, "just cleared out a whole wave of Empty Men. If she can do that, maybe she could *send the Stone Men home.* Of *course* I want to wake her up!"

"Hey, what's happening back there?" Binley said from the cockpit, finally speaking up.

"I don't think she can do that, Andy," Paul said, ignoring Binley. "She's powerful, more powerful than Sophie, but Sophie didn't even have a hint of that kind of clout. And doing what she did back there has clearly drained her completely. Let her sleep."

"Fucking *hell*," Andy spat, shaking his head. "This is bollocks. We have to do something! At the very least, Paul, you and I should try and . . . you know?"

"What?" Paul asked, looking confused.

"Well, you know," Andy said, suddenly embarrassed again. "See what the deal is? No?"

Paul looked horrified.

"Andy . . . are you serious?" he said. "Are you really talking about trying to find out who this new Stone Man's Target will be?"

"Well . . . I don't like it either, but . . . I mean, aren't we supposed to . . ."

Paul's mouth moved silently, shocked.

"Sometimes, man," he said eventually. "I know you get it, but *sometimes* you still . . ."

"What?"

Paul shook his head and raised his hands, letting it go.

"We're leaving the mainland," he sighed. "So I don't think we'll be able to do anything about it anyway. Until Maria wakes up, we need to assume it isn't safe to even try and connect to their circuit without her. Surely?"

Andy lightly slapped at the metal wall of the cargo hold.

"Yeah," he said. "*Fuck.* I can't believe they're . . . *ahhh*, it was always gonna fucking happen," he sighed. "Always gonna fucking happen." Then he paused, realising something. Late to the party, as ever, but at least he got there in the end. "Paul, are *you*, uh . . ." He shrugged. "You okay?"

Paul smiled.

"Yes, yes I am," he said. "Thanks for asking. And look, when Maria *does* wake up—"

Linda's voice cut him off.

"Christ," she said.

Andy saw Edgwick sit up stiffly upright with his hands raised, palms out. He turned to see where the soldier was looking.

Holbrooks was holding a gun in his shaking hands, pointing it around the helicopter.

"She stays . . . asleep," he said.

"No one move," Edgwick said quietly.

"The signals," Holbrooks said, his eyes on Paul. His voice was quiet and shaking. Dangerous. "Not just the between the Stone Sensitives. The connection to *them*—" His eyes darted upwards briefly—"goes both ways. Doesn't it? Paul? Andy? I think you've known that for quite a long time. Or maybe not; do you even *know* what you do anymore?" A line of spit ran from the corner of his mouth, unnoticed. *"If the signal goes both ways, how do you know they aren't using you right now?"*

"Craig," Paul said, instinctively trying to pull Linda further away from the doctor. "What . . . there's no need for this. You aren't making sense—"

"You don't go near Maria," Holbrooks said, his eyes seeming to pulse white in the dim light of the chopper's interior.

"No one's going to, doctor," Edgwick said. "That's been decided—"

"Holbrooks—" Binley began in the front seat, but Holbrooks spoke over him.

"Keep doing what you're doing, Binley," Holbrooks said, his voice trembling breathily. "If you move, I'll shoot them, and then you. Fletchamstead can fly this thing alone, or at the very least you can fly with a bullet in your knee. Edgwick, I'm sorry, but I need you to move over to that wall by Winter and Wyken. Pointer, get over there."

"What the *fuck*—"

"Just come over here, Andy," Paul interrupted, his eyes on Holbrooks. Andy moved over to join the others as Edgwick did the same. The soldier's gaze held the doctor, his expression relaxed, his eyes unwavering. Andy saw that the doctor was watching Edgwick right back, clearly understanding that the big soldier was the largest threat; Fletchamstead—seated in the front—was even bigger, but he'd have to clamber around the front seats to do anything, and Holbrooks would easily have time to shoot him.

"Whatever you say, Craig," Edgwick said calmly. "We're all playing it your way. No one's going anywhere near Maria. We can all relax—"

"Raise your hands, please, Edgwick," Holbrooks said quickly. Andy saw Edgwick's hand was by his sidearm. The soldier hesitated for a moment, and then did as he was told.

"You had that in your jacket," Linda said, her own voice shaking a little. "I saw your hand in there, I'm a bloody idiot, you were being weird and I should have said something—"

"He had the highest clearance at the Project," Edgwick muttered bitterly, as if cursing at himself for not knowing. "Which meant he had access to the—"

"Everyone ... everyone shut up," Holbrooks hissed, his breathing speeding up. The gun shook uncontrollably for a moment and Paul took a silent gasp of air as he noticed Edgwick stiffen to spring, but then Holbrooks' shakes subsided and the moment passed. "Just sit there and shut up." He nodded at the gun. "I brought this for *me*, alright? In case I—" He screwed up his eyes for a moment, winced, opened them. "I need to decide what to do. Winter, Pointer, even fucking *Wyken and Edgwick*, if any of you look like you're trying anything with Constance here," he said, nudging Maria lightly with his foot without looking at her, "I'll shoot you." He blinked a few times. "Sorry, Edgwick. I don't want to. You either, Ms Wyken."

Of course, even when literally staring down the barrel of a gun, Andy couldn't let the obvious implication slide.

"And . . . you don't want to shoot me or Paul either, Craig," he asked. "Right?"

Silence again, apart from Holbrooks' heavy breathing and the sound of the helicopter's droning blades.

"*Craig,*" Andy repeated earnestly.

"Andy—" Paul said.

"No, Paul," Andy said leaning forward. "He doesn't want to shoot us, he knows us. We worked together, we're *colleagues*—"

"It isn't ... personal ..." Holbrooks said. His lip was trembling. "But I'm not so sure ... at *all* ... that you two can be trusted anymore." He looked at Edgwick. "You saw what happened at Ladybower, Edgwick. *Paul brought the Empty Men right to us.* After he messed around boosting this silly bitch *here* ..." He jabbed a finger on his free hand towards Maria then paused for a moment, chewing his lip, a trace of the rational doctor coming through as he heard the venom spewing from his own mouth. Holbrooks suddenly let out a sob, blinking fast and furrowing his brow. "Was that really an accident?"

Andy could see why Holbrooks was creating this insane narrative. The doctor was scared to death and desperate for a solution. If he could convince himself that Paul—or Andy—was the key to it all, then killing Paul—or Andy—would take that fear away.

"I think—" Edgwick began.

"The system we used before the Project was *working,*" Holbrooks moaned. "Identify Targets, terminate. You two got cut off? Fine, we had replacements to help hunt down Targets. We could kept doing the same thing. Maybe they would have given up eventually. Instead ... *instead* ..." Holbrooks breathed in heavily through his nose. "... we kept Caementum here. And I think they adapted their plan." Andy didn't know what to say; if they just let Holbrooks talk, he might calm down. He also might also wind himself up into an even greater frenzy and shoot him or Paul. "And what did we really learn, by keeping you two alive? Keeping Caementum going in circles? What of any real *use?*" Holbrooks suddenly pointed at Andy with the gun, jabbing it in his direction.

"*NO—*" Andy cried out, flinching against a bullet that didn't come.

"We should have followed the system with you two," Holbrooks continued, and Andy breathed out, shaking hard. "Before the project, before *I* had to ... to deal with all the ..." He trailed off, his eyes beginning to water before he sniffed his tears back. *"I'm not letting you wake her up."* Holbrooks finally hissed, teeth gritted.

"Don't worry, Craig," Paul said, blinking rapidly. "We're not going to, Craig, we already said, remember? We can all just sit here until we get to the Chisel."

If he lets us, Andy thought. *The way he's talking—*

"Not the same mistake," Holbrooks muttered, seemingly to himself. "Not again." He scowled at Andy, considering him and shaking his head bitterly. "We never should have woken you up," he sobbed, but the last part of the sentence seemed to blur into slow motion as, for the second time within half an hour, the nausea slammed into Andy's brain and he slumped to the helicopter's metal floor as the vision hit him.

He saw it much more clearly this time. Saw *them*. Plural.

He was horrified, but not surprised. When one came, more came soon after. This was their way.

As the world around him came back online, along with his control over his limbs, an urgent but slurred thought penetrated his fear:

Holbrooks will have collapsed too, he thought frantically, *he'll have dropped the gun—*

No, of course Holbrooks was still sitting there, wide-eyed and holding his pistol. Holbrooks wasn't Stone Sensitive, and furthermore, he had used the break in proceedings to take the collapsed Edgwick's sidearm too; the big soldier's gun was now lying on the floor at Holbrooks' side.

"What's happening back there!?" Binley yelled from the front. "Is everyone—"

"Don't . . . talk, Private," Holbrooks stammered. He looked at Paul.

"No," Paul groaned, "that was—"

"Paul," Andy breathed. He was trying to get up, using the wall for support.

"Yeah. I saw them," Paul said.

"We didn't feel them coming, Paul."

"Maybe they travelled inside that building that appeared at Ground Zero," Paul said. "Maybe that's why. They were hidden by their transport."

"What do you mean, you saw *them*?" Linda asked. Her face was ashen. "Them who?"

"The Blues," Andy sighed, his face ashen as he turned to Maria. "They're back."

"There was something else though—" Paul began.

"Shut up!" Holbrooks snapped. "Were you trying something just now, Winter? Were you trying to wake her up? *Tell me.*" He raised the gun higher.

"Was I *trying to bring anything here?*" Andy asked, incredulous. "How would I even do that?"

Out of the corner of his eye Andy noticed Edgwick tensing, preparing to pounce. Andy could see it would be a heroic but doomed effort. The soldier was too far away from the doctor and would be shot before he made it.

"Doctor," Linda said quietly. "Don't you think Maria could be a help—"

"Don't involve yourself in this, Wyken," Holbrooks said softly. "Warrender couldn't fix the problem, and Constance won't be able to—"

"Sophie saved my life," Andy said firmly, his nostrils flaring. *And what was the point of that*, the voice in his head snarled at him yet again, so loud Andy couldn't ignore it.

He stared at Holbrooks' gun.

Wouldn't that, the voice said, *just be easier than* this?

"Isn't that *funny*, though," Holbrooks continued, ignoring Andy and screwing up one eye, "that all the other GALE people we collected for the Goodnight Protocol, all those innocent people that trusted us to put them under and keep them safe, they're all *dead* and you're not, Pointer, now how is that? The coma trick *somehow* didn't work with them when it did with you, now isn't that just—"

"You *know*," Andy said, his voice suddenly low. It was beginning to shake. "You know why I'm still here, fucker, you were there for the Fourth Arrival, the Crawlers, all of it." His finger came up, aiming like his own gun. "And you ever mention Sophie around me again, gun or no gun, I will—"

"Crawlers? Fourth Arrival?" Linda asked. She was looking at the faces around her for answers. "We're *in* the Fourth Arrival now, what do you—" Andy saw the penny drop in her expression. "This isn't the Fourth Arrival, is it?"

"No," Paul said. "It's the Fifth."

She looked at him in amazement.

"There was a Fourth," Andy said. "No one knew about it."

"Pointer," Holbrooks said. It was barely audible over the sound of the blades. The doctor turned to Andy and now he could see the depth of the man's sorrow in his horrified gaze. Holbrooks was desperate for this to end by any means necessary, and the world went into slow motion as Andy saw the doctor's face suddenly relax. Holbrooks' rational side had just conceded to the crazy barrage in his mind.

Holbrooks had made his mind up; Andy or Paul had to die, and right now.

Andy had time to think *this is it* and realise that he was absolutely ready as the suddenly relaxed, calm Holbrooks straightened his arm to fire. Then he seemed to change his mind over the choice of target and swung the barrel towards Paul. Andy moved without thinking, just as Edgwick leapt. Edgwick was much faster, his combat-ready body diving towards Holbrooks, but Andy wasn't going for the doctor; he threw his body across Paul. Linda gasped just before the gun went off, a deafening detonation inside the metal space—nanoseconds before Edgwick collided with the doctor's scrawny arm—and as Andy's ears exploded with white noise and he felt no pain from a bullet he realised that the combination of the helicopter's movement and Holbrooks' woozy state meant that the shot was never going to hit its intended target. He heard a small, wet bursting sound immediately followed by the crack of metal on metal as the lead slug entered and exited Linda's body through her stomach and embedded itself in the helicopter's internal wall. She fell backwards, eyes blinking rapidly.

"Wuh ... wuh ..." she gasped, looking down at her wound and beginning to shake.

"No," Paul mumbled, before Linda collapsed sideways into his arms.

Edgwick was already upon Holbrooks, punching the skinny man hard in the face. The doctor dropped onto the metal floor.

Andy stared in shock at Linda and Paul, his friend cradling Linda's head and looking down into her wide and blinking eyes. The sounds around him were muffled and strange thanks to the deafening ringing in his ears from the gunshot; the tissue had protected his eardrums only a little.

"He's going to fix you, hold on, hold on," Paul babbled as Edgwick threw unwanted items out of the military-issue first aid kit he'd scrabbled from the back of the helicopter.

"Andy!" Edgwick barked, waking Andy from his daze.

"*Yes*, I'm here, yes—"

"Take your belt off," Edgwick told him, "and tie Holbrooks' hands behind his back, now—"

"Got it, got it, yes," Andy babbled, moving over to the doctor's now-unconscious body and turning him over to tie his hands, positioning him alongside the still-sleeping Maria like sardines in a can.

"Is it ..." Linda began. She was blinking but not delirious, alert but pale as a sheet. "Is it bad?" she asked Paul. Edgwick shuffled over to Linda on his knees, holding a bottle of clear liquid, two fabric things that looked like giant tampons, a syringe and a needle and thread.

"Deep breath," Edgwick said through gritted teeth as he leaned over her and felt around Linda's back. Linda cried out, a ragged shriek that mingled perfectly with the screeching in Paul's ears. "Good news, it went right through," Edgwick said, answering for Paul and breathing heavily as he began to fiddle with the items he'd brought over. "It was a .22 calibre, small bullet, and it looks like it might have avoided major organs too, if we're lucky. Try to relax as much as possible. I'm gonna get this closed up." But the soldier accidentally caught Andy's eye and looked away much too quickly. Blood was spreading in a pool on the floor around Linda. "I'm going to fix it," Edgwick said, taking Linda's hand. "Okay?"

"The Chisel has a full medical bay," Binley yelled from the front, speaking to Linda. "Hold on—"

"This is morphine," Edgwick said, ignoring Binley and holding up a syringe. "Paul, roll her over too and lift up her blouse at the back."

"Ah, no, *no*—" Linda grimaced, protesting desperately.

"Sorry, I have to clean this," Edgwick said, unscrewing the bottle.

"Sorry, Linda," Paul said, doing as he was told, pulling up the crimson-soaked fabric as Edgwick poured some of the contents into the gruesome but mercifully small exit wound without hesitation. Linda screamed, an awful high-pitched noise that made the hairs on Andy's arms stand on end. "Good, good, one more and it's done," Edgwick breathed as he handed one of the tampon-looking things to Paul. "Field dressing," he said. "Put this under the exit hole when you lay her down." Paul laid the now-sobbing Linda back on the floor, looking sick with worry. Edgwick lifted up the front of her blouse, revealing her pale stomach, and as Andy watched, hands over his mouth, he saw a fresh spout of blood pop out and run down her side.

"*Breathe . . .*" Edgwick cooed as he poured the bottle again, its clear liquid washing away the latest fresh rivulet of red, the two fluids mingling like Linda's guttural screams with the drone of the chopper's blades. The bullet hole was momentarily revealed as a tiny, ragged extra belly button before it immediately began to fill with blood once more. "Good, good, now we're going to make you feel better," Edgwick said, his sweating face belying his breathy but calm tone. He handed Andy the other field dressing. "Press this down on the front and keep it tight," he said, picking up the syringe.

"Got it," Andy said, taking the dressing with a shaking hand and placing it over the hole. Linda screamed again. "Sorry," Andy said stupidly, feeling like he was going to throw up.

"Linda," Edgwick said, I'm going to inject you now and you're going to feel a hell of a lot better, okay? Then I'm going to stitch you up."

"Okay," Linda gasped. Her eyes looked up at Paul and Andy watched as her hand searched for his. Paul took it and squeezed it hard as Edgwick injected Linda with the painkiller. A few moments later her face relaxed only a little; it was clear that her physical discomfort had eased, but not her terror.

"We're going to get you to the Chisel," Paul told her earnestly. "Edgwick is going to stop the bleeding and you're going to be okay. Okay?"

"Yeah," Andy chimed in, "yeah you're going to be okay—"

"*Ohhhhh*," Linda breathed, "that stuff is . . ."

"The morphine?" Andy asked. "It's helping?"

"Yeah . . . it hurts *so* much, but . . ." She winced, looked back at him. "It's better. It's better . . ." Now she tightened her grip on his hand. "Tell Selena what happened," she said. "My daughter. Okay?" Her eyes filled with tears. "I haven't seen her in . . . if I don't—"

"I will, but you're going to be okay," Paul said, but then stiffened as Linda's eyelids started to flutter and her pupils rolled back in their sockets.

"Linda—"

"Stay with us," Edgwick said loudly, and Linda's eyes opened again.

"I'm here, I'm here—" Linda gasped.

"Keep talking," Edgwick said. "I need you to stay with us."

"*Talk* to her, Paul," Andy said.

"Yes, talk . . . talk to me," Linda said, her voice shaking as she forced a frightened smile.

"Sure," Paul said, forcing a shaking smile. "Let's talk about . . ." He swallowed tears. Andy saw his friend trying desperately to be strong. His heart broke for Paul. "Tell me, tell me all about—"

"No, no," Linda said deliriously, shaking her head slightly, her expression a pained smile. "*You* have to . . . tell *me* . . ."

"Yes, tell her, Paul—" Andy babbled idiotically, not even knowing what Paul was supposed to tell her.

"*Listen,*" Linda breathed, cutting Andy off and talking with great effort. "Paul, I thought . . . you were bloody *dead* . . . Paul. And you're *not*. So now . . . *you bloody well tell me* . . . what happened *that day?* My last morning at the Project . . . all the chaos and shouting. You didn't die . . . but the Stone Man went home . . . so what happened and then what the hell . . . *uhhh* . . . have you been *doing* all this time?" She let out a huge breath, her body relaxing, and then grimaced as she relaxed too much. "*Go on.*"

Paul, pale-faced, glanced at Andy.

"Go on," Andy echoed, but now his voice was a squeak. The situation was hellish and the subject they were about to broach only brought with it the most painful thoughts; but of course, they were inside the black helicopter now. Andy knew that only painful things could be expected. "It's okay."

"Okay," Paul said.

Edgwick stitched, and Paul talked.

By the time Paul was finishing his story, Edgwick's stitching was complete, the first aid kit put away, and even Andy was listening closely, sitting on the unconscious doctor's back for good measure, having partially hogtied him. Linda's breathing was easier now and she didn't look to be in as much pain, but her eyes had remained focused on Paul's throughout the telling. That was good, but Andy thought she looked even paler now, even though it looked like Edgwick had managed to stop the bleeding. So much blood surrounded them on the floor, so much so that Paul's jeans were visibly wet and sticky with it; had Linda already lost too much?

"So . . . yeah," Paul said, finishing clumsily.

Linda didn't reply. Instead, her eyes moved to Andy.

"I'm so sorry," she said quietly.

Andy looked amazed, seeing this possibly dying woman offering *him* sympathy . . . and that was when Maria suddenly shot bolt upright at the waist, awake and gasping.

She sat up so quickly that everyone in the helicopter jumped in surprise, including Linda, who let out a bark of pain. Maria wheezed in lungfuls of air and blinked rapidly, lungs working like bellows as she turned her head back and forth, trying to understand her new surroundings. Edgwick was the first to respond.

"Maria, it's alright—"

But she was shaking her head frantically, looking about herself for someone that wasn't there, so confused that she didn't even notice Linda's current position on the floor or the trussed-up doctor in the corner. Her hand shot up as if to say *be quiet, I'm trying to listen*. When she clearly couldn't find the resolution she wanted, her hands flew to her head in frustration, clutching her hair as she barked a single word at the top of her lungs:

"*ERIC!*"

Andy's mouth flew open but immediately froze as the latest jolt shot through the bodies of the Stone Sensitives inside the helicopter.

No, for the love of God no, not now, Andy thought as his head slumped mercifully backwards onto the wall and not forwards onto Linda's wounded body. As the faces spun in the darkness he saw several drop into place; of course, seven stone men, seven Targets. Five white faces, one brown, one black.

Then the darkness faded, and Andy was already trying to get up and clamber over to Maria, hearing Edgwick's groggy voice as the soldier tried to get himself back online.

"—leave her alone, can't you see she's doing something—"

"Maria? *Maria!*" Andy yelled, ignoring Edgwick. Maria was sitting with her eyes screwed tightly shut, looking as if she were concentrating with all of her mental might. "*Maria, listen to me!*" Andy barked, and now Maria's eyes flew open, and they were blazing with fury.

"*Shut up!*" she bellowed. "I'm trying to talk him, I need to concentrate!"

Andy looked startled.

"...who?"

Maria's head suddenly jerked up as if she'd heard someone.

"Wait, he's back, shut up," she hissed, and then closed her eyes again, her fists balled up in the air by her face. Andy looked dumbly around the helicopter's cargo bay. No one spoke.

"... who's she's talking to?" Andy asked. He looked down at Linda.

"Don't ... look at me," she croaked. "I've no ... idea."

Maria was talking to someone only she could see and hear? Crazy in any other time and place, but not today. Andy was struggling so much to hold himself back from bothering Maria that he was swaying on the spot.

"Let her work, Andy," Paul whispered to him. "Just ... let her work."

Andy folded his hands under his armpits to keep them occupied and sat back, not taking his eyes off Maria. A minute or two passed and then her eyes flew open again, turning to face all of them, an expression written all over her face that told Andy with total certainly that things were about to get much, much worse.

Then Maria dived towards the cockpit, yelling at Binley.

"We have to land!" she bellowed. "Right now!"

"What?" Binley snapped. "We're over a bloody loch! This isn't a watercraft!"

"We can't land!" Fletchhamstead added uselessly from the co-pilot's seat, his enormous frame at odds with his high voice.

"Get us lower then, you have to get us lower, as low as you can!" Maria yelled, looking out through the window for whatever danger was coming. "Trust me! Do it! DO IT!"

Binley, confused, looked over his shoulder to Edgwick for confirmation.

"Do as she says," Edgwick said.

"But sir, there's just water below—"

"That's an order!" Edgwick interrupted. "Just get us as low as you can, and we'll land as soon as possible, we'll figure the rest out when we ... just do it! Quickly, now!"

"Everyone grab something and hold on *tight*," Binley said quietly, clearly irked, and glanced at the terrified-looking Fletchamstead before the helicopter began to drop. Andy grabbed a fistful of netting as his stomach headed towards his mouth, watching as Paul, seated behind Linda now, gripped her under her armpits as she moaned gently in pain, gravity playing havoc with her wound. Edgwick gripped the netting too as he called to Maria. "What's happening?" he asked. "Why do we need to be low?"

"It's . . . it's . . ." Maria gasped, looking around the cargo bay at everyone and clearly trying to remember how she got there. "Eric, in Coventry! He warned me! Something terrible is about to happen, he said if we were in the air we had to land—"

"Fuck," Andy breathed. "Like what?"

"Something to do with the Stone Man," she said, "there's a new one, it's doing something, making something happen, it's talking to the . . . I can't describe it—"

Andy felt the helicopter beginning to level off and looked through the windscreen, seeing how close they were to the water now, Binley having expertly—

Andy froze, along with everyone in the back of the chopper. There had been a distinct change in pressure, and it wasn't from the aircraft's rapid descent.

WHOOMF.

Something moved through them all at lightning speed, a goose-walking-over-your-grave pins and needles sensation that made all the hairs on Andy's body stand up on end, and then there was a sound like someone slopping the last of the car wash bucket over a windscreen. A crisp, burnt smell filled the chopper, and for a crazy moment Andy thought a blood vessel had burst in his eye or something to that effect.

Why else would he only see red?

Then he realised that both men in the front of the helicopter were gone, and the windscreen was covered in an explosion of now-dried blood. Where Holbrooks had been laying there was now a spray of red crust coating a lab coat, trousers, shoes, and the two fastened belts that had been used to restrain him. That elevator-dropping-quickly sensation in Andy's stomach intensified. A warning beep began to sound rapidly.

Oh fuck, Andy thought, *oh fuck, oh Jesus—*

Edgwick was lunging forward and clambering over the backs of the front seats, trying to shift his immense bulk into the pilot's seat and failing as his huge backpack kept trapping him between the seat backs. Andy gripped the netting with both hands and his body began to lift up as gravity seized the helicopter. He saw Paul wrap his legs around Linda's waist and grab the wall netting tightly in his fists; Linda's body came up off the floor, saved only from flying up into the back end of the helicopter by Paul's thighs, and she bellowed in pain.

"Fuuuuuck!"

Andy tried to yell too but he had no air. Edgwick had made it into the front seat and was fiddling with the controls—*yes, maybe*, Andy thought, as he felt a change in the speed and angle of descent—but the beeping sound became maddening and the light coming through the windscreen suddenly became much darker, as if the world was ending.

Maybe just your world, he had time to think, before Edgwick interrupted his panicked thoughts by yelling:

"Go limp—"

There was a dull thud like a hammer blow to the brain, then a rushing noise, then cold. As Andy's mind went black, his brain made the rapid and simple association: the black helicopter had finally completed its task, and as his world began to end he realised that it was not a dark harbinger after all; it was a blessing. Now he would finally join Sophie, *Sophie*, and as the darkness claimed him his thoughts were of her, the day she—

Chapter Eight

The Threads of the Caeterus

*** ***

Andy.
One Year Ago.
Project Orobouros.

Andy lay on the bed in Paul's cabin, listening to its—he had to agree with Paul on this one—rather soothing rumbling sounds as it continued its endless circuit of the hangar. He was throwing peanuts up into the air and trying to catch them in his mouth as they waited for the latest volunteer to arrive. He didn't know why he was still throwing them; both times he'd managed to catch one lying on his back like that, it had felt like he was choking.

"What'd you say?" Paul asked. Over the last year, ever since Carl Baker's death, this response had become more and more frequent, to the point where Andy had grown to expect it. Talking to Paul often felt a little like talking to an elderly relative in the early stages of dementia. Paul continued to work slowly away on his handheld grip strength trainer in the cabin's corner. Andy sighed and repeated himself.

"I said: four years? Who fucking waits four years to volunteer?"

Paul looked up as he considered the question, and Andy's breath caught a little. That happened more and more these days too; Paul would look at Andy a certain way, in a certain light—being sweaty from the effort even a little grip strength device required certainly didn't help—and Andy would realise just how much more his friend had deteriorated over the last twelve months or so. Surely they were going to stop Paul boosting people now? He looked like a dead man walking. "The woman they're bringing over today, Paul. She didn't volunteer for *four years*." For an impatient man, Andy somehow found he had endless reserves of patience for Paul.

"Who? The one I saw the other day ... Linda?" He waved Andy off the bed out of his way, rising from his seat and staggering over to lie down. He stumbled a little but quickly caught one of the many handholds that had been reinstalled in the cabin. Andy thought it was good Paul used the grip strength gadget. It was the only dedicated exercise he was allowed now, and the interior of the cabin looked like that of a home help patient. Handholds adorned nearly every surface. "She didn't come here for four years, I think. Three, maybe? "

"No—" Andy began to snap as Paul lay down. "No," he softened, "not Linda. The *big deal* woman. The one who's supposed to be like Carl. Remember?"

"Ah. Ah, yeah." Paul breathed out and closed his eyes. Once, Andy guessed, the bed would have creaked under the old, larger Paul's bodyweight. Now it barely registered his presence.

"What do you think she was doing all that time?"

"Who knows," Paul said softly, and Andy knew that was the conversation done for a while. That was okay. Paul needed to rest;

the companion cabin would be here any minute to collect Andy. Then, to his surprise, Paul spoke again: "She's nice. That Linda."

"Oh yeah?"

"Mm. She's been cut off though. And no big deal when we shook hands."

"Ah," Andy said, not really interested. Another volunteer with nothing in the tank. There had been a lot of those over the years. Once he'd have been interested in the being-cut-off element, but other cut-offs had shed little light on his own condition. Volunteers outside of Carl Baker's bracket—meaning all of them, even the ones that who'd shown echoes of the same ability—weren't his main source of interest. Give him another Carl, now, one who was actually confirmed to be the real deal, and *oh, what he could do . . .*

At least there were still some volunteers, though. The numbers had dwindled since he and Paul had begun the search for a new Carl Baker. Straub had claimed it was due to the amount of rumours online of bad things happening to *Be Prepared* appeal volunteers; Andy thought it was simply because most of the Stone Sensitives that existed had already come forward. They were down to the dregs now.

"I asked Straub if she thought Linda would be a Target if they came back," Paul said.

"Let me guess," Andy said, trying to watch the pursuing Stone Man through the window for more than ten seconds. He couldn't do it. Even after all this time, he never, ever relaxed inside the cabin. How had Paul managed it? Just another reason why Andy's admiration for Paul Winter was now boundless. The cabin began its turn and the Stone Man's impossibly fluid body disappeared from view. "She didn't give you an answer."

"Of course."

The cabin continued to rumble.

"Think we'll be finished in time for kick-off?" Andy asked. Paul was sometimes allowed to watch certain TV programmes now, and Straub had sprung for all the sports packages. Andy liked to watch football with Paul. It was good to see his friend come alive when the Blades scored.

"If this is anything like the others," Paul muttered, "I think we'll be done before coverage even starts." He caught himself. "I meant, as in, it'll turn out to be a waste of time. I don't mean like with Carl—"

"I know, I know, it's alright," Andy soothed, seeing how shaken Paul was from even that little burst of guilt. "And don't forget, Carl was—"

"Yeah. Yeah."

The autopsy had shown Carl Baker had been a heavy recreational drug user, something he'd failed to inform the brass when he volunteered at the project. His test scores had been so good he'd been rushed through the system to Paul before they'd performed what perhaps would have been the most important tests in hindsight: blood and urine. He also had, as subsequent investigations revealed, a history of concussions from years spent playing rugby with his smaller stature. Those concussions eventually forced him to stop playing the game he loved, which presumably had led him into heavy drug usage. His brain had become a perfect piñata, one that had been smashed wide open by the circuit they'd made with the Stone Man. The incident had led to increased screening at the project and compulsory MRIs for everyone who was going to be boosted by Paul, regardless of their suspected gifts. Such procedures had been previously reserved for volunteers who complained of headaches or Stone Sensitives of particular interest who warranted further study.

They'd been so *close* with Carl, though, Andy thought. So much had been there, ready to be unlocked. They could have communicated with it, *actually talked to the frickin' Stone Man.*

"Four years," Andy muttered again, sitting in the chair. "What's with these people? Where's their sense of duty?" Something grey caught his eye as he looked through the cabin window at the hangar floor; for a moment he nearly leapt to his feet, thinking Caementum was somehow gaining on them ... but of course, it was just the companion cabin beginning its journey over.

"People have ... short memories," Paul breathed, lightly dozing. He drifted off a lot now. "Who's going to leave their ... lives for, what, weeks, maybe months when there ... hasn't been an Arrival? When other people're ... dealing with it?" he sighed. "Then two years pass since the last Arrival. Then three. Then—"

"Maybe so," Andy interrupted. "Still bollocks, in my book."

Paul snorted a little.

This boost is the last one, Andy thought, watching the companion cabin approach. *I don't care what Straub says, or what Paul says. I won't take part in any more if they try and make him, even if he wants to.* As he heard the clunk of the companion cabin locking alongside them, that nasty voice in his head spoke up. He hadn't heard it for a while, leering and snarking and always calling him out on his worst instincts:

Really, Andy? You'd abandon your best chance of solving this puzzle? So what the fuck would you do with your life instead, then?

The doorbell rang.

"Paul," Andy called, "they're here, mate."

"I'm awake," Paul said, struggling to sit up. Andy crossed to the bed and helped him. "Come in," he called. The door opened and Straub stepped inside, followed by Holbrooks, a guard, and a tall blonde woman with piercing eyes who looked to be around Andy's age. She wore the Project's uniform and the polo shirt's sleeves revealed a pair of lightly muscled arms; not toned, but thicker than the average woman's, the look of someone with a past involving a lot of physical activity. She was striking, to say the least. Andy stood up straight.

"Hello," he said, realising that he hadn't even looked at Straub or Holbrooks since this stranger walked in, and also that he was staring. That was stupid, rude even; better say something.

But nothing came to mind.

He suddenly felt anxious; what the fuck was this?

"I'm Andy," he said, and that would do, but why the hell had he said it so loudly? "This is Paul."

"Hi," Paul said. He sounded totally unfazed, which was crazy to Andy. Couldn't he feel the woman's presence? It was different to Carl Baker, it was—

Then he realised what was happening. He was aware of the woman's Stone Sensitive nature of course, the way most reasonable-level Stone Sensitives seemed to be when it came to being near each other. But this was nothing to do with that. The woman just had... yes. The previous word was correct: *presence.*

"Hello both," the woman said, and when she smiled Andy found himself needing one of Paul's nearby handholds. Instead he completely forgot Stone Sensitive protocol and went to take the blonde woman's hand, who politely pulled hers away. "Ah . . ." she said, chuckling nervously.

"Mr Pointer?" Straub asked. "Is everything okay?"

"Fine, yeah, fine," he said quickly, then addressed the blonde woman. "Sorry, they told you about the shock, of course."

"Yes," she said, smiling kindly. "I'm told most Stone Sensitives seemed to get a little zap from one another when making physical contact, but, ah . . ." She looked at Straub. "You said the handshake today had to be. . . ?"

"Yes, I did," Straub said, giving Andy a confused side-eye. "We're going to try things a little differently today. We want you to shake hands together for the first time, at the same time, in a physical version of the circuit. It's a theory we wanted to try, seeing as we want you all to be working as a unit—"

"Oh, wait, I'm so rude," the younger woman said, "I didn't introduce . . . I'm Sophie."

"My fault," Straub said. "I'm rather excited to get you all started and I'm afraid I somewhat rushed the formalities. This is Paul Winter and this is Andy Pointer, who you will refer to outside of this cabin as *Dispensatori* when discussing him or speaking *to* him." Andy realised he was still wearing his cap and shades inside the cabin and took them off. He hoped for a star-struck look to cross Sophie's face. It didn't come. "Unfortunately, Andy's former notoriety makes the codename a necessity, but considering what you're about to be doing and how you're going to connect, that will be unnecessary inside the cabin. Gentlemen," Straub said, holding a hand to the newcomer, "this is Sophie Warrender. We're *very* excited for her to work with you. Now let's get you hooked up."

Andy felt a little flutter in his chest, and then realised Straub was referring to the electrodes.

* * *

"Ready?" Straub asked.

They were seated in a circle of three folding chairs that had been brought in for the occasion. Holbrooks and his team were now ensconced in the corner and Straub was standing nearby with her escort. A small video camera went about its business on a tripod. Andy had forced himself to stop looking at Sophie; he didn't want her to feel uncomfortable. She looked surprisingly relaxed, regardless. He'd never seen that in the handful of people who'd visited Paul's cabin over the last year. Knowing the Stone Man was walking just a few feet away usually put people on edge, but Sophie just seemed focused. Andy was concentrating on Paul instead, given that it was too hard not to look at Sophie when they were all seated on top of each other like this.

Get it together, he told himself, staring at the Paul instead. *You're Dispensatori. Be professional.* That did it, but what the bloody hell was going on with him? He'd seen pretty women on the base before, so it couldn't just be her looks, even if it had literally been years since he'd had any sexual contact with a woman.

Then Andy noticed Paul screwing his face up in confusion.

"What?" he asked.

"Huh?"

"You're staring at me like I'm some sort of arsehole."

"Oh. I was just checking you were okay mate."

"Mm."

He turned away to see Sophie looking at *him* now.

"You okay?" he blurted.

"Good. Excited, actually."

"Yeah. Me too."

Fucking hell, what do I sound like?

"Anytime you're ready," Holbrooks said. Was the doctor sweating? Sophie immediately gave Holbrooks a thumbs-up. She tried to hide it, but Andy saw her hand shaking. Not just excited, then. Paul and Andy gave thumbs-ups too.

"One," Holbrooks said. "Two."

Just stare at the floor—

"Three."

Andy just had time to think *bloody hell, I completely forgot what we were actually doing* before the three of them clasped their hands together. Then the next thing he knew he was staring at the wall, his hand placed under his cheek, one arm straight out, and one knee raised. He knew this. It was the recovery position. Why was he in the—

"Easy," Holbrooks was saying, "Easy, Andy, nice and steady." He felt hands gently cupping his armpits and realised that Straub's escort was helping him to his feet. He'd fallen off his chair? He looked around; one of Holbrooks' team was helping Sophie up, and Paul was already seated on the bed, drinking from a cup of water. Andy caught his eye, and was relieved when Paul looked up and grinned, then raised his eyebrows and nodded twice.

"We blacked out?" he asked.

"It was a little more dramatic than that," Straub said, breathing heavily and sounding relieved, "but essentially: yes. How do you all feel?"

Andy waved the soldier off him, finding his own feet.

"I'm okay," he said.

"Paul?"

"She's better than Baker," Paul croaked, ignoring Straub's question. "*Much* better."

"Sophie? I know that must be a shock for your first—"

"Yes, but ... wow," Sophie said. "I feel ..." She stopped and suddenly wrapped her arms around herself, looking from wall to wall like a trapped animal.

"It's alright," Andy said, stepping forward but catching himself; he'd nearly taken her by the shoulders to comfort her. He put his hands behind his back. "We're moving and it can't catch up to us. You're just more aware of it now." Sophie nodded, but her eyes showed a frightened little girl that Andy didn't think came out very often—

No, not *think*. He *knew* that now, didn't he?

He blinked, cocking his head for a moment. Sophie was looking at Andy with curiosity too, as if considering him.

The force of the connection, Andy thought. He'd been able to put up a mental block between himself and Carl, and the now-dead man had done the same, but their first connection hadn't been powerful enough to knock him out. Andy suddenly felt exposed, and it wasn't from the presence of the Stone Man outside.

He didn't want her to know him. Not the real him.

He looked at Paul, who was talking to Straub about something; he hadn't had the same insight, then? Though Paul was different, after all—

"You were going to die," Sophie said quietly, squinting softly at Andy. "You didn't want to, but you were going to."

Andy's mouth dropped open. He didn't have a response, and as panic set in, instinct took over and he did what he'd always done; put on a show.

"See?" he said, red-faced and false-laughing, turning to everyone else in the room. "What did I keep telling all of you?"

But Sophie didn't take her eyes off him.

"The first connection is always the most dramatic," Straub said, and even she was still breathing hard. Four years into Project Ouroboros—a year since Carl Baker—and here was a lead. "Don't worry. It's not always—"

"I'm fine, really," Sophie said. "I want to go again." She caught herself. "As soon as Paul and Andy are ready, of course."

"I'm ready now," Andy said. "Like you say, Brigadier, the first one is always the worst. Right? Next time will be a piece of piss. Sorry," he added quickly, embarrassed by such vulgarity before someone he didn't know, but when Sophie smiled again as she waved his apology away, Andy knew that he was suddenly in deep trouble.

That *smile.*

"Give me something to eat," Paul said from the bed, "just something with some sugar in it, and I'll be good to go."

"Doctor?" Straub asked.

"Readings say yes," Holbrooks said. "We'll need to reattach some of these cables, but we can be ready in five minutes."

Good, Andy thought, but then panic seized his entire body.

Just don't let her see you. Oh my God, don't let her see you.

***

If the completed circuit had been electric with Carl Baker before, this was nuclear.

Once they'd held hands and breathed down into the theta brainwave state—guided by one of Holbrooks' meditation experts—Andy was able to sit for a moment and simply take in the sense of still, raw *power* that seemed to be coursing through his body. Through *all* of their bodies. They weren't even holding hands now; the initial connection had been made. Paul and Andy had never needed to hold hands during the Arrivals, and they certainly didn't need to now Sophie was here.

Away to his right, Paul was hopeful. Andy couldn't tell what form that hope took, but as the feeling trickled to Andy along Paul's mental thread he got a vague sense of it; if they could talk to the Stone Man, they could perhaps *reason* with it, find out more about it, and that could mean—

Andy stopped. He realised that he was being drawn into Paul, and he didn't know if his friend was aware. There had to be boundaries.

To his left, Sophie's thread was thrilled and frightened. Andy didn't know what would happen to her when he actually flashed into the Stone Man, as part of Sophie would go with him, he knew. She'd been briefed, read his and Paul's reports; she knew what had gone wrong before. Andy had to stay in the driving seat. All he had to do is not let himself be caught up in it again.

Walking towards them but always at the same distance—its presence was like sitting next to the sun—was the Stone Man. It was clearer than ever, even clearer than with Carl, so bright and sharp that Andy knew with certainty that he could flash into it at will. They were going to do it. They were—

Sophie's thread sung to him, an unintentional communiqué of a new emotion: fear had suddenly given way to terror, feeling Andy's intention to go towards the Stone Man. He couldn't blame her for being afraid.

—Don't worry Sophie—

The message was so much easier to send that it startled him; Sophie too, her surprise travelling down the invisible, ethereal thread between them like a fly's distressed struggles travelling along a spiderweb. She'd been told they would likely be able to communicate telepathically, of course, but a briefing couldn't prepare you for having someone else speak inside your mind. Andy wanted to tell her *it's good, you're doing this, you're the one making this possible*, but he didn't want to startle her any more than he already had. This was so smooth, the cogs and gears of his and Paul's consciousness all beautifully oiled and moving together with hers to create—

Andy suddenly understood it. Cogs and gears; those was Paul and Andy. Sophie was the one putting it all together.

She was a watchmaker.

He could already feel the light sense of waning power in the Stone Man, but much more noticeable were the threads coming off the monster, flying away into the ether to God only knew where. Andy had done his best to explain it to Holbrooks and the rest of Straub's boffins. The consensus was that he should not— not yet at least—try and connect with those distant threads. Baker's brain might have been set up for failure, but they didn't want to risk Andy's, or draw attention from the Caeterus. Andy's job today was to connect to the Stone Man and talk to it if he could. That was all.

That's all, Andy scoffed in his mind. *I'm only about to talk to the Stone Man.*

He took the mental equivalent of a deep breath, and dived in.

Sophie's thread became taut. The inside of the cabin became the outside and he was now seeing its turning wheels; he was now flashed-in, and his mind was drawn inexorably towards the vehicle's precious cargo. That sensation was immediately squashed by a terrifying fact; the Stone Man's threads—or the threads of the Caeterus—those invisible, intangible alien equivalents of fibre optic cable to the nth power, were twitching, sensing . . . and beginning to turn inwards.

They began to search for him.

Flashing in may have been easier, clearer, but the same applied to Andy; *he* was clearer, easier to spot, and now it seemed he was actively drawing outside attention. Sophie's thread, and now Paul's, began to twang sharply in fear. Andy didn't think the

Caeterus could see him yet—they only knew something was wrong—but soon they would. He didn't have long, but the rush of energy was coming now, already making him delirious with power. No, he had to stay in the moment—

He stilled his mind and, amazingly, began to calm down. This wasn't due to the meditation classes, either. He still felt the thrill of the Stone Man's energy field (the Stone Man's mixed with *Paul's*, he reminded himself) but thanks to Sophie's governing, containing energy, that soothing oil in the gears, he no longer became lost in it. His Stone Man eyes showed him the hangar, the steadily rolling cabin ahead, but his mind had to go deeper inside the beast. He had a greater sense of presence now, he discovered; an awareness of the Stone Man's inner world. Not in the sense that he could feel its body or its limbs, but that he could almost physically root around in there.

But could he talk to it?

—Andy—

No response.

—Dak, da-da-dak dak—

Nothing. The Stone Man felt ... empty.

Opinion had always been divided at the Project, from Paul to Straub to the rank and file; did the Stone Man have a mind? He didn't have much longer to settle the on-base debate; the Caeterus's own threads were moving closer still, creeping towards Andy's consciousness like malevolent, sentient ivy, and as it was it looked like there was nothing after all—

No. There *was* something. Further down inside the darkness of the Stone Man, so deep that Andy almost missed it. He couldn't tell what it was, but a glancing stroke of his mind had revealed an edge of it, a deep rebound of his mental sonar. It was in the Stone Man's depths.

Stay. In. The moment.

Easier said than done. The heart in his physical body was beating so hard that Andy could feel it in in his current imaginary chest. He had to decide what to do. He couldn't think and those threads were closing in, he didn't have the tools—

And then something came down Paul's thread; his friend was giving an extra little bit of juice, uncalled for but sorely needed. He felt strengthened—

—Thank you—

Suddenly the edge, that *something* down in the dark vacuum of the Stone Man's self, became clearer, he could see the direction of it, and then he knew that Sophie was helping him put it all together. The Watchmaker, making the system tick ... but whatever it was looked so far away. He could go deeper, he knew that, but it still felt as it if wouldn't be enough, as though, if he were to physically reach for it, the tips of his grasping fingers would just ... come ... short. It was maddening. And on the Caeterus's threads came. There was no *time.* He needed—

Sophie was preparing something, away on the other end of her thread. What was she doing?

Pop.

Sophie was with him in the darkness too.

Not like Carl, elbowing him out of the way, but just there. Supporting him. He couldn't see her—he couldn't see himself— but it was as if they were standing in a darkened room and she was breathing on the back of his neck. Whatever lay down below in the dark became clearer still. He was suddenly a palaeontologist, and below was the tip of a Tyrannosaurus skull, poking out from the sand. Precision, deftness of touch; these things would be required to unearth correctly, carefully. He needed—

Then there came a connection akin to Sophie putting a hand on his shoulder. He could feel her fear, but even more strongly, her will to overcome. It electrified him—it told him that of course they could get to it, but the Caeterus were nearly on them—

He couldn't be seen by them. That would mean being put into a coma again and that would set back everything they were trying to do. Would it even work twice? He began to tell Sophie that they had to get out of there, but the message was already communicated to her as soon as he thought it. It was as if they were separate bodies of water now merging into one lake, and even more so when he felt Sophie's own amazement at her mind's—or her body's—automatic response.

Something in Sophie shifted, and the Caeterus's threads stopped heading inwards. It was as if she and Andy had been hidden.

—How are you doing that—

—(I don't know)—

—This is amazing—

—(Stay focused)—

But even so, Sophie's amazement mixed with his. He felt her instinctively going deeper.

Except her exploration was of Andy, not the Stone Man.

It was automatic. Effortless, natural. He felt a memory from the back of his mind leap into her, her mental fingers unknowingly plucking one of the brightest, clearest treasures in there, and he heard it speak aloud in his voice:

—the Quarry Response got to hide got to hide
you're dying—

She recoiled, and as he moved towards her to steady her, the same process unintentionally repeated in reverse, from her to him:

—*(Dad! Hold on!)*—

Then she was pulling back, settling them both down, the Watchmaker putting everything back into smooth motion.

—*(It's alright)*—*(I don't know how I'm doing this but I'm buying you time)*—*(you have to talk to it)*—*(unlock whatever's down there)*—

—Yes, yes—

But something else hit him, then more, then *more*, unstoppable—growing up in Oxford, riding horses, her love of anim . . .a *vet,* Sophie was a *vet*—and he actively had to push away from it. She could not be contained. Everything she was suddenly became an irresistible force to him, and he was too drawn to her. He began to turn away but her aura unintentionally held him there, washing over him just by being close to it. In whatever state they currently inhabited, boundaries were a mere concept; he knew from experience that they had to be actively willed into existence. She was now managing to create a barrier, amazingly, but despite her best efforts the force of herself could only be contained so much. Being near to it was like a soothing caress.

He managed to turn away and tried to plunge down towards whatever lay below in the depths of the Stone Man ... but he couldn't. It was so cold down in the darkness.

Up here there was a warmth he had never known before.

He turned back to Sophie's energy.

—(Go)—(What are you doing)—(We don't have time for this)—

He didn't move towards her. He would never, ever go against her will. They remained at a distance, but even so, it was like the warmth of a Caribbean sunrise.

—(Andy)—(Go!)—

—I'm going—

But he couldn't move.

—(Dispensatori!)— (Do your job!)—

That jolted him. He *was Dispensatori*. That was his meaning. But the jolt came too late.

—(Do)—(do your)—(your)—(your job)—

He had listened too late. She was beginning to see him. All of him. He began to panic, realising that his own boundaries were down, she would know everything he really was, Everything—

—(Dispen . . .)—

She softened. Opened.

—(Andy)—

The force of her became stronger as she responded to . . . him. She knew him, and she still moved closer.

—Oh—wow—

Knowledge flowed between them, a lifetime of truths. A single thought formed, given and received from either pole.

—(So)—Much—(Pain)—

Then Andy found something unyielding in the flow, a tiny, ultra-protected part that resisted the exchange of knowledge. He couldn't see inside the walls of it, but even they themselves were built of great suffering.

This. *This* was why she hadn't come to the Project for four years.

His heart broke for her, wanting to ease her pain; of course he wanted to, he'd just spent a lifetime knowing her inside a single moment. He asked, the voice of his mind breathless, even as the rest of him reeled at the impossible exchange that was occurring:

—What's hidden in there—

The answer came back in a wave of guilt, an expression of sorrow that she had to be the one to withhold something:

—*(No)—(I'm so sorry)*—

—No, no—you don't have to—

Then something else came screaming in, a dousing, icy bucketful of angry and terrified thought:

What the fuck are you two twatting around at

Paul. Desperate, frightened. They rushed back to individuality, stepping out of one another, speechless, a bond of decades suddenly severed—

The Caeterus's reaching, grasping threads were about to fasten onto them, having closed in while Sophie's protective instinct had been elsewhere. They were moments away from seizing them—

Get out of there

Paul's thread strained as extra energy came down it, and Sophie quickly used it to briefly halt the Caeterus's threads' descent; they suddenly froze, confused, their Quarry hidden, and the incredible tension in Sophie's thread told Andy just how much she was struggling to keep them there; he knew what her limits were, knew *her*. The threads of the Caeterus were too close, too strong ... and yes, whatever he'd seen so tantalisingly below in the depths of the Stone Man really was out of reach.

—Paul—maybe Paul can give us—

—*(They're too close)—(I need to)—(ah)—(we need to regroup)*—

He understood. The Watchmaker might be able to work miracles, but she was still learning.

—Okay, let's go, let's go—

He turned to flee back along his own thread, and then stopped. He reached for her, found her, and she gripped him back firmly.

They fled together.

***

The cabin upon their return to their bodies was bright and harsh, but not as harsh as Paul's voice, even as weak and wheezing as it was now.

"What the ... hell did ... you do?" he snapped. "You were ... onto something! I could feel it! I had to ... *fuck* ..." He raised his hand and one of Holbrooks' orderlies helped him up and over to the bed. Andy didn't answer Paul's question even though guilt tried to hit him, knowing that Paul had to spend extra precious energy to save the day; he tried to catch Sophie's eye, desperate for her to confirm that the amazing bonding experience they'd just been through hadn't been imagined. It couldn't have been ... yet, in the cold light of physical reality, magic always craves confirmation. "Knock that shit ... on the head," Paul croaked— he'd noticed it, then—but Andy was already pulling off his electrodes and standing up, ignoring all of Paul and Straub and Holbrooks' simultaneous questions. His heart hammered and it wasn't from the effect of coming back to his body. The colours in the room were brighter. The presence of the people around him felt energised. This was more surreal than flashing into the Stone Man.

This was what all the songs and movies and books talked about. Jesus Christ, Jesus *Christ,* it was real! It was fucking *real!*

But Sophie seemed to be actively avoiding his gaze. His whole body went cold. *No.* This couldn't be yet another situation he'd misread. Not this. That had been ... elemental. There was no doubt, no denial. So why was she—

Then she finally looked at him, and he understood.

She was furious.

What?

... and she was pale. Deathly pale. She was swaying in her seat.

"Holbrooks," he said quickly. "Check on Sophie."

"Easy," Holbrooks said, rushing over to Sophie. "Easy. You're not used to this. Your vitals are all good but you look like your blood sugar just took a dive."

"I'm okay," Sophie said. "Give me ten minutes and I can go again."

"I don't think Paul's—"

"Let me eat, nap, and I can go," Paul said from the bed, his eyes closed. He looked half-dead.

"You're all done for the day," Straub said. "You'll be having thorough checks and Sophie and Andy will be on the wards tonight for observation before we plan our next move." Andy felt relieved. Paul didn't look like he could stand, let alone go again. He'd thought beforehand that this would be the last time, but after that, when they'd been so close . . . could he really insist that Paul *didn't* go again?

You'd let your friend do *that again?* the voice asked.

The answer wasn't immediately *no*, and Andy was disgusted with himself.

But the question was moot; Paul would insist anyway after what had just happened, and Straub was already asking Andy about that; Paul was flat out and Sophie was leaning forward, eyes closed and sucking on some sort of astronaut-food-pouch thing that Holbrooks had given her.

"What happened, Andy?"

"There's something inside the Stone Man, Brigadier," Andy said, taking his eyes off Sophie. Her anger was making him panic. "It's way down deep, and I don't know if we can reach it."

"Something?" Straub asked. "Like . . . a mind?"

"I don't know. Maybe. It was too far away to tell. Too deep. The circuit between the three of us was . . . extremely strong, and I think we'll only get better with time, but . . ." He considered it, trying to stay focused on thoughts of the Stone Man. Whatever was down there *had* felt too far away, hadn't it? Even if they hadn't gotten carried away and—

Oh. Oh, fucking hell.

He suddenly understood why Sophie was furious. He'd blown it. She'd told him to get on with the job, and he hadn't; he'd frozen in her presence, and the whole thing had gone off the rails. But she hadn't pulled away either; she'd opened to *him*—

"The circuit between the three of you is good?"

"Yeah, it is, yeah," Andy stammered. "Paul's boost, my abilities, and Sophie aligning the two of us, it's like she moves everyone's ... I don't know, energy? She shunts it all into place, like gears coming together. Clockwork."

"Tik-Tok the Machine Man," Straub said, surprising Andy.

"Well, exactly," he said. "And she's our Watchmaker. Doctor?" Andy said, turning to Holbrooks. "How have we not seen anyone quite like her before?" Holbrooks glanced at Straub, received the okay, and answered Andy.

"Sophie has been on ... medication for many years now," Holbrooks said. *You'd know all about self-medicating, doc*, a tired and nasty voice inside Andy smirked.

"Antidepressants," Sophie said, but Andy already knew. Of course he did.

"Yes," Holbrooks shrugged. "We think those, combined with the rarity of Sophie's genetic bracket, have led to a unique brain chemistry." He sighed. "Ironically, we'd looked at that element right at the start of our research but it was abandoned when trials proved inconclusive and unproductive ... it seems that we may have been wrong, simply because of the time factor involved; perhaps the amount of time taking them—in Sophie's case years—made all the difference."

"I've been on antidepressants too though, for years now," Andy said.

"You have," Straub said, "which also suggests that a lot of the work we put into the List is now somewhat useless. We thought we'd clarified some of the rules, the brackets, but it turns out we possibly haven't."

"The List?" Andy asked. "It's finished?"

"Yes. And that isn't your concern right now," Straub told him briskly. "Your priority is cracking *that*." She pointed out the window, where the Stone Man was now disappearing from view once more as the cabin turned. If it was seven per cent less of anything, it certainly didn't look it. "Alright. All of you will be in your quarters for the rest of the day. Someone will come to see you in a few hours to do your bloodwork, etc. and you'll be getting MRIs too. In the meantime: rest." Straub stepped back, out of the path of Paul's cabin door. "After you," she said to Andy. "Can you stand, Sophie?" Sophie did, holding her head, but steady on her feet. Andy tried again to catch her eye, but Sophie's cold shoulder turned towards the door too quickly. Angry or not, how could she pretend that whatever just happened hadn't happened? Didn't she feel it?

He couldn't talk to her now. Not in front of Straub. Andy followed Sophie into the companion cabin. She didn't look his way until they disembarked at the docking station on the other side of the hangar, before she was led politely away by her escorts (never guards, always escorts). She'd been walking away from him down the corridor towards her quarters, with Andy hovering at the hallway crossroads.

"Sir?" Andy's escort politely asked. Andy might have technically been a higher-up on the base, and he wasn't always escorted everywhere on site, but on days like today he absolutely was. Straub always said they wanted to "keep an eye on him during times of high stress".

"One second," Andy hissed, watching Sophie go and feeling a dull, heavy ache inside. This wasn't some unrequited stalker shit; they'd shared a mind. He knew how she felt. So why was she—

There. Right before she turned into the right-hand corridor, she looked back. Their eyes met, and now Andy saw no trace of anger there.

Instead, she looked frightened.

***

When he saw her later by the vending machine, her anger was back in force.

"Sophie?"

He hadn't intended to run into her. When she spun round at the sound of her name, surprise had been in her bright, piercing eyes. There was a flash of a delighted smile upon seeing him ... but it quickly turned into a scowl.

"Yes, *Dispensatori*," she said tersely.

"Can I talk to you for a second?"

She set her jaw, glancing awkwardly at the soldier close behind her, and at Andy's escort.

"Yeah," Andy said, "hang on—guys? Can you back up and give us some privacy for a second? We're just going to talk."

"Sir," one of them said, and both men took a step backwards.

"... maybe few more, chaps?"

The soldiers exchanged a glance, and then backed all the way up to the wall.

"Thanks."

"What is it?" Sophie whispered. *Don't panic*, he told himself, *you know this woman better than any other person you have ever known in your entire life, and she knows you the same way. Just talk.* It was an insane concept, one he still couldn't quite understand even now he'd had the last few hours to think about it, so his brain fell back on its default panic option: shit jokes.

"I just wanted to show you these guys actually kind of have to do what I tell them," he false-chuckled.

Sophie's expression was steel. Andy's fake smile vanished.

"I'm sorry, Sophie," he said. "I should have listened to you." Sophie shook her head.

"I didn't come here—" she began loudly, but then lowered her voice to a whisper. "I didn't come here to piss about, Andy. I came to make a difference. I'm a very busy person, very busy. I have a life. I didn't decide to give it up for something I don't care about, I'm here because I *do* care. I'm not an idiot. I don't expect to be heard from again if something goes wrong here." Andy was taken aback. She really was serious about this. "The people I love, the people *they* love . . . they all might have needed someone like me to step up and help save the country, and as cheesy as that bloody sounds it's true."

"Why did you volunteer?" Andy blurted. It was a hole in his knowledge. "Something to do with your—"

"None of your fucking business," she snapped. "Alright?" It was like a knife to him, and she saw it. "Sorry," she said, sighing. "That's just . . . that's mine, okay? That's mine."

"Okay. I really am sorry," he said . . . and then decided to chance it. "And I think you know that's true. Don't you? You know I would really be sorry. Right?"

Her brow furrowed in confusion; Andy saw it and the bottom dropped out of his world.

She *didn't* know. It was all in his head.

"Well . . . of *course* I know," she said, looking at him as if he'd asked if water was wet. "Why would you even ask that?"

If *none of your fucking business* was a knife, this was a caress. Sophie saw Andy's growing smile and put a stop to it.

"Same way you now know how I work, yes?"

"Of course—"

"You now know how I do things?"

"Yes."

"Then why are you asking me why I'm angry?"

Andy blinked.

"Because . . . I think I know but then my interpretation jumps in the way—"

"Then think. *Really* think. Go on."

Andy did. He got it.

"Because . . . you're a professional," he breathed. "You take great pride in what you do, which gets you results. And this is something—for whatever reason you wish to keep secret, which is fine, that's fine—" he added very quickly, "that matters to you a lot. This was your first performance in front of Straub . . . and you want her to know what you can do . . . so she puts her faith . . . in you . . ." He trailed off, understanding, but not adding *because you're also a bit of a Head Girl type whose happiest childhood memories were getting praise from teacher in front of the class, and you were desperate to do well on your first go and you were afraid of screwing up.* More came to him: she always did her homework early, the kind of kid he hated at school because he was always the opposite, but the kind of person who, as an adult, he admired. She didn't want to be ordinary, but she wanted to raise other people up too—

"That's right," she said, breathing out heavily. She suddenly cocked her head slightly, and Andy knew she was going through the same mental process. Her eyes squinted, un-squinted, and her mouth opened slightly. She saw him.

He didn't know how she was still standing there.

"You know what Paul and I did, too," he said.

"Yes." Then the magic words—a truth that, of course, he knew, but hearing her say it out loud was everything—"I would have done exactly the same thing, Andy. All of it."

Tears came to Andy's eyes and he looked away.

"What the fuck is happening," he mumbled. Electricity shot through his body—the regular kind—and he realised she had taken his hand. He looked back to her and saw that she also held his soul.

"If we hadn't done what we'd just done," she said softly, "this would be an insane conversation, and you would be some kind of loony stalker. I'd be saying *you don't even know me*. But we both know that couldn't be further from the truth." Andy didn't dare speak. This was everything he'd wanted to hear. "But ... Andy. Listen to me. This cannot happen again. Not yet. We can't screw up like that. I know how much you love your friend, I know the reasons why ..." She paused, suddenly cocked her head again, looking down. "Which apparently means I care a great deal about him too." She looked up. "Even if you don't care about the mission here, which, *Jesus*, I guess I know you do, bloody hell this is weird ... look, this mission here is vital and we have to keep it together for Paul too. He's dying. So, no matter what's happening between us—no matter how insane—it has to *wait*. It has to. Do you understand?"

"Yes." If she'd said *you have to paint your backside blue and do a naked dance on the roof of the Ricoh Arena* he'd have still said yes. "And I do know how important it all is, Sophie. I died to save the country, you know," he added.

Sophie couldn't stop the smile from coming to her face.

"You look good for it," she said.

"And I do care about all of those things you said," Andy said. "But even when they're talking about communicating with the

Stone Man—and believe me, I want to—my main priority is saving Paul. It's the only way we can because God knows these arseholes aren't going to put him in a coma and send the Stone Man home. They'd rather run him into the ground first. *He'd rather run himself into the ground trying.*"

"Then we have to get this right on the next try," she said. "I don't think he has much more than that in him."

"I agree. And I love you."

The words were out before he could stop them.

Then he was glad they were out. They had to be said. He'd never said that to anyone in his life other than his parents. A great weight left his shoulders and then immediately returned as Sophie's brow furrowed again.

"That's the shit I'm talking about!" she hissed. "No more of that. Not yet."

"... okay. Of course."

"Jesus *Christ*," she said, and then leaned in closer, her voice so quiet he could barely hear it. "I love you too, okay? Mr known-me-for-a-matter-of-hours. This is ..." She ran her hands through her hair and shook her head. "Now. Keep a lid on that stuff. We have work to do."

He was so shocked to actually hear it that the question came to his lips immediately:

"But *how*?"

"How what?"

"How can you know all of me and still ..."

"Oh. Oh, Andy ..." She smiled. Her hand came up and stroked his cheek. "You really are a mess, aren't you? Because ..." Her hand came down and her finger tapped his chest. "I can see in *here*, in ways you probably don't even know about. Because of what you want to be. Because of what I saw of myself when you looked through my eyes. Because I can see the elephant, and not the rider." Andy didn't know the metaphor, then realised that she did, and therefore he now did. "Because behind your rampant ego, and insecurity, you are made of iron and don't even know it. Because after everything . . . you really *were* going to jump out of that fucking window." She leaned in, suddenly chest to chest, and kissed him briefly on the mouth. She began to step back, but he couldn't let her; his hands came up, his fingers plunging into her blonde hair, and he stepped in to kiss her back. She melted against him, her firm body pressing onto his, and in that moment, *Dispensatori*'s purpose changed. She was indescribable. As they kissed, each breathing the other in, Andy's mind was—for the first time he could remember—blissfully, perfectly silent.

It was an effect more dramatic than anything that had ever happened to him.

Well, to be fair, he thought as Sophie finally stepped away, *Paul never kissed you. Thank Christ.*

"Now," Sophie said, smiling and taking him in, even as the sudden physical space between them was painful, "all business. Until we're done. Okay?" Andy didn't answer, partially from being stunned by her kiss, and partially from an idea that had just slapped him upside the head.

Holy shit. The space between them.

"Andy?"

It had to be worth a try.

"Andy?"

"Wait," he said, turning away from her. "Hey, bud?"

"Yes sir, *Dispensatori*, Sir," the now-smirking escort/guard said.

"Can you radio Straub for me?" he said. "Ask her for a meeting in her office. It's urgent. We'll meet her there now. She won't be doing anything more important than this, I guarantee it."

"Is everything alright, sir? The Brigadier will ask."

"Yes, yes," Andy said, feeling excited. Truly alive, he realised. "Everything's great. Let's head over there now though. Lead on, Macduff, let's go."

"Andy, what is it?" Sophie asked, taking his hand. They both noticed it, smiled . . . and separated.

"I just had an idea," he grinned. "Come on, I'll tell you on the way."

Chapter Nine

Forty Feet and Closing

***

Andy.
Project Orobouros.
One Year Ago, Continued.

Once Andy had finished pitching his big idea in Straub's now partially-crowded office, he half expected her to do the standard *no way, absolutely out of the question* bit he'd seen in so many movies, the initial resistance that occurs whenever the rookie hero comes up with a risky idea. He should have known better; Straub had shown time and again—from the moment of their very first meeting, in fact—that she was prepared to take chances. She'd listened to Andy's pitch as he paced up and down, his chair empty, Sophie's filled. Holbrooks was leaning against the wall, Straub was sitting on her side of the desk, and Paul's face was visible via Wi-Fi on an iPad propped up on Straub's desk. There was one of the higher-up soldiers in the room too, and Andy finally remembered his name: Edgwick. A big man made more distinct by his red hair; lightly-thinning and neatly-clipped on top with a matching moustache below. Andy had exchanged pleasantries with him a few times; he seemed like an okay fella.

When Andy finished his pitch, Straub simply said:

"Doctor?"

Andy had noticed Sophie watching him as he talked, smiling. It had taken him a moment to recognise the expression: pride.

"I believe the current minimum distance between Caementum and the cabin is set to forty feet," Holbrooks said. "How close are *you* saying, Mr Pointer?"

"Touching distance," Andy said, the riskiest part of his pitch. "At least for me and Sophie. Paul would of course stay inside the cabin, but we keep the doors open."

His plan was simple but went against every protocol that had been set up thus far. Distance, Andy believed, was the issue when it came to getting deeper into the Stone Man's inner world, to find what was hidden down below, but he'd previously only been thinking about it from the point of view of *mental* closeness; the possible solution had come to him when Sophie had pressed up against him briefly in the hallway. Could the answer be to simply get their physical bodies closer to Caementum, without any metal walls in between them? From the moment of Project Ouroboros' first inception the concept had been to keep Paul and any other Stone Sensitives *away* from the Stone Man. It had been such a founding principle that the idea of getting closer to it had never been properly considered. After all, the cabin was already riskily close as it was; there was always a scramble team tracking just behind the Stone Man and two men in the separate front section of the cabin, ready to unload Paul in the unlikely event of an issue. Now here Andy was talking about being on the floor of the hangar, within touching range of the creature from his nightmares?

"You'd have me and Sophie on the back of a Jeep, exposed, driving between the cabin and Caementum," Andy said. "Your job would be to keep us close to it, but of course moving. Any issues, you get us out of there."

"Edgwick?" Straub asked.

"Logistically it couldn't be easier," Edgwick said, shrugging. "The question here is Stone Man related, and that's obviously . . ." He waved a hand at Holbrooks, who shrugged too.

"Caemtentum has never shown any interest in the companion cabin," Holbrooks said, "even when it's crossed his path. It stands to reason that his only focus is Mr Winter—"

"His?" Straub asked quietly.

"Its, sorry, its," Holbrooks said quickly, looking flustered. Paul wasn't the only one getting worn down, it seemed. "Sorry, it's been a long . . ." His head gave a small, rapid shake. "Look, I don't see any issue with this plan, barring technical failure, and we already have measures in place to deal with that. My only reservation is that, personally, I can't see it working. All past prolonged flashing-in proximity tests with Stone Sensitives suggest a distance threshold with most of them of—"

"Around one hundred feet, yes," Straub interrupted, bristling a little, clearly irked at someone telling her Stone knowledge as if she didn't already have it . . . but that wasn't like her, Andy thought. Even Straub looked tired, then. When did the woman ever sleep? Holbrooks, for that matter? Straub briefly mentioned her husband from time to time; did she ever see the man?

"Sorry, Brigadier," Holbrooks said, holding up his hands. "Of course." He turned to the others present. "Studies seem to show that, once GALE subjects are within roughly one hundred feet of range from Caementum, any effect of the Stone Man's presence on an individual is at maximum. The cabin has always been within that range. So ..." He spread his hands. "Sorry, *Dispensatori*," he said. "I just don't see why getting even closer would make this any different. That said, I do think it's worth a try, if the Brigadier deems it low risk."

"Not wanting to sound like a bighead," Sophie said, "but you didn't have someone like me in the circuit when you did those tests, did you? Or even a Carl Baker. That's got to make a difference, surely?"

"I have to agree," Andy said. "The way the three of us work as a unit is unlike anything else I've experienced with the Stone Man. The rush I got from it the second time would have been too much without Sophie." He smiled at her, thrilling as he saw her swell a little with pride. Perhaps they weren't that different in many ways. "She changes everything."

"The plan isn't without risk," Straub said, "but this is too important not to try. Mr Winter?"

"It sounds ... fine," Paul's voice croaked over the iPad's tiny speakers. "I won't have to be any ... closer to it, will I?"

"Only a little bit, but yes," Andy said, wincing a little as he braced for resistance. "We'd have to slow the cabin to a range only just big enough to fit our Jeep in between the cabin and the Stone Man."

"Ah." That was Straub. Paul looked even more pale.

"We have the scramble team inside your part of the cabin, Paul," Andy said quickly. "They can pick you up and *carry* you across the bloody hangar if they need to. This still has to be worth it." He saw Sophie's expression; what was she—*oh*. He took her hint. *Be human.* "I know it's frightening, mate," he gently said to Paul. "But this could be part of what gets you out of—"

"I know," Paul interrupted. "It's okay ... I want to do it."

"Sophie?" Straub asked.

"Other than my concern for Paul?" Sophie replied. "I can't *wait* to get back out there."

"You're not frightened?"

"Oh, very much so, yes," Sophie said calmly.

"And what about you?" Straub asked Andy. "Are you sure you're okay with this? *Dispensatori* . . . sorry to bring this up, but I read your psych reports week to week. I know how you feel about Caementum. You haven't been physically face-to-face with him, truly, for several years. Are you sure you can handle this?"

An image suddenly came to Andy: the hangar lights, high above, blotted out by the towering form of the Stone Man as it loomed over him, those protrusions beginning to emerge from its chest as it—

He looked at Sophie. She nodded almost imperceptibly, and he had his answer.

"Yes," he replied. The task at hand suddenly became even more important. If they had a breakthrough, it meant he was one step closer to being able to leave with *Sophie.*

That's *what you'd do next*, he thought. *Go have a life.*

"Like she said: we didn't have a Sophie Warrender onside before."

"Alright," Straub said, sitting up, which implied that she had been slouching previously; Straub, however, was the only person Andy had ever met who managed to straighten up from an already sitting-up-straight position. "We're done here. Edgwick, make the necessary arrangements and update me later today once they're in place. I want this operation commencing at 0700 hours tomorrow. *Dispensatori*, Mr Winter, if you could hang back a moment please, I'd like to talk with you. Everyone else, you may leave."

"Wait, I leave too?" Sophie asked.

"Yes, Miss Warrender, your escort is outside."

She looked at Andy, confused.

"It's okay," he said. She didn't like it, he knew, but he could tell her about it her later. Straub was onside, and he wanted to keep it that way. No disagreeing with her.

"Mm," Sophie murmured tersely, giving Straub a brief *look*. Andy nearly choked. She gave *Straub* the side-eye!

"And I was going to . . . get ready for the Mardi Gras later," Paul wheezed, and Andy felt a sense of even greater resolve; that was the old Paul coming through. If this plan had done that, then they were on the right path. Sophie stood and gave Andy a smile that he saw before she caught herself and turned it into a serious *go get 'em, work colleague* expression. The change was so obvious that they both had to stifle a laugh as Sophie, Edgwick and Holbrooks left the room.

"Firstly," Straub said to Andy, "if you think I don't see those glances between you two, you're an idiot." The smile vanished from Andy's face. "My base. My rules. No fraternisation. None. Especially between members of *this* team."

"I'll do my . . . best," Paul muttered, and Andy turned his laugh into a cough. Straub reddened slightly—a miracle—but Andy thought it may have been her supressing a laugh herself.

"Secondly," Straub said, "I wanted to ask you both something out of earshot of the others. There's an element of this plan that hasn't been discussed here, and I consider it a professional courtesy—even, I daresay, a personal one—to bring it up with you both without Holbrooks here."

"A personal one?" Andy said, raising his eyebrows.

"Holbrooks is a good man, and in my opinion, a genius," Straub said, ignoring Andy. "He might not believe in this plan, but I know from our discussions that if our objective here—to plunder whatever intel the Stone Man might have—results in the death of Mr Winter, he would believe it's worth it, even if that meant Caementum leaving. If you asked him, he would talk about the greater good and say it would be what Mr Winter wanted." She turned to Paul's face onscreen. "I believe in Andy's plan, but I'm not sure I agree with Dr Holbrooks' opinion on all counts. I want to ask you, Mr Winter—Paul—are you still prepared to die, doing this?" She looked up at Andy. "And are you prepared to let him, Andy?"

"I am, and he is," Paul said. Andy stared at Paul's pale, haggard face onscreen. Did Paul think Andy actually *was* prepared to do that?

"If he says that, then yes," Andy said. "I am."

"I still want to have my appointment today," Paul said. "With Linda."

"Linda ..." Straub said, looking confused. She tapped at her computer's keyboard. "Wyken? This will be the fifth time you've seen her, I think?" Straub said, checking her notes. "We were about to begin her discharge procedure. She's only borderline Stone Sensitive since she was cut off during ... I believe the Third Arrival. Your boost did almost nothing for her, according to this. I'm surprised they even booked her in for the last appointment, we must have not updated the system. What would be the point, Paul?"

"You think she'll be ... a Target, then?" Paul asked. The air in the room became frosty. "I know from ... personal experience what ... being cut off can mean."

"Says here," Straub said, ignoring the question, "that the last time you saw her, you tried to warn her. Give her information." Paul scowled onscreen. Straub tapped her desk. She said something under her breath, and Andy thought it might have been *men.* "Alright. You can still see her, and only because I'm concerned about the outcome of the next encounter with Caementum. We owe you far more than that, and it's the least we can do . . . which makes what I have to say next all the harder. We can't risk you giving any information, Paul. Anything. We can't take any chances at all, even as a possible last request for you. If you want to see Linda today, you'll have to wear the deterrent." Andy sat upright in his seat, outraged, but Straub silenced him by holding up a hand.

He knew what deterrent meant. Paul had been a little too loose-lipped with volunteers, hinting about them potentially becoming Targets if they worked with the government and ended up cut off. They'd warned Paul, and Paul had told Andy: *deterrent* meant *shock collar.*

"I will," Paul said. "I'll wear it."

"You have to be kidding!" Andy barked.

"It's alright," Paul said, looking more beaten than ever. "Won't say anything, so . . . won't have to zap me."

"That's not the point—"

"Thank you for understanding, Paul," Straub said. "It's not something I would do lightly. I have to do my job." She looked at Andy, who was fuming. "Very well. I'll see you in the morning."

"You'd really do that to him?" Andy asked her as Paul's image disappeared offscreen. "After all he's been through?"

"If it means doing what needs to done," Straub said, "then yes. He understands that. Why don't you?"

Andy looked at her, horrified.

"You can't—"

It was pointless. Straub, someone Andy had come to know well over the last few years—as much as anyone could know Straub—now looked like a stranger.

"Would you put one on me?" he asked quietly. "If that meant *doing what needs to be done*? After all *I've* done?"

"This meeting is concluded," Straub said.

"Did you put forward my request? About being able to leave for a week?"

Straub pressed a button on her desk.

"Escort for Mr Pointer, please." The office door opened and a soldier entered. The visual of the armed man blocking the doorway said it all. A slow, sinking feeling settled into Andy's chest.

"You're never going to let me leave, are you?" he said quietly, turning back to Straub. "Not as long as you think you need me? After everything I've—"

"Don't be dramatic," Straub said, turning away from him and facing her computer monitor. "I'll see you at 0700 hours, Mr Pointer." Andy stood stock still for another moment, watching her, and then turned and stormed past the soldier and out of the office, blood thrumming in his head. As he heard his escort fall into step behind him, all he could think about was what he'd said to Sophie earlier; that he believed in the project, in the work they were doing. He'd meant it. This place had given him something he'd never had: purpose. He'd also said that getting Paul out was his greatest priority.

All of that had changed in the space of an afternoon.

Getting Paul out was now the only priority. Paul ... and Sophie.

Fuck you, Brigadier, he thought grimly. *And fuck this place too.*

***

Sitting in the Jeep at the entrance to the hangar, Andy remembered Paul describing the first day of playing cat and mouse with the Stone Man. On the floor of the hangar before the cabin was even built, riding around in the back of a Jeep. *The worst part*, Paul had said, *was worrying about how the Stone Man might respond. Four years after the First Arrival even, we still know next to nothing about it, but back then, man ... We'd seen its chest expand when it harvested a spine; we didn't know if its arms could shoot out and grab me or something. What if it could shoot laser beams and take out the Jeep? The first few minutes were frightening but exciting, because they were all about hoping the plan would work. Once it worked, the next few hours were hell. Just waiting for that unknown disaster.*

Andy felt very glad that they now knew the Stone Man didn't have Go-Go Gadget arms or laserbeam eyes.

"Roger," Edgwick said into his radio, sitting in the driver's seat of Andy's Jeep. Andy and Sophie could hear him but not easily see him; their seats had been removed, turned around to face backwards, and then reattached to the floor of the vehicle. What they needed to see would be behind the Jeep, not in front. "We're off, Private," Edgwick said to the soldier in the passenger seat. "*Dispensatori*, Miss Warrender. It's showtime."

"Let's do it," Sophie said. Andy tried to catch her eye but she was staring straight ahead, clearly not allowing any distractions this time. Lucky her; Andy's brain was *all* distractions, from the whirl of emotions whenever he thought of Sophie to an overriding, low-level terror. The hangar wall they were facing steadily grew further away as the Jeep—Andy and Paul always called them *Jeeps* even though it wasn't their proper name—slowly set off across the dirt floor towards the centre of the huge hangar. The glass-fronted room away to their right—Observation

2—was full; he saw some faces he recognised, some he didn't. Straub was in there. He'd expected to see O'Reardon as well, one of Holbrooks' higher-ups, but instead Holbrooks himself was in her place. Head honcho didn't want to be too close to the action, it seemed. That meant O'Reardon was inside the cabin, riding with Paul.

High above, the enormous ceiling lights continued to blaze in that cavernous space. If Sophie was frightened, she wasn't showing it, but then she'd never seen the Stone Man up close, not truly. Never seen it harvest. Once connected, Andy would know how she really felt. He turned around in his seat to watch their approach; the bright interior light of Paul's endlessly moving cabin caught his eye first, the wide-open rear access door revealing Paul's living room, the man himself seated in a chair, framed by the doorway. Andy raised a hand; Paul returned it weakly. This *had* to be worth it. Paul was surely about to give the biggest push of his life.

He took a deep breath and looked left. There it was, growing ever closer. Larger.

The Stone Man's feet lightly kicked up dirt with each step forward and flattened it down hard as it pounded its way along after the cabin. The mass of the thing—not just its size but its sense of weight and heft—was, as always, frightening and awe-inspiring at the same time. There was never any forward lean to it; it walked fully erect, head high. It had been pursuing Paul for four years and had never shown any signs of eagerness or haste. Slow, relentless, implacable ... but now, apparently, flawed? Slowing? Andy couldn't believe that. He just couldn't. He was about to try and find out what was inside it, though, and knew he'd better hope there *were* some chinks in that armour.

But what armour.

Sophie turned now too and breathed in sharply as she saw the Stone Man. Andy knew what she was thinking, no psychic link required: seeing the Stone Man in the open air, without glass or plastic shielding in between ... it was just something else. Its presence hit you. He could feel something in his bones responding.

"It's ..." Sophie began, and then stopped. She never finished the sentence.

Andy had to turn back around to keep the Stone Man in his eyeline as the Jeep began to draw alongside it, and then moved to around ten feet ahead.

"Stand by," Straub's voice said over the radio.

"Roger."

No one spoke. The Jeep's engine, the rumbling of the cabin, and the heavy, pounding feet of the Stone Man behind them to their left; these were the only sounds.

"Move into centre," Straub then said, and Edgwick moved the vehicle sideways into the gap between the cabin and Caementum. Andy took a last look at Paul, directly in front of him now, and tried to give his friend another thumbs-up, but Paul wasn't looking. Paul was looking behind the Jeep with a death stare, jaw set. Andy then realised that once he turned around, the Stone Man would be walking directly towards him. He took a deep breath and slowly spun to face it.

Good God, it was huge. It looked like something out of a nightmare dream sequence in a movie, one of motion in an endless loop: the Jeep was moving at walking pace and the wall of the hangar to his right seemed to never stop, the Stone Man never coming closer than ten feet away, but that was more than close enough. He imagined it suddenly getting closer ... *closer* ...

"In position," Edgwick said into the radio, interrupting Andy's thoughts.

"Roger that," Straub said. "Reducing cabin distance."

Andy heard the cabin's alarm, warning of the reduction in speed. He glanced back again; the cabin had moved so close to the Jeep that they were nearly rear bumper to front bumper.

He hasn't ever been this close to it. Andy wondered what Paul must be thinking . . . then realised he'd never been this close to the moving Stone Man either, and started worrying about himself, which he was rather good at. But then—

Sophie—

"You okay?" he asked. She wasn't. Her face was ashen.

Yep, it's a little different when you're face to face, isn't it—

Andy felt ashamed as the thought came, unbidden; he squashed it down. He wanted to take her hand, but he didn't. They'd made an agreement. She looked at him, then laughed nervously.

"Yeah," she said. "Yeah. Let's do this." Her attitude was fantastic. It was time to step up.

"Whenever you're ready *Dispensatori*, Miss Warrender, Mr Winter," Straub said over the radio. "Good luck." The engines were quiet, almost drowned out by the sound of the tyres rolling. And of course, that *other* sound.

Thud. Thud. Thud. Thud.

The Stone Man walked.

Andy turned around in his seat to look. Paul's chair had armrests, and Paul was gripping them. His knuckles were white as he looked straight ahead. Was it because they were so close? Or because he knew this might be his last dance?

Don't stop, Paul had told him last night. *No matter what. Don't you fucking dare. If you're my friend, you promise me that you don't stop for me. Promise me.*

Andy had promised.

Promise me too, Sophie had said.

Andy had promised.

Paul closed his eyes, nodding, and Andy sat back in his seat, giving Sophie the thumbs-up. They closed their eyes too. In Paul's cabin the night before, they'd tested their own circuit, making sure to not connect to the Stone Man and increasing the distance between them as much as the space inside the cabin would allow. It had been even easier to form than the first time. What else did Sophie mean they could do? If they got better each time . . . what other abilities could they unlock?

In the darkness of his mind, Andy felt Sophie creating their threads, those super-fine and hard to grasp cables that, once connected, were raw energy. *Pop,* there was Paul. *Pop,* there was Sophie. And then the world inside his mind lit up as Sophie fed out a line towards the Stone Man and it connected; the three of them found Caementum.

Its own existing threads were like flowing fire, red and spitting, as well as its own little slowly-leaking streams of precious energy, the two kinds flying away into the ether.

The three of them took a moment to let their connection to it settle, Paul slowly feeding them and giving the circuit fuel, allowing it to happen. Sophie, making it stronger, more tangible, malleable. Andy, gaining control, capability. All of them feeling the Stone Man's energy . . . but Andy had to stop himself turning towards Sophie's light, drawn like a fly to a bug zapper. He settled back into his position in the circuit and let the minds of the other two hum away distantly at the end of their threads, the crackling like electricity in power lines. Sophie, thrilled and terrified. Paul, grim and *oh God,* Paul was frightened and

—ready to die—

Paul hadn't meant to send it, but his state of mind had been too strong not to feel. Andy couldn't allow himself to turn towards his friend in Stone Space either, even though he kept instinctively doing it; falling into the others' threads felt like catching yourself falling asleep on the sofa. It was a creeping thing, but also pleasant. *Connection.*

—(let's go)—

Sophie. Fearful but pressing forward.

—Yes—

He had to ignore all the oh-so-tempting threads coming off Caementum, leading away into an eternity that, if he were to follow, he knew would never be able come back from. Carl Baker had seen what lay beyond them, and Andy had never truly believed that Baker's haemorrhage was due to his battered brain.

Besides, what he needed was *inside* the Stone Man.

—Cover me—

It was meant to be a light-hearted comment, but he meant it; key to the plan was Sophie's ability to hide them as much as her ability to connect and make the unit work.

—(I've got you)—

The double meaning of her words washed over him but he plunged into the Stone Man all the same.

It was better this time. Much better. The plan was—

—It's working—

He found it immediately, down there in the dark. That same edge of something, and yes! It looked like it was within reach!

The Caeterus's threads twitched and began to turn inward, sensing his intention.

Sophie redoubled her efforts and they stopped. He was covered.

—(You're all good)—(don't worry)—(go)—

Her thread sang of the truth though; it was taking a lot of effort. This closer, open physical proximity to the Stone Man brought a greater risk of detection, and Sophie was having to work harder. Paul too—

—I'm fine—

—*(Me too)—(go)—*

—Jesus—alright—

He dived towards that edge below, feeling a pressure build around him as he descended. Beneath him, that edge began to grow closer ... but not quickly enough. It *was* closer than before, but still far away. He knew he could reach it, but how long did they have? How long could Paul and Sophie last?

Dive, he told himself, even as knew he wasn't actually diving into anything. All of the sensations he was experiencing couldn't be described in physical terms. There were no tangible, solid, real-world connections between himself, Paul and Sophie, but he could perceive the mental connections between as *threads* all the same. The only way he could perceive mentally moving through the darkness inside the Stone Man was as diving downwards. And the thing that lay below him, the edge that he could see, he perceived as being part of ...

—a cage—

The pressure suddenly increased, and Sophie gasped in his mind; she'd slipped, lost control for a moment, and the Stone Man's own threads—the awareness of the Caeterus—had jabbed suddenly closer, as if razor-sharp teeth had suddenly snapped shut a few feet away from Andy. Sophie cried out with the effort of obscuring Andy from them at such close range.

—*(Ahhh)—(aaaaaAAAAAAAHH)*—

—*Sophie*—

Then Paul—

—I   have   you—

Sophie's tension eased a little, but now Paul's thread was taut as a drumskin. The Caeterus's threads had slowed greatly, but now they were still moving inwards, and already so close. He didn't wait for further checks on his team. They'd agreed, and he'd promised them both. He dived deep, and fast, and that was when the pain began.

—Hgggggggg—

He kept going but it felt like swimming through concrete, the pressure on his mind's eye like a spike being jammed into it. He tried to think-scream but then it was *there*, the outer corner of the cage, and he groped for it but couldn't focus because of the pain, the fucking *pain*—

Sophie and Paul reached down, salving his mind, but the distraction from their concealment task meant the Caeterus's threads were coming in quickly again, their dim awareness becoming sharper, hungrier, and as Sophie and Paul shared Andy's agony, taking on the burden, their distant screams travelled so faintly along the threads that Andy understood he was very deep indeed. The edge of the cage was there, buried in darkness . . . Andy's grasping hands found it.

He pulled.

The pain lanced into him and he let go, and even as he bellowed, Sophie and Paul's threads told him what was happening; the Caeterus had come roaring towards them. Andy's team were screaming from the effort of keeping the Caeterus out.

—*(ANDY   ANDY   QUICKLY PLEASE)*—

He was trying but oh God it *hurt,* it hurt so much, so many blades on him, in him, slicing, but his hands found the box once more and tugged, hard, and it gave a little—

BANG.

The pain stopped.

The box was now out of his grasp, far below him once more.

. . . what?

How had—

He'd been pushed back up.

—Sophie, Paul—

—*(. . .)*—

— . . .—

They couldn't speak, but he could hear them holding on, stopping the Caeterus from fully—

The Caeterus were all around him.

The ends of their threads felt dark, cold, sharp, and unspeakably powerful. Could they see him? Not fully; Paul and Sophie were keeping them from touching him, but the Caeterus's threads were a hair's breadth away. The sensation of their proximity turned Andy's consciousness to ice. The threads were impassive, utterly clinical. They regarded the shadow of his shape, wondering what he was, what he would do next. Andy couldn't think.

He dived downwards again, towards the box—

Something immense came sideways out of the darkness to meet him— whatever had pushed him back up—and now it shoved all three of them together—

Pop.

Andy fell sideways against Sophie. She let out a *whuff* sound as his weight fell onto her. She was strong enough to almost catch him though, and as he pushed himself upright and looked into her stunned, blinking eyes he had time to think *it threw us out* before Sophie's answer was already in his mind—

—*(Get back in there)*—

And then he was diving back into the darkness, even though he'd felt the sheer force which had removed him . . . but this time, it was ready. *Caementum* was ready. He was flung back out with so much power that when he slammed back into his body once more, his limbs locked up.

His body began to spasm.

He couldn't feel the other two, the circuit now dead, but he could hear Sophie making choking, gagging sounds next to him. Her too, then. Through squinting eyes he saw the Stone Man walking towards the Jeep as always, but it was suddenly getting further away—

"Edgwick—"

That shout came from the soldier that Andy didn't know in the passenger seat, and as Andy heard it he understood three things at once: Edgwick was Stone Sensitive, the sheer force of Andy's removal from the Stone Man had blasted him too, and

Edgwick's body was locking up like his, Sophie's, and presumably Paul's. Andy understood this because the Jeep was now accelerating the short distance towards the cabin, Edgwick's locked and spasming leg jamming his foot onto the accelerator. Andy wanted to turn to see Paul but he couldn't move and then *BANG*, he was jolted forward in his seat as the Jeep slammed into the back of Paul's cabin.

"Edgwick! Edgwick!" The soldier in the passenger seat obviously wasn't Stone Sensitive, given that he could yell. Andy tried to look at Sophie but he couldn't turn his head as the Jeep's engine became deafening, pushing the cabin forward, its wheels spinning in the dirt, and he realised Paul was in trouble.

There had never been any point in making the cabin tank-like; the Stone Man could rip through any known substance like tissue paper. Reinforcing it was pointless and only created logistical issues. So the goal with the cabin had been to make it as light as possible. It was designed to never stop moving, after all. Why would they want it to be heavy?

With a superhuman effort, Andy managed to turn his head and take in the sight; the passenger-solider trying to turn the wheel enough to move the Jeep away from the cabin and failing against the locked-in strength of Edgwick's larger arms. Paul, teeth gritted in his chair in the open back of the cabin, his terrified eyes finding Andy's ... and Andy realised the cabin was about to begin its automated turn.

The sync light on top of the cabin turned red as someone, either the personnel in the booth or the emergency personnel in the front cab, took over, understanding that they needed control, but the rear edge of the hanger was approaching; they still had to turn or they would run into the end wall, but they had to turn quickly or—

It wasn't quickly enough. The cabin was light, but even so its height, taller than a high-top van, made it top-heavy. The onward force of the Jeep pushed the cabin's back end sideways as the larger vehicle turned, and for a moment it looked as if they would have a narrow escape as the cabin skidded sideways, away from the Jeep, a disaster averted in slow motion. But then as the cabin tried to handle the conflicting directions of the kinetic energy exerted on it, it wobbled, the wheels on one side left the floor, and it hung half-suspended for a moment as the Jeep continued towards the hangar wall at now-unimpeded speed, accelerating helplessly courtesy of Edgwick's locked-up foot.

The cabin slowly toppled over and smashed into the dirt floor with a deafening crash. The Jeep slammed into the hangar wall with a louder one.

Stunned, Andy tried to blink the white spots out of his eyesight. He couldn't get his breath and there was a sharp pain in his sternum; the noise of the Jeep's screaming engine filled his ears. He got his eyes to focus just in time to take in the sight of the Stone Man beginning to turn as it walked.

It was heading towards the downed cabin.

The Jeep's engine suddenly dropped back to idling speed and Andy realised therefore Edgwick was no longer locking up, as Andy's own painfully tight fists released themselves. The fit was over. Pandemonium reigned inside the hangar; personnel were pouring out of the observation rooms, yelling.

Paul, Andy thought, *Sophie—*

But Sophie was okay, desperately fiddling with her seatbelt catch the same way Andy now was; he couldn't see Paul through the cabin's doorway anymore because of the angle it had crashed, lying at the end of a long arc of freshly turned earth.

The Stone Man was four steps away from it. The crashed Jeep was at thirty feet. The backup units already racing in would not get Paul out of there in time and Andy *couldn't get his fucking seatbelt undone—*

Sophie's hand gripped his hard, just as a great rending and screeching came from the cabin, along with the sound of sparking electrical circuits blowing. The Stone Man was walking through the vehicle's exposed underbelly. Without a word Andy and Sophie's minds leapt forward and found Paul's stunned brain; the circuit formed like lightning, two words from Sophie painted in Andy's brain in neon letters one hundred feet high—

—(SAVE HIM)—

—and Andy's reeling mind interpreted those words into thoughtless action as Paul's awakening mind gave them everything he had left. The circuit became truly alive.

The following happened in nanoseconds:

Not knowing what else to do, Andy tried to plunge down towards the cage in the depths but the Caeterus's threads cut him off, forcing him to dance desperately around them with the speed of terror as Sophie ran interference as best she could. He tried again, the threads whipping around him like living barbed wire, the cage below maddeningly out of reach, and as he darted left in in the darkness, kept high above the cage, he suddenly felt his consciousness *snag.*

What—

The heightened arousal of the moment bathed everything in stark clarity. Andy felt again and realised that he'd discovered something they hadn't even been looking for. They'd been so busy trying to go deep inside, they'd never even thought to look at the *edges* of the Stone Man's essence.

He'd found Caementum's weak spot. The leak.

There was no time to do anything other than thrust his mind inside the break in the Stone Man's mental armour. Instantly, Andy was battered by a stream of inexplicable information that he knew to be commands. He couldn't stop them and give his own— they were far too powerful to compete with—but he could *interfere* with them. He leapt into their path and broke the chain of information, absorbing it as his body, sitting helpless in the Jeep, began to buck. Blood burst from his nose in a gush, and in his mind he dug himself deeper into the Stone Man's weak spot and *twisted*.

He was dimly aware of something wet spraying onto his face from the right; blood had burst from Sophie's nose, her thrashing head flinging crimson liquid left and right as something inside the Stone Man—something important—finally gave way for good.

—HOLD   ON—

And the Stone.

Man.

Stopped.

The space inside the Stone Man suddenly became thick and choking, some of sort of internal protocol of the Caeterus's own being activated as the physical air inside the hangar itself turned icy cold. The stream of information that had been battering Andy inside Stone Space suddenly froze, and a sound began to ring out through both the physical and mental worlds Andy simultaneously inhabited. It wasn't a deep tone, like the noises that had accompanied different stages of the Stone Men's progress; this was a reedy, octaves-higher-but-still deafening klaxon. Andy suddenly felt as if he was being buried; the Stone Man's insides were shutting down, closing over him—even the threads of the Caeterus were retreating—but the klaxon-screech was deafening, stopping him from getting his bearings. He could feel the sensations on his body but he didn't know how to get back to it, which way to go to, he couldn't feel Sophie and Paul's threads, and down below him still, he knew, was the cage, mocking him. If he dove towards it now he'd never—

A thread pinged at him out of the darkness.

—Get   out   NOW—

Paul's voice sounded weak but alert, and he was right. Whatever the name was for the inside of the Stone Man, it was dying fast, and Andy couldn't be there when it did. Paul's voice, his thread, called Andy back towards the outer world, a literal lifeline, and as Andy grabbed it he tried to comprehend what had just happened. The three of them had done what the combined military might of the British government had never been able to do—*they'd stopped the Stone Man*—but as he ascended up and out of Stone Space once more any amazement he had suddenly turned to terror: he still couldn't feel Sophie.

—Sophie—

His eyes opened as he returned to his body, feeling his lungs working, his heartbeat racing as he sat up and spun around in his seat to grab Sophie's shoulders. Her face and polo shirt were streaked with blood, but her eyes were half-open and half-aware.

"Sophie!"

"Pa ..." she breathed, blinking fast. "Poll," she said. Andy's head whipped around to the stricken cabin.

Military personnel were swarming over it, and Paul was already halfway across the hangar floor, being raced away on a stretcher towards a waiting medical truck. Was Paul ... no. A hand raised up from the stretcher, wobbling uncertainly in the air.

The hand turned into a thumbs-up. Andy looked at the Stone Man, waiting to be proved awfully, terribly wrong. It still stood, frozen mid-stride, one of its legs firmly embedded in the mangled base of the still-sparking cabin.

Andy saw with horror that, stationary as it was, it had stopped in the middle of bending forward at the waist, both arms outstretched.

Reaching.

"He's okay," Andy gasped, turning back to Sophie, still holding her shoulders. "We saved him, Sophie!" He had to shout to be heard over the Stone Man's awful high-klaxon noise ... and then, suddenly, that stopped too. He looked at Caementum again. Still no movement. He watched, triple-checking the result even though he knew the answer. He'd been inside it at the end.

"Sophie ..." he said breathlessly. "I think we broke it." It wasn't the right word. "I think we *killed* it."

"Killed ... it ..." she smiled. "Good." Andy began to shake as the adrenaline worked its way through his system. Joy, relief, terror—

Movement coming from the inside of the cabin caught his eye. The soldiers were freeing O'Reardon, the scientist—Andy had been right about her being inside the cabin—and she was thrashing in their arms like a lunatic, shouting.

"Ya!" O'Reardon barked, her hands closing into fists in the air, opening and grasping at nothing. "Ya! Gone! Ya! Gone!" O'Reardon was Stone Sensitive too, then, and it seemed whatever force had pushed them out of the Stone Man hadn't just hit those in the circuit, as Edgwick's reaction had proved—

Edgwick—

The soldier was already clambering out of the Jeep's driver's seat, red-faced and wincing but otherwise unscathed. He took one look at Andy and Sophie and snatched up his radio, even though Andy could already see a medic truck zooming towards them. "Medical evac immediately," Edgwick slurred pointlessly. Andy stroked Sophie's face—and why the fuck not after what had just happened?—and her hand came up to touch the back of his. She smiled.

"Kiss me," she said.

He moved eagerly towards her, but even in the headiest rush of love, the amount of fresh blood around her mouth made him pause.

"Uh—"

Sophie let out a guffaw and pulled his head down to meet hers, and he found he cared very little about the blood after all. He had never known a kiss like it.

As he drew away, grinning as he looked down into her eyes, he saw her eyelids were closing. Her whole face suddenly went limp.

"Sophie?"

She let out a long, slow, shuddering breath and became still.

"Sophie!"

Her eyes flew open.

"Christ!" She gasped. "What, what?" She tried to sit up. "Is Paul—"

Andy was so relieved that tears sprang to his eyes.

"Oh . . . oh, thank God," he said. "I thought you—"

"Sorry, sorry," Sophie said, tears coming to her eyes too as she stroked his face. "I didn't mean to scare you! That was just really, really nice." She smiled. "Kiss me again."

THE STONE GIANT

***

Chapter Ten

Dark Times on the Road

✳✳✳

Eric and Harry.
The A45, Coventry.
Now.

"Get right up against the side, Harry."

"... are you sure you're going to—"

"*Get up against the side.*"

"Whadiffit ricochets?"

"That's why I'm standing over *here*. If it ricochets, it'll fire off over *there*."

"Okay, man," Harry drunkenly slurred. "Okay. Just don't ... wandyoudda get hurt."

Harry wriggled back up to the edge of his dirty-silver prison without further complaint, although he seemed to jar his injured ribs as he did so, letting out a little gasp. His movements looked sluggish, but Eric thought that was good; it meant the booze would be taking the edge off his friend's pain. Harry's last few sips of his oversized hip flask had been a great deal shallower than before, clearly running out of booze. For once, the thought made Eric sad. If Harry needed it for his last moments—

Eric looked at the machine gun in his hands. He didn't even know if it would still fire; he'd extracted it from the crusty red glued-together mess that was the remains of the soldiers standing the other side of the Barrier. It was entirely conceivable that the same flash-dried gunk was now gumming up the gun's interior workings. Getting the weapon had been Harry's suggestion; Eric had spent the last hour or so desperately trying to get the bubble open, but to no avail. He was covered in sweat, his jaw ached from grinding his teeth, and when he'd returned to the car to get some water he'd caught a glimpse of himself in the rear view mirror; his eyes were heavily bloodshot.

The bubble around Harry remained as intact as when it had first appeared. He'd tried to use it to contact Maria, the same way he had with the Barrier. It hadn't worked; it hadn't even *begun* to work. Something bad must have happened to Maria; had saving Harry once before burnt her out? When she'd faded from Eric's mind the first time it had felt like she was running out of juice … without the Barrier, he didn't know if he could find her again, which was frightening, although not as frightening as the situation in which they currently found themselves.

Neither Eric nor Harry had said anything to each other until Harry had suggested fetching the gun. He'd simply sat and sipped, watching Eric worry at the bubble. Eric thought Harry almost— *almost*—had an air of resolve, of a man who has finally come to the end of a very long and tiring road. Eric wanted to believe that.

"Okay. Ready?" Eric asked.

"Yep." Harry put his flask down and covered his ears.

Eric was lying on the floor, sighting down the gun and using his stump to help keep it upright while he ignored the pain in both shoulders. He'd set the fire rate to fully automatic. He didn't think this was going to work, but if he was going to shoot at the bubble, he was going to empty the fucking clip.

He'd poked once more at the torn-up napkins he'd stuffed into his ears—he'd found them in the Honda—and pulled the trigger. The gun jumped violently in his hands.

Pa-pa-pa-pa-pa-pa-pa-pa-pa—

The recoil sent a searing pain into his aching shoulder, much worse than the pistol had, but Eric held on.

Pa-pa-pa-pa-pa-pa-pa-pa-pa-powwwww...

The brutal sound rang away across the eerily silent land around the A45. Eric opened his eyes, seeing the turning surface of the impenetrable bubble still there, unmarked. If there had been a sound when the bullets ricocheted harmlessly off it, it had been drowned out by the incredible noise of the machine gun. He let the weapon fall sideways and dropped his face onto his bicep. He lay there for a few moments.

Eventually, he realised Harry hadn't said anything. Eric looked up. The older man was picking his hip flask back up and giving it a light shake.

"Lil' bit left in here," he said. "Gonna make it last." He paused. "Hey. I have a question."

"... sure, Harry." Eric sat up and wiped his face with his remaining hand.

"Why *us*, d'you think?" Harry said, staring at the hip flask. Eric waited for him to continue, but Harry didn't.

"... I don't know what you mean, Harry. Sorry. Can you ... can you elaborate, bud?"

"Why do they want us?" Now Harry looked up. "You're the guy who's read 'bout all this ... bullshit."

"Do you ... do you really want to talk about this? Now?"

"Is there a theory about it?"

"...yes."

Harry grunted.

"Out with it."

Eric took a deep, shaking breath.

"Some people think we come from those things," he said. Harry didn't respond. "That they're our forebears."

"Well, well. Isn't that something."

"Two arms, two legs and a head, walking upright. In all of the universe, of all the infinite possibilities ... it would be a major coincidence if we just happened to match the same basic layout. There's a name for it that existed even before the First Arrival, we see it in nature: *divergent evolution*."

"That so."

Eric talking continued on autopilot. It at least briefly meant that he didn't have to deal with Harry's certain and impending doom.

"Groups ... groups from the same ancestor evolve and develop differences. If they aren't related to us in some way, why else would they need or want our genes—" Now he stopped. "Jesus, *Jesus*, Harry, I'm so—"

"But what," Harry said, now taking a sip from his flask, "about the things we saw inside Ground Zero? The big stone-like things with all the legs? 'Cos I don't remember *anyone*, Stone or human, having that many legs, unless we're talking about some serious inbreeding."

"... I don't know, Harry. They do rather, uh, screw up the theory, yes ..."

"She's waiting for you," Harry said suddenly. "This Maria woman. Isle of Skye. Long way 'way. You gotta go."

Eric chuckled darkly and shook his head.

"Absolutely no fucking chance," he said. "I'm not going anywhere without you."

Harry tapped at the inside of the bubble with his hip flask.

"Then ... duzzen' look like you're going too far, eh?" He giggled foolishly, before his face suddenly and dramatically fell. "Shit," he said. "*Shit.*"

His spine, Eric thought. A Stone Man was going to take Harry's spine and Harry was going to die screaming because Eric hadn't had the—

"Still got those ... keys, right?" Harry asked. "To the lockup? My paintings?"

"Yeah," Eric said, patting his pocket. "I won't forget." He blinked back tears as he put his hands on his hips and looked at the Barrier in the sky. "I don't know if ..." He stopped himself. If Harry was going to die, did he need to hear that Eric thought he had zero chance of surviving and being able to honour Harry's wishes?

"Where d'you reckon the Barrier's gone to now?" Harry asked.

"I don't know, Harry."

"Mm. Whaddya think they're gonna ... do next?"

"... I don't know, Harry."

"Mm."

Silence. Then Harry said something under his breath.

"What?" Eric asked.

"I said ... do you think it'll hurt?"

Harry's eyes were wet. Eric tried to find a response that didn't give away what Straub had told him: that it was going to hurt an unimaginable amount.

"Harry—"

He broke off as Harry's eyes suddenly rolled over white.

"Harry?"

The moment was brief, and Harry eyes were already back and blinking, looking around himself.

"I saw . . ."

He suddenly grabbed his flask and raised it all the way up, his gullet working as he put away the last of it.

"What? What did you see?" Harry finished emptying the flask and threw it away, bouncing it off the bubble's inner surface. He gasped and wiped his lips, closing his eyes, and opened his mouth to speak, but couldn't. His lips pressed back together tightly, and then his finger jabbed downwards twice, poking the concrete surface beneath him.

Harry had seen the road.

That meant he'd seen through a Stone Man's—

Eric looked back up the A45, his heartbeat suddenly tripling. He saw what was approaching.

It was so far away they couldn't feel its terrible, heavy footsteps yet, but now he was looking back along the straight stretch of dual carriageway, the tall, imposing figure walking towards them could not be missed. It didn't hurry, of course; instead its steps were steady and in a perfect rhythm, as if it had all the time in the world. Even at a long distance, shrunk visually to a mere thumbnail, its size and presence were clearly evident, so much so that Eric backed up a step.

A Blue Stone Man was walking along the A45 and heading for Harry.

Eric turned to his friend; Harry's jaw was set as he watched the Blue approach. Eric could see the vein pulsing rapidly in Harry's neck.

"*Jesus,*" he whispered. He licked his lips.

Eric turned and strode over to the second pile of bloody soldier-rags and kicked at it with his foot. He pulled out the gun, wincing as his shoulders protested, and he held it by his hip as he walked back towards his friend.

"I-I thought we just tried—" Harry began.

"It's not going to do to you what it did to Jenny," Eric lied, knowing exactly what the Blue was about to do to Harry. His voice was shaking but there was no point in hiding it.

"How do you know?"

Eric didn't want to mention Straub.

"In all the years I spent reading every Stone rumour and theory," he said, "none of them ever talked about the Stone Men doing to anyone what the Stone Giant did to Jenny, taking—" he hesitated. "Taking someone from the feet up like that. I think that one was different. Her bubble looked different to yours, too."

"So what do ..." Harry let out a groan and ran his hands through his tight, greying curls. "What do Blues do?"

"I don't know," Eric lied. "But I think with you on the floor, under the bubble ..." He had to put the gun down. It was heavy and his adrenaline was pumping so hard he suddenly felt nauseous. "I think it might have to take you out of the bubble, or remove it, or something."

Harry sat up.

"So I can get away, you think?" His eyes were bright, filling with hope as he scrabbled closer to Eric. "You think we can escape, man?"

Oh, Eric thought. *Oh, Harry.*

"No," Eric said, and his voice was as heavy as a tombstone. "I'm so sorry, Harry. It's found you. Even if it took the bubble away, those things ... they have these other barriers they used in the past, ones that aren't solid but still make it so you can't leave the immediate area. Ones you can't see." He couldn't continue looking into Harry's face as it fell. He looked at the gun in his hands. "If Maria could help us it might be different," he said, "but I think something's happened to her." Harry slowly sat back down, the light that had briefly flared in his eyes dying. "The gun," Eric said "I'm going to try and use it … to make it quick. If I get a window. I'll be ready. I promise."

Harry slowly turned his head to look back down the road. The Blue was already larger, and now both men could feel the very faint, rhythmic pounding of its footsteps.

"I've had dreams like this," Harry said quietly. "Nightmares."

"Me too."

They watched it.

"Siddown," Harry sighed. Eric began to sit, then paused.

"Hold on," he said, then thumbed off the safety on the large gun before bracing it over his forearm stump. He aimed off to the roadside and pulled the trigger, stepping back awkwardly as the recoil shoved him in the chest. The shot rang out around them, loud and damning and terribly, terribly final. "I had to check," Eric said, "in case—"

"I get it," Harry mumbled. "Don't wannit jamming."

Eric wished Harry hadn't had to hear it in that context, but better that than risking the awful possibility of not being able to take the shot when needed. He sat on the ground next to Harry's bubble, laying the gun down. The edges of Eric's vision kept fading over white and he had to keep blinking away tears.

Harry was going to die and there wasn't a damn thing Eric could do about it.

The Blue continued to approach, its footsteps becoming more palpable through the ground now; Eric thought he was just beginning to make out their sound.

"I can't believe this shit," Harry mumbled. "Shoulda saved most of the, the fucking thing, the fuckin' hip flask for this." He looked up at Eric. "Is it safe for you to be here? When that thing arrives?"

"I don't know. I think so, if it's . . ." He trailed off.

"A lotta *don't know* answers coming from you, man," Harry chuckled breathily, but it was forced, shaking. "You're supposed to be the expert on this stuff." Harry was trying to be dignified, and Eric wanted to talk to him, but he didn't want to take any of Harry's airtime. He had so little left. "Can you try the woman again?" Harry asked. "Maria?"

"Of course, of course," Eric said quickly. "I'll keep trying until . . ." He shut up, placed his hand on the bubble, called to Maria. Nothing. Was it because the small barrier wasn't as strong as the big one? It didn't matter right now. He opened his eyes to see Harry staring at him. Eric shook his head.

"Give her another go in a second?" Harry asked. His breathing was shallow and rapid now.

"Yeah."

They sat in silence. Now the Blue's footsteps were clearly audible.

Crunching. Heavy.

"You still gonna . . . go to Skye?" Harry asked, sniffing. He wiped his eyes and Eric pretended not to notice.

"Yeah. And Harry . . . thank you. For all your help. I'll do everything I can to get there."

"Good," Harry grunted, and now his face became stern, angry. "You promise me you will."

Eric froze.

". . . I promise, Harry."

"And don't waste any time on me. Okay? If . . ." He wagged a finger in Eric's direction, scowling, eyes wet. "If there's anything of me left afterwards, okay? Not like, not like. . ." He closed his eyes, swaying a little, booze playing tag with his memories. ". . . *Jenny*, if there's anything of me left . . . don't fuggabout burying it. Okay? Just leave it. It won't be me. It'll just be a body, right? I'll be gone. So you just get out of here. Take the car as far as you can get."

"Harry . . . I don't know if I could just—"

Harry screwed up his face and flapped a hand at Eric.

"I've told you," he said. "Told you, told you, so do it. Right?"

"Okay."

"Try Maria again."

Eric did. Nothing.

The Blue grew closer, larger.

The ground was shaking with each of its steps now, less than a hundred metres away. Harry took in a deep breath and blew out the air between his tightened lips.

"I wish . . ." He paused. "Do you think it would have picked me anyway?" he asked. "If I was further away? If I hadn't been in Coventry?"

"Distance never mattered to them," Eric said, watching the Blue. He was shaking and he wasn't even the Target. He couldn't begin to imagine how Harry was feeling. It was so unreal that he kept expecting—hoping—to wake up. That was the only way this could be stopped. "They picked people very far away before."

"Maybe because I was right next to the big red one when it turned up?"

Harry's voice was muffled. Eric turned to see his friend's face was in his hands. Harry's shoulders were shaking rapidly.

"Maybe," Eric his voice cracking. Harry looked up sharply.

"Don't," Harry said, and now tears were coating his cheeks. "Don't. Keep it together, you prick. Might need you to shoot straight so *fucking keep it together.* Okay? Okay?"

Eric sniffed and nodded quickly, wiping his own eyes. A reason, he suddenly needed to give a *reason* for Harry, a reason to justify—

dumpf. dumpf. dumpf. dumpf.

The footsteps sounded as relentless as the thing making them, and Eric suddenly couldn't breathe as the reality *finally* seized him: they had run out of time. The Blue would be on them in under a minute. He could barely think, but still he searched to try and find something to make Harry know—

"When I was shot!" he babbled, putting both hands on the bubble and pushing his face to it, staring at Harry through its awful surface. "You hadn't stitched me up, cleaned it, a *flesh wound*, Harry! Who else would have done it for me? And even if it *wouldn't* have bled out without you, we've rooted through all sorts of rubble and filth since then!" His voice was pleading. "The infection would have been serious, people die on battlefields from less than that! I might not have seen anyone for days to help, still might not! I think you . . . you probably saved my life, Harry. Right? So anything I do now from here on in, anything I do to help against . . ." He waved a hand frantically at the Blue, the bubble, the Barrier above them. "It's because of *you.*" Harry just stared back at him, tears flowing freely. "*It wasn't a waste*, Harry," Eric continued. "It wasn't. I promise."

Dumpf. Dumpf. Dumpf. Dumpf.

"That's a nice try, Eric," Harry sniffed. "A nice try. Might even be true. Try . . . please try Maria one more time?"

"Yes, yes, of course—"

He did. Nothing happened. To Eric's right, the Blue was huge. It was about thirty seconds away from them. As the ground shook, the thudding sound of the Blue's footsteps mixed with the low crunch of cracking concrete.

"Harry," Eric breathed, ". . . Harry . . ."

DUMPF. DUMPF. DUMPF. DUMPF.

"It's okay," Harry said, wiping his face with his sleeve. "Fuck it, mate. Thanks." He shook his head and threw out his arms in front of him, shaking them out too. "I was part of . . . something important."

He had to raise his voice over those terrible, rhythmic thuds in the ground. Harry looked at Eric now, his whole face shaking. "Thanks."

Eric bellowed and began to slap at the bubble over and over with his hand, willing it to open and searching for Maria at the same time, but there was just nothing. Nothing. With awful timing, the Blue moved in front of the sun, its immense shape now cast in shadow as it came within twenty feet of the bubble. *"Get ready,"* Harry said, gritting his teeth. "I'm . . . I'm counting on you to . . . to . . ." His eyes darted between the Blue and Eric. He couldn't speak any more. He was shaking too much.

"I'll be ready, I'll be ready," Eric gasped, snatching up the gun and rushing away from the ditch to about five feet from the bubble. Breathing in rapid snorts he squatted down to one knee, bracing the rifle's stock against his shoulder and holding up the barrel with his stump underneath. He would sight through it when . . . when what? When the process began? Would he even get a chance to shoot?

DUMPF. DUMPF. DUMPF. DUMPF.

The rifle shook in his hand and his finger felt weak on the trigger. The Blue Stone Man walked the last few feet towards

Harry's bubble, the difference in their heights even greater due to Harry sitting at the bottom of the shallow roadside ditch.

"I got you, Harry!" Eric screamed uselessly, desperate to let Harry know he was there. "I got you!"

But Harry wasn't listening. His eyes suddenly widened, and he found his voice.

"DO IT!" Harry suddenly screamed at the Blue, veins bulging in his neck and forehead. "DO IT! FUCK YOU! FUCK YOU, FUCK ALL YOUSE, FUCK YOU!"

"TELL 'EM!" Eric screamed, joining in, his voice cracking as his vision blurred with saltwater. "YOU TELL EM, HARRY!"

"COME ON!" Harry yelled. "CHOKE ON IT! CHOKE—"

DUMPF.

The Blue stopped and so did Harry's yelling.

His eyes rolled over white the instant the Blue's foot touched the edge of the bubble.

It stood there for a moment, frozen in front of a roadside ditch by the bottom of a hedge just outside of Coventry. Eric froze too, his mouth hanging uselessly open.

Harry's back arched sharply. His head then jerked sideways and he fell against the inside of the bubble, smashing violently against it.

"Harry!"

Harry was no more aware of his surroundings than the Shufflers had been. He turned and flopped against the inside of the bubble, trying to find purchase, and then managed to get his hands under himself. He began to rise to his feet, emerging from the ditch. The bubble expanded upwards with him. He was saying something:

"GCCATAAGACAATACC—"

The entirety of the bubble didn't grow, just the topmost half of it, while the bottom part that Eric could see remained round. Harry swayed on his feet like a charmed snake as the bubble continued to elongate, undulating like the blob in a lava lamp. Harry's head, Eric saw with horror, lolled back on his neck the same way the Shufflers' had, right before they disappeared into the Prism forever. Harry took a staggering step up and out of the ditch and the bubble came with him—lurching forward and rippling like struck jelly—as he stood before the Blue. The behemoth simply waited, arms by its side, head high above Harry, who began to rock from side to side. The movement was stiff-legged, wobbling from foot to foot, his head and arms still loose and dangling. It was grotesque, but Eric realised that Harry was turning around—

"Ah!"

Eric cried out as the air around him became unbearably cold. The Blue's head lowered slightly, as if it were looking at a spot on Harry's neck, and then a cacophonous drone filled the air around them. Eric moaned aloud, an agonised, helpless sound that was lost in the noise as two rectangular shapes began to protrude from the Stone Man's chest, coming together to form a single extension that aligned with, and moved towards, the base of Harry's skull as he faced away from the Blue. The elongated bubble still surrounded Harry but was now much closer to him, its surface perhaps only inches away from Harry's rolled-over, unseeing eyes. The noise emanating from the Blue on that empty road was the sound of madness and death.

Eric sighted the down the rifle and fired twice. The first bullet careened uselessly off the stretched-out bubble near Harry's shoulder, pinging away to Eric's left. The second ricocheted off the impervious Blue's head as its chest protrusion finally touched

Eric's friend, nuzzling between Harry's neck and shoulder blades. Smoke began to rise from Harry's skin.

His eyes suddenly rolled back down, looking straight ahead, and Harry began to scream.

Contact made—the process begun—the bubble vanished.

Now—

Eric took a quick, shuddering breath, hugged the rifle's stock tightly under his armpit and pulled the trigger once more. The weapon was set to fully automatic but it was unnecessary; the shot was near-perfect and one bullet would have done it. The top of Harry's head exploded in a spray of blood and bone that coated the high hedge beside him.

Eric screamed and held the trigger, emptying the clip uselessly into the Blue, the bullets ricocheting away into the ether across the road. Once the rifle's cacophony ended, Eric let out a moan and put his hand to his face. Harry's body hung in front of the Blue as smoke continued to rise from his neck, arms hanging limply by his side as the Stone Man continued its terrible task.

It didn't vanish.

But why would it vanish when it no longer needed a signal to follow? It had made physical contact and was in the process taking that which it wanted; not even the bubble was needed any more. Eric dropped to his knees, clawing at his face in horror as the cacophony rang out all around him, helplessly watching the Blue harvesting Harry Regis's spine.

Were you quick enough?

Harry had only screamed for a moment.

You spared him a longer death. You did.

But how much pain had his friend felt in that single moment?

He had to leave. Now. Harry had made him promise not to hang around, but there was the other question: what happened when the Blue finished? The Stone Men apparently used to vanish after they reached their Targets, but all bets were now off thanks to the Prism. How could he know that the Blue wouldn't immediately get the Prism to put another bubble around *him*?

Eric got up and staggered over to the car, his stump-wrist leaving him unable to cover both ears from the terrible noise.

Just go, he thought. *Don't think. You promised Harry.*

Skye was an extremely long way away, and he didn't know how far he would get by car. If the Barrier had burst everyone who wasn't a Stone Sensitive for miles around, he thought the roads further outside of Coventry would be very clogged indeed. Such merely-logistical concerns were lifelines for his battered psyche, and as he opened the car door and turned to look at Harry and the Blue, it occurred to Eric that, once he reached the Isle of Skye—if he could at all—then he would have a decision to make. He would see what the purpose of his journey there turned out to be and what it had to offer; what the chances of success in any further struggle against the Stone Men were once he had all the information.

From there he would decide whether or not to take his own life.

Knowing this was finally an option—something he'd always dismissed in his quest to find out the truth about Theresa and Aaron—felt comforting, like a bed that was waiting for him at the end of a long, long day. He'd promised Theresa he'd find out the truth, and he'd promised Jenny revenge. He was one for two. That was okay. If he kept his promise to Harry and got to Skye as soon as he could, he'd be two out of three, and everyone knew what the old song had to say about that.

You don't mean it, the voice said. *You can't give up now; you won't give up now.*

The Blue's chest was pulling out of Harry's neck now, retracting backwards, and once it came free Harry's near-decapitated body dropped heavily forward like a meat mannequin with its strings cut.

You won't give up now, the voice repeated. *Will you?*

The protrusion re-separated back into two and continued to disappear back into the Blue's body. Once it finally vanished, the deafening distorted-brass sound ended, and the road was silent once more. A breeze blew, catching Harry's clothes and skittering dust over the concrete. The Blue stood still, its head still slightly angled downwards to look at the point where Harry's neck had once been. Eric braced himself, having seen the Stone Giant vanish and expecting that harsh, cold sting again, but it didn't happen; the temperature around him had actually returned to normal.

The Blue's head slowly rotated on its shoulders without looking up.

There was no sound to accompany this movement, slow and gentle and deeply unsettling. Eric froze.

The Blue's head continued to turn until it was, without question, looking directly at Eric.

He pressed his back up against the driver's door, keeping himself upright. If the Blue took a single step towards him, Eric would try to get into the car and get away as quickly as he could. Had Harry left the keys in the ignition? Oh *God*, please—

Now the cold snap came; it was like ice was being pressed against every inch of his skin at once, and as Eric cried out the Blue disappeared.

After a few seconds, Eric let out a pent-up breath. Had the Blue gone back to the Prism, like the Stone Giant had, or to wherever the hell those things originally came from? He guessed he would find out. Eric's eyes fell on Harry's body, seeing his partially-destroyed head and the perfectly-cauterised rectangular hole in his neck; a portion of the top of his spine had indeed been removed. The little food remaining in Eric's stomach came up and he turned to vomit onto the road.

Get moving.

Eric wiped his mouth, popped open the driver's door, and got in without looking at Harry again. There. Promise kept. The question still came again:

Will you end it when you get to Skye?

He didn't know yet.

Eric looked through the glass of the windscreen, at the military vehicles and their crappy wooden blockade—he could drive around those, at least—and the segment of road beyond where the crowd had stood. The concrete there was now a carpet of crusty red, embedded with detritus like mobile phones and TV cameras as well as clothes.

He could get past that, too.

But what about the roads ahead, like Harry had said?

Will you end it when you get to Skye?

"Let's get to Skye first," Eric said aloud to the car's interior. His voice didn't sound right. He checked the radio and found it was still broadcasting only static. He turned it off. Silence would be good for now.

Eric set off along the A45, finally leaving Coventry behind him.

Chapter Eleven

Out of Gas, and the Best Thing About Travelling is Making New Friends

***

Eric was twenty-five stunned and empty-headed minutes outside of Coventry before he realised that he should have taken one of the soldiers' radios.

The resulting rage that leapt into his throat died halfway to his mouth, smothered, and instead he just let out a heavy, heavy sigh. He had until the next junction to make a decision: keep on heading north, or turn around and go back, burning up precious fuel. The Barrier could have killed every petrol station staff member for a hundred miles, and what if it had somehow fried their electrics too? If he could contact the military—even Straub had to be an ally in this situation, as much as he loathed the idea—then great, but how much good would the radio be anyway? The army radio's signal would surely be as useless as the car's, probably even more so now the Barrier had expanded. Turning back would also waste precious time too, time he could have used to bury Harry—

Remembering Harry stopped him thinking for a little while.

By the time he came back to himself he'd already passed the next junction, and that made his mind up for him. Soon, he knew, he would hit stationary traffic, or enough of it to impede his progress. He'd passed a few unmoving cars on the way, all embedded to a greater or lesser degree in the metal roadside barriers, windows covered with red from the inside. One in particular had hit him hard: red in every single window, including two smaller red patches in the back.

The question kept trying to push to the forefront of his mind: how much further did the Barrier go? How many people were dead? He ignored it as best he could, but he still kept an eye open for any swirling, ethereal surfaces hanging in the air ahead of him. The last thing he wanted to do was hit the Barrier doing seventy.

The low number of cars that had been heading *out* of Coventry made sense; so few people lived there now, let alone people with transport, that any evacuation of that area would be minor. Now he was heading towards the M6, the number of crashed cars was beginning to increase. The Midlands in general had taken a hit since the time known as the March of the Stone Men, with the cities surrounding Ground Zero all seeing mass emigration over the years, but soon the roads would be impassable. Amazingly, some of the stationary cars he'd passed had been facing *towards* Coventry. There had actually been looky-loos that had wanted to go towards the Barrier and gawk at it.

Blessedly, Jenny's car being automatic meant that Eric could just put his foot down. Driving was tough with one hand and now two painful shoulders, but the painkillers were making it just about bearable. There was a map in the glove compartment, but Eric wasn't even using that right now; he was heading towards the M6 toll road on autopilot, the old instruction of *that way will be quicker* from his gig-driving days going through his brain, but as he approached the roundabout he realised two things: not only had the M6 Toll been almost unnecessary since the first three Arrivals, but also the now-unmanned tollgate barriers might be down. Exhaustion was affecting his thinking—

Sooner or later, he knew, he would reach the first dead traffic bottleneck, and he would have to get out and walk until he could find a crashed motorbike intact enough to take him all the way to Scotland. He knew how to ride a bike, and he'd already figured out a system to operate the clutch; if he rode relatively slowly, he could tie some fabric, torn from his T-shirt if need be, around his wrist and the clutch lever. It would be far from perfect, but it would still beat walking all the way to Scotland. If he could find an automatic scooter, even better—

He realised the vision was coming just in time to slam on the brakes in the middle of the motorway and kill the engine with a hand that suddenly could barely grasp the keys.

He managed it just in time; had he still been driving when his body locked up that way—even at the slower speed he was travelling—he'd have been killed. He tried to remind himself as the convulsions began that the visions were always brief, that even if his breathing stopped he could comfortably hold it for the minute or so that the visions lasted. He tried even harder to not think about what another vision meant: someone else was being selected. *Don't get distracted from the mission. Light or no light, you couldn't even open Harry's bubble, let alone Jenny's golden one, so—*

The thought cut off as he realised that the light he was seeing was again golden.

The convulsion suddenly peaked, shooting through his whole body, and now his vision began to grey as he realised he was passing out. He had time to think *you can't* before he was out.

When he came round the clock on the dashboard told him that about thirty minutes had passed.

He was hearing something familiar, and he didn't think it was coming from outside.

"Then get out and *check*," he suddenly said aloud, his now-ragged voice sounding like a stranger's in the silence of Jenny's Honda. As he opened the car door he caught sight of his reflection in the windscreen. He looked like something out of a prisoner of war movie.

He got out, standing by the car in the middle of the motorway that would take him to the M6. Four more grey lanes spread away to his right. A towering motorway sign stood nearby, an object completely forgettable in a past life but impressive and imposing when observed from ground level on a silent road. He could see more crashed cars ahead as the tarmac stretched silently towards the horizon, perhaps a little closer together now, but still not impassable by another vehicle.

Eric listened.

The sound was only faint, but he'd heard it before, and once heard it couldn't be unheard. He spun slowly on the spot, trying to identify where it was coming from ... then he slowly covered his ears. Yes. The sound was inside his head.

It had been much louder the first time he'd listened to it: that strange, metallic screaming sound he'd heard when he'd touched the Barrier, coming from those barely-glimpsed phantom threads he'd sensed in his mind. But he could hear them now in thin air? Was this because the Barrier had expanded? *Maria!* He tried to reach out for her with his mind again but found nothing; he might as well have been willing laser beams to fly from his fingers.

If you can't contact Maria, he thought, *at least listen.*

He'd understood snatches of it before, maybe now he could—

Maybe, a voice in his head sneered, *it'll tell you what they did with Harry's—*

"Shut *up*," Eric hissed aloud to himself, trying to concentrate. Did *they* know he was listening? He didn't want to attract any attention, but they hadn't seemed to notice him eavesdropping before; he'd have known it, he was certain. He stood on the silent motorway and tried listen to and catch meaning in the awful, screeching, all-treble sound in his head. Doing so now, without the Barrier's hateful surface to touch, was much more difficult.

What are you all doing, *you bastards,* he thought, screwing up his fists. *Tell me.*

He couldn't get it. He was about to give up—an urge now more familiar and instinctive than it had been for the last few years—before an understanding reached him, felt almost physically in the back of his skull.

They were discussing a course of action.

Information was being passed back and forth. Eric's eyes widened: they were trying to decide what, if any, new approach was needed. But why—

Then he had it. Eric grinned with dark satisfaction.

"You're *worried* about something," he whispered, amazed.

Grim satisfaction took hold of him. He didn't know what they were worried about, but if they were that was very, very good. And there was something else they were talking about, wasn't there? What was—

There was another familiar sensation; a tug in his scalp, one that urged him to traverse the factory-agricultural land to his left that lined this part of the motorway. It was urgent—whoever lay inside another awful bubble, a golden one perhaps, was very close—but of course he would not be deterred from his promise.

And *yet* . . .

What if he could open *their* bubble?

It was a ridiculous thought. Why could he open this new bubble and not Harry and Jenny's? It was pointless.

But he didn't know for *sure*.

Ahead lay the road. Away to his left lay another trapped person.

You promised Harry.

He had. And he *would* get to the Isle of Skye. But this was person was so close, surely he *had* to try? The thirst in his mouth and the growling hunger in his belly also raised a very good point: he was starving, delirious even. He *had* to eat, and very soon. If there was someone in a bubble away to his left, they were probably at home, or near home. That would mean supplies, and without them he wouldn't even get halfway to Scotland ... but eventually he would reach a service station on the motorway, no? *They'd* be open. There would be cars, too, undamaged ones; people would have been standing at the pumps, keys in their pockets, when the Barrier hit—

He caught his own excitement at the prospect and damped it down, ashamed. Besides, he was so weakened that the last vision had knocked him out. What if another one came and he couldn't stop the car in time? He looked at the darkening sky beyond the Barrier above him; he would soon need shelter as well as food and water. It was still considerably earlier than his usual bedtime, but he was beyond exhausted. He had to head towards the bubble, which would most likely be in a somewhat populated area, which would mean—

Sure, he thought, *this is just about food and water. Who are you kidding?*

"Shut up," Eric said quietly. Unnerved by how many times he'd spoken to himself in the last hour or so, he climbed over the roadside fence, pushed through the government-issue trees, and began to follow the light in his head. He remembered doing this with Harry and stamped the thought down viciously.

***

It was a farmhouse.

There were no animals in sight, and no crops in the surrounding fields, so Eric wasn't sure it was a working farm. One thing he knew for certain was that there *was* a bubble inside the place. He could feel it like the heat from a nearby furnace. As he walked down the hedge-lined driveway towards the building, he saw two small, ancient-looking stables. There were no horses inside as far as he could tell. Parked outside was a Land Rover Discovery, devoid of dried blood on the inside of the windscreen. He paused and listened; he couldn't hear anyone moving around or talking inside the house. The modern double-glazed windows set into the farmhouse's much older brickwork were clear of blood too, but didn't reveal anyone inside.

"Hello?" Eric called, waiting a moment. *Someone* was there, he knew, inside one of those hateful bubbles, but was anyone with them? He thought he heard movement. "Is someone there? I know I look bad right now, but I promise I just need some food and water." A door suddenly banged open somewhere inside, there was a flash of movement through the window, and then a blonde-haired woman was rushing around the corner towards him, freezing on the spot at the sight of Eric, and perhaps also at the little jolt that had just passed between them on sight; he had certainly felt it, at least.

"Hello," she said, her voice shaking. "Who are you?"

"I'm Eric,"

"What happened to you?" she asked. She wasn't much shorter than Eric and was stocky.

"I was attacked," Eric said, holding up his hand and his stump. He saw her looking at the spot where his hand used to be. "That's been like that for years," he lied, "the attacker didn't do that."

"They attacked you?"

"Yeah. I was trying to get out of Coventry, and they took my car."

"You saw what happened?" She glanced back into the house, anxious, as if she wanted to tell him something but was frightened to.

"Yes. And I think maybe someone inside your house is in trouble, aren't they?"

The woman's face turned white.

"How do you know that—" She began to back away.

"Because I can feel it," he said, just wanting to lie down again. "I saw someone in Coventry that was in the same situation, and I could feel them too. I think maybe you've experienced some weird stuff yourself when the Stone Men came before, right? So you know the kind of thing I'm talking about?" The woman looked uncertain; Eric realised that, other than the person trapped in the bubble, she was possibly here by herself . . . and now this bashed-up and bloodied stranger was standing in her driveway.

"Look," he said, as kindly as he could manage. "I know there's someone inside and they're trapped in a light-bubble thing." The woman's hand went to her mouth. "I'm not in the slightest bit interested in doing you any harm, I promise." He didn't mention the fact that, given that she looked to weigh about the same as he did and he felt like a stiff breeze would blow him over, his odds of successfully doing her harm were pretty low. "But if you have any spare food and some water, I'd really appreciate it." He pointed at the small, empty stables. "And if I can do a Mary and Joseph and shelter in there while I sleep for a bit, that would be great."

"What happened to the other person you saw?" she asked. "The one in the bubble?"

Shit, Eric thought.

"I couldn't get her out," he sighed, and as the woman's face fell he added quickly, "But I'm trying to get to Skye. There's a woman there who *can* help, I think. The government has a base there . . . sorry, who's inside the bubble?"

"What came through here?" the woman asked, ignoring the question. "I felt something come through here earlier. The TV isn't working, my phone—"

"I don't know, I felt it too," Eric lied. There was no point in freaking her out more than she clearly already was.

"Are the Stone Men back?" she asked quietly. "I saw . . . faces."

Eric's shoulders slumped.

"Yeah," he said. "They are."

The woman's face screwed up, but not in despair; it was anger and impotent frustration.

"I knew it, I told him," she hissed, screwing up her fists. "Even here was too close to Coventry, I *told* him. The idiot, I never should have . . ." She trailed off and looked at Eric. "I'm Esther," she said, sounding defeated as the anger bled rapidly from her and worry replaced it. "Come inside. I'll make you a sandwich and I'll show you the . . ." She couldn't finish. "Just follow me."

She turned and headed towards the house. Eric followed.

She led him indoors and into the living room. It was a cosy space, but the metallic alien screeching sound was quieter indoors somehow, which made no sense because it was *inside* Eric's head. He realised then that it was actually drowning out his tinnitus, which was almost a relief. Esther's living room looked as if it had been furnished a long time ago by someone far older than her. With some TLC it would have been nice; exposed beams in the low ceiling, old-fashioned wall-lights casting a cosy glow. But the sofas were fraying, the rug in the centre of the room was threadbare, and the picture frames on the walls were full of those cross-stitch pictures Eric's grandma used to do. What had she called them? Samplers or something? Eric couldn't remember. He was too busy staring in horror at the bubble in front of him.

Like Jenny's, it was a faintly glowing gold. The bottom part of it disappeared into the dusty wooden floorboards. A few feet away, a wooden chair lay shattered into pieces. The sight of the bubble alone would brought a sense of revulsion and fear, but its inhabitant reminded Eric so much of his greatest failure that a sickening wave of hopelessness sluiced through him.

Slightly obscured by its moving, shining surface, Eric could see the prisoner sitting on the floor, their back propped up against the solid light. A Nintendo Switch lay on the floor to their left.

It was a boy.

"This is Aiden," Esther said. "He's eight."

***

Interlude

Colin Renwick Checks Out

***

Colin Renwick's shaking hand froze on the edge of the revolving door.

Whatever you see, he told himself, *stick to the plan. You can do this. You've been in more frightening situations than this, and you were fine.*

He briefly brought the worst one to mind; the retreating blade stall in ridiculously low visibility over Honduras. He'd been convinced beyond any doubt then—even as his body went through the correct procedures on, ironically, autopilot—that he was going to die. Not that Becky would have minded, of course, but the kids would have been devastated. They'd have been four and seven, then. Old enough to know what had happened, and to be scarred for life as a result.

Which is why you have to keep it together now, he thought. There had just been so much blood, that was why he'd freaked out so badly. So much blood all around him. *On* him. In his food.

He'd known very early on in life that he'd wanted to be a pilot. He'd assumed, in the manner of many little boys, that he would join the army or the air force. Either way, he wanted to fly a helicopter. Not a plane; they didn't have *giant* propellers, and therefore just weren't cool enough. Even twin prop planes didn't appeal to him; he could vividly remember his mother getting him a toy seaplane as a kid and looking into her smiling face as he felt the disappointment wash over him; he thought he'd be getting a toy Apache. It was his earliest memory of using tact: "Thanks, Mummy!" he'd yelled convincingly, and she'd grinned with delight.

It was the blood that had always been the problem.

He'd had cuts and scratches as a kid, of course. They were a little scary, but no big deal, until the time his father pulled a pint glass out of the kitchen cupboard during Colin's fourth-ever New Year's Eve. He'd been allowed to stay up late for the occasion, and although he'd been starting to get sleepy, he'd been determined to make the most of it. He'd come into the kitchen to chance his arm and ask for more crisps when he saw the pint glass slip from his father's tipsy fingers and shatter onto the kitchen tiles.

"What was that?" his mother had called from the other room, over the music and hubbub.

"Pint glass," his dad had called back. "Where's the dustpan?"

"It's in the garage."

"Why's it in the bloody garage?"

No answer. His father had shaken his head and held a finger up to Colin.

"*Touche pas,*" his father said, and then jabbed the same finger towards the shattered glass on the floor. Colin knew the words were French—his dad was always saying silly little things in French—and while Colin didn't know the exact translation, he understood from the pointing and his Dad's tone that he was not to touch the broken shards.

"*Oui*," Colin had said back, the only French word he did know other than *non,* and his dad had grinned and given a drunken thumbs-up before leaving the room. And it had occurred to Colin how happy Dad would be if he not only cleared up the glass, but showed how clever he was by not getting cut—

The blood had been everywhere.

The year had nearly ended in the hospital, but some butterfly stitches, a bandage, and a lot of tears meant that they'd made it back in time for the whole Renwick family to be together at midnight to sing "Auld Lang Syne" (or "Old Man Time", as Colin thought it was called until he turned eleven). Even so, the terror had never left him; the dark redness of his own body's fluids, the sheer amount of it, the pain and the mental association of imminent death. His parents had called him *squeamish,* but by the time he was nine they'd started trying to get him treatment for it and learned the correct word: *haemophobia.* The therapy helped—*we caught it young*, his parents would later tell people proudly—but it had never fully left him. It had meant that a career in the army was out, certainly, and so commercial flight became the plan. No biggie. It still meant getting to fly a helicopter as long as he became qualified, and qualified he became. He kept his haemophobia quiet, and it had never been an issue at work.

Today Colin's worst nightmare actually happened.

He'd been eating in the hotel bar. It had been busy, with all the TVs on despite no feed appearing on them. The hotel didn't dare switch them off in case the signal came back. No one wanted to miss an update on the world-stopping news coming out of Coventry: a Fourth Arrival, the city encased in a wall of energy. The bar itself was fairly bare bones, but pleasant enough; the room was covered with endless stock photos of world-famous landmarks, and one of the walls featured a mural of a jazz band, despite this particular venue not even having a stage. It was cheap enough but nice enough, a hotel just outside of Oxford for business travellers on a budget. For Colin, it was home for five days of the week; since the divorce, he hadn't been able to face living in Newcastle anymore. He'd originally moved there *for* Becky; to him, the place might as well be called Beckycastle. Getting out of there had meant moving away from the kids too, and that had been painful beyond belief, but he needed to get away in order to grieve for his relationship. Collecting his children every other weekend from a woman he still loved was agonising enough. He'd taken the first job he could, flying charter work out of Oxford. He'd only been doing it for a month and was still trying to find somewhere nice to rent, somewhere with a safe garden for the kids, somewhere they'd be happy to come and stay. He'd begun to believe he could make it work. He couldn't stay in love with Becky forever, after all, and maybe in a year or so he could move back up north. Maybe it had even been for the best. He just wasn't a particularly big fan of the Grand Royal, Oxford, because despite its name it was neither of those things.

There had been maybe hundred or so people in the bar, enough to pack it; some eating, others having coffee and reading the newspaper. Only a few, Colin surmised, were guests who had checked in the night before. The rest would be people who had simply had enough of the nightmare traffic and decided to get off and have a break, maybe even a room. Colin was glad to have his little table in the corner; all the other seats were taken.

After the plane crash the day before, all commercial air traffic had been grounded until further notice. Then the phones had gone down, and Colin was left with only a partial certainty that he had at least that day off. He'd decided he was going to start drinking, and if the TV news signal came back on and announced all flights could return to the air, he'd keep his phone switched off anyway.

He was halfway through his meal and had finished his first pint—his first in a while—and raised his left hand to catch the barman's eye, pointing at his empty glass with his right.

The barman gave him a thumbs-up, and then exploded.

Then everyone exploded.

The sound of the room went from a bustling hubbub, to a loud *pop* followed by a faint squelching sound, to the only noise being the lounge music playing quietly over the bar's speakers and Colin's own heartbeat. Then there was a series of distant bangs from outside, the sound of metal slamming into metal. He sat there for nearly a minute, not breathing. He didn't dare look down at himself. He could feel there was something sticky and crusty all over his face, and then dimly understood that it belonged to the couples who had been seated at the tables either side of him.

Every surface in the room was coated with red, even the clothing that had been left behind. The tables, the benches along the far wall. The jazz band mural was almost completely obscured, with only the tops of the heads of the musicians rising above the fade of crimson where the spray had failed to reach. It was like something from the half-remembered nightmares he'd had on that New Year's Eve over four decades ago. For a moment he thought he *was* dreaming. This wasn't *possible.* Then he remembered two things at once: the Arrival going on in Coventry, and that something had landed in his mouth when everyone in the room burst.

Colin leapt to his feet, gasping, but the vomit was already coming. He ran to the double doors leading the foyer, kicking over a table and chairs as he went, and nearly falling face down in the unspeakable carpet of freshly-crusted crimson as his foot became tangled in someone's left-behind jeans. He twisted, managing to stay upright, and then plunged through the twin doors, rushing past the reception smeared with unspeakable gore, and into the ground floor toilets. Turning the tap to maximum, he bent at the waist and blasted his face with water, scrubbing frantically with his fingernails at the muck coating his cheeks and eyelids and then putting his mouth below the jet, rinsing and spitting and rinsing and spitting. He nearly caught a glimpse of himself in the mirror but mercifully managed to look away in time.

Immediate concerns taken care of, he knew this wasn't enough. Panic did not come easily to Colin, ironically; it was one of his great natural blessings for his job, and even now, when he found himself living his worst nightmare and nearly everything inside him had become a screaming, useless idiot, his internal Pilot was breaking things down for him.

Get upstairs, it said. *Get undressed, brush your teeth, and shower this off. Don't think about anything else until you have.*

Roger that. Colin turned and bolted for the stairs.

Thirty minutes later, Colin was changed, packed, and standing by the revolving door that would take him out to the street. Had he been childless, he probably would still have been curled up in a ball on the floor of the shower. As it was, the thought of his kids had forced him to stand and get shakily on with things.

He'd opened the window to his hotel room but hadn't looked outside, not yet; he could deal with that when he went out there. There was no need to face the potentially red-soaked pavements now, but he could listen.

He heard nothing. No cars, no screams.

He'd tried the hotel landline and checked his own phone multiple times, but they were working about as well as the TV. He'd at least managed to speak to the kids the day before, when the Arrival had started; they'd been at home with their mother. In a rare moment, he'd asked to speak to her, and she'd promised—in her usual icy fashion—that they wouldn't go anywhere until the government said it was okay.

If they were alive, then they were at home. He couldn't consider any other possibility.

The airport was close by; a few minutes by car, if the road allowed, or an hour or so from the hotel on foot if need be. The helicopter—AJT Air's, not his, of course—was there. He had the hanger keys. If everyone there had gone the same way as everyone here—

The room swam for a moment and Colin put his hand on the wall to steady himself as the Pilot told him what to do.

Go on, it said. *You nearly had it—*

If everyone there had gone the same way as here, then he would take the bird. Even if they hadn't, he'd take it anyway. He was flying to Newcastle, government be damned.

And you know what you have to do first, don't you?

Yeah. He just had to walk downstairs, past the bar that had become his own personal Room 101, and out along the street that might be just as bad. For the kids, he could do it.

It's just a little blood, the Pilot had said, but that was a step too far in the self-talk stakes, and they both knew it. It was never 'just' a little blood.

And now here he was, one hand on the hotel's revolving entrance door. He realised he was holding his breath as if the air outside were toxic. He breathed out, then realised the air actually might now *be* toxic for all he knew, and held his breath again.

First step, the Pilot said. *Step outside.*

Colin pushed the revolving door and stepped into its orbit, pulling his carry-on luggage beside him, dressed in shirt and trousers and looking as if he was heading out to conclude a business trip. His eyes were closed, but he felt the air on his face as he stepped outside.

Okay, the Pilot said. *Open them.*

The street was empty. The Grand Royal wasn't in the centre of town, after all; it was on a back road opposite some kind of warehouse, one whose entrance, blessedly, was on another side of the building. To its right was a car park. There were no people, and the roads here were empty. A single car was part-embedded in a low wall about two hundred metres down the road, its front end crushed. Colin looked away quickly but it was too late; he had already seen the windscreen, completely opaque with red. Worse, his confused mind briefly wondered why the horn wasn't constantly blaring the way it usually is after a crash in the movies, but then he understood why: there was no intact body inside the car anymore to be leaning on the steering wheel.

What's the next step, the Pilot asked, cool, calm and collected as always; Colin's usual *modus operandi*, at least when Becky wasn't pushing his buttons. He briefly lit up, wondering if Becky might be burst herself, then admonished himself for thinking that. If she was burst, the kids were alone—and worse, they'd have seen it.

And the fact she'd be dead, the Pilot added helpfully.

Yes. She'd be dead, and that wouldn't be good at all. He tried to concentrate and think about the Pilot's previous question, discovering it was already easier to do so.

Next step is to get to the car, he thought, *and drive as close to the airport as quickly as I can.*

And if you run into traffic, the pilot asked, *even traffic where all the cars are like that one down there?*

Colin took a deep breath.

Then I get out and walk.

Part THREE

CONNECTIONS

Chapter Twelve

The Last Days of Stone Disco, and More Contact is Made

***

Andy and Sophie.
Project Orobouros.
One Year Ago.

Andy stared at the view as he sat side by side with Sophie, high up on one of the hills overlooking Project Ouroboros. It seemed impossibly peaceful after the madness they'd just experienced.

They'd stopped it. They'd *stopped the Stone Man.* He hadn't been able to get the thought out of his head.

Andy was desperately glad that Straub and co. had left them alone while the clean-up was going on. Later there would be questions, tests. But not now.

"Okay. We have to talk about it," Sophie said eventually.

"Go on." Even though he knew what she meant.

"What do you think," she asked, "after all that? Did it have a mind?"

Amazingly, neither of them had broached the subject until now. All they'd done was hold hands and take in the relative silence of the hills around them. It was, as far as Andy was concerned, a staggeringly wonderful day. He didn't know that living could feel like this, Christ! All the mad partying in New York, the highlights of his heyday post-First Arrival, that had been insane fun, but this was . . . magic.

"Caementum—or the Caeterus—certainly seemed to take action when we made contact," Andy said, scratching at his ankle tag. Sophie had one on too. "But that could have been an automatic, built-in security process or something."

"We stopped it," Sophie said, her voice full of wonder as she echoed the thought that had been dancing non-stop around Andy's mind.

Andy smiled.

"So you said."

She'd kept repeating it in the hangar; Andy felt the same amazement, though.

They'd stopped the Stone Man! He hadn't been able to find much out in the short time since they'd done it—in fact, he'd been so much of a pest with his questions that Straub had given him and Sophie their current Project Ouroboros equivalent of shore leave just to get rid of him for an hour or two—but he had managed to find out one thing.

Now that it was shut down, the Stone Man was as light as a feather. When they tried to move it using machinery, it fell over effortlessly. They'd already known it could seemingly alter its own mass, but this was utterly unexpected.

Had they killed it? It certainly looked that way. He didn't know for sure yet—all the scientists were still losing their minds and it was only an hour or so since they'd halted Caementum in his tracks so he would have to wait for the full debrief—but, to his mind, the Stone Man was dead. No Stone Man, no project. Surely it was all over . . . but something told him it wouldn't be. There was still the risk of another Arrival, after all. Would Straub and co. ever let their guard down? The autopsy of the project would go on for years, and Andy would have to be a part of it. Once, that idea would have been fine with him; the Project had been his purpose. But now his purpose had dramatically changed. Yes, he could be here with Sophie, but it wouldn't be a life until they left.

Until you're allowed *to leave,* he thought.

He plucked a blade of grass. From here he could see the tiny people below them, ants ferrying hither and yon, a constant movement ever since the explosive development in the hangar. The day was surprisingly warm, and the clouds were few. Andy felt good.

It wasn't all he felt, though. Dead or not, the Stone Man was still leaking that something to somewhere. The circuit wasn't anywhere near as strong now, but somehow he was still lightly connected to it. Another reason they'd make him stay, if he told them about it. Sophie too.

"But that noise it made when we stopped it," Andy said. "It doesn't mean it actually had any . . . you know. *Feelings* about what was happening. I think we'd have felt them too if it did, no?"

"True," Sophie said. "Do you think Paul's barrier is still here?"

That was the question, the all-important one. Paul's barrier, the one the Stone Man had put up all those years ago when Paul was first Targeted, to stop him ever leaving. They wouldn't know if it was still there until Paul got out of the infirmary, checked the area, and told them. All he'd been able to glean from the staff was that Paul was awake and stable. That was a relief. But even if the barrier was gone . . .

"Or do you think," Sophie asked, almost reading his mind, and Andy wondered if in fact she still could, "that they wouldn't let him leave even if it was gone?"

"This is what I'm worried about," Andy said, looking grimly at the scurrying staff below. "They aren't going to care about what he's done for this place. If they're prepared to put a shock collar on him, they're prepared to keep him for whatever reason they see fit. Me, too. You, even. Sure, you're a volunteer now, but if they decide it's in the national interest, they can do whatever they like with you. He flicked the small blade of grass away.

"But would Straub really let them do that?" Sophie asked. "You three are . . . well, I know how you two feel about her." When Andy whirled around, indignant, Sophie simply smiled and tapped the side of her head. "Don't even try to deny it," she said.

"And what's that then? How do we feel?"

"You want to impress her," Sophie said. "Be *good boys* for her, both of you. She's your captain."

"Jesus. Some captain."

Then Sophie quietly moaned. She put her hand to her forehead.

"You okay?" Andy asked her.

"Still have a headache," she said.

"Me too, a little."

"*Uhh*, mine's getting really bad. I need to get one of Holbrooks' goons to get me some major painkillers. Don't worry, don't worry," she said, waving away Andy's impending fretting. "I'll get it all checked out when things calm down."

"Promise?"

"I promise."

They fell silent.

"So what's next?" Andy asked quietly.

"How do you mean?"

"I mean for us." He was amazed at how effortlessly he'd asked such an important and frightening question. Things were very different once you knew someone's soul. "You said we couldn't do anything while we had a job to do. Looks to me like, in my opinion at least, that job is done, no?"

Sophie nodded, watching the business going on below.

"Looks that way," she said, matter-of-factly. "And I did mean it when I said it."

The directness . . . he was head-over-heels for her.

"I've paid my dues, Sophie," he said, taking her hand. As she turned, her gaze washed over him like a warm shower on a cold day. "And I don't want to do this anymore. I've been awake here long enough, nearly died once, and in the hangar, when I thought I'd just watched you . . ." He shook his head. Sophie squeezed his fingers and smiled.

"I'm here," she said.

"Well, when I saw *that*, it was like the fucking world was ending, quite frankly. I can't go through that again, and they can't *make* us work. They can't."

"So what do we do? Demand to leave? Andy, I want to help here."

"Even if it kills Paul?"

"Ouch," she said, turning away. "If you'd asked me when I got here, I would have said yes. But I know him now like I know you . . . and no, I don't think I can."

Paul said to not stop, no matter what, Andy thought, but didn't say it. The Stone Man was dead, and that was a concept Paul hadn't even entertained at the time. He surely would have thought differently if he'd known that was a possibility, wouldn't he?

"But what if they won't let him go?" Sophie asked. "He doesn't need to *do* anything, unlike us, who can refuse to cooperate. Paul just needs to be present and to be touched. If we can leave—if they let us—but won't let Paul, do we leave him here?" They stared at each other. She cocked her head and smirked at him. "Hell, I already know your answer."

"Yeah," Andy said. "Dammit." Her smile grew, and she stroked his hand.

"You're a good friend to him."

"Meh."

Sophie laughed.

"It's not fair though," Andy said, half-joking. "You know everything about me, and yet you've managed to keep the reason why you didn't come here for so long a secret . . ." He'd hoped that bringing it up in a semi-serious way would get her to open up, but instead Sophie screwed up her face and pulled her hand away. "Ah, look, shit," Andy babbled, wanting to make it right. "I'm sorry, I shouldn't have—"

"No," she said, putting a hand to her head. "It's not that . . . I don't feel . . ."

"The headache again? Don't worry," Andy said, an arm around her shoulders and a hand on her hip; the hip felt slender, her shoulder firm. He'd never forget how it felt to touch her. "You're okay, they're going to give you all the scans—"

"It's not the headache," she whispered, and she was terrified. "Something's coming."

The air began to fizz.

"*No,*" Andy said, grabbing Sophie's shoulders, his gaze darting around. Not *now,* it was all over—

"Wait, it can't be coming here," he said, "we're not at Ground Zero and that's where . . ."

But the fizzing sound continued, filling the natural basin of the hills and reverberating, growing louder. All the racing soldiers down below suddenly became still. Someone was barking orders, but their words were muted by the noise. *Fizzing*, Andy thought, *we've never heard that—*

There was a sudden, sharp screech, and the fizzing stopped. There were no Stone Men in sight.

"Could that have been from Caementum?" Sophie asked.

"I don't think so," Andy said, his entire body tense as he scanned his surroundings. "I think we'd have felt it."

"Yeah—there!" Sophie gasped, pointing to the other side of the Project.

"What . . ." Andy breathed.

On the hill opposite, near a pair of the huge white metal turbines that gave the Project its wind farm facade, two large creatures had appeared out of thin air. They were unlike anything that had arrived before.

They looked like huge roundish boulders at first, made of smooth ridges and a grey—from Andy's vantage point—stone-like material. After a moment though he saw that they appeared to be held up on five or six protrusions that kept them upright; legs, perhaps, ones he hadn't immediately spotted because they were curled in tightly together underneath the larger . . . was that a torso? A body? Both of them stood at least eight feet tall—maybe taller, it was hard to tell from there—and they had no discernible features like a head or arms. The nearest thing Andy could think of to compare them with was a jellyfish, but that would suggest they were transparent, which they were not.

"It called them," Sophie said, grabbing the shoulder of Andy's polo shirt in her fist, but he didn't take his eyes off the things on the hill. "The Stone Man. That noise it made as it was dying." Now he turned to her.

"A distress signal," he said.

Chaos broke out down below; officers yelling, vehicles starting and the activity—busy before—became a frenzy as soldiers ran to get weapons and set up a barricade.

"What does this mean?" Sophie asked him, the vein in her neck throbbing. Andy looked from her to the visitors as something else arrived: an idea.

"It means we run," he said, gripping both of her hands tightly. He looked into her eyes as he spoke. "There will never be a better time than right now."

"What? But those things—"

"We've got to be quick," Andy said, the words coming fast and breathless as knelt upright in front of her. "There's chaos down there and if there was ever a chance to get away, it's *now*. Come with me. We'll get the tags off somehow, but first we need to get far enough away to do that before things clear up here and they come after us."

"Andy . . ." Sophie said, blinking and trying to find the words, ". . . Andy . . ."

"I'm *done*, Sophie," he said. "I told you. There will be other GALE people they can use. They have the List now, and although it's not perfect you know soon they're going to start drafting the public in, they won't give people a choice. I've paid my fucking dues and they'll never let me leave as long as I'm still useful. You either."

"But you said we couldn't leave Paul!"

"What? Of course we can't! They'll use him all up. That's the main reason I want to do this! I'm saying," he pointed at the base, "that we go and *get* him. Now."

"But his barrier—"

"The fucking Stone Man is dead!" he cried. "The barrier will surely be gone, we at least have to try!"

Sophie looked at the hive of frantic activity down below, weighing up their odds.

"They weren't prepared for an Arrival here . . ." she said.

"Exactly," Andy told her. "Come on. We'll get out of here. You and me."

"Andy," she said, taking his shoulders now. "I want to *help* them."

"*And I can't leave without you,*" Andy pleaded, feeling his stomach drop through the grassy floor beneath him at the thought of it. "I'd have to be on the run when I leave, Sophie, at least until all this ends and I'm no longer needed. That could be years, if ever. Don't you get it? You've changed everything. They'll never let either of us leave after what we did today, and things are already at the point of shock collars, do you understand that? And if I go without you, you won't be able to find me and I might never . . ."

"The tags—"

"There'll be a way to get them off, we'll find it! This is the only chance we'll have, the head start we'll get until they're done with whatever is happening . . ."

Sophie's chest was heaving as she looked down at the chaos below.

"Do you . . . *have* to go?" she said.

"I can't do this anymore," Andy said quietly. "And I have to save Paul. I know you want to stay but I don't think you know what you're letting yourself in for. Come with me."

"*Ah,* this is—" Sophie gasped, clenching her fists in frustration. Andy watched, his heart in his throat. Then she shook her head and stood up.

"Come on," she said, standing up and looking angry. "Like you said: we don't have much time, and it's now or never."

"You're . . . you're coming?"

"Yes, *goddammit.* I came here to fucking . . . *ahh,*" she said again. "But I can't leave you." Her hand suddenly flew out and slapped him across the face. It wasn't hard and didn't hurt, but he recoiled in surprise. "But that's for making me choose. Sorry, but this was . . ." She breathed out heavily. "Okay. I'm with you."

"I . . . I don't . . ."

"Transport," she said, helping him. "We'll need transport."

"Right, yes," he babbled, nodding, exhilarated. "Do you know where—"

"There are trucks round the back of B barracks, they leave the keys in there."

"Right," Andy said, watching the mayhem as fresh soldiers swarmed out of the barracks towards the new arrivals. "You get a truck while I go and get Paul from the infirmary, meet us outside the rec building, that way I'll be able to get a straight run to the first checkpoint with as few obstacles as possible."

"But if the gate's down—"

"Believe me, their attention is occupied right now, so if *Dispensatori* drives up screaming *open the fucking gates* in the middle of this madness they're going to make a rapid judgement call, I guarantee it. And if they don't open them, I'm going to smash through them." There were so many *what if*s in this hastily arranged plan, not the least of which was Paul's barrier, but it surely would be gone? It had to be worth a shot. Paul had not been in his right mind for many months; Andy had to make the right decision for him. At least, he had to hope it was right and apologise later if necessary. "Ready?"

Hope. It filled him, charged him, and that was the moment then he heard and then saw the black helicopter, rising into the sky.

It was carrying a large metal crate, suspended by several immense chains slung from its underbelly. It was obvious what was inside. He watched the helicopter leave, carrying its cargo away, and while the hanging attachment was a unusual addition Andy did not know what this moment would come to represent to him in the future.

He would never forget the next moment either, the way the world froze as Sophie saw his distraction and leapt into his arms, kissing him deeply, because as she did so Andy forgot all about the black helicopter, and this would be the first and last time that would ever happen.

He opened his eyes and saw her beautiful, breathless face. Over her shoulder the black helicopter began to disappear into the horizon.

"Let's go," she said.

They ran.

***

They almost made it to the point where they would branch off in their separate directions when they ran into Straub and two armed guards.

Andy briefly thought about running, but he caught Sophie's eye, her almost-imperceptible shake of the head, and waited.

"*Dispensatori!*" Straub barked, in relief not anger. Soldiers ran past, carrying more material for the makeshift barricade that was being set up on the hill, surrounding the new Arrivals. *What's the point of that,* he thought in the midst of the chaos and noise. *They'll just smash—* "Warrender! No time to explain—"

"We saw, don't worry—"

He winced at the noise as a helicopter flew overhead.

"Where is that helicopter taking Caementum?"

Straub ignored him and thrust a finger at the arrivals, sitting above her on the hill behind. From here they looked a lot larger, maybe eight or nine feet tall.

"Can you read those things," she said. "Now Caementum is down—"

"Caementum!" Andy barked. "Where is it going?"

"We've triggered the Permutatio Protocol," Straub told him, "and that's all you need to know! Now—"

"But what about Paul?" Sophie asked. "Is he still connected to it? What's happening?"

"Keeping the Stone Man secure is our number one priority." Straub snapped over the noise. "Winter is second, and he knows that." She pointed up at the new arrivals. "Now get scanning those things! I need—"

"We aren't doing anything until you tell us what's happening with the Stone Man," Andy said, his disgust for Straub now complete. The limits of her concern for Paul were clear. "Your choice."

"Are you disobeying a direct order, Pointer?" Straub stepped close. She had to look up into his eyes, but didn't look any less fierce. "Do you understand what that means?"

"Tell us what's going on," Andy repeated, not answering the question, but not looking away either. Straub glared at him.

"It's being taken to the least populated space on earth, a region of Greenland," she said. "We struck a deal with their government in case something like this happened."

"But it's *connected* with Paul now! You don't know what—"

"He was prepared for whatever may happen," Straub said, her eyes still on Andy. "We're monitoring him in the medical centre right now. Now: do your duty, *Dispensatori*," Straub said. "You too, Miss Warrender." Andy looked to the horizon, trying to see the black helicopter disappearing; he couldn't. The cries of O'Reardon's Stone-induced madness had been proved correct; the Stone Man was indeed *gone.* "The way you help your friend right now," Straub said, "is to make sure those things on the hill aren't here for him." That did it. Andy read Sophie's face and knew what she was thinking: *stick with the plan. Bide our time.*

"*Have the surrounding areas been cleared of civilians, over,*" Straub barked into her radio, and then waited for an answer that Andy couldn't hear. "*Roger,*" she said eventually. "*Green, red and purple to maintain outer civilian perimeter until further notice. Over.*" She turned back to Andy and Sophie. "Scan the arrivals." She said. "Now. That's an order."

"Yes, *Ma'am*," Andy said, scowling and doffing an imaginary cap. Straub simply stepped back out of his line of vision without a word, talking into her radio and giving him and Sophie a clearer view of the still-unmoving visitors on the hill. The portable-and-almost-certainly-pointless barricade the soldiers had erected around them was finished and science crews were already charging up the hill to join them, pushing carts and lugging various pieces of equipment.

Andy held out a hand to Sophie—not because he needed to—and she took it. Her grip was warm, her pulse beating hard and fast.

"Do you need Winter?" Straub asked, as if he were nothing more than a battery after all.

"Let's try without him first," Sophie said quickly, seeing the look on Andy's face. "We'll know if we need a boost to get in there, right?"

"Right," Andy said. He closed his eyes. Sophie did the same.

It was immediately clear that they didn't need Paul to get Andy inside the new visitors.

Flashing into them was even easier than flashing into the Stone Man ... but there was nothing to see. Only darkness. Not even a glimpse of anything down in the darkness and no visual. Only a static noise, and not one like the screaming of the Caeterus that he'd heard in the past either. He waited a moment, gaining his bearings inside this new space, but it was just a void. There were two important things missing too: the threads heading back to the Caeterus—*so no live feedback, then?*—but, more worryingly, no sense of anything leaking.

Unlike the Stone Man, these things were at full capacity.

"They're similar to the Stone Men," he said out loud, "but fundamentally different at the same time. They're ... Sophie?" He sent the mental image of a hand back down the thread towards her, calling her into the space, lending her some of his ability to see; it wouldn't be as clear to her, but she could get an idea of it. He wanted her to confirm an idea. He waited a moment and then she was there with him. Her aura entered the darkness like a roaring fire on a winter's night.

—Can you feel that—

She took a moment, feeling whatever lay between herself and the edges of the things they were inside. There was a residual something that hung in the space, the last echoes of a received signal.

—*(They were called here, weren't they)*—

—Yes. I think these are backup—

"I think," he said out loud, opening his eyes, "you're going to have some big trouble when those things wake up. I think you're looking at the Stone rescue team."

"Then it's a good job we shipped Caementum out," said Straub.

"Sure, but what do they do when they wake up and Caementum isn't here?"

"Obviously, I don't know," Straub said, "but what I do know is that you're going to stay here and monitor them until they do wake up, if they wake up at all. Keep on it. You," she said, stopping a hurrying soldier in his tracks. "Stay here with Linehan and keep an eye on these two. Radio me immediately if anything happens."

"Keep an eye on us?" Andy asked angrily. "Like guards? I thought we always had *escorts*."

". . . indeed."

Andy saw it then. Straub knew what they were planning to do.

She hurried away without another word. The guards, one of them presumably Linehan, moved around behind Andy and Sophie, so they could see the goings-on up on the hill.

"Carry on please, Sir," Linehan said. His voice was shaking. He was clearly scared to death. Andy looked at Sophie and took her hand again, their minds meeting.

—*(What the hell do we do now)*—

—We do our job until we get a window to get him out of here—there's no way we're getting away with the same trick with these things as we did with Caementum—they're juiced to the gills—and if we can't stop them that means we can't help—so that means the plan is the same—we just have to warn everybody when they start to stir—but stay ready because it will be chaos again—then we move—

—*(Okay)*—

She paused for a moment.

—*(Coming here was the best decision I ever made)*—

Andy glowed. He wondered if she could see it, there in the darkness.

—I'm very glad you decided to—eventually—

It was a half-tease again, another opening for him to tell him why she'd taken so long, but she didn't take it.

—(Then count your blessings)—(and get to work)—(dickhead)—

Andy smirked. They continued to listen to the static inside the visitors, but nothing they could explore or pick up on. It was as if the new arrivals were dead too; perhaps they died in transit? After all, they'd arrived a long way from Ground Zero, something that had always been presumed impossible before. Why else would the Stone Men land in Coventry when their Targets had been as far away as Edinburgh? Maybe they'd pushed it this time to come directly to the Stone Man's aid and the toll had been too much? An hour passed and Andy began to believe that was true. All the same, Andy and Sophie remained wary of each other, careful while inside in the most personal of spaces, lest they became lost in each other. If they did, they would be useless as an early warning system.

Then:

"Oh," Andy gasped quietly, automatic and unbidden, and Sophie let out a gasp.

"Sir?" Linehan asked, but Andy and Sophie just looked at each other in shock, blinking dumbly.

The inside of the arrivals had filled with light, there had been a *CRACK* sound, and the static had died.

Then Andy and Sophie had been firmly and immediately pushed out.

"They're waking up—"

"Movement!" came the cry from above. The arrivals began to stand.

There was no deafening, distorted brass, no sudden snap of cold; the creatures simply rose by around three feet as the legs supporting their seemingly mushroom-shaped bodies began to extend and spread. At first the only movement was vertical but as the legs creaked outwards, knuckled at three points along their trunk, they shifted slightly left and right, like a baby deer learning to stand.

"Sophie—"

The two of them tried to dive back into the arrivals, but it was useless. They couldn't even get a purchase on them now. The two creatures—

"Crabs," Sophie gasped. "They move like crabs."

They did, gingerly turning left and right, seemingly taking in their surroundings, stretching their legs out. They truly were different to the Stone Men in design, and not just by the number of limbs. The Stone Men had always woken, straightened, and begun walking smoothly. These more complicated creatures seemed to need to calibrate their bodies after their travel. They took a few shuddering, half-committed steps away from each other, and then became still. Orders were barked over the guards' radios behind Andy and Sophie.

"All personnel—"

Andy seized the moment and sent the message to Sophie, loud and clear:

—Follow my lead—

"Uhh," he said, taking a staggering step backwards against Linehan. "Oh God, that feels . . ."

"You felt it too?" Sophie asked, rushing close to him and giving a jaw-droppingly bad performance of frantic concern. In the midst of chaos, however, it was enough, and that was just as well. Focused and driven Sophie may have been, but she was shit at acting.

"Sir?" Linehan asked, wide-eyed, pale faced, and clearly a rookie in the Stone game. A new transfer, perhaps? "Sir, what's happening, Sir?"

"You need to . . . get up there," Andy croaked, clutching at Linehan's arm for added effect. "It's all about to . . . kick . . ." He closed his eyes but kept enough of a squint to be able to see a ghost-image of what was going on.

"Sir! Sir, what's happening—"

Fortunately for Andy, in that exact moment it did in fact—coincidentally and with perfect timing for his lie—all kick off on the hill.

The sounds shouting and running intensified as both of the arrivals began to walk—no, *crawl* was a better word, those long, knuckled legs dragging low under their hulking, featureless torsos, leaving long tracks in the earth with every step—towards one of the enormous white wind turbines nearby. They would pause, twitch, then freeze, as if sensing around themselves, then crawl a few more feet. Andy wasn't sure if the movement towards the turbine was intentional or just a continuation of the calibration process, but as one of them bumped up against the turbine, seemingly accidentally, both of them froze, then began to rapidly twitch in sync. Communicating? It seemed like it, as immediately the other visitor—the other *Crawler*, Andy thought—scuttled around to the other side of the turbine so that both Crawlers now surrounded it. They gingerly put their legs against it, testing it ... and then each of them wrapped a long, sinewy, knuckled leg around the outside of the turbine. They weren't long enough, by some way, to wrap completely around the immense metal column, but then their legs suddenly tensed. There were wrenching sounds, then a pause followed by a cacophonous clanging and snapping noise as the Crawlers crushed the column inwards like a used aluminium can. Soldiers scattered as the turbine fell, its metal screeching as it dropped heavily to earth, landing with a deafening crash as the massive metal structure smashed into the hill's grassy surface.

"You can't do anything here!" Sophie said to the soldiers, holding Andy upright at the waist where he had fake-fallen to the floor. "I'll get him to medical, you need to be up there!" The soldiers looked at each other, then up at the hill to see the

Crawlers, now a little more awake and online, beginning to move in searching circles around the hillside, testing here and there with their legs. Now and then they would pause, dig up a little earth, then test the freshly turned ground with the stump of one of their footless legs before moving on. They looked dazed, searching on a blind, muted instinct, but Andy didn't think that would last long. A white-coated scientist, holding some kind of measuring device aloft, had been inching fearlessly towards the Crawlers, flanked by two armed soldiers, the trio moving far beyond the military pack behind them. They were being ignored, but then the three men made the terrible mistake of moving one step two close.

The nearest Crawler to them suddenly spun on the spot and froze.

One of its front legs twitched, as if sensing, and then the enormous creature darted forward so quickly that the three men only had time to turn away before it was upon them. Two of its legs shot out like pistons, moving with pneumatic drill-like speed between the three of them, a quick tattoo of blows that instantly dropped the scientist and soldiers to the ground, the force of each strike folding the men in half backwards. They didn't even have the breath to scream, but their limbs had time to twitch before the Crawler beat that terrible rhythm on each of their downed bodies for several seconds. The raw force of it thrummed through the ground and down the hill to Andy and Sophie and their escorts, all of whom cried out in horror as the men were pulped instantly beneath the Crawlers' feet.

"*Oh my God!*" Sophie yelled.

"*All personnel,*" barked a voice over the escorts' radios, "*attend point of arrival immediately, all units—*"

"Can ... can you move him yourself?" a breathless Linehan said, meaning Andy, as he and his partner began to move nervously towards the hill, away from Sophie.

"Yes, yes, ah, yes," Sophie babbled, composing herself and bending down to attend to Andy. The two soldiers nodded, then turned and ran towards the chaos on the hill. Gunshots began to ring out. "They're gone," Sophie said. Andy opened his eyes.

"What happened up there—"

"Don't ask, no time," Sophie said, clearly shaken.

"I'll get Paul," Andy reiterated. "You get the wheels. Meet where we said."

"Got it." She helped him up.

"Get something hefty if you can," he added as they broke away. "In case we have to break the gate."

"I ... I love you," she stammered, her face pale.

The air rang with noise and in the midst of it all she stood, blonde hair blowing gently in the breeze. On the hill to his left, alien creatures moved, and all Andy could see was Sophie.

"I love you too."

They ran.

***

Andy flew down the medical centre corridor, searching for Paul while the Crawlers continued to cause chaos on the hillside.

The building was empty of personnel as the alert signal rang through the hallways. The sounds of the now wheeled-out heavy artillery had begun outside. Concussive booms rattled through the facility, mingling with the blatting alarm. Andy didn't know which room Paul was in; other than his *very* carefully-concealed annual trips out to the barrier to check it was still there, the man had never left the cabin. The entire project had literally been built around him, after all. Andy got no signal from his friend as he checked room after room; did they have Paul in some specialist section he didn't know about?

Wait. Of course. He'd forgotten in his panic. Andy stopped running and closed his eyes. He knew how to find Paul. His consciousness spread out around him. Cut off or not, Andy could *always* find Paul.

There.

Andy immediately knew something was wrong. He redoubled his efforts and flew down the rest of the corridor, turning left at the end. Now he was closer, he could hear the noise coming from what he knew to be Paul's room; the booming sounds of the heavy artillery outside had been drowning it out.

Paul was screaming at the top of his lungs.

Andy barrelled past two, three, four, five doors, grabbed the handle of the sixth and smashed into it, banging his head painfully on the glass as he realised he hadn't used his passcard. He fumbled it out on its lanyard from under his shirt, and as his hands fiddled it into place, he thought for one crazy moment that the wire-laced glass panel in the door was somehow distorting the image beyond. It had to be, because what he was seeing was impossible: Paul was pinned against the wall, arms and legs spread wide like Da Vinci's Vitruvian Man, and his face was a picture of agony.

He was also suspended in mid-air.

The cardlock disengaged and Andy yanked the door open, tumbling into Paul's room. By the foot of the bed an orderly was yelling into a radio, shuffling from foot to foot and obviously too terrified to go anywhere near his charge.

"Paul, Paul!" Andy bellowed, rushing over and grabbing his arm. That was a mistake; Andy's mind filled with Paul's pain, the unspeakable tension. He instinctively recoiled and as his vision cleared he saw that the wall behind Paul was deeply cracked, that Paul was in fact wedged into the plasterboard. "Paul, what's happening? What's—"

Then it hit him: Caementum was being taken away, and Paul was still it's partial energy source. Their bond was being stretched by the disappearing black helicopter.

The wall cracked some more, and Paul was sharply yanked another few millimetres inside the plaster. His screams became a series of chokes. He was dying. Was this the dying breath of the Stone Man too? A last-gasp lunge for—

It didn't matter.

Andy raised both hands and was about to dive for Paul's arm once more when his friend's choking stopped and his eyes flew open. He saw Andy.

"I can't . . . feel . . . it—"

He fell forwards as an enormous bang—far louder than the heavy artillery outside—ripped through the facility. Andy had time to smell the smoke and to understand that all of the electrics in the room had blown out, before something else exploded deep inside his brain and he was knocked to the floor.

Everything went dark.

***

Sophie ran headlong for the back of B barracks; the transports were ahead. Her heart was beating fast and she was frightened, but her body was loving every moment of this. It had been so long since she really *ran*; even amongst the terror of this latest Arrival, she felt alive.

Where will we go, her brain whispered. She hadn't wanted to leave the Project, but every single nerve ending in her was sparking with the sudden thrill of adventure—not just of the unknown, but of facing it with the man she loved. The fact that they may not even survive the day was secondary.

Sophie Warrender, she thought, *who knew that by coming here you would get a whole new life back—*

BANG.

The same force hit Sophie, and the same darkness took her.

***

Andy didn't know how long he was out but when he came to he was being lugged into the recovery position by an orderly simultaneously yelling into her radio. Immediately he was getting up, pushing the orderly away and looking for Paul; his friend was now on the floor, also placed in the recovery position, a crater left in the wall where he'd previously been embedded. Andy scrambled over to Paul before dropping to his knees and putting two fingers on his neck; this was instinct, and as he understood that Paul was alive— spent and unconscious—he realised that checking in such a way was pointless. If Paul was gone, Andy would already know.

Andy breathed out and fumbled around mentally for Sophie, even as he reeled from what he'd just seen. Paul had been dragged? And what was that enormous bang? Were the Crawlers on the hill still—

He couldn't feel Sophie.

Every other thought stopped.

Don't worry, he thought. *Focus.*

He did.

Nothing.

As panic set in, he selfishly grabbed Paul's wrist to see if that helped. It didn't, but Paul's eyes now opened. They saw the terror in Andy's.

"...Andy...?"

"Paul, *I can't feel her*," Andy gasped. "I can't feel her on the base."

And with that he was up and lunging towards the door, flinging it open and running along a darkened corridor that stank of fused electrics and blown connections. All of the keylock lights were off. Part of him idly wondered if the Crawlers had somehow taken out the power, but that part was smothered by the all-pervading fear that something had happened to Sophie.

He didn't stop running when he made it outside, not to survey the scene or wonder why all the shouting and firing had stopped. He didn't stop when anyone called to him; he would not stop until he reached the back of B barracks where he knew Sophie had been headed, didn't stop until B barracks hove into view, his breath like metal in his lungs now as he rounded the building and saw the row of parked trucks, didn't stop when he saw the figure laying splayed face-down on the ground because that might not be Sophie, even with the long blonde hair and *oh please God in heaven don't let it be—*

He dropped onto his knees out of a flat run, sliding the last few feet and screeching to halt next to Sophie's body, leaving a trail in the dirt behind him.

"Sophie, Sophie, Sophie," he babbled, checking her spine before turning her over, layman's check but he had to see her face and he knew that you had to be careful with the neck, always careful—

Her face was streaked with fresh blood but much, much worse this time. It had come from her ears as well as her nose, covering the entirety of her lower face and neck. Her head rolled loosely on the grass as Andy's breath and heart died in his chest, but her eyes fluttered open, very briefly, for the last time, and she saw him.

"It's dark," she muttered, and then her eyes closed for good.

"Sophie! Sophie! Sophie!" Andy barked, pleading her name over and over as if he could stop her departure from him by willpower alone. "No, no, *no, no . . .*"

He took her hand. Gripped it tight. Tighter.

There was no response from the darkness.

***

There was a knock at the door. Andy didn't respond.

Instead, he continued to stare at the point on the ceiling where it met the magnolia walls. There were no adornments in the room save for a wall-mounted TV and an armchair for reading. There were few thoughts in his blasted-clean mind, and for that he was extremely grateful. He knew he was in shock, and that later the thoughts would come, and they would be unbearable. The seemingly-unending tears of grief were drying on his sore face, but he knew this was only the briefest of reprieves.

Knock-knock.

But would it have been different, he wondered yet again, *if we were together at the moment the blast hit?* Perhaps the effect of whatever that force was would have been shared between them, reducing the impact on Sophie's already beaten-up brain? Or maybe if she'd had a little more time in between stopping the Stone Man and the Arrival? The other thought slipped through, the one that would haunt him for the rest of his life: could something have been done if he'd marched Sophie to medical the second she said anything about a headache? Why didn't he take greater notice of that? How hadn't he—oh God, oh *God*—

He heard the door open; someone entering without his invitation. He glanced at the doorway without lifting his head; of course, it was Straub.

"Hello Andy," she said. She was by herself. "I'll leave if you wish."

"Do what you want, Brigadier," Andy said, staring back at the ceiling. "It's your house."

Straub didn't bite, and instead moved to the armchair.

"Do you mind if I sit?"

"Why are you *asking* me these questions?" Andy sighed. "You say jump, I say how high. Why are you pretending that I have any kind of authority? Do what the fuck you like."

Straub nodded and sat down.

"Any witnesses?"

"Sorry?"

"The Crawlers, the things on the hill. Any witnesses? Civilian drones in the area?"

"We don't know for certain, but all signs so far suggest we were lucky. The arrivals' time active was brief, although the falling wind turbine got some attention. We've cooked up a cover story for that."

"Ah. That's good. No home visits needed to permanently compromise any unfortunate hikers that happened to be nearby, then. That's the term you use, right? *Compromise*?"

Straub just stared at him.

"We've spoken to her family," she said gently. "Once we have the latest Arrivals packed and taken to Ground Zero, the Warrenders will be coming here to make arrangements."

"Do they know what happened?" Andy asked, his voice dangerously quiet. "Her brain haemorrhage?"

"They will know that it happened during research," Straub said, straight-faced. "They'll know that Sophie signed a disclaimer and that she knew the risks going in." Anger began to flare in Andy, and then died quickly. He didn't have the energy, and it was half-truthful: Sophie did know the risks. And she'd faced them with total courage.

Whatever did she see in you, a voice in his mind asked him, coming home like an old friend. *You're a coward and always have been.* It was right. Of course Sophie must not have actually seen *all* of him, the way he hadn't been able to see that one piece of her; whatever reason she'd had for not coming—

"I came to ask if you had any questions, Andy."

"I know everything I need to know."

In the last few hours Andy had endured enough high-ranking visitors to know the essentials: the electrics in the base had been fried, large parts of the National Grid had briefly been shut down the moment that energy wave hit, and Paul was okay and recovering in medical. Apparently, he said he felt the best he'd felt in a while. Andy could piece together the rest: the bond between the Stone Man and Paul severed as the black helicopter flew away, detonating some sort of energy release; presumably the last of whatever was stored inside the thing.

The force, luckily for everyone on base—and perhaps the rest of the country—had shut down the previously invincible Crawlers. They'd fallen sideways, frozen and upended like dead spiders; and the energy wave hadn't only affected the Crawlers;

the few other Stone Sensitives on base, Edgwick included, were in the medical facility. He, Paul and Sophie hadn't been the only ones, then—

Sophie—

"What happened to Caementum," Andy asked quickly. "It's in Greenland?"

"I still have to be careful what I tell you," Straub said, "until we know it's fully and unequivocally dormant. You could still be in the circuit for all I know."

Andy raised his head and scowled at her.

"Come on," he said. "Fucking hell. It's dead—"

Straub sighed.

"It arrived in Greenland and it won't be coming back for the foreseeable future," Straub said. "While the first blast seemed to emanate *away* from the chopper—"

"*First* blast?"

"Yes. During the final leg of the Stone Man's journey a second, smaller burst emanated from it. seemingly affecting the navigational systems of the aircraft carrying it. It crashed. Pilots ejected and survived but we can't move Caementum right now."

"Why not?"

"It's forty feet down, for starters," Straub said. "That thing was giving off so much power it sunk straight into the earth. Worse, it's still giving off some kind of radiation; anything electronic that goes near it gets wiped. Even anything that has touched it remotely—for example, trying to winch it out with a cable: zap. Caementum is bleeding out. The levels of energy stored within that thing must be unimaginable, which somewhat explains how unstoppable it's always been. It's almost as if it's expending the last of its power as it tries to find another power source—a Hail Mary move, if you will. We've a long way to go before we run out of options but it's a daunting start. The locals have been told it's just an aircraft crash site. Like I said, it's the least populated area on earth, so there shouldn't be too many questions."

"So what do you do when there's another Arrival?" Andy sneered, lying back on the bed. Straub, in many ways, was the perfect visitor; somewhat he thought deserving of having all his bitterness poured over them. "Who do you dump it on next?"

"People have been able to smelt lead without electricity for millennia," Straub said. "If we can't get it out and the Caeterus send another rescue team of monstrosities to fetch it, then we'll do our damnedest to make sure they can't get it out either. We're prepping to have molten lead on standby, ready to pour and set at the first sign of an Arrival. Whatever Caementum's leaking can't stop *that*. We have to hope that even a fully-active Stone Man would struggle to get out of a several-feet-thick lead coffin, and a Stone Man that's dead or dormant? It would hopefully at least take time to escape, time we'd badly need."

Andy didn't respond.

"Where are the Crawlers now?"

"The what?"

"The new arrivals."

"I see. They're being prepped for departure and analysis; this base is compromised, Andy. It's been discussed and decided that we're moving operations to the Isle of Skye. There's an existing training ground there that's being converted as we speak—"

"Are the dead Crawlers going there too?"

"—as we need a separate facility for research and training with new Stone Sensitives," Straub said, continuing without answering the question, as Andy had known she would. *Need to know*, and all of that. "They're already calling it the Chisel. Project

Ouroboros will be kept open for another eighteen months or so, maximum, in order to study the geology of the site, even its electromagnetic properties. Arrivals could only occur in Coventry before; why could they do it here? Ground Zero is for research at the point of Arrival; now Project Ouroboros has to be the same."

"So I'm being sent to the Isle of Skye now," Andy said. "Just when I thought things couldn't get any better."

"Well," Straub said, crossing her legs and looking out of the window. The sun caught her face and Andy noticed again how much she'd aged in the last few years. For a brief moment, he almost felt guilty. Almost. "You'll be dividing your time between there and here. We still need strong Sensitives. You can't be a Hunter for Targets, we've known that since the Third Arrival, but we don't need that right now. And anyway, who knows . . . maybe your experiences recently have changed that. We'll see." She'd wisely said *experiences* rather than *connecting with Sophie*. Andy had been waiting for Straub to say *Sophie* from the moment she entered, needing an excuse to snap. Straub paused, then played her trump card. "Paul has said he's staying."

"Like he has a fucking choice."

"Actually, Andy," Straub said, sitting up straight and looking Andy in the eye. "You both do."

Andy sat up in bed.

"What?"

"I'm giving you the same choice I gave him: if you want to go, you can go."

"His barrier—"

"We haven't been able to get him out there to check yet," Straub said, shrugging slightly. "He's still too weak. But given the huge discharge of energy, your own report of the Stone Man feeling like it died inside this morning during the . . . exercise, and the hole in the wall that Paul left, we very much doubt there will be a barrier here any longer."

He could leave? Alone?

"You'd have to sign an extensive NDA," Straub continued, "and, as with all the others, any discussion of what went on here will be punishable by treason. There would be no TV, no book deals for you this time. You would be an ordinary citizen. The Stone Man is dormant in another country, and if you want my honest opinion, my gut feeling—no disrespect—is that while we do want you to continue working with us, you'll be less important to us than previously. You and Paul—and Sophie's family—will even be given honours, although of course they will be strictly off-record."

Andy just blinked, trying to comprehend it. A thought began to creep in, and Andy's mind twisted as it tried to dance out of its way.

"Andy," Straub said softly, "it doesn't take a genius to know what you and Sophie were planning. Where you were found, and when. You were going to run. There's no punishment," Straub added quickly and calmly, holding up her hands. "You had one hell of a forty-eight hours and I'm putting it on record that you were in an altered state after all of your recent connections and disconnections. I have to admit, though," she said, cricking her neck and straightening her back, "that I'm surprised. You seemed so content here. You believed in the work."

"I did." Andy scowled.

You can leave though—

"I understand. This news is meant to help you, Andy; take some time to think about it. Paul still wants to stay, but that's Paul. This is obviously your choice, and an important one. Take all the time you need to decide. You can stay here while you do."

He could leave. He could leave. But here he was, being given what he'd claimed to want, and it scared him to death. All those grown-up thoughts of finally not needing the spotlight had turned out to be nothing but vapour. Out there he was no one, would have to rebuild from nothing. Here, he could be *Dispensatori*, and to his disgust he found that to be the better alternative. The thought that had been trying to penetrate finally shucked and jived in just the right way to get around Andy's weakened defences; he'd found and lost his first true love within forty-eight hours, and now he was realising what he truly had left:

Nothing.

He wept as the self-deception began again, and he seized its protection and held it tight. It had been a while.

It's different if you're making a choice *to be here. You won't feel trapped. It's a choice. You're doing it for Paul. That's why. You're doing it for him.*

He put his hands to his face. Straub shifted awkwardly in her chair, and then stood and crossed over to the side of the bed.

She began to stroke the top of his head.

"I can't imagine what you're going through, Andy," she said. "I'm so sorry for your loss."

"Jesus," Andy sobbed, the words muffled by his palms. "Look ... look at you ... I thought you didn't have ... work friends ..."

"I don't," she said softly. "There's only one man on this earth who comes before the work, and he was stupid enough to marry me. But I do have feelings Andy, and believe me when I say that right now, my heart is breaking for you." She stepped back from the bed. "Try to get some rest," she said. "I'm arranging for a grief counsellor for Sophie's family, and you'll get a visit too."

She left without another word, leaving Andy alone in the darkness behind his squeezed-shut, watering eyelids. He tried to reach out for Sophie on instinct, in case some last vestige of her was still in the ether, but he felt nothing at all. All he had were the memories of a lifetime together that never existed, and he dropped into them now, a blanket to be wrapped around him of both comfort and sorrow.

Andy dropped into the darkness.

Chapter Thirteen

Just Passing Through

***

Andy Pointer.
Loch Alsh, Scotland.
Now.

The pain was muffled by the darkness. It was a blessing.

Then he was awake and vomiting.

He felt an awful coldness sloshing out from inside him, and then he was coughing in sweet, sweet air as someone rolled him onto his side. He was soaked from head to toe, and freezing cold, shivering on top of grass and soil. What had happened?

He thought of the black helicopter as the memory of the worst day of his life began to fade, mingling with the present in his confusion:

You were flying to Skye in the black—no, *a different helicopter, you were in the air*—

WE CRASHED—

He went to sit upright but a hand firmly pressed him back to the grass.

"Wait a second," said Edgwick, breathing hard. "Just wait." Andy did. His head hurt; he thought he was cut. No, he'd banged it earlier hadn't he, before—

He squinted, though it hurt to let in the light. They were on the banks of a large body of water, surrounded by grass and trees. What had Binley said? A lake? No, a loch. They had been over Scotland before Maria had warned them to descend. Andy didn't know what the difference between a loch and a lake was, and he considered the possible reasons before realising that he was delirious. He decided to just go with it until he remembered—

"Paul!" He sat up again and this time he pushed Edgwick's restraining hand off him, the sudden upward movement making his head yelp with pain. His hand went to his temple and came away a little bloody—he *was* cut then, but not as badly as he'd feared. As the throbbing died down, he scanned around: to his immediate right was Edgwick, standing up and running down to the water's edge. Andy got up and followed him, passing Maria who was on all fours, soaked and coughing; then he saw Paul, emerging from the water.

He held Linda in his arms. She wasn't moving, and her visible left-hand side was covered in rapidly-spreading blood from the waist down. Clearly, Edgwick's stitching and dressing had given way. Behind him, Maria let out a cry and ran towards the pair. Andy got to his feet, speechless. He didn't know Linda, but this didn't look good. He was mostly relieved that Paul was okay, his friend now kneeling and lowering Linda gently onto the grass as Edgwick approached. Edgwick dropped too and began the same resuscitation drill he'd performed on Andy.

It's too late, Andy thought, but ran down to the group anyway as best he could, his left leg aching. He knew he should be horrified but he couldn't shake the overriding feeling of relief . . .

and wonder. He was alive, Paul was alive, how were they this lucky, and *what the hell had just happened?*

Just for once, a weary but familiar voice said inside his head, *can't you think like a human being?*

Linda's eyes were open, staring up at the people around her as Andy approached.

"It's okay, it's okay," Maria said, sobbing, taking Linda's hand, but the older woman's eyes were only on Paul, who took her other hand and pressed it to his chest. Linda couldn't speak, and her breaths were beginning to hitch faster and faster. "We're nearly there Linda, we're nearly there," Maria said. Linda's eyes went to Maria now, wide but understanding. Tears were running freely down Paul's face. Edgwick lifted Linda's bloodied shirt to inspect the wound; Andy caught a glimpse and wished he hadn't. Her stitches had been torn wide open in the crash, a buttonhole now dragged aside to form an opening that could house an infant's fist. Edgwick looked at Paul, solemnly shook his head, and stood without a word. He moved away, letting Paul and Maria be closer to the dying woman as he turned to face the loch and put his hands on the back of his head. Maria gasped and put a hand over her mouth. Andy looked to the water where the ripples were still rolling outwards, the only sign that their aircraft had splashed down other than the cloud of smoke that was already dissipating in the air. Had whatever had hit them blown something important in the helicopter too then? *Or some of the pilots' bodies gummed up the works,* he thought grimly, and immediately wished he hadn't. He couldn't help it though: how many pints of fluid were inside two human bodies? How many pints of *anything* could be dumped over a helicopter's dashboard before it went haywire, even if it did congeal immediately afterwards—

Stop it.

He would. Linda may have been a stranger to him, but the woman had brought Maria to them. She'd given them a fighting chance. She deserved—

No, you freak, the voice hissed at him. *She's a person and she's fucking* dying. *She doesn't need to earn your compassion with how much she contributed.* Late to understand as always, Andy crouched down between Paul and Maria, and Linda's eyes found him. As his knees touched down, his hands rested on Paul and Maria's backs.

All four of their bodies arched as the circuit completed.

Andy gasped and realised that he wasn't gasping with his mouth. He was in the darkness again. Away to his right was Paul's thread, familiar as always. Ahead, *very* faint but there nonetheless, was Linda's thread, humming with fear but also . . . weariness?

And then there was Maria.

Her thread was an electrified cable, her presence an inferno, so bright and fierce that Andy had to move away from it, scurrying into the shadows. Good God, Paul hadn't been wrong; as much as he hated to admit it, Maria made Sophie look like an amateur.

—*(What is this)*—

That was Maria. She was scared out of her mind, not knowing what she was doing, but then Paul was there too—

—**It's alright**—

He was barely holding it together.

—**This is a circuit—it's safe—we're connected—there isn't time to explain—do you understand why—**

The response was breathless, too shocked to give anything but a one-word answer.

—*(Yes)*—

—You—me—Andy—and Linda—can you feel her—

Andy waited.

—*(Yes)*—

Linda was only a distant echo; she was barely a Stone Sensitive, unable to join their circuit even with Maria's involvement. They couldn't hear her if she was trying to communicate, and Andy didn't think Linda could hear them either, but he knew what to do. Of course he did, with Maria here. *Christ*, if Sophie had poured oil over the gears of the system they made together, Maria turned the gears *themselves* into mercury. They might not be able to talk to Linda here, but Andy thought he could move them all closer to Linda with Maria's help; *yes*, it would be easy. Silently taking their threads, he moved Paul and Maria forward, hanging back himself—because they were Linda's friends, not Andy's, and even he managed to understand his place now and then—and Linda's thread trembled in response.

—Think of comfort—

He told them this. They understood.

—Think of peace—of rest—

Andy began to feel it pour along the threads, raw and unfettered, to him, their Pilot. He took their energy, shaped it, formed it into something that could be processed and passed on, amazed at how easy it was. He rolled up their vibes and dropped them seamlessly onto Maria's thread—she was the great connector after all, the Watchmaker— and they shot away along it towards Linda's distant presence.

After a moment, Linda's thread began to relax, the last of her fear dissipating and rolling out of her like a wave, purged. It hit Andy hard and he scowled in the darkness, not wanting this—he was only here to ease the passing of a stranger—and he began to thrash against it, Linda's memories coming to him, carried by the feedback of Paul and Maria's energy flowing to their friend.

Linda's life poured into him, all of her joy and grief—*Selena, her daughter, she's in America, she would be seeing all the news from the UK and worrying about Linda, what would she have been thinking during all of this, would she even get to know what had finally happened*—and the lid of Andy's own pain suddenly burst open in automatic and uncommonly empathic response. He cried out, wanting to withdraw, trying to break the connection, but the other two wouldn't let him, dammit. They wanted to stay with Linda until the end, and now Andy began to struggle and thrash.

—Let me go—

Maria found him in the dark. She could split her consciousness like that, between him and Linda? Andy marvelled at her power, at the warmth that flowed through the circuit, even as Maria examined it, testing out this new ability and holding it up to the light to see it more clearly, even as she soothed her dying friend. She found Andy's pain, its harsh edges jutting from its burial spot like shards of broken glass.

Of course, she found the sharpest first—the day the black helicopter left and the Crawlers came—and then rifled through Andy's mental files of all the days since at computer speed, trying instinctively to get a handle on it all, to understand him:

—(Let me help you too)—

He tried to stop her, tried to tell *Paul* to stop her, but it was useless. She moved through his memory:

—*Sophie, left in an irreversible vegetative state, getting the best treatment she possibly could at the project. Her family given the option to pull the plug and opting not to do so. Andy, reading to her every time he was on-site, often being flown back from the Chisel just so he could see her. Finally bringing himself to meet her family, knowing them intimately, loving them, yet having to act as if he didn't because he'd never met them before—*

—*the doctors saying there was no point in reading to her, that her brain activity showed she wouldn't hear it but Andy kept reading to her anyway—*

—*spending the last year between the Chisel and the remnants of the Project, working with Paul once he healed. Trying to identify new Stone Sensitives and helping out with research on both the Ground Zero site and at Ladybower; being pretty much useless but kept around just in case. The dedicated infirmary for potential Sleepers always kept ready: a more central destination than the Isle of Skye, Straub said, and there simply isn't the room at Ground Zero—*

—*Paul having his quarters on the Isle of Skye and at Ladybower made up to look like the cabin, Andy worrying about it—*

—Paul leaving, taking a two week vacation, unable to bring himself to contact anyone from his old life ... and lasting four days before he came running back with his tail between his legs. Andy knowing Paul should have taken the counselling beforehand—

—Not finding any new Stone Sensitives, enduring long, long days, trying all sorts of ways to see if they could access an individual circuit with each other and the volunteers. The testing, the worst yet, once Paul was back to full health. Holbrooks and co. trying to see if adrenaline or stress responses, if forced fight or flight triggers could spark a connection. Past trauma stuff, regression. The special forces guys they brought into help for a few months (Conway, that sadistic bastard) until Andy said no more—

Andy felt Maria move away from him, mentally gasping as she found the trail of his side of the story going cold; she was confused, learning of Andy's stewardship of Sophie for the last year, knowing how to give Andy the comfort she'd given Linda without knowing what she was comforting him *for*.

—(But Sophie died)—

A line from Maria pinged into Andy's head, and his resistance suddenly crumbled as her understanding fell upon him. She wasn't just communicating the words, she was communicating what the words *meant* to her, method of delivery lending them weight that mere advice never could:

—(The only way out)—(is through)—

He had to say it.

—Yes—she died—

—*(But)—(I don't understand)—(when)*—

That was all he would say for now; Paul took over for him, opening to Maria and solemnly passing on his knowledge. His voice in Andy's mind was leaden, consumed with the sensation of Linda beginning to die.

—This morning—

He paused, uncertain whether to continue. Andy reassured him.

—She's right Paul—

The only way out was through.

—Show her—

Paul opened his memory to her.

It had started yesterday at the Isle of Skye. Maria took their circuit there.

Like a movie flickering bright in their minds, they began to watch the beginning of the end of Sophie's life; Paul and Maria held Andy and Linda tight, wrapped in peace, Linda leaving, Andy agonisingly present in Paul's last memory of the Chisel.

The morning of the Fifth Arrival.

***

Chapter Fourteen

Two Extremely Difficult Days

***

Paul.
The Chisel, Isle of Skye.
Yesterday Morning.

One thing about Skye that Paul always liked; the crisp morning air. It had taken him a long time to get used to the concept of being outdoors—of not being inside his bloody barrier at the Project, even—and although he still wasn't fully comfortable yet, how could he not enjoy a coffee first thing with the sea breeze on his face? Even if couldn't seem to shake the tension in his shoulders today; he was trying to walk it off. The fact that he even could go for a stroll was a testament to how much his health had improved since he got out of the cabin.

The facility on Skye was considerably smaller than the sprawling setup they'd had at the Ladybower Reservoir. A single building lay surrounded by high, razor wire-topped perimeter walls away to his right, but still a building big enough for five leisurely laps of it to be nice exercise. Time to finish a big coffee, too, but today Paul wanted to go a little farther. He ambled away from the building and up to the main gate. Steve was seated in the sentry post, listening to a cheap, tinny radio wittering away with the sound of Talksport. Beyond him, the road wound away between the long grass to where it met the main thoroughfare, which would take a wanderer on their merry way to the Skye bridge. On the other side of that, the mainland, and a normal life, should Paul choose to have it. The concept was still too big. He liked island life. Here, he could pretend his old life never existed. They weren't massively close to the water, but the sea still filled the horizon, grey and beautiful on that breezy, lightly chilly morning.

"Morning, Steve."

"Paul," Steve said, raising a hand. "Heading out?"

"No, just wanted the pleasure of seeing your beautiful smile."

Steve gave a wide, forced grin, and hit the button on his console. The gate quietly began to clank and retract.

"Cheers bud," Paul said, giving Steve the thumbs-up and heading through the slowly widening gap. He had until 9.30 and his appointment: guided meditation. There were no restrictions for Paul and Andy here, though his friend wasn't present today. Andy had been at Ladybower yesterday and wasn't due back until Monday. Paul's freedom of movement certainly wouldn't be the same if the Stone Man were still up to its old tricks, he knew. For all the gruelling stress experiments on Paul, Andy, and the few volunteers that still trickled in, everyone here knew that the Chisel was a bust, and funding for failed experiments didn't last forever. Even keeping Project Ouroboros running as a dedicated emergency Sleeper destination on the mainland cost money, but the powers that be saw that as a worthwhile investment. After all, the Stone Men could come back today, tomorrow, or in twenty years' time. He didn't think they'd ever close *that* place.

When they closed the Chisel, Paul would have to go home and start again.

Steve suddenly called after him as he passed the plexiglass booth.

"You okay?"

Paul paused; it had been a serious question. He and Steve weren't close by any stretch, talk never going any deeper than good-natured ribbing about football—Paul was still Sheffield and Steve was what Paul saw as the typical Man U fan, as northern as the Oxford and Cambridge boat race—and this kind of enquiry was uncommon. More uncommon still, Paul didn't immediately say *yeah, fine.*

He wasn't okay, was he. He hadn't felt this tense in a while.

"Why'd you ask?"

Steve shrugged".

"You just seem off," he said. "You're all hunched up. They working you too hard?"

"Same as always," Paul said, "but . . ." How could he explain it? He'd not felt right since last night. "I just feel . . ." He looked around himself, trying to find the words, and as his gaze moved to the sea his hand went limp and his coffee mug fell to the ground. It shattered on the concrete with a flat *plink* sound as Paul stopped breathing.

Steve got up from his seat.

"Paul?"

Paul just continued to stare at the giant figure that had appeared on the horizon.

It was immense; Paul couldn't accurately guess at its size, but it had to be at least as tall as the tallest skyscraper, maybe taller. It was humanoid, white, with elongated limbs, and appeared to be slightly transparent; Paul could just make out the shape of the clouds behind it. It didn't move. It made no sound. It simply stood there, silent, as if considering the country that lay before it.

"Paul?" Steve couldn't see what Paul was seeing; his back was to the water, the booth's rear wall opaque. Paul tried to speak but his throat had turned into parchment. He swallowed hard and found his voice.

"Radio the mainland," he said, his usual baritone reduced to a squeak. "Now. *Tell them there's an Arrival.*"

***

Paul.
Project Orobouros.
This Morning: Fifth Arrival, Day Two.

The twenty-four hours that followed were surreal for Paul; a delirium that came both from numbly living through something he'd feared for the last five years and doing so on snatches of sleep. He'd never really, *truly* believed they'd seen the last of the Arrivals, so to find himself in the midst of one wasn't entirely unexpected, albeit unexpected in the same way that having a winning lottery ticket isn't entirely unexpected.

After all, just having a ticket means there's a chance you can win, and Britain had already hit the dark jackpot four times. *But surely not a fifth?*

And yet, here he was.

Immediately flown away from the Isle of Skye.

Back to the mainland. Back to the skeleton-crewed Project Ouroboros.

Back to work with an equally horrified and flustered Andy (who had been dragged away, of course, from reading by Sophie's unaware and vegetative side) and Straub, who along with her team had observed the pair of them trying for several non-stop hours to get a bead on this mysterious new Arrival. The re-emergence of the Stone sensations in Paul's body had been like the creeping shock of an old, familiar illness returning. He and Andy had been cut off from the wider circuit during the Second Arrival, yes, but no one knew if that still held true anymore; Sophie's influence had done something to them, certainly, and without a regular Stone Man-based Arrival to confirm or deny their abilities—unlike these seemingly intangible *Empty Men*—they were still in the dark. He didn't know which to hope for. He badly wanted to help—*defined himself by the desire to help*, according to his government-provided therapist—but the idea of not having to choose was a great relief. He and Andy hadn't been able to offer any insights so far, and now the pair of them were on another Straub-mandated one hour break, the Brigadier giving the order disappearing to put out fires. Was she still even on-base? Paul didn't know. He'd tried to sit down and rest but couldn't and was now wearing a path into the government-issue carpet of his temporary barracks quarters as he paced endlessly. He didn't even know what time it was now—he knew it was the next day, at least—but he was just too wired to sleep.

Andy was elsewhere. Paul had let him go without enquiry.

Paul didn't like being back at Ladybower. Not just because it was on the mainland, but because whenever he was there, he was disgusted to find there was still a creeping, cowardly part of him that actually wanted to run back to the hangar, to the now-defunct cabin, and crawl up inside it. Plus, no connection had ever been found in any of the geological testing that had been performed between Ground Zero and Ladybower, and whenever Paul was brought back there it was only as a just-in-case-this-guy-gets-something request. He wouldn't have minded those days if he'd been able to hang around with Andy in the endless downtime in between tests—they could have played cards or something—but Andy had always disappeared to read to Sophie. Paul had asked Andy once how he knew Sophie liked the kind of books he was reading to her, and Andy had sharply responded that he absolutely did, thank you. Paul hadn't mentioned it again.

Today was different though; today there was a goddamn Fifth Arrival going on. They'd even triggered the Goodnight Protocol; Paul had seen the potential Sleepers arriving at Project Orobouros as they'd been flown in, the military gathering as many as possible to be put under and thus—hopefully—protected. Other LION-bracket Hunters were around, but Paul didn't know what they were doing. They'd probably be under by now. He'd been all set to be put under as well—and for the first time too—before word got back over the intermittent radio that Paul and Andy's sleep should be delayed. They were required to stay awake in an advisory capacity for a little longer and—now both Paul and Andy were at Project Orobouros with its purpose-built wards—could be put under at short notice if need be.

No one had been keeping Paul the loop since he'd gone on enforced break, the one hour now edging towards two; the only updates he'd had for a while came sporadically from the TV when the signal kicked back in. If he was being kept awake to advise, then use him to advise. The Empty Men were all apparently moving inland now too, so why didn't Straub—

"Fuck this," he suddenly said aloud, and headed for the door. He'd been told to wait inside, but there was a vending machine down the hall and since he'd arrived at the base yesterday, he'd barely eaten. Sleep hadn't come easily either. He opened the door and stomped off down the corridor; Andy was nearby, he didn't need his Stone Sensitivity to tell him that. The room where Sophie "slept" was two corridors over, the Sleeper wards situated in the corridor before that.

A soldier Paul knew—Binley—hurried past.

"Hey, Binley," Paul said. "Any word on the next intake of Sleepers?"

"Last ones arrived a few hours ago," Binley said shakily. Everyone on base was tense. "Word from above is that no more are coming, we can't reach any more with comms as bad as they are. I think this is it. The last few are being prepped now. You'll be sent for shortly to help with the briefing."

"Are there—"

Paul blinked as the hallway flickered white for a moment, spots dancing before his eyes as tiredness and hunger finally started to make their presence felt.

"You okay?" Binley asked, clearly wanting to be away, and Paul began to say *yes, can everyone please stop asking me that* when he realised that Binley was somehow in front of the flickering whiteness in his eyes. *Eh?* It was like seeing static appear in real life, or strobing snow; then he saw that it was forming into shapes, human-shaped ones that defied all ordinary laws of proportion. They were so tall they filled the narrow hallway, and so numerous that Paul couldn't even begin to count them. He blinked and shook his head. He wanted it to be fatigue and fear taking over his mind, making him see the things he'd only heard described. Then the whiteness grew solid and removed all doubt.

The Empty Men were here, materializing at the end of the hallway, and they were legion.

Paul jabbed a finger out behind Binley.

"Look!" he yelled. "Look!"

But Binley's eyes were already widening as he looked at the corridor behind Paul.

"Jesus—"

Paul began to turn but a glimpse of flickering whiteness to his right told him he didn't have to; the Empty Men were filling the hallway all around him, and he and Binley were right in their midst. He blinked, freezing for a moment in panic, and then the Empty Men surrounded him so closely that they obscured Binley from sight. The soldier's outline could only just be seen, and then an Empty Man moved onto Paul, filling his vision, and he felt as if poison had been dumped directly into his veins. He fell back against the wall, incapable of speech, and the Empty Man followed, covering him like a blanket. He felt it reaching into his bones, rummaging around in there like someone ransacking a bargain basement ... and then it was gone, moving away from him, leaving Paul gasping like a freshly-caught fish. It had freed him? It was already passing into the wall, its ghostly compatriots following, leaving Binley standing alone and terrified in the hallway. It hadn't affected Binley at all? Paul became aware of the distant yelling just before the alarm sounded, the corridor ringing with its deafening sound.

"Paul, you okay—"

"Yeah!" he gasped. "They're ... where did they go?"

"They went through the fucking wall!" Binley yelled over the clanging din as he snatched up his radio. "They went through the fucking *wall!* They're all—"

"Sleepers!" Paul yelled. "They're heading for the Sleepers!"

Binley turned without another word and ran off up the corridor. Paul followed, willing his body back online as he lumbered after the young soldier, amazed that he was alive; was that all the creature could do to him or had that been a lucky escape? He stumbled around the corner, and as he did he saw the next corridor half-filled with white humanoid figures, bleeding away into the walls that divided the Sleepers' wards and the hallway. The Empty Men glided silently along, their feet disappearing into the floor as they sailed eerily out of the alarm-clanging corridor, beginning to branch off now, separating; each of the rooms on the right-hand side of the corridor held Sleepers.

The Empty Men were separating to cover each one.

Binley was much further ahead than Paul and, to the older man's amazement, the soldier disappeared into the white mass without hesitation in order to get to the first ward door. The man's bravery was incredible in the face of such unspeakable unknowns, but then Paul had seen that Binley had no physical response to the Empty Men whatsoever. The soldier disappeared behind the whiteness, but Paul could still just about see him opening the ward door and dashing through it; by the time Paul caught up, the Empty Men had all followed Binley's lead and were inside the ward as well. Paul ran through the door.

He froze in the archway, realising the endeavour was pointless.

The large room full of sleeping people and beeping machinery rang with blaring alarms as Binley frantically moved about the nearest bed. He was trying to figure out how to safely move it away without disconnecting the vital equipment. All the Sleepers were on life support and in a coma. The Sleeper in question was a dark-haired white woman who looked to be in her early sixties. Her facial expression was peaceful, blissfully unaware of the towering monstrosity that was already silently gliding towards her bed. Its compatriots were spreading out around the tiny ward, splitting apart to creep towards a bed each. Some were already disappearing through the wall at the end of the room as they stalked into the next ward. Binley bellowed in frustration as he looked up from his struggles to see the approaching Empty Man stop by the foot of the sleeping woman's bed. Its shoulders were hunched, Paul now saw from this angle, its head sticking forward like a vulture's. Then it slowly straightened up.

They were never going to be able to move these people in time. It was already too late.

"Help me!" Binley screamed, but it was pointless. The Empty Man poured itself onto the sleeping woman, who immediately began to buck and choke on the bed. Binley tried to yank the cables free, panicking, but some kind of tube was connected to the woman's face, visible even through the white semi-translucent body that now draped itself across her. Binley, confused and terrified, tried to just *yank* the bed, even though the woman was still hooked up to the nearby equipment. The Empty Man went with her, and Paul watched as Binley plunged his hands into the whiteness to try and pull it away, his fingers of course finding nothing. Paul looked across the room; all the Sleepers were now coated in white, and the sound of them choking in unison was audible even over the alarm's screaming. Dark fluid began to pool under their nostrils, at the corners of their eyes.

Andy—

Paul spun and dashed out the door and down the hallway. Binley screamed after him, but he knew that going back was the only thing more pointless than trying to stop the Empty Men getting to Andy.

Unlike the Sleepers, Andy was awake. Like the Sleepers, Andy was on the high-level mental GALE list.

Paul rounded the end of the hallway and dashed down the next corridor towards Sophie's room. There were no Empty Men in sight, but they could already have passed through the wall. Did Andy know what was happening? Had the Empty Men reached him yet? If not, then maybe Paul could at least get him away. Andy might have heard the alarm, but Paul knew there was no way he would leave Sophie's side in an emergency without knowing what was going on, and if he hadn't been told—

Paul slapped his keycard onto the panel and the door clicked open. He yanked it free and froze when he saw Sophie lying on her bed, her face pale and gaunt behind the oxygen mask. Andy was in the corner, sitting on the floor with his back propped up against the wall. He'd clearly fallen and slid down to a seated position, where he now twitched and bucked like the Sleepers.

His entire body was coated in white. An Empty Man had him.

***

Andy's world was filled with the whiteness of the Empty Man and he knew he was dying. He was vaguely aware of a large figure moving in his peripheral vision; Paul? Andy wanted to yell *stay away* but couldn't breathe, wanted to hold up his hands to keep Paul back but couldn't move his arms. As his body twitched helplessly, he found that his only wish was that it be quick. If he were to die, he would rather do it here, next to Sophie. Something was about to happen to his insides. He didn't know what it was, but he could feel the Empty Man at work and knew that things were about to give way in a manner they shouldn't; his body temperature was also heating up fast, very fast.

This wouldn't, in fact, be quick at all, and it would be very painful.

Paul was yelling something but Andy couldn't hear it over his own gagging noises. He felt Paul's hands on his ankles but they immediately disappeared, followed by a loud thud as Paul collapsed to the floor. The heat in Andy's body slowly became unbearable as Paul gripped his ankles again, less tightly this time, but once more touching the Empty Man meant Paul couldn't hold on.

Thanks for trying mate, Andy thought, and as the pain began he realised that both the people he cared most about were here, at his end. That was something, but *oh God*, it hurt.

The pain halted. Something had interfered with the awful process underway.

Sophie's presence was there.

Andy tried to let out a gasp, but he couldn't. The Empty Man still had him, but it was no longer tangible.

Sophie was *there*.

—Sophie—

There was no response. Sophie's essence—her energy—was there, but her shattered mind was gone. Whatever was happening, whatever her brain was doing was drawn by the electricity of Andy's fear, their connection firing up whatever remained of her instincts.

She was protecting him.

The Empty Man began to withdraw, unable to find Andy any longer, but all Andy cared about was reaching Sophie, to whatever degree she was there, and he flailed desperately around in the darkness, calling to her.

—Sophie—Sophie—I love you—I love you—I
knew you could hear me—Sophie—please—
come back—please come back—

Still nothing. The inner darkness was just beginning to fade as the outer whiteness around him continued to withdraw; his physical eye could see the Empty Man reforming and moving away, could see Paul sitting up on the floor in amazement.

Wait, he thought. *What's—*

His mind's eye saw two hazy lights lying in the retreating inner shadows for him. Two memories. Sophie's last gift for him.

—What did you want me to know Sophie—
stay and tell me please—

But she was already gone. She'd been gone for a long time. These energy-archived messages had been waiting for him since the day her brain had been destroyed, her dying intentions lying unsent in the conveyor belt of her thoughts. He knew he had only a moment to see them; Sophie was finally dying, her few remaining motor functions destroyed by her body's final effort. His mind leapt forward and seized the nearest one—

And then he is in a car with someone, Father, on the way home from a CrossFit meet, terrified as this loved one begins to buck behind the wheel—

—standing in a hospital, watching the First Arrival on the waiting room TV, then by the Father's hospital bedside as Father says don't let them see you and then Father is dying.

But then Father doesn't die.

Father is left unresponsive. Unable even to communicate through as much as a blink, Father the former athlete, the always-active giant in her world. Sophie is left to care for him, changing his adult diapers, bathing him, carrying out all the relevant chores so that this shell can continue to breathe for another day. He wouldn't want this, she knows, but her duty is her duty, and all the while she religiously follows Father's last words:

Don't let them see you.

So she ignores the TV ads for the Be Prepared appeal, the government's requests for volunteers, taking a carer's pay while her career and her own athletic dreams lie abandoned in service of the man she adores. She does it willingly and without complaint, though with no small amount of sorrow for herself, even if that pales in comparison to the grief of seeing her father this way.

Then the Second Arrival begins.

Sophie watches it play out from her father's home while the man himself lies in a bed pushed against the living room wall. He stares blankly at the ceiling, she stares at the TV, looking away only to see if the Stone Men's appearance repeats its effect on her father. The visions hit her and she falls, and when her fit passes and she comes to, she clambers immediately to her feet and rushes to her father's bedside. Her father was not one of the faces she just saw in her mind, but if their searching and scanning affected him again ...

They didn't. He's exactly the same shell that he was moments before, and she should be relieved, but she isn't. She's disgusted with herself to find that she is disappointed.

She squashes those feelings down. She vows to be even more attentive.

Months pass.

She's in the back garden. Her father is inside, sleeping. She's still physically strong but now she notices herself groaning when she bends down, feels a tightness in the backs of her legs that wasn't there before. She used to be able to do weighted chin-ups. She's not sure now if she could even try. She misses the patients from her former job so much, especially the dogs. The looks of relief on the owner's faces when she told them it's just an allergic reaction, it's only a skin tag, or this will require surgery but they're going to be fine, or best of all, it went great and you can take them home this afternoon. That seems like a life that belonged to someone else, a woman she liked and forgot, replaced by someone who spends their life surrounded by the smell of disinfectant wipes, piss and shit. She pauses for a moment and realises that both of those lives actually had plenty of the same smells, and that both of them were lives of important service, but she's still miserable beyond belief.

Then the sight of her back garden suddenly vanishes, the vision of the tumbling faces begins, and she realises a Third Arrival is underway.

She manages to make it inside the house; the TV was left on, and of course it's the only thing showing onscreen, regular scheduling thrust aside for only the third alien visitation in human history. There are seven Stone Men this time, standing motionless in the middle of Coventry, and even though once again they are miles away she can feel them scanning.

Her father's face stands out in her mind amongst the swirl.

Have they finally selected him?

She thinks they have.

She knows she can hide him, even as her body collapses to the floor. Her mind moves to protect him . . . and stops.

It will always be this way, she realises. Every time they come back. He will always be in danger.

The pillow is already in her hands before she knows what she's doing.

When she finally becomes present once more, the fabric pressed over her father's unresponsive face, she begins crying and apologising even as she tells herself it is a kindness, the best way to protect him.

But it also means her freedom, and Sophie is the one making it happen.

She cannot balance these thoughts in her mind.

Three years pass, four years after the First Arrival.

Sophie's support group is ending for the week. It's a secret group, its existence divulged in confidence by her therapist after several years together, and even then, the group's function is only implied: I've spoken to them and they're happy to meet with you. No real names, no real phone numbers, and you didn't hear about this from me.

It's a euthanasia support group.

It's only Sophie's tenth session, but she has already come to look forward to it each week like a long, cool drink after a time in the desert. To know she's not alone—that it was, at least in part, a kindness—is everything.

Someone else new comes this week. Sophie doesn't know from where—nobody ever does, for obvious reasons—an elderly man, Simon, who shares his story about doing the right thing, as the group calls it, for his wife. It's nothing unfamiliar, but maybe it's the day, the time, something about this particular man's story from this particular man's mouth that makes the very familiar resonate in a way it never has before . . . but most likely it is the way Simon, a former ambulance worker of forty years, repeatedly uses the same word throughout his story that finally tells Sophie exactly how she can finally let it all go.

The word is service.

The next day Sophie Googles the Be Prepared appeal's phone number.

The ads are hardly ever on TV anymore, but the appeal is still going. Within days, she's on her way to London—

Slumped against the wall, Andy managed to wrench himself free of Sophie's memory, gasping from the after-effects of the Empty Man as he remembered where Sophie's energy ended and his began. He coughed, blinked, and found himself under the strip lights in her room as he turned over what he had just seen, still trying to cling to the darkness within her as he understood the answer Sophie had finally passed on.

There was little time left; she was nearly gone. He could still feel the other memory nearby in her mind, but the darkness had almost faded entirely and Andy could hardly see Sophie's gift anymore, most of his sight now filled by Sophie's room at Project Ouroboros once more. Paul was calling Andy's name and shaking his shoulders, but he knew he had seconds to seize the other remaining message from the dropbox of Sophie's dying brain. He grabbed it, and it was flimsy and barely tangible, but it was real and strong and oh-so bittersweet.

It was the knowledge of how much she loved him, and Andy tried fruitlessly to stay in the darkness with it, clutching it tight as the memory—and Sophie—finally died.

***

Chapter Fifteen

Now What

***

Andy.
Loch Alsh.
Now.

Linda's life thread detached from Andy, Paul and Maria's circuit inside Stone Space, its passing as gentle and effortless as a butterfly taking flight from a branch. Paul and Maria's pain at her departure came down their threads now, singing mournfully to Andy, but he was too lost in his own grief of losing Sophie. His and Paul's memories of this morning tangled together. He didn't know if it was possible to suffocate in Stone Space, but Andy's mind felt as if it couldn't breathe for the pain that Maria was making him relive.

Maria was far more powerful than Sophie; even as her conscious mind grieved, her automated subconscious processes had been rooting around, seeking connections to latch onto; the raw, efficient power of her gift trying to improve their circuit like a computer running a diagnostic program. Andy's pain would only get in the way of the system running at peak efficiency; it was a bug that needed to be drawn out.

She was too good at it. This was too much. Andy immediately tried to pull out of the circuit.

Something snagged him. Maria—the bleeding heart—trying to hold onto him, calling to him from the circuit. Did she think she was comforting him?

—GET OFF ME—

"—GET OFF ME!"

Andy's mouth screamed the words aloud as his mind returned fully to his body, finally tearing free of Paul and Maria's circuit. The bright green of the trees surrounding the loch filled his eyes, standing in stark contrast to the darkness as he commanded his hands to wrench themselves away from Paul and Maria's backs. Had Maria been more experienced in that kind of connection, Andy knew, the physical removal of his hands wouldn't have made any difference. Fortunately for Andy, Maria simply cried out as she too returned to herself, blinking and turning to face him as the memories she'd just unwittingly stolen settled into her mind.

"*Don't ever stop me!*" Andy gasped at her. "*When I want to leave—*"

"Andy," Paul snapped. Andy glared at him, chest pitching as he breathed heavily ... and then saw Linda's body lying on the now-crimson grass. Paul and Maria's eyes were bloodshot, and a few feet away, Edgwick stared reproachfully.

Look at Paul, for God's sake, he thought. *Look at Maria.*

"I'm ... really sorry for your loss," he said quietly, covering his face as fresh tears sprang up, but not for Linda. He'd just had to lose Sophie all over again. But then an internal voice spoke up in his mind, a long-denied sentiment that spoke softly, kindly; self-talk that was usually so much more unkind:

She'd already been lost for a long time, Andy. You know it, don't you?

"Thank you," Maria said quietly. "But . . . yours—"

"No," Andy said quickly, before adding, "Thank you."

Maria stared uncertainly at him, then her head twitched and she held up her hand, her attention caught; the bandaged splint around her broken fingers had come loose in the water. "What happened to my hand?" she asked dreamily, and then paused. "Wait. I remember."

Paul wiped his face and drew in a large, whooping breath.

"There are rocks in the water," Paul said. "Big ones." He looked at Andy. "We can't leave her out here for . . ." He couldn't finish the sentence. *For the animals* was just too brutal. "You and me, we're going to get those rocks, and we're going to bury Linda with them. Okay?" His sorrowful eyes searched Andy's face, his bottom lip trembling like a child's, before adding, "Please?"

"Yeah," Andy said, blowing his nose into the hem of his shirt. "Of course, mate." He couldn't meet Maria's eye; instead he spoke to Edgwick. "Edgwick . . . Maria's fingers. Is the first aid in your pack—"

"Yeah," Edgwick said softly, moving over to Maria. "You two handle the rocks. I'll fix Maria up, and then I'll help with the carrying." Andy nodded and offered Paul his hand, The big man took it and stood before collapsing onto Andy, bearhugging him. Andy returned it, and they stood by the water in each other's arms, wet and shivering.

"I don't know if I can take any more, Andy," Paul whispered. "They're too big. They destroy everything." Paul took another whooping, shuddering breath. *"We can't beat them."* Andy opened his mouth to say something like *we can, we just have to keep going,* but the fading remnants of the circuit and physical proximity to Paul meant his true, honest response bled from him. Paul felt it and released Andy, stepping back. "So . . . what *are* we doing this for then?" he asked quietly, as if Andy had responded out loud.

It was a great question . . . and to Andy's surprise, he thought he might have the beginnings of an answer, found through reliving this morning once more through the lens of Maria's observation. What a gift it was; as Herculean as it had been to endure, the second trip around Sophie's final message had been lent a greater clarity via the circuit between the trio. He'd been able to see through the filter of his own grief; to truly feel the love she'd sent him.

She was freed from her physical prison at last, saving him in the process. So what did that mean for him now; what was left?

She saved you for a reason, the voice said, that gentle tone piping up once more.

No, he replied. *Not now.*

"Because . . . we can't just roll over for them, Paul," Andy said, finally. It didn't feel like a real answer to his friend's question, but it would do. "Look what they've done to our friends. To us." In the past Andy had sometimes thought that, despite all the pain and fear, the Stone Men had in many ways given his life meaning. But then they took Sophie away, and now all he wanted to do was hurt them back. Worse: they'd taken her twice.

Anger alone won't be enough, the voice began, but Andy spoke over it. "And I need you," he heard himself say, and that part was definitely true. "We regroup at the Chisel, okay?"

"Uh-huh." Paul sounded like a kid who'd just scraped his knee. It was awful to hear, and Andy realised that Paul needed *him.* "We're going to be walking buddy," he said, trying sound strong. "I don't think it's too far, a few hours maybe?"

"We bury Linda first—"

"Yes, yes of course. But then we move. And we'll have to process everything at some point, but later. Later. Okay?"

"...yes."

Andy glanced at Maria and Edgwick. They were talking, Edgwick asking her questions and Maria calmly answering them. She'd moved round to Linda's head and was stroking her hair with one hand while Edgwick reset the fingers on the other. Andy couldn't hear them, psychically or otherwise, but Maria's tears had already stopped. He'd felt her steel inside the circuit, but bloody hell; what was the woman made of? She'd clearly tapped into some hitherto unknown part of herself once Paul fully boosted her. What did that *do* to a person? He also noticed that Maria wasn't shivering, and even Edgwick was.

"Let's ... let's get the rocks," Paul said, turning and heading towards the water. Andy followed, and caught Maria staring as he passed them.

"Fingers okay?" Andy asked her loudly and unconvincingly. He would not talk about it, and wanted her to know.

"No," she said calmly, as Edgwick worked. "They really hurt. But I think they'll be okay when they're all bandaged up."

"Okay."

"...sorry."

Andy paused.

"I couldn't help it," Maria said. "It drew me in, I didn't want to—"

"Later," Andy said firmly, looking down. "Rocks now. Do you have painkillers, Edgwick?"

"Yes," Edgwick said as he worked, nodding at the first-aid kit. He recommenced sucking on his big ginger moustache as he concentrated on the job at hand. "Morphine will take you out too much, Maria, but the other stuff is pretty strong. I'll hook you up in a second."

"Thanks," she said, her expression blank. She suddenly seemed to think of something, and squinted at Edgwick, cocking her head to one side.

"You're the ... *TIN man* ... ?" she said. Edgwick froze.

"Well. I'm TIN, yes," he said slowly, "but ... how do you know that?"

"Linda's memories," Andy said. "We were connected. When she ..." He trailed off as he looked at Paul wading into the freezing cold water without hesitation.

Maria looked confused for a second, then her brow unknotted as Linda's recent past explained it all to her inside her brain. She breathed out.

"I don't know how I'm processing this," she said. "It's crazy."

"I think for now," Edgwick said, "you just worry about putting one foot in front of the other. We have a long walk ahead."

Andy agreed. He was freezing. It wasn't a warm day, the loch itself had been like ice, and he was about to wade back into it; he could see Paul already shin-deep, bent over and fishing out large rocks. The sooner they got walking, the sooner he could start to dry off.

"How far do you think we are from the Chisel, Edgwick?" Andy asked.

"I have a map in my pack," Edgwick said, finishing Maria's splint. He stood up. "That feel secure?" he asked her.

"Yes."

"Good." Edgwick turned back to Andy. "I'll have a look when we're done making this cairn, but if I'm not mistaken, we're at the back end of Loch Alsh. That means we're about three hours on foot to the Skye Bridge, unless we can catch a ride and the roads aren't backed up around here."

"Do you know what happened?" Andy asked Maria. "You seem . . . pretty keyed in."

"Yes, did something hit us?" Edgwick asked her.

"Yes," she said. "It was the energy wall that was around Coventry. It's expanded." She looked at them both, her brow furrowing. "Could you not tell what it was when it passed through us?"

"No," Andy said.

She looked at Edgwick.

"Me neither," he said. Maria looked up and pointed.

"See?" she said. They followed her finger to see, far above, a faint, shimmering, silvery movement in the sky. The Barrier hung above them.

"Fucking hell . . ." Andy breathed.

"That came all the way from *Coventry?*" Edgwick said darkly. "But . . . we're in Scotland." He lowered his gaze to Maria. "How much farther does it go?"

Coventry. If they could communicate with Maria's guy there—

"Can you try and contact whoever you were talking to—" Andy asked, squatting down to talk to Maria, but she leapt into the air with a shriek.

"Fuck *me*—" Andy barked in fright, his hand on his chest.

"*Coventry!*" Maria cried, her eyes widening. Andy half-expected her to freak out, but then her face immediately returned to that dazed expression she'd had ever since Andy had broken the circuit. "Eric . . . his friend Harry, I have to help them! I need to see what's . . ."

She closed her eyes.

"If you can see into Coventry," Andy said, breathing out, "we need you to try and see what's going on there. Can you do that? Uh, and also help, uh, Eric and Harry there—"

"I can't see it clearly," she said, her eyes still closed. "I can't focus after . . . after Linda. It's too chaotic in there, like my brain is sorting all this new stuff into place. It's getting easier, but for now . . ." She shivered, cocking her head in that curious way again. "I think when whatever's happening in my head is finished it's very possible I might get really upset, so if that happens, please bear with me. Okay?"

"Oh. Okay," Andy said, still trying to comprehend that she could just see around the country like that. He'd been able to visualise the Stone Men's path a little bit during the first three Arrivals, but this . . . "Okay, good. Give it a try. Do you need help?"

"I think right now," Maria said, her eyes still closed, "that would only make things worse, give me something else to sort out. I don't think I need Paul close by to do it."

Andy and Edgwick stared at each other silently. *Jesus*, Andy mouthed. Edgwick shrugged and shook his head. Maria suddenly screwed up her forehead and hissed between her teeth.

"*Dammit*," she cursed, the first time she'd sounded truly human for several minutes. "I can't contact either of them. One of them is under a . . . it's like a little ball of light, I was hoping I could use it to talk to them, same as the big Barrier—wait, I think that might be *Harry* trapped inside the light—"

"Wait . . . the big what?"

Maria scowled at the interruption.

"That's what Eric called it, shush a second," she said. She fell silent. Then: "*Eric. Harry.* Shit!" She swayed for a moment. "This really hurts."

"A ball of light? Like the ... *Barrier?*" Andy asked, using her word.

"Yes. But small. Eric used the big one to talk to me, like it was sonar or a phone booth or something, when he was close to it I could ... *oh* ..." Her hand flew to her mouth. "I can't hide Harry." She whispered something that sounded to Andy like the word *please.* "*No.* The ball of silver light, it's like a marker." She gritted her teeth and grunted, then breathed out. "I can't remove it either. I think it's Harry in there ... he won't be able to get out, oh *no* ..."

"Can you see where the Barrier stops?" Andy asked, stepping closer to her. He was scared to hear the answer, but he had to know.

"*Wait a second,*" Maria whispered, and now she began shivering before sitting up straight. "I can see the big building now, the Prism, that's what Eric knows it as," she said, her voice low and trembling. "The one in Coventry that appeared. It was hidden before, but now we're under the ..." She trailed off, and her mouth fell open a little. "I can see dark shapes." She gritted her teeth. "Hang *on* ..." she said, and Andy felt the circuit sing between them briefly, straining—

He saw it. Felt *Paul* seeing it. Maria was showing them.

Six Stone Men. Walking away from the *Prism*, as Maria had called it. Andy should have been amazed at what Maria was managing to do, but instead a relieving understanding washed over him: the Stone Men had started walking ... but they weren't walking after *him.*

"Wait," he heard Maria say. "There's one more."

"I don't see—" He heard his voice come from his mouth; he opened his eyes and saw the loch once more, Maria's vision lying faintly over the landscape like a projection. He saw Maria. Her body was shaking.

Andy realised that his was too; his fists were clenching tightly, but he allowed the connection with Maria to continue. "Another Blue?" he asked, "There's seven of them now? I can't see—"

"No," Maria said. "A new one. A *big* one. I can't see it clearly, but..."

She tried to show him, but the vision was so blurry for Andy that he only saw an immense shadowy outline. The perspective had to be wrong, too; compared to the other blues, the shadow looked to be at least twenty feet tall, surely? "*The Stone Giant*, Eric called it," Maria said, and Andy's face became white. He took a step back from the vision hanging in the air before him, but he couldn't back away from it; it was inside his eyes. "It's not moving," Maria said, her voice beginning to rattle. "It's ju-just standing by the puh-Prism. I think... Andy, the buh-Blues are... I think they're listening to it."

The lynchpin, Andy thought, and as his own hands began to curl up involuntarily towards his chest he knew this had to stop. He looked at Maria who was beginning to hitch at the waist.

"Maria. Stop."

"Yes."

She opened her eyes. Andy felt the tension bleed out of him as the vision vanished.

That shadowy shape *couldn't* have been as big as it looked, not if it was a Stone Man. Just because Eric called it a giant didn't mean it actually was, either. As his shakes began to subside he watched as Maria walked in a small circle, trying to see the last of the effects off.

"Let's ... let's not do that again," Andy said, "without Paul a little closer. Okay?"

"Okay," Maria said, taking slow breaths.

"They're talking?" Edgwick asked.

"There are definitely signals moving back and forth at varying intervals," Maria said, "and it looks like most of it's broadcast out from the big one. I think it's running things. I saw it, remember, right before the Barrier hit us. The Stone Giant set it all off." She furrowed her brow, trying to describe it. "It's like there are ... I don't know ... lines between them all. *Threads.*" Andy and Edgwick exchanged a glance; Edgwick had never been in a circuit, Andy knew, but the soldier knew the terminology *Dispensatori* used. Edgwick had read Andy's reports. "They're between all of them," Maria said, "but all the threads go back to that big Stone Man, standing out like lasers, and the building ..." She sighed in wonder. "It's like a giant router, that's what it is. It makes everything ..."

"Accurate," Andy said, wiping his face with his hand. "That explains the ball of light or whatever around the guy outside of Cov. *Shit.*"

"Harry," Maria said. "He's Eric's friend and he has a name."

"What do you mean?" Edgwick asked Andy, ignoring Maria.

"They're putting down markers," Andy said, throwing up his hands. The anger was growing. "Me and Paul, then later Sophie too ... we changed the game. Now this is their response."

"One of them is heading for that ball of light right now," she whispered, then looked at Andy. "What happens when they get to them?"

"I don't know about any ball of light," Andy said sadly, "but whoever the Stone Men visits, dies. It's not something you ever want to see." He didn't add what he thought: *next time you start rummaging around in my memories, take a look at that one and see how much you like it.*

Maria slapped her hands on the grass in frustration and stood up. "Why can't I *talk* to them now! He boosted me!" she cried, pointing at Paul down at the water. "Why do I feel . . ."

"Tired?"

"Yes!"

"One of the first things they told me when they woke me up," Andy said. "You have to be Stone-match fit. You've done a lot in the last few hours, and you just said that your brain is—"

"That's not good enough!" Maria cried. "Harry is going to die if I don't open that bubble!"

"I don't think this is like the Empty Men, Maria," Edgwick said kindly. "Possibly not the Stone Men either, and *Dispensatori* here and Paul are experts in that field. Hiding mental signals, same as Warrender, is one thing . . . but the few reports on the anomaly— sorry, the *Barrier*—that we got said that it was solid, impenetrable. We have to assume the same is true for the smaller ones, too." He shrugged. "These are *physical* things, not mental."

"Paul and I learned the hard way," Andy said quietly. "You can't save everyone."

Signals, though. Threads. The Stone Men, in a network, with the Stone Giant as the potential lynchpin.

"What is it?" Maria asked, seeing Andy's furrowed brow.

"The circuit we made with you just now," Andy said thoughtfully. "We did that with Sophie. That's how we stopped the original Stone Man . . . it *had* been weakened . . ."

"But Maria's stronger than Warrender, right?" Edgwick asked.

"...yes."

"What are you thinking, Andy?" Maria asked, sounding eager. Andy sighed as he realised that yes, his idea made sense, but he was frightened to try it. He wanted to distract Maria away from worrying about some stranger in Coventry, to say *shouldn't you be more upset about your friend right now* ... but that was the old Andy talking again, and besides, he understood some of the fire in Maria's eyes. *Something's happened to you*, he thought as he looked at her. *I didn't even know you before, but it's still obvious that you've been changed. It's clear even you're surprised by it.*

"You might not be able to hide the bubble or remove it," he said, speaking slowly, reluctantly, "but maybe if we can make a circuit, with Paul properly in this time, and get me to flash into the—"

"Into the Stone Man walking towards Harry!" Maria cried, interrupting him.

"Well, potentially," Andy said, "but I was going to say that we try and flash me into the Stone *Giant*. If it really does have influence over the other Stone Men then we could potentially stop all of them at once." Andy didn't add that he didn't know how long this would take, and that if this Harry was only just outside of Coventry then it would probably be too late to save him ... but they could save all the other Targets.

"Let's do it then!" Maria barked, sitting down again and crossing her legs, patting the grass frantically for Andy to join her. "Come on! Now!"

Andy looked up and saw Paul, heading slowly back towards them with an armful of rocks.

"Okay," And said, sighing and sitting down. "Let's try it. But you can tell Paul what we're doing."

***

Chapter Sixteen

A Flying Visit to Coventry, and the Difference Between Men and Giants

***

They sat in a circle. Behind them, Edgwick began another trip down to the loch, continuing the task Paul had started. He'd taken the rocks from Paul as Maria had explained the plan, and by the time she'd finished, Edgwick was already ankle deep in the water. Paul hadn't said a word, quietly sitting down.

"Ready?" Andy asked.

"Do I need to know anything?" Maria said.

"Sophie didn't," he said, "and based on what you just did a few minutes ago, I'm not worried. But," he added, holding up a finger, "*stay out of* my *head*. I know how easy it can be to follow instincts in there . . . but that's private. Okay?"

"Okay," Maria said, looking confused. "I'll be ready this time. I won't get drawn in."

". . . okay."

They took each other's hands.

Right, Andy thought nervously as the darkness rushed in, *show me Coven—*

Paul and Maria's threads snapped onto him so hard it felt as if they were barbed. He cried out but already he was rushing away under a great light—*what the fuck was that*—and then he realised he was flying underneath the Barrier. He tried to see how far it went but it they were already hurtling towards the centre of a dark mass he knew to be the UK; he needed a higher aerial view. He caught glimpses of smaller dots of light—the small light prisons Maria mentioned, the bubbles?—but again they flew by before he could properly look. Paul's thread hummed with power in a way it hadn't before, a now-healthy Paul, channelled and amplified by Maria, so much that Andy almost began to panic, but Maria was there.

—(Focus, Andy)—

She really hadn't needed telling what to do. This was so *fast,* and already one of the tiny balls of light was growing closer. Maria was driving the view.

—(That's the one)—(get ready)—

How was she this calm? He could feel pieces of Linda in Maria's thread, he realised, and Maria's computer-mind still scurrying around sorting and segmenting her memories, her brain running a defragmenting program on auto. How would Maria be once that was done? The ball of light flew by and now they were skimming along darkened streets, so minimised in detail that the houses and lampposts were only towering shadows, but ahead of them all a looming shape began to grow. As it came closer, larger, Andy began to make out a colour.

The shape was Blue, it was walking towards the small ball of light, and Andy was flying towards this Stone Man way too fast.

—(It's right there)—(let's try this one first)—

—Maria—slow down—this isn't the plan—

—(No time)—(it's right there)—

When Andy, Paul and Sophie had gone into Caementum it had been steady, gradual; this was lightspeed by comparison. What would happen if they slammed into it? Andy's hands, situated on the grass by the loch, began to lightly claw at the grass. He felt the green blades beneath his fingers and opened his eyes a moment; still the vision remained in front of him like a haze, unclear, but through he could see Paul and Maria. No shaking from Maria, but her chest was heaving in a rapid in-out in-out staccato motion. Paul's head was dropped, his arms limp on the grass, his upper torso slumped as if he were asleep. Andy closed his eyes again.

—Maria—okay but we have to be careful—

—(You can do it)—

The Blue Stone Man was bigger than Caementum, as it had always been; Andy began to recoil, his threads strung between Maria and Paul growing taut. He had never actually seen the Blue that had pursued him, not up close, but he'd felt the Quarry Response as that Blue had found him from miles away. Panic surged as it all flooded back.

—Maria—

—Andy—are you okay—

That was Paul. His thread told Andy that Paul was frightened too. Andy had always denied having PTSD; that was for soldiers, he thought, people who'd actually been in warzones.

—(He's fine)—

Andy tried to tell Maria off for answering for him, but the Blue was now filling his vision, clear as day in the darkness around it—where was it walking? A road?—and before he could say *please stop* Maria had already breathlessly pushed him inside the thing. Andy screamed:

—STOP—

Then he was surrounded by faint blue light.

He was inside the Blue Stone Man.

It actually felt so much better than seeing it looming in front of him, but he still made a mental note to speak to Maria about ignoring his wishes. He heard that ugliest of sounds, the rhythm he'd always heard inside Caementum's head; whatever morse code-like signal the Stone Men followed that faintly sung of a Target's genetic stock. A road appeared before him; he recognised it! Unlike the visions of the UK that he, Paul and Maria had conjured up, the Blue's sight was camera-clear. It was heading onto the A45 now, out of Coventry, the white centre line of the road slowly ticking by at a steady walking pace. He froze for a moment, then relaxed. It wasn't the only way the Blue differed from Caementum. Paul's Stone Man had been leaking energy, and had a seemingly endless number of threads that flew away into the ether; the Caeterus, it seemed, were myriad. But the Blue had only one thread. Andy felt it disappearing back towards the city. Towards the Stone Giant. Towards the lynchpin.

—*(Hurry)*—

—Back off—

Maria fell silent as Andy angrily began to feel around for a weak spot to slip into, to gum up the flow of internal commands as he had with the dying Stone Man. He already knew this was different; the sense of raw power compared to Caementum's was notable. Not that the original Stone Man had been a slouch by any measure, but the Blue felt fresh and well-maintained. He didn't know what the Blues had been up to since they'd gone home after the first three Arrivals, but he had a hunch that they hadn't been doing years of endless laps like Caementum. He felt for somewhere to jam a mental spanner into the works, but it was impossible. The Blue in motion was a seamless flow, a solid-state organism whose internal stream of mental data was simply impenetrable. If they'd been able to try this before it was walking, perhaps, while it was dormant and waiting, might he have been able to get in? Now the thing had its Target and was en route at full steam, he could tell that, even if he could get further inside, his consciousness would be squashed flat. Andy probed some more and felt his body back at Loch Alsh arch and clench.

—Andy—what's happening with you—

Andy opened his eyes at the sound of Paul's voice in Stone Space. His friend's body was still seated as before, but now Paul bent-forward neck was beginning to pop up and down at irregular intervals, as if he had the hiccups. Maria' head was repeatedly twitching to the right, over and over, and Andy saw his own fingers were digging down into the grass below, stiffening and pushing. He closed his eyes

—Nothing—Let's just be quick—

He felt for the Blue's thread, trying another approach; could it be detached? No. Maybe at the other end?

The other end.

—Take us to the city centre Maria—the Stone
Giant in Coventry is the lynchpin—

—(But if you can't stop this one then how can you stop the bigger)—

—You said it wasn't moving—

—(It isn't)—

—Then that means its dormant—that might make the difference—go to the Stone Giant—

—(Yes)—(Yes)—

There was a pause as Maria tried to recalibrate. Then Andy opened his eyes as he heard Maria's body screeching outside of Stone Space. Maria was clutching at her chest with clawed fingers, gritting her teeth.

"We can stop," Andy said aloud, "it's too soon, Maria, after you—"

—(Get back in here)—

Andy returned to Stone Space.

—Help her Paul—

—I'm here—

—(This hurts a lot)—(just keep going)—

Then they were moving out of the Blue and flying towards the centre of Coventry, and if they were a little slower than before, Andy didn't ask why. Maria was already struggling physically and mentally with wielding her new gifts like this. They might not get another chance to try this before the Stone Giant fully woke up. Even so, as the immense dark shape of the Prism hove into view at frightening speed, Andy marvelled at just what the hell they were doing. *Sophie*, he thought, *you hyper-*

competitive little sod. You'd have hated being shown up this badly. Maria is extremely good at this.

There he saw it. All of his thoughts vanished in the face of fear as saw the Stone Giant standing motionless at the base of the angular edifice before them, and *Giant* was indeed the right word. Even at a rapidly-closing distance, Andy could see that it really was as big as he previously thought.

What can that *thing do*, he wondered, and the thought sped out along his circuit.

—Stay focused Andy—

Andy heard Paul talking but couldn't listen to him. He was in horrified awe. This wasn't just a Stone Man at a larger scale; the Stone Giant's ratios were different, thicker in the torso and the shoulders, and as they zoomed towards its completely stationary body Andy could see that its stone-like frame was a harsh, ugly red.

It was a Stone Man from his nightmares.

He tried to keep himself under control, knowing that Maria wouldn't slow down and reminding himself that, once he'd been inside the Blue, it was actually quite peaceful . . . but wait—

—Hold on Andy—she's right—you can do it—

But Andy wasn't so sure. Couldn't they feel it, how this one was different? He checked Maria's thread, and the answer he found there was frightening; Maria almost lost in a kind of determined mania. Paul's thread was trembling like a plucked guitar string but Maria seemed beyond listening at all, having to use everything she had left to be able to operate at this level. Andy began to babble.

—I don't think—I don't think this is—

But the Stone Giant was rushing towards his face, and Andy only had time to realise that this was, in fact, *definitely* a very bad idea before they were plunging inside the monster and Andy's world was filled with a terrible sound that he had hoped to never hear again.

That awful, metallic screeching.

It was so loud it drowned out the immediate screams of Andy, Paul and Maria; Andy's sight became jet black and there was the feeling of being cut and clawed at before a sensation of immense concussive force smashed them out of both the Stone Giant and their shared vision, slamming Andy back into physical awareness and the scenery of Loch Alsh. He blinked at the sight of the clouds and the Barrier in the sky above him—directly in his eyeline, as he had been knocked flat onto his back—and as he tried to catch his breath, his hearing came back. He heard Maria and Paul gasping.

"M-Maria". That was Paul. "Your eyes."

Andy got to a sitting up position and met Maria's gaze; her eyes were heavily bloodshot, looking as if she'd suffered some kind of awful infection.

"Are . . . they bad?" she asked.

"It'll pass," Andy said, whooping in air, "they'll heal. We've seen this a few times. Do you feel okay?"

"I'm okay," she whispered, but she was pale now, fragile. "Guess I'm not . . . Stone-match fit yet."

"It's not just that though," Paul gasped darkly. "That thing didn't just push us out, it tore us out of itself and then punched our brain halfway across the fucking country. Andy . . ." Paul eyes weren't red, but they were terrified. "*It did that and it hasn't even fully woken up yet.*" There was the sound of rocks being dropped onto grass, and Edgwick was walking over.

"What happened*aaaaah!*" he clapped his hand to his head just as everyone in Andy's circuit did the same. Even Edgwick heard it, then; the metallic, alien screaming.

It had followed them out of the vision, out of Coventry, all the way to the loch.

"What's happening!" Maria yelled, unfamiliar with Stone experience as Andy got to his knees, dazed and looking around himself for invisible attackers.

"It followed us out!" Andy shouted back, and flinched as he felt the Stone Giant's invisible presence crawling over the grass towards them from all directions; unseen but very much there, closing in. "Maria! You've got to hide us!" Paul sat up too, his hands clasped uselessly over his ears. The hairs on Andy's neck and arms rose as if the red monstrosity itself were looming behind him, arms spread to swallow him up and begin its unspeakable embrace. Maria screwed up her eyes and fists and Andy felt her counter-force cover them all like a blanket ... but one that was all too thin. The trap of the Stone Giant's presence continued to close, cold and calculating and terribly, terribly *keen.*

"Andy," Paul gasped, holding up his forearms for Andy to see. They were shaking violently, and his hands curled into fists so tight that his knuckles were white. "I'm not doing ... this ..." Andy didn't need to be told; his own fists were balling up painfully tight, as if someone were sending electrical pulses directly into his muscles.

"*Aah,*" Andy gasped as his toes curled in on themselves too, his feet arching painfully inside his soaking-wet shoes. He cried out as his back arched again, violently this time. "*Maria!*"

"I can't do it!" she gasped, clutching at her stomach too now and bending at the waist. "This is . . . *ah!* Oh my God, it's too . . ."

As Andy's knees began to pull into his chest, to his amazement he saw Paul managing to crawl painfully slowly along on his locked-in elbows, knuckling his whole body forwards like a worm made of right angles until he'd crossed the few feet over to Maria from where he'd fallen.

"*Guh!*" Andy gasped as he forced his arching body to follow Paul's lead, body-hobbling towards Maria too and getting close enough to get a hand onto her arm. Paul got the back of his hand against Maria's knee and the blanket of her protection suddenly became thicker, stronger . . . but the alien screaming continued. "Edgwick!" Maria barked. "Get closer!" The big soldier already followed their lead, screaming as his own hobble-crawl was faster and neater, the practiced discipline of military life enabling him to force himself into greater physical feats than the rest of them could. He even managed to fully straighten his arm as he drew closer, reaching out to slap a hand onto Maria's back . . . but the mental blanket of protection suddenly wavered. "Wait, don't!" she snapped. "You're . . . that complicates it, get off!" Edgwick removed his hand and the thickening of Maria's protection resumed; was the screaming less? It was—

Then it was gone.

"*Ohhhhhhhhhh,*" Andy breathed, all the air leaving him in a rush of delightful relief as his body suddenly turned into a loose, relaxed noodle in comparison to a moment ago.

Nobody moved, and all that could be heard was the sound of their rapid breathing and the loch's gently lapping waters.

"What did you *do?*" Edgwick asked.

"Don't do that again," Maria hissed to the soldier.

"What?"

"When we're in a circuit," she said, "don't try and get in there as well. It confuses things. You're not . . ." She trailed off, suddenly embarrassed. "No offence. It just works best with us three only."

"None taken," Edgwick said. Maria raised her head, paused.

"It's okay to let go, everyone" she said. "I have it now."

"You're hiding us right now?"

"I've been hiding us since before the helicopter crashed," she said, grimacing and massaging her temples. "It's . . . instinct now. You know how you're only aware of your breathing when you think about—look, I have this now too. It's just more to handle, but I can."

The three men exchanged a glance, and then Paul and Andy removed their hands.

Maria slumped onto her back, holding her head. "Harry," she moaned. "He's doomed."

I don't think we're looking much better, Andy thought.

"You have to let us know when it gets too much," Andy said. "Not just for your sake. If you burn up with all this, then we're fucked."

Maria didn't answer.

"That was close," Paul said. "I don't think we can risk that again."

"Definitely not," Maria said. "It's looking for us now. We *really* got its interest. I felt it."

"Do you think we'd have ended up in one of the light-bubble things?"

"I don't know."

"I saw them," Andy said. "Did you two? There are more of them."

Everyone fell silent, not wanting to acknowledge what they'd just felt: such raw power as the Stone Giant pushed them out, the horror of its long-distance gaze.

"They're hunting again," Paul said quietly.

"I know."

"It's *all* starting again."

"Then we have to regroup and do something about it, don't we?" Andy suddenly snapped, his shock evaporating as the anger boiled right through it. Targets. Hunting.

Patrick Marshall.

Paul, Maria and Edgwick had all stopped and were staring at Andy. Waiting for him to lead. He'd been *Dispensatori*, after all . . . but what was he now after everything that had been stripped from him?

Was this *what Sophie saved you for, then*, the gentle voice said.

Andy was used to his brain sniping at him, finding the negative in anything he might have achieved, and generally trying to tear him down. This voice was new. It felt, for once, like it was on Andy's side; was this what the Project therapist had been trying to tell him? She'd said the same line during every session; Andy had always assumed that it was because she wasn't a very good therapist; it never occurred to him that she was saying it because Andy needed to get it:

To be loving to someone and be loved in return you have to feel like you are loveable. If you don't, you'll sabotage everything because you'll feel like you don't deserve it.

Sophie had shown him how much she loved him.

They were still staring at him.

"Uh . . ." Too late. He'd get it next time, use it. Right now, they had to move. "Look . . . uh . . . well, it's too late to save the man in that bubble, okay? But maybe not the other Targets out there, if they're further away in terms of walking distance from Coventry. Okay? So we can stand here and shit ourselves, or . . . or . . ." He waved a hand in the air. Paul moved towards Andy and put a hand on his back.

"I know," he said softly. "I know you still see him. It's okay."

Patrick Marshall. The Stone Man's first Target.

"Not . . . not *all* the time," he muttered. "Not like I used to."

"Let me say a few words for Linda," Paul said. "Then we go."

Andy looked at Linda's body, already covered to her shins with rocks. With him, Paul and Edgwick working together, it wouldn't take long. It meant a lot to Paul, and perhaps still Maria, to a degree.

"I want to help," Maria said, as if reading his mind, and perhaps she was.

"Your fingers—"

"I'm helping," Maria said firmly. She stood up and began to head for the shore.

"This won't take long," Paul said to Andy, but his eyes were on Linda. "Thanks, Andy."

"For what?"

"For not insisting we go to the Chisel right now."

"Oh. Yeah. No worries."

Paul walked away, and Andy tried to remember a time when he *would* have insisted that. He couldn't. That was something. Then he thought again of the screaming they'd heard, of the effortless way the Stone Giant had slapped them aside as if they were annoying flies.

Perfect, he thought. *I start being a good guy right before the fucking world ends.*

***

Chapter Seventeen

Grounded for Life

***

"Hello," Aiden said, squinting to see Eric. His cheeks were bright red from crying.

"Hi Aiden," Eric croaked. He couldn't find his voice.

Aiden. It was much, much too close to *Aaron.* His nephew, Theresa's son. The *Aaron* who would have only been three years younger than this *Aiden* had Eric managed to save him.

Esther crouched down next to Eric, addressing her son and interrupting Eric's thoughts. That was good.

"Eric says he knows someone that might be able to help," she said, doing a decent job of faking optimism and hiding her fear. "He's going to the government people. Okay? We're lucky he came here, because now he knows you're here and he can tell them." Aiden's eyes didn't leave Eric all through this.

"You know the government?" Aiden asked, his voice small.

"Yeah."

"When will they get here?" the boy asked.

LUKE SMITHERD

"I've got to go to Scotland first," Eric mumbled. First? Hadn't he really already decided that once he got there—like he promised Harry—his journey would finally end?

"How long will that take?" Aiden asked.

"The, uh . . . the roads are pretty bad . . ."

"Did you drive?" the boy asked.

"At first, but I left my car."

"You could take Mum's car," Aiden said, sitting up. His hair was the same colour as his mother's, and if he was eight then he was small for his age. He was wearing a black T-shirt with the Star Wars logo on it and only a pair of boxer shorts below, obviously caught half-dressed when the bubble appeared. "Then you'd get there quicker."

"You could definitely take it," Esther said eagerly. "You could sleep here for a few hours and then take the car, right?"

But Eric was looking at Aiden and wondering why he hadn't seen the boy's face in his vision, trying to manufacture hope.

You didn't see Jenny's face either, though. You just saw the light of her bubble.

True . . . and that wasn't good. Because he'd been hoping that not seeing Aiden's face meant that there wasn't a Stone Man on its way. Yes, they were some distance from Coventry, but still only what, less than ten hours of walking? Eight?

If Harry had still been here, his brain threw up helpfully, *he might have been able to see through their eyes and tell you.*

"Are you okay?" Esther asked.

". . . yes," Eric lied, for Aiden's sake . . . but then, as he Eric looked at Aiden's bubble, an idea suddenly formed.

Jenny's bubble. Harry's bubble. Different levels, different bubbles; even the Barrier was a giant bubble, different again, right?

And while he hadn't been able to use *Harry's* bubble the way he wanted, he'd been able to use the Barrier to—

Eric suddenly moved towards Aiden and the boy flinched; Esther darted into Eric's path and he backed up.

"It's okay," he babbled, "I think I can use the bubble to . . . I'm going to put my hand on it, okay?" he said, seeing the confusion and fear in Esther's face. "Have you touched it?"

"No," she said, relaxing a little. "I didn't . . . it felt dangerous."

"You were probably right," Eric said. "I can touch it, but some people can't. If it feels dangerous, then absolutely *don't* touch it." He turned his back on Aiden for a moment. "I saw someone do it," he said under his breath, "and . . ." He shook his head slightly. Esther breathed in sharply and nodded.

"I tried to break it," she said. "I even broke a chair over it, but it didn't—"

"It won't," he said. "You can't break them."

"Was the big one that over Coventry like this?" she asked. "I saw it on the news before it finally stopped. I mean, you got out of there, didn't you?"

"Yes and no, on both counts," he told her. "I'll explain later, but I want to try something right now, okay?"

"Yes, yes," she said eagerly. "Anything if you think it can help him."

Eric turned back to the bubble, its horrible churning light hurting his eyes. If his idea worked then maybe, in the long run, it *would* help the boy. *If the kid even* has *very long*, Eric thought, but that wasn't helpful. He squatted down and Aiden leaned closer, seeing Eric clearly now.

"I'm hungry," he said.

"Hang in there," Eric replied, his own stomach rumbling. The promised sandwich hadn't materialised, but this wasn't the time.

He took a slow breath, raised his hand, and flattened it against the bubble's surface. It was much easier now, but the harmless sizzling sound began all the same. Aiden let out a little yelp at the noise.

"Ssh ..." Eric said gently, his eyes closed; the screeching in his head had doubled in volume the moment his hand touched the bubble. He winced; until then he'd been able to ignore it to a degree, but now that was impossible. He heard that undercurrent in their communications again; that mild concern. *Maria*, he thought. *They have to be worried about Maria.* The thought was gladdening. He took a moment to test the strength of the thing, to first see if he could open it himself, but he knew immediately that would not be happening. The golden light felt just as strong as Jenny's.

Okay then. Plan A.

Maria, he thought, pressing his hand even more tightly onto the golden glow, desperately hoping that it really *was* a better conduit than Harry's had been. *Can you hear me?*

Nothing. Dammit!

"Oh! What's that noise?" Aiden asked. Eric opened his eyes in surprise.

"What do you mean, Aiden?" he asked carefully. "You heard something when I put my hand on the bubble? The fizzing?"

"As well as that, that other sound, it's horrible," Aiden said, wrinkling his nose. "It's like the noise lots of noisy birds make, but like ... metal birds."

Eric looked at Esther, who was watching intensely.

"Can you hear it?" he asked her.

"Hear what?"

He turned back to the boy.

"Can you understand what they're saying, Aiden? Just a little? Maybe just like the feeling of what they mean?"

Aiden thought about it.

"No," he said. "It's just a noise." He looked at Eric's hand. "Does it change if I touch it then?" Aiden lifted his hand and pressed it flat against his side of the bubble.

Right underneath Eric's.

The farmhouse living room disappeared and a shadowy vision of the UK appeared below Eric as if he were hanging in a darkened sky. He cried out, as did Aiden, and he jerked his hand away the bubble's surface. He blinked, seeing Aiden once more, holding his hand on the other side of the golden prison.

"What happened?" Esther gasped, but Eric was staring at the boy. He had it.

A golden prison like Jenny's; not silver like Harry's. The boy was *DIGGS*.

Eric was already putting his hand back on the bubble, excited, the impossible surface fizzing once more at his touch.

"It's alright, Esther," Eric snapped, and nodded frantically towards his hand while he looked at Aiden. "There, put your hand back there," he said.

"I don't want to."

"Do you want to get out?"

"Yes."

"Then *do it*." Part of Eric heard the way he was speaking to the boy, but that part wasn't in the driving seat. Aiden looked at his mother.

"Listen to him, Aiden," she said, uncertain. "He's here to help us."

Aiden hesitated, then put his hand flat against where Eric's pressed against the solid light. The vision of the country flooded

Eric's eyes once more; this time it was a little clearer, and he could see ... bubbles? No, there were lights, but they were a different kind of brightness.

There were hundreds of them. Maybe thousands. Potential *Quarries*. Maria would be one of them, he knew, even as part of his brain whispered *is that all that's left*—

"What is it?" Aiden whispered.

"Quiet," Eric snapped. He heard Esther moving behind him and realised, mission or not, that he had to watch his tone or the mother would—

One light stood out to him from all the others. It was no brighter, or larger, but it was moving. Even though it appeared, from Eric's vantage point, to be crossing the country very slowly, the fact it was covering that amount of distance meant that it was actually travelling very fast, surely faster even than a car—

Oh my God, Eric thought. *They're flying. They're in a plane.*

It was hard to see the shape of the country accurately, but it looked as if the plane was currently over the southwest, hardly any distance at all from where Eric was, as the crow flies at least. And it was heading north! Eric tried to remain calm as his fried nerves all fired at once, willing whatever form he had inside the vision to move towards the swiftly travelling light, but he couldn't. He was frozen in place.

"Aiden," he said aloud. "Can you move closer to that light there? The moving one?"

Aiden tried.

"No." His voice was an even smaller whisper than before.

"It's okay Aiden," Esther said, supportive even though she couldn't know what was happening. "You're doing great."

Eric wanted to scream with frustration. A goddamn *plane*! If he could just talk to it he could be on Skye in an hour!

"Hey," he whispered aloud, trying fruitlessly to talk to the speeding light. "*Hey.* Can you—"

That wasn't going to work. He was talking in a Midlands living room, not on this astral plane or whatever the hell it was. He wet his lips and concentrated as hard as he could.

"Aiden," he said slowly. "If you can't move us closer, can you focus on that moving light there? Concentrate on it and do your best to think of nothing else?" Aiden didn't answer, and Eric began to feel the boy's fear somehow creeping to him through the bubble. How was that possible? There was no time to wonder. "I know that's hard," Eric added, forcing a kind tone. "Can you do it?"

There was a pause, and then something shifted. The other lights—the country—seemed to fade, and all Eric saw was that slowly speeding, glowing dot.

"That's it," Eric whispered. "Good."

Hello, he thought.

***

Colin Renwick had been humming anxiously to himself ever since take-off. It was a help for his nerves, something he had never needed before behind the stick, but then he'd never flown without a fully-functioning radio before. He kept telling himself that, today at least, there was almost no one else in the air, but even so it went against everything he knew about flying. He had his bearings, if nothing else, and for now that was all he needed. The one-step-at-a-time technique had worked fine thus far; it had helped him get to the hangar, helped him walk past the remains of the few onsite security guards who had been there that day— which had been a nightmare—and it had got him into the air. Now he was managing—just—to keep his thoughts clear. Every time his fear over *just what the hell had happened* to everyone, his friends, his family, and *please God no* his kids, he just returned to the same system and let the Pilot do the talking, always with the same question:

What's the next step?

Land at Newcastle Airport. A scary concept indeed without a radio—landing without talking to the fucking *tower?*—but again, if no one else was up in the air—

Hello.

Colin sat bolt upright in his seat, listening to his headphones. Someone was—

Can you hear me?

It wasn't in his headphones. It was in his head. He was finally cracking.

I'm talking quietly, the voice said, *because I think you might be flying and I don't want you to freak out and crash. My name's Eric Hatton, you're not going crazy, and I'm communicating with you through some kind of . . . I don't know, it's something to do with the Stone Men. I need your help.*

Colin remained frozen in place, the controls thrumming gently under his hands. He didn't dare respond.

Please, the voice said. *I'm pretty sure you can hear me. Don't be scared.* A pause. *Hello?*

This wasn't in Colin's plan. This wasn't the next step.

Fuck it, the Pilot said.

Hello, Colin thought back, and gasped as he felt the thought zip away over the miles between him and his caller.

***

Once Colin had calmed down—but still only just keeping it together—he'd told Eric his name and begun to explain about what had happened in the hotel, but once he'd mentioned that he'd been sitting in a crowded bar, Eric interrupted Colin and said that there was a kid listening. Thankfully, Colin hadn't asked how this was possible, and had immediately pivoted and explained where he was going. Newcastle, to see his kids. North. Eric had explained who he was trying to get to, and why, and where. Esther had interrupted a few times, but Eric had been wary of breaking the connection and had ignored her. The third time she'd asked what was happening, Aiden had answered for him.

"He's talking to a man, Mum," he'd said quietly. "A pilot." Aiden had handled it all fantastically, perhaps because of a child's capacity for accepting the impossible.

"What? How?" Esther asked.

"It's the *bubble*, Mum," Aiden said, a slight and very specific exasperation in his voice that only children can use towards adults.

Who's that, Colin asked.

It's Aiden, he's helping me talk to you, Eric thought back. *He's been a big help*, he added, feeling bad for snapping at the kid earlier. He felt Aiden swell a little in response.

I have to go to Newcastle, Colin insisted, uncertain . . . but Eric felt the man only needed a little push. Kids or no kids, when someone magically starts talking in your head and you're pretty sure you haven't gone crazy, you tend to listen. Eric knew it from experience. *I'm not happy about being in the air at all after the plane crash yesterday, that thing in Coventry did something to that passenger jet, it was on the news. I don't want any diversions, I don't want to be up longer than I have to be. I'm staying at as low an altitude as I can, way lower than that thing would have been, but even so—*

Plane crash? Eric asked. *What plane crash?*

You didn't hear?

No, Eric thought, but there wasn't time to discuss it. If Colin was flying, then at least lower-altitude flight was currently possible. *But Colin ...* he didn't know how to say it without terrifying Aiden. *Trust me when I say this. If you want your kids to be okay, if you want them to have the best possible shot, you need to give me a ride so I can help Maria Constance. It's not too far out of your way. She told me to go to her, and believe me, she has some tricks up her sleeve.*

What does she need you for, Colin asked, and Eric didn't have an answer.

I don't know ... he thought. *But if she told me to go there, then she needs me, and we need to get her as much help as we can.*

There was silence over the connection. Before Eric's eyes, the little glowing dot was still moving ... or was it? It had stopped? How was that possible? Of course. Colin was in a helicopter then, not a plane. And if he was hovering, that meant he was thinking about it.

Colin?

Silence.

I don't even have your coordinates, Colin said.

Do you have a map? A roadmap?

Yes.

Then I can give you road directions. And I can do something you'll see from the air; a fire, smoke, would that work?

... yes.

Great—

This is crazy. This is crazy.

I know—

What happened to the people, Eric, Colin interrupted, clearly choosing his words carefully for Aiden's sake. Even in Eric's mind, Colin's voice shook. *You know . . . in the bar, what did that?*

I'll tell you when I see you, Eric thought back, *because I know exactly what happened. Gives you an extra incentive to come get me, eh?*

A pause.

I won't stay with you. I'll drop you off and then I'm going.

That's fine, that's fine, Eric babbled, amazed at his good fortune. He'd been staring down the barrel of a possible days-long walk; now he'd be *flying* there!

"What does he mean?" Aiden asked. "About the people in a bar?"

"He means people who had too much to drink," Eric said aloud, the mental connection with Colin still comfortably staying in place thanks to the bubble. "It's okay. Esther," Eric continued, his eyes still closed. "Do you have anything you can build a fire with?"

"Yes," she said quickly. "There's a ton of boxes I bought for the move, we were going to leave in a few months. An old wooden bed-frame too, and the bits from the chair I smashed. I can find more stuff too."

"Good. Get one going in the yard. I'll come and help you in a second."

"Okay." Esther hurried out.

Do you have something you can write with? Eric asked Colin.

Yeah. Hang on.

Eric gave Colin much information as he could, including landmarks, even though it was probably unnecessary; with the junction number and the fire, surely Colin should have no problem finding them.

Think that'll be enough?

I think so.

Okay, Eric thought, *I'm going to go now; if I can contact you this way then maybe I can contact her, I'm going to try again.*

He had no idea how, though; Colin had stood out because of the way his light was moving. Even if the kid had the hang of focusing on a distant person now, Maria would be a needle in a haystack of lights.

What if I can't find you? Colin asked.

If I don't hear a helicopter in half an hour, I'll call you this way again, Eric thought, before adding, *if you can't find me, keep circling though, wide circles. It makes it easier to spot you in here.*

Spot me in where?

I'll tell you that later too, Eric thought. *I need to go.*

. . . okay.

Colin?

Yeah?

Eric didn't know how, but he was picking up something from Colin.

It's going to be okay, Eric thought. *We're going to fix this.*

Step by step, Colin said.

What?

I'll tell you that *later.*

Okay.

Eric let go. Below him, Colin's little light continued northwards through the sky over the dark vision of the UK.

"Wow," Aiden breathed.

"Yeah," Eric replied, moving his hand away from the bubble and opening his eyes. The living room came back. Through the golden haze, Aiden still looked scared, but he was smiling a little. "You're doing really well, Aiden. Think you can do another?"

"I think so."

"Good lad. This one might be a bit harder though."

"Will it hurt?"

"If it does, you tell me, and we'll stop, okay?"

"Okay," Aiden said quietly, putting his hand back on the inside of the bubble. Eric covered the boy's palm on the outside. Together, they looked down at the lights as they winked into view. "Which one do you want me to concentrate on?"

"I just want you to try and take them all in," Eric said. "I don't know which one we need, but the woman we're trying to talk to is *very* powerful. I'm hoping that if we really think hard, really concentrate just like you did when were able to link up to Colin, and say her name in our heads together, she might hear us. Think you can do that?"

"Like at a birthday party? With the rabbit?"

". . . with the what?"

"I went to a birthday party last year," Aiden said. "And they had magician and the magician said he could make a puppet appear, but we all had to say his name together. And we did and the puppet appeared."

It was a brief story from a different world, one Eric wasn't sure was ever coming back.

"Yeah," he said quietly. "Just like that. What was the puppet's name?"

". . . I can't remember."

"That's okay. This woman's name is Maria Constance. *Maria Constance.* Okay?"

"Okay."

"When I count to three, we do it. Give me one second first though."

"Okay."

Eric breathed out, looking at all the little lights below him. He couldn't see the biggest light of all, the Barrier, and he wasn't sure what that meant. Was it because he was underneath it? He tried to remember Maria's voice, how it had come to him from far away. Where he'd felt it in his head.

"Ready?"

"Yes."

"Okay. One."

The little lights continued to twinkle below him.

Two."

One of them was Maria Constance.

"*Three.*"

✳✳✳

Chapter Eighteen

Everyone Talking at Once

***

"If they can teleport," Paul asked quietly, "why do they ever walk anywhere? Why not just teleport?"

It was now several hours since the crash and Linda's burial; they'd been walking for some time, Andy and Paul walking together along the roadside, hanging back a little behind Maria and Edgwick. The pair in front weren't talking; they'd all passed a crashed bus earlier and that had killed any growing conversation. They hadn't been able to see inside through the red-encrusted windows. Their soaking wet and freezing clothes had dried a little by now, but still were damp enough to make Andy feel miserable; even he wanted to talk now, if only to take his mind off his discomfort.

"You mean the Blue teleporting back to the Prism?"

"Yeah."

Andy considered it.

"Maybe they can teleport *back* but not teleport out," he said.

"How would that work?"

Andy considered this question too.

"Like a bungee run. You ever see those? Where you run along with a bungee cord tied to you as far as you can go, and then it pulls you back?"

"Ah, yeah. I've seen those."

"So maybe they can be yanked *back* but getting *there* takes more precision."

"Hmm." Paul pondered the suggestion. "Yeah, that could be it, you know." They carried on in silence for a moment. "Man," Paul added, chuckling darkly. "I really would kill for some sort of a manual on those bloody things." Andy laughed, glad to hear Paul laugh even a little. He'd caught Paul crying earlier, hanging at the back of the group. He'd asked if he was okay, and Paul had denied any issue, but Andy had felt Paul's grief over Linda earlier; he knew how much the man was struggling. Andy didn't think Paul had been in love with Linda, but she had certainly been someone he cared for a great deal.

So much loss.

Yes, what is *the point of this*, the ugly voice asked. It seemed to have tagged itself back in ever since Andy started walking, its nagging question completing its latest loop around his head. *For all the bullshit earlier, really, come on: what* was *the point of Sophie saving you? Don't you want to just lie down by the side of the road here?*

But that second screening of his memories on the shores of the loch. That distanced viewing; the feeling of Sophie wrapping him up once more, of the sheer *effort* it took from her, the moment experienced through Maria's eyes and outside of the all-distorting filter of his grief ... yet he couldn't admit to himself how it had made him feel.

Doing so would mean not allowing himself to lie down until this was done, taking the option of surrender off the table. That would mean—

He watched as Maria suddenly staggered about five feet sideways as if she'd been punched in the side of the head.

Edgwick spun round and darted over to catch her, but even as Andy and Paul began to run forward, he thought he caught the echo of something in the air; two voices, one high, one low, screaming *Maria Constance*. Maria was already shaking her arm free of Edgwick by the time they reached her, holding up a hand and lowering her head.

"Eric?" she asked.

"Is that the guy?" Andy asked, stepping towards her. "Is that the guy from Coventry?"

"Shut up," Maria hissed dismissively, trying to listen. "It's hard to hear him, *Eric?*"

"Do you need us to—" Paul began, but Maria flapped a hand at him too, scowling.

"I don't know, this is harder than before, keeping us hidden is making it . . . *Eric, can you hear me?*"

"Is that the guy?" Andy repeated, frustrated. "Is that the guy who—"

"Shut up!" Maria hissed again, and Andy felt his insides jolt as the road disappeared and he was pulled into Maria's vision, Paul's proximity presenting the sight in high definition. *Holy shit,* he thought, amazed. *I didn't even have to do anything. She did that like it was nothing.* There was no dim shape of the UK this time; all he could see was a single bright light, close up, surrounded by darkness. He knew immediately it was one of the light prisons they'd seen earlier.

—Maria—you said this was dangerous—

—(That's what you two are in here for)—
(we're going to be quick and I'm going to need
you to help me)—

She wasn't lying. Her voice sounded pained, like before ... but more capable. Paul was helping, she'd had a mental break since they'd been walking, but even so Andy could already feel the tension coming from Maria's thread. He felt Paul take on some of the strain,

—Do it—just be quick—

Andy shut up and concentrated, but a thought occurred to him; *he* was *Dispensatori*, not Maria. Shouldn't he be the one who could do this? Was Maria, the Watchmaker, somehow accessing *his* gift? He felt a strain settle into his mind; was that him helping her, or just Maria helping herself? He thought about Carl Baker.

A stranger's voice spoke in Andy's head.

Maria, oh my God, a man's voice said. It had to be Eric. *I can hardly hear you.*

—(I'm doing a lot more at the same time than I
was before)—(it doesn't matter)—(I have to be
quick)—

Okay, yes, Eric said, sounding frantic. *I'm on my way, a helicopter is going to take me to you! What's on the Isle of Skye—*

—(a government facility)—(we're going there
to regroup with the military)—

I know that, Eric snapped, *I saw Brigadier Straub—*

Andy couldn't help but cut in.

—You saw Straub—

Who's that talking? Eric asked.

—*(That's Andy Pointer)*—*(he's here with me)*—*(listen Eric I have to)*—

Andy Pointer is with you? Eric gasped. Are you fucking kidding me? The Andy Pointer?

—Hi—it's always nice to—

—*(SHUT UP ANDY)*—

Eric fell silent in Andy's head, uncertain.

Uh, Eric said quickly, okay, so where is the facility, is it hard to find—

—Head over the Skye Bridge and keep going—

Who's that talking, Eric interrupted.

—*(that's Paul)*—*(he boosts the abilities of Stone Sensitives)*—

What?! Eric said, sounding suddenly even more energised, you can make Stone Sensitives stronger at what they do? Like anyone?

—Most of the time, yes—

Oh my God, Eric cried, yes! He sounded suddenly joyous. Paul, can you hear me?

—Yes—

Okay, Eric said, there's this kid with me here, he's under a bubble thing, I can open these bubbles a little bit but I can't open them all the way, I can't get him out! But if you boosted me Paul . . .

—I can't do it remotely—we have to touch—you'd have to meet me and then go back to help the boy—but it's possible—but listen to me Eric—you need to know where you're going—when you cross the Skye bridge you keep going and you'll pass two blue shipping containers by the roadside—you take the *next right*—it isn't signposted—okay—

Yes, I got it, Eric babbled, *I'll go that way!*

—(Eric)—

That was Maria again.

—(Where is the other man that was with you)—(the one that was trapped in the bubble)—

There was silence for a moment.

I couldn't get him out, Eric said eventually. *I couldn't get the bubble open.*

—(I'm so sorry)—

You did your best, Eric said quietly. *I . . . took care of it as soon as I could. He didn't suffer—*

—(Eric)—(we have to go)—(I'm sorry)—(it's not safe to be in here)—

I didn't get that, Eric said. *Can you repeat it?*

—(I said)—

Sorry . . . the noise, Eric said, his voice now even more faint. *Their form of talking, it's getting louder!*

Only silence came over the connection, then—Andy was sure he wasn't hearing it correctly—the sound of a child's frantic, horrified breathing.

Shit, Eric said. He sounded as frightened as the child did. *Oh shit, Maria, it's so loud—*

Andy knew he had to stop this.

—Disconnect, Maria—

Andy tried to pull them out. Maria stopped him.

—(I can)—(hear the boy)—

Oh God . . . it's seen you, Eric babbled.

Andy didn't have to ask who it was. This had to stop.

—Maria—take us out *now*—

It's coming, it's seen all of us, Maria, hide, hide—

Eric's voice vanished in their minds as the presence of the Stone Giant suddenly flooded the connection, devoid of emotion but vast and *oh God*, so powerful. Andy's vision began to cloud over red—

Maria finally flew down their threads and poured herself over them, shaking and strained but *there* and faster this time, ready for the assault, and then they were hidden and out. Andy gasped as he opened his eyes and the Scottish roadside filled his sight once more. Edgwick stood nearby, his hands held up by his face.

"Fuck me," he said, breathing hard. "You were all hyperventilating. What was it? I felt something a second ago, all the hairs on my—"

But Andy was already rounding on Maria, pointing a finger in her face.

"Don't *ever* do that again without asking us," he barked. "And when I say disconnect me, *you fucking disconnect me!* Okay?"

"Andy—" Paul began, but Andy whipped around to face him.

"No, Paul!" he snapped, slapped the side of his head with his palm. "This is my mind! *Mine!* Not hers! I have a right to say where I get taken and where I don't!"

"Okay," Paul said. "You're right. You're right about that, absolutely. But let's not—"

"I don't get trapped again! Ever!"

Paul didn't respond. He just nodded slowly and held up his hands. Andy turned back to face Maria, who was looking at the floor. Her face was screwed up from concentrating, and she was shaking.

"You're right," she said, nodding towards the floor. "I'm sorry. I won't do that again. It's not right. I just heard the kid and I . . ."

The anger bled out through Andy's feet. He could see the strain Maria was under. It didn't excuse what she did, but—

"Are you okay?"

"Yes," she said. "It wasn't as close as before, but I still need to . . . *ahhh* . . . oh, no," she finished, breathing out and looking up. Her eyes were even more bloodshot than they had been a minute ago. "*Oh no,*" she repeated, gritting her teeth and screwing her eyes shut.

"What?"

"The Stone Giant," she said, and bit her bottom lip. "It saw Eric."

There was silence except for the breeze.

"But we . . . we disconnected from him though, right?" Andy asked. "He got out before—"

"No . . ." Maria said quietly. "I didn't disconnect anyone. *It* did. It found him first. I couldn't hide all of us in time." Her fingers began to twist together. "First his friend. Now him . . ." She shook her head. "I can't find him again. He's gone."

She suddenly turned away from the three horrified men and walked a few steps away before pausing. "Let's . . . let's just get going," she said, speaking over her shoulder. Her voice was cold; it made Andy think of the analytical, alien eye of the Stone Giant. The old question came back, the one he and Paul had always wondered about Caementum during their attempts to communicate, the one they'd never answered: *did it have a mind?*

"No more stops until we get there," Maria said. "No more delays. Okay?"

She turned away without another word and walked off along the road.

Chapter Nineteen

Eric's Problems Double

***

Esther was upstairs grabbing pieces of her old bed-frame and thinking about how, yet again, Darren's *insistence* on buying this cursed place—and her reluctant agreement to go along with it—had come back to bite her in the backside. Now Darren was gone, buggered off to Thailand with whatever good-time girl had promised him the earth while he was there on business, and Esther was left—quite literally, in that current moment—to pick up the pieces. Her job managing the warehouse was an hour's commute both ways, the farmhouse was always falling apart at the seams, and she had come to hate both, but right now she would double the amount of hassle those things brought her—quadruple it—if she could get Aiden out of that awful prison of light.

Please, God, she prayed silently, let the madman downstairs be telling the truth.

Then she heard two things, and neither of them was anything to do with the Almighty: the first was a loud bang that sounded like the TV being knocked off its stand, and the second was Aiden screaming. She was already flying halfway down the stairs before Aiden's wordless yells turned into a single short sentence.

"Mum! Help him!"

She fell into the living room to see Eric lying on top of the fallen TV, his eyes rolling back in his head, arms wrapped around himself. Aiden was up against the bubble, hands and face pressed into it, helplessly watching Eric as he thrashed around on the floor.

"*It was red, Mum!*" Aiden screamed. *"Something came in and everything went re—"*

Aiden froze. Esther did too. Something had appeared on the floor, something they had already witnessed once inside their house. Aiden had described it to her afterwards; Esther had been outside hanging washing while it happened. *Why didn't you move*, she'd asked him through her own terrified tears; the answer was that he had been too scared. He hadn't been right for days beforehand either, but how could she have had any idea that *this* was going to happen? Aiden had panic attacks often, ever since Darren had left, and she'd thought it was another one of those. He'd calmed down a bit too, just for a moment, and she'd seized the chance to dry out the sheet she'd had to wash due to him wetting the bed the night before. If she'd waited just a moment more ... but right now, that didn't matter. What *did* matter was that it was happening again.

A circle of light had appeared on the floor around Eric.

It was a grimy silver colour, whereas Aiden's was golden, but Esther was already rushing forward to grab Eric, to move him out of the circle ... then she stopped.

"Mum! What are you doing, get him!"

Eric continued to twitch. Esther watched him, unmoving.

"MUM! GET HIM OUT!"

She wasn't hesitating for her own sake. She'd seen what had happened when Eric and Aiden had connected through the bubble, when Eric had touched the bubble alone. *Touch* seemed to be an important thing here; if she touched Eric, would she start fitting too? If she did, Aiden was dead. He would starve inside the bubble, if it never went away. If she were to grab Eric's arm to move him, she would have to reach inside the circumference of the dirty light. Would she be trapped too, dooming her son?

She suddenly turned and ran out of the living room as Aiden screamed after her. Rushing to the back door, she pelted across the tiny courtyard and round to the back of the house, where the washing line hung. Yanking the still-drying sheet free, she unhooked both ends of the line and coiled half of it up before charging back towards the house, trailing the rest of the line behind her.

"Mum!" Aiden called as she rushed back inside. Esther dashed over to Eric without a word and began to fashion a makeshift noose with one end of the line. She was sweating, breathing hard as she noticed that the dirty-silver circle on the floor had now formed a wall about two inches high while Eric continued to twitch on the floor. Leaning forward, she stretched out the shaking hand that held the noose and dropped it over one of Eric's feet, hooking it round and under his ankle like a clumsy game of Don't Touch the Wire. *"Yes! Yes!"* Aiden yelled. Esther gripped the washing line with both hands, wrapping it around her forearms, bent her knees and *pulled.* The line dug painfully into her skin; Eric wasn't a big man, but he was still an unconscious adult. Esther was strong, but it took a great effort and it hurt a lot to only move Eric about two feet.

The circle surrounding him moved along the floor with Eric as he did, perfectly in sync, and continued to rise.

"Mum! Mum!"

"I see it," Esther said calmly, gritting her teeth and pulling again. Eric slid towards her, and again the circle came with him. "Come *on*—" She yanked yet again, and Eric moved across the wooden floor, his soon-to-be prison of light following him like an inverse shadow. "*Dammit!*" She dropped the washing line and plunged her hands into her thick blonde hair, desperate and trying to think.

"Mum, please!"

"Shush," Esther said softly. Aiden did. Esther never, ever raised her voice to her son. Whenever she became mad or stressed, she also became quiet. "Thank you."

She couldn't let Eric end up in a bubble too—

Screw it, she thought, and darted around to Eric's twitching and lolling head. Taking a deep breath, she reached down and grabbed his arm. She froze, expecting her own fitting to begin. It didn't happen. Immediately, she began dragging Eric back towards Aiden's bubble.

"Mum, don't touch the—"

"I won't," she breathed, turning around and holding Eric by the elbow with both hands. Crying out with the effort, she yanked his body forwards, releasing his arm at the apex of the movement. It fell against the bubble, then bounced lightly away, his remaining hand sliding to the bottom of the glowing dome, where it lay on the floor, twitching. Carefully, avoiding the deadly golden light and the edge of Eric's own slowly-growing circle of dirty silver, she gingerly lifted Eric's forearm and slapped his unconscious palm flat against Aiden's bubble.

"Sweetheart," Esther said to Aiden, breathing hard but trying to keep her voice calm. "Touch his hand from the other side. Call the woman he called."

"No," Aiden said, "it's dangerous—"

"*Darling,*" Esther said, closing her eyes and breathing in through her nose, "the danger has already happened here. Do it or . . . just do it. *Please,*" she finished. She was shaking with the effort of holding Eric's arm, tired out, but she could feel the air pressure in the room changing. In a moment, the bubble would close, and both Aiden and Eric would be doomed . . . or she herself would be taking a helicopter to the Isle of Skye. The thought of leaving Aiden filled her with dread, but the thought of him starving to death was even more unthinkable. Crying, his bottom lip trembling with fear, Aiden crawled forward and put his hand against Eric's. "That's it," Maria gasped, forcing a smile. "You can do it, son. Now call her. Like you did before."

"I'm scared—"

"Aiden," Esther said, looking her son in the eye. "Be brave."

Aiden nodded and closed his fear-filled eyes.

***

The Skye Bridge lay before them: a simple, lengthy, up-and-over, no-frills stretch of concrete that would carry them to their destination. Andy, Paul, Maria and Edgwick were all too tired to talk about the view, the sea stretching out either side of the narrow road as they reached the edge of the mainland. The rolling hills and greenery of Skye rose up in the distance and along the horizon. The road up to the bridge still carried a few crashed and stationary cars, but not too many; once word of an Arrival had gotten out, it seemed, most people this far from Coventry had stayed home. Andy would have dearly loved to have been able to drive some of the way, but not only were the few vehicles they'd passed all too damaged—empty roads did not lend themselves to people driving slowly at the moment a murderous Barrier passed through their cars—but even if they hadn't been, the thought of getting inside a vehicle filled with the burst and dried remains of its previous driver was far from appealing.

Andy pointed wordlessly at the bridge, tired beyond measure; Paul nodded and even the hyper-focused Maria managed a thumbs-up.

"Not much further," Edgwick said.

"What?" Maria asked.

Andy wasn't sure who she was talking to.

"I said not much further—"

"No, not you—" Maria suddenly held up a hand, eyes wide. "Wait."

Andy and Paul moved forward, understanding what was happening; someone was communicating again. Eric?

"Come close," Maria breathed, and Paul and Andy stepped towards her.

"Show us—" Andy began, but Maria cut him off.

"We're just talking, nothing to see," she said, "just stand there and be quiet, it's easier to focus and hide you at the same time right now."

Andy bristled ... but then he felt it, Paul and even Edgwick doing so too, turning on the spot in fear as they looked pointlessly around themselves.

The Stone Giant was already closing in.

It was much faster this time; it must have been already looking, constantly searching for them, and now Maria was busy in Stone Space—

"It's here—" Edgwick began, breathing in sharply, but Maria flapped her hands frantically. Edgwick shut up. She stepped away some more, and Andy felt the searching eye of the Stone Giant move with her, focusing in like an iris with Maria at the centre. "I can see ... I can see ..." she fell quiet for a moment, breathing hard. "I can see *their* thread," she said, and Andy thought for the briefest moment that a grin flashed across Maria's mouth. "The signal they're following. Listen to me, listen to me ... I think I can ... I can ..." She snapped her fingers over and over, turning on the spot. "Eric's in trouble and I think I can save him," she finished.

"Paul," Andy whispered, the hairs on his neck standing on end as if they were alive, "I'm giving her ten more seconds and then I'm snapping her out of it. If she gets taken out long distance, this is all over." He could see the sweat standing out on Maria's brow.

"Maybe she knows what she's doing," Paul whispered.

"*Does* she?" Andy hissed back. Maria continued babbling to someone Andy couldn't see.

"Okay, okay, *okay*," she was saying "If I can see their signal, their thread ... what it looks like ... I can copy it ..."

"What's she talking about—" Andy whispered, but Paul shushed him.

"When I say *now*," Maria said to the air, "you tell your Mum to move him, okay? Don't move him until I have it fully ready, but when I say, pull him out of there as hard as she can. You hear me?"

"What are you *doing?!*" Andy yelled, and Maria's eyes flew open.

"A switcheroo," she snarled, and then closed her eyes as she began to repeat herself. "*Eric is* there, *he's* there, *he's* right there—"

The air around felt alive with static electricity, as if the Stone Giant itself were about to appear before them, and Andy felt the edge of something remembered, that he had never wanted to feel again: the urge to hide, to go to earth. As the crippling muscle cramps returned, as they had at the loch, all three men began to crouch in the road, to curl up in a gnarled ball. Andy saw the terror in Paul's eyes and it was indescribable, even as the big man tried to fight it. Here was the one thing Paul feared the most returning once more: to be the Target of the Stone Man. Andy tried to say Paul's name, but the words wouldn't come. He looked at Maria to beg her to stop, yet Maria continued her madwoman's refrain: "*Eric is* there*, Eric is* there, *Eric is* there—"

That was it. Maria was going to get them all killed for this guy.

Andy had to move now while he still could, before the locking up became too much to withstand. He bellowed, straining so hard to stand and move that the tendons in his neck and legs stood out like mooring ropes in a storm. Then he launched himself at Maria.

"*Andy, no!*" Paul croaked, trying to catch Andy's arm, but Andy was too quick. Paul's fingers caught nothing but Andy's slipstream.

Maria breathed in sharply just before Andy rugby tackled her, her eyes flying open once more, so wide this time that Andy, Paul and Edgwick could see the thick tops of the red veins around the edges of the whites.

"N—"

Andy collided with Maria, hard, knocking the wind from her and cutting the word *now* off before it could be completed. They both fell to the concrete and the connection dropped, the encroaching presence of the Stone Giant disappearing as quickly as the breath from Maria's lungs.

***

In Esther's living room the strength of this mystery woman's—this *Maria*'s signal was so great that for a moment even Esther's brain was picking it up too and she could see it: before her lay Eric, twitching and bucking on top of the fallen TV's broken screen, yet at the same time she saw *another* Eric laid over the original, stacked perfectly above his outline, slightly transparent and visible only when Eric's spasming body moved out of alignment with his doppelgänger. When Esther blinked, it took a moment for the second Eric to come back, and Esther understood that she was not seeing him with her eyes. Maria was duplicating the Stone Men's signal.

"Oh my God ..." Esther whispered as the penny dropped. "She's making a decoy..."

The second Eric became more solid but still wasn't perfect; it would glitch briefly, winking in and out of existence, before returning fully. It was clear that, however this Maria woman was doing this, it wasn't something she could do for long. "Now?" Esther called to Aiden? "Do I move him now? What does she say?"

"Wait!" Aiden yelled. "She said to wait!"

"Okay, okay," Esther said, crouching like a sumo wrestler, eyes locked on Eric and ready to pounce. She had moved around to his feet and had her hands frozen in mid-air, a few inches away from Eric's ankles; the circle of light had raised about six inches from the floor now and Esther felt that it could close over him at any second. She didn't want to have her arm waiting inside the shining radius when it did, but she could snap her arm in to grab him Eric's ankles lightning quick when Aiden gave her the cue. She'd just have to hope that the timing wasn't disastrously wrong ... then she remembered the line, the bloody *washing line*, and snatched it up, coiling it around her arms once more, the other end still tied to Eric's foot. A few seconds passed. Aiden suddenly sat upright like he'd heard something, opened his mouth ... and then froze.

"Now?" Esther yelled. "Was that the signal? Now?"

Aiden looked worried.

"I don't know," he said, blinking as if he were listening. "She's gone."

"What?" She looked down at the two Erics. The frozen, illusory version of him was almost fully solid now ... but wait, was it starting to fade? "Now? It's fading, Aiden, do I go *now,* what is she waiting for?"

"I don't know!"

"Shit—"

Fuck it. *Esther* decided it was now. She turned her back on Eric, the thin, harsh washing line running over her shoulder and biting into her forearms with a sudden, white-hot pain as she ran forward as fast as she could, pulling it taught with Eric tied to the other end. She cried out as she ran ten feet towards the door, surely enough to get Eric out of the circle, but as she turned around she heard both a faint *snap* sound and Aiden crying out in dismay.

Spinning on her heels, she saw Aiden with his hands over his mouth as he sat inside his golden prison, staring at the newly-formed, larger bubble made of cloudy-silver light that sat right next to his.

Eric was firmly encased inside it.

Another, more solid Eric lay a few feet away, and as the Eric inside the bubble finished slowly vanishing from sight, Aiden pulled his hands from his face and fell backwards with a moan of relief. Esther fell to her knees and let out a moan of her own. Tears threatened to come, but she stopped them. Esther never cried in front of Aiden, not even during those hellish few months after Darren left. That had always been kept to her bedroom, face stuffed into her pillow, crying it all out to bleed the poison away while her steel re-formed inside her; a good thing too, given the events of this afternoon.

Eric groaned and began to stir on the floor. Aiden sat up too at the sound, and Esther got to her feet as Eric let out a gasp and put his hand on the wiry rope around his ankle.

"*Shit,*" he gasped as the sharp pain of the thin plastic line cutting off his circulation began to register.

"I'll get some scissors," Esther breathed, crossing to a wooden unit in the corner of the room as Eric turned to see the now-empty, brand-new bubble behind him.

"Oh my God," he said.

"Yeah," Aiden said quietly. "Maria and Mum saved you. Maria confused them, Mum pulled you out."

But Eric was just looking at the bubble, his hand on his chest, horrified.

"*Fuck...*"

"Not in front of Aiden, please," Esther said quietly, squatting down and working the tips of the scissors under the washing line. Eric winced a little as she did it, turning back to face her.

"Thanks," he said, breathing out heavily.

"You're welcome," she said, snipping the line free, and then looking up into Eric's eyes, her own blazing. "Thank me by saving my son."

***

Andy hadn't meant to hurt Maria but he outweighed her by a good thirty pounds; Andy wasn't big, but Maria was small, and because he hadn't been in full control of his limbs his body had slammed into hers with considerable force. She cried out as she hit the concrete, but instead of rounding on Andy for his assault, she immediately began trying to scrabble out from under him.

"Get off!" she cried. "Get *off!*"

"Stop!" Andy yelled back, "Stop what you're doing! You have to, you're going to—*get off me!*" he shouted, realising that not only was his body back under his control but that Paul and Edgwick's were too; they were grabbing him, pulling him to his feet. Maria leapt up, spun away, and moved a few feet back, eyes screwed up and head down. "She's going to get us all killed!" Andy shouted. "You can feel it—"

"It's gone!" Edgwick yelled. "Calm down, calm down—"

Andy shook free of them and stepped back himself, eyes blazing, but his head went up as he tested the air. The presence of the Stone Giant was indeed gone.

"You're *welcome*," he hissed petulantly, pointing at them both, then turning to see Maria pacing on the spot. "She's going to do it again—" he began, and started towards her once more, but before Paul and Edgwick could stop him, Maria suddenly looked up and opened her eyes, staring Andy down.

"Eric's gone," she said, her voice dangerous and low. "I *had* him, I could have *saved* him if you'd given me one second more. I can't get him back—"

"Good!" Andy replied. "Stop trying, it's dangerous to be in there. That's the second time we nearly died in there, and you nearly screwed us all for the sake of one guy we don't even know."

"Yeah?" Maria said, face flushed. "You're pretty good at deciding who dies for the sake of everyone else, right? You're the guy? You're comfortable with that? Good for you. *I'm* not."

The blood left Andy's face.

"How do you know that? Who told you that?" He stepped closer to her. "Are you reading my mind? Can you do that?" He pointed a finger at her. "I fucking told you—"

"And I'm telling you," Maria said, standing up straight and marching so close to Andy that she had to tip her chin right back to look him in the eye. "*Don't* mess with anything *I'm* trying to do. You said to me *don't do this, don't do that?* That's fine, I won't. So don't you fucking *dare* make decisions for me either. But how do you want it, Andy? You want to run the show? *Absolutely fine*, I have *zero* problem with that, and I mean it. You're *Dispensatori*, right, after all. You're the top guy, the point man, the *shop window*, and me and him—" She pointed at Paul. "—are the engine room, the *goods in the back*. Again: you're *Dispensatori*. Fine. *But* the problem is this, and I really hate to say it: I was inside *there*," she said, pointing a shaking finger at his head, and again Andy bristled, but let her talk. "And even if I didn't mean to be, I've felt what's going on. And right now it seems to me that you possibly don't actually *want* to be *Dispensatori* anymore."

"You don't know what I do or don't want to be," Andy said quietly, but it was pointless. And he *wanted* her to keep talking.

"And what you want to be is your choice," Maria said, stepping forward, bloodshot eyes blazing. "However, I'm all that's keeping you alive right now, yes? I'm keeping you hidden. *Right now*, I'm keeping you hidden. Constantly, all the time, and it makes me feel *so, so* . . ." She closed her eyes and held up her hands. "It's not nice at all, Andy," she finished, looking at him once more. Her eyes were shining a little and suddenly the steam in Andy's chest began to dissipate. "It reaches out of me and it coats all of you and I'm spread so *thin*. I'm more aware of all the aspects of this situation than any of you know so *listen to me*," she said, her face screwing up as the anger returned. "What do you call it," she asked, her head cocking to one side as she searched through memories that weren't hers. Andy saw this and nearly bit, but he didn't, waiting for her to finish. "A *circuit*, we're supposed to be a circuit, right? That means we're a team." She nearly prodded him in the chest, but her finger just stopped short. "And if we don't have a leader that means we have to back the decisions each other makes."

"It nearly had us—"

"And we trust each other's judgement," she interrupted, "or we're going to be screwed. And yes, that *was* close for us, closer than I wanted, but I had to try. And that isn't the point, anyway." Andy's shoulders rose and fell rapidly. Maria stared up at him, and he could feel the eyes of Paul and Edgwick on his back. *"What do you want to be, Andy?* Are you fully in on this? Is your *heart* in this? Because if you want to be *Dispensatori*, we certainly need it. But that means facing your fears, making decisions, taking risks. Listening to everyone whenever possible." She sighed. "Can I mention Sophie without you attacking me?"

"... go on."

"I felt her messages too. What she saw in you. I think you're an utter prick right now ... but *I saw them too.* You *can* do this, Andy. We need the Andy Pointer that—" Her brow furrowed as she tried to pick the right phrase from a memory that wasn't her own. "—was absolutely going to jump out of that fucking window. We need *Dispensatori.*"

Andy blinked and looked at Paul, who stared back.

As always, he went back to his default response.

"Well, shit," he said, forcing a chuckle that was so false and sad that he was even more embarrassed by it. "Tell me ... uhh ... tell me how you really feel, eh?" He looked around for smiles that weren't there. He face fell ... but the gentle voice spoke up.

Let her go, it said. *She saved you for this.*

The black helicopter was still flying away in Andy's mind. He let it.

"Okay," he said, sniffing back tears. Edgwick was there. "Okay. And yes: we trust each other's judgement." He held out a hand for Maria to shake. She looked down, slightly surprised, then back up at him. She snorted, and her shoulders dropped as she shook her head and took his hand. There was no jolt—they were already circuit-bonded—but something passed between them on that empty roadside just the same. "But no more risks," Andy said, because of course he had to salvage *something* from her dressing-down, not realising that he just had. "Unless we *all* agree first."

"Sure," she said.

"And . . . maybe they got him out in time," Andy said quietly.

"Let's hope so," Maria said, after a pause. "I think the bubble was closing, though."

Andy turned around to look at Paul and Edgwick, but they had already turned and begun to walk towards the bridge.

***

Eric sat on the sofa, hungrily devouring a cheese and pickle sandwich. Beside him, as a bonus, was a bag of Wotsits. In other, normal days, Eric would have balked at the idea of going double cheese like that, but right now it felt like a banquet. As the food began to work its way into his system he was already feeling even sleepier. Colin had to still be a little way off; could he maybe grab ten minutes? Maybe even twenty?

Esther was in the kitchen making Eric a packed lunch for the road while he ate, and Aiden had even calmed down enough to pick up his Nintendo Switch and begin playing on it. Eric felt bad about breaking the TV; the signals might not have been getting through, but at least the kid could have watched some DVDs or something. Being stuck in a death-bubble was bad enough, but not having anything to watch would make it even worse.

If you don't get him out soon, Eric thought, *entertainment is going to be the least of his troubles.*

"You're going to come back to get me, right?" Aiden suddenly asked quietly.

Eric froze mid-bite, staring at the boy.

"Yes," he said. His voice sounded small, but his response was immediate and sincere.

But you can't beat them, he thought.

"Do you promise?"

The P word. There it was again. A shiver went down Eric's back ... but in truth, he knew something had changed in him the moment he saw the boy in the bubble and looked into his eyes, seeing Theresa and Aaron—and Jenny and Harry—staring back at him.

"Yes," he said.

Aiden nodded gently, understanding that an important agreement had been reached.

"Now will you promise *me* something?" Eric tried.

"What?"

"You don't try and contact Maria again unless it's absolutely necessary. It's not safe in there, as you just saw."

"I don't think I can without you."

"Good. You're already in a bubble so I don't know what else can happen, but I don't think it's good to be in that ... space, that other place." He waved a hand around his head to show what he meant, and Aiden nodded. "They're scared of something, you know."

"What?"

Eric noticed the kid didn't say *who*. Although he wasn't able to get the gist of it like Eric could, Aiden had heard the noise, after all.

"I think it's the lady we spoke to," Eric said. "I think they're scared of her. She's got gifts; I think we all do to a degree, but hers, and maybe the people she's with ... I think we can do something about everything that's happening." Eric didn't fully believe it, but he was choosing to try. "So don't give up, okay? There are good people working hard to save you."

"I hope so," Aiden said. "I don't want my Mum to be alone. She gets sad."

Eric was saved from responding by Esther walking into the room.

"Eric," she said, "come and have a look at this and tell me if there's anything else you want." She walked out of the room. Eric stood gratefully and followed, but when he entered the kitchen Esther beckoned him towards her without a word, silently opening the door to the small courtyard and disappearing through it. Eric followed once more.

"Okay," Esther said quietly, carefully closing the door behind Eric. "You said you saw other people in bubbles?" She folded her arms across her chest, hugging herself against the chill. The sun was low now, and the limited heat was draining from the day.

"Yeah. Yeah, I did."

"What happened to them?" She'd saved him from responding to Aiden but Eric didn't know if this was worse. He looked anywhere but at Esther. "You can tell me," she said, taking a deep breath. "I just want to know."

"They got out," Eric told her, the lie coming quickly and surprisingly easily. "Their bubbles eventually vanished."

"I'd believe you," Esther said, "if I hadn't seen your face when you saw *Aiden's* bubble." Eric turned away, shaking his head, but Esther sidestepped around into his line of vision "Hey," she said, not letting him escape. "I saved your life, I think. So: tell me the truth."

"Esther—"

"Tell me."

Eric closed his eyes.

"The Stone Men killed them," he said, having to take deep breaths himself now as his whole face screwed up tight. He heard Esther gasp but he kept going, trying to hold the tears back, the awful dam he'd built threatening to burst. "And they'll kill Aiden too if I can't get back to him in time." *Time?* He didn't even know if the Stone Man coming for Aiden had started walking, if it had even been *made* yet. If it was one of the already-existing Stone Men then there was no chance. If it had yet to be made, Aiden earmarked for the Stone Man that would built using pieces of Harry's spine, perhaps even now being constructed— "What you *need* to know is this," Eric said, opening his eyes and talking quickly to cut off his own thoughts. Esther's hands were over her mouth. *This is what you wanted*, he thought sadly. "If they come for him before I get him out ... what you need to do is ..." Her eyes pleaded with him above her fingers. "There's a window of time you see, and it's very short, and what you need to is ... you need to be ready to ..."

Eric was almost certain Esther didn't have a gun. The only way she could do the unthinkable would be up close and by hand.

"You can't stop it," he said finally. "There's nothing you can do. All you can do is help it be quick. I'm sorry." Esther let out a moan. "But I'm going to do my absolute best to ..." No, dammit. He'd promised. "I'm going to come back and save him," Eric finished, and now he was locked into it. The knowledge was heavy and frightening and he felt his chest tighten a little as he said it, and yet the burden somehow gave him strength. It was an odd feeling.

Esther's hands came away from her mouth and she grabbed a handful of her sweater, rubbing her eyes with it.

"*Please*," she said. "Please do."

There was silence in the small courtyard, save for the wind and the very faint noise of an approaching helicopter's rotary blades.

Chapter Twenty

Nowhere Left to Walk

***

Andy, Paul, Maria and Edgwick stood at the top of the approach to the Skye Bridge, the vast expanse of water ahead of them churning noisily away. It made Andy feel tiny, but even that paled in comparison to the Barrier, now he could see its outer wall in the distance; the waves smashed up against it, throwing up spray as they were repelled by its solid light.

They had reached the Barrier's edge, and from their vantage point they could now confirm it; the Barrier came down just a short way onto the mainland-side of the bridge.

It had cut the country off from the outside world.

It stretched away endlessly to the east and west, shooting straight up from the earth on the distant bank and above them, curving high up and over their heads and away to the south. It covered everything, shimmering in the rapidly-disappearing sun.

They would not be able to reach the Chisel.

"Oh . . ." Andy began, and then didn't finish.

"Yep," Edgwick agreed, his voice solemn. He handed Andy his binoculars. On the far side of the bridge Andy could now see a cluster of civilian cars, looky-loos from this remote, rural island, come to see the sight of a lifetime. Several military vehicles were parked there too, their personnel preventing the island's civilians from getting onto the bridge and approaching the Barrier's outer surface. A helicopter was hovering near the far end of the bridge; Andy recognised it as being from the Chisel. Standing close to the Barrier's outside was a handful of people, some of them wearing fatigues, some of them in civilian dress using various bits of tech.

"We can't get there, can we," Maria intoned. "It . . . it's covered the whole mainland, hasn't it." This was the first of them any of them had admitted out loud what they'd all known the moment they felt the Barrier pass through the helicopter.

No one responded. The sound of the sea and its accompanying breeze filled Andy's ears, his still-damp clothes cold and clammy against his skin.

"Maybe . . ." Andy began, handing Edgwick his binoculars back and trying to deny an idea so big and terrible that it was almost unthinkable. "Maybe that's a different Barrier to the one from Coventry," he tried, the truth feeling heavier than a cement truck. They all fell silent again. The edge of the Barrier was a only a brief walk away. Andy didn't know if it was the presence of Maria or merely instinct, but he *knew* everyone was thinking the same thing, talking around it. How could they think anything else?

"This is why that plane crashed at the start of all this," Maria said, extrapolating. "The ferry that everyone jumped off, too, back when the Empty Men arrived. They'd felt this was coming. It's like that . . . what did the conspiracy people call it, that thing that happened to the people the Stone Men were coming to see?"

"The Quarry Response?"

"That's it," Maria said. "They got the Quarry Response when they tried to get out before the *solid* Barrier came. Those poor people," she added sadly. Her easy empathy was a fascinating and alien concept to Andy. "They got caught up in it at the wrong time."

"You know about the conspiracy stuff?" Andy asked her.

"A little bit," Maria said, shrugging. "I did kind of have a reason to, wouldn't you say?"

"What was the point of the Empty Men, though?" Paul asked quietly, almost to himself, his voice full of awe.

"Can we not talk about the Empty Men, please?" Maria said softly. "I saw one kill my friend, up close."

"Okay. Sorry."

Silence.

"Besides," Maria continued suddenly, clearly unable to help herself and scowling as a result. "They don't even make any sense. If the Barrier was going to kill people, then why would the Empty Men even be needed?"

No one answered for a moment, unsure whether to respond given Maria's previous instruction.

"Well . . ." Andy began, looking at Paul, who shrugged. "Maybe the Empty Men were more of a precision tool, if the purpose of the Barrier was to . . ." He trailed off. To continue would be to acknowledge the truth. "Let's just get down there," he said. "We'll be able to figure it out once we get to the Chisel . . . if we can," Andy muttered, his eyes on the endless Barrier. He was surprised to not feel relieved; they were stuck after all, *oh well, nothing we can do.*

Uh-uh, the gentle voice said. *It's WWDD, now: What Would Dispensatori Do?*

Shit.

"Maybe you can do something to it, Maria," he said, but his voice was solid. "Get us through, and then if we get some dry clothes and a proper copy of the List, then maybe we can—"

"They're going to confirm the worst news you've ever heard," Edgwick said softly. He was looking through his binoculars and his voice was quieter than Andy had ever known it. "And then they're going to sign off on the stupidest *plan* you've ever heard."

"What plan?" Maria asked.

Andy turned to her, surprised.

"Surely you know?" he said, tapping the side of his head. "You've been in here. You've surely figured it out? I thought that was the reason you haven't asked what we're going to the Chisel *for*."

Maria shuffled on the spot a little.

"To be honest, yes," she said. "But I was hoping I was wrong. It seemed like the only logical answer, but I didn't want to confirm it." She shrugged. "I was actually hoping you were going to come up with something better."

"Nope."

"It can't be any dumber," Paul said, "than my driving-in-circles-in-a-field-in-Sheffield idea."

"That was a great plan," Andy said. The scope of the Barrier seemed to be making a sense of giddiness seize the group. It was that, he guessed, or go crazy. He looked at Maria. "You didn't need any of my memories to know what's waiting on the Isle of Skye, did you? *That* was pretty obvious." Maria shivered and took a deep breath.

"No," she said, her face darkening. "I didn't, and it was. Let's go, shall we?"

"Even better news," Edgwick muttered, squinting through his binoculars, "I've just seen the Brigadier."

"Straub?"

"Yep." Edgwick shrugged. "At least she's on the other side of that thing."

"Fucking *hell*," Andy breathed ... but he didn't mean it. The thought that the Brigadier was there was strangely comforting.

"Linda mentioned that name when we were on the road," Maria said, mentioning their lost ally for the first time since they'd built her cairn of rocks. She tapped the side of her own head. "But now it rings a *big* bell in here. Straub ... let me see ..." Her brow furrowed and Andy watched her putting things into place.

"Oh," she said finally. "Oh dear."

They walked down to the mainland end of the Skye Bridge.

***

Andy recognised some of the scientists milling about on the bridge but he was too amazed by the sight before him for his attention to linger on *that*. The Barrier was still staggering to see as it disappeared through the concrete of the Bridge's nearside and down into the sea below, the water continuing to wash up against it as with a dam. All that was stunning, of course, but not as stunning as the vision standing before Andy on the other side of the swirling, watery-silver wall.

Straub's face and eyes were red. She'd been crying.

"Ma'am," Edgwick said, saluting, but Straub waved him away from attention without a word.

"Brigadier," Andy said, trying to find his voice. *Straub crying*—"What are you doing here?"

"I got word you were coming and flew in from Coventry," Straub said, a faint tremor in her voice. "If I hadn't, we wouldn't have got out in time. If we'd been in the air when it hit—"

"We tried that," Paul said. "It was . . . rough."

"Holbrooks, then?" Straub asked. All four travellers exchanged a glance, and then Paul shook his head.

"No," he said. "Binley and Fletchamstead were with us too. And a former Project volunteer. Linda, uh . . ." He coughed a little and cleared his throat. "Linda Wyken." Straub nodded solemnly. Binley, Holbrooks, Fletchamstead and Linda were now notable by their absence; Straub didn't need to ask what had happened.

"I'm very sorry to hear that, Paul," she said.

"Thank you."

"Someone told you we were coming?" Andy said, confused.

"Someone in Coventry told me—"

"Eric?" Maria asked, speaking up. "You spoke to him? When?"

"A few hours ago," Straub said. "I don't know where he is now or if he's—"

"I only just spoke to him," Maria said, before adding, "sorry, I mean remotely, it's hard to explain—"

"He's still coming here?" Straub asked, brightening. "That could be very important."

Only Andy and Maria exchanged an uneasy stare this time.

"We don't know," Maria said. "He might be. He ran into some trouble and we got cut off."

Straub raised an eyebrow at Andy and Paul.

"Always a sod when that happens, isn't it . . ." She rubbed the back of her neck, a nervous smile running across her face then quickly vanishing. She gestured weakly at the Barrier. "We have divers checking where it ends in the water, but we don't expect to find an edge. Eric Hatton told us about the solid spheres of light the Stone Men have started using; there's no reason to believe this isn't a sphere too, albeit a lot larger."

"Brigadier," Andy said again, before hesitating; he didn't want to ask the question. "I've ... *Laura*," he said, and Straub's head twitched a little as he used her first name. Edgwick shuffled on the spot uncomfortably at the sound of it. "I've never seen you like this," Andy said softly. "What's—"

"Project Ouroboros," Straub asked Edgwick suddenly, ignoring Andy. "How many of the Sleepers survived?"

"None, Ma'am," Edgwick said quietly. Straub bit her lip and nodded.

"Yet here *you* are," Straub said to Andy, that worried smile running across her face again. "They can't seem to get you, can they?"

"It was Sophie," Andy said. "She ... yeah."

"Why didn't the induced comas work, Brigadier?" Paul asked. "Are there any theories?"

"Many. All inconclusive," Straub said. "Maybe they hadn't been under long enough. Maybe the Empty Men were different, had different senses. Maybe it was something to do with the anomaly in Coventry, more accurate searches and Targeting. The limited evidence we have seems to suggest it might be the latter, especially when it comes to Targets in general, but we just don't know."

"Evidence?"

"Before all the comms shut down almost completely," Straub said, putting her hands behind her back and looking at the sky. She was breathing heavily, but slowly. "The police reports we'd managed to gather, as well as our own findings, showed a very clear pattern. Everyone we know of that was killed by the Empty Men was GALE, the ones we couldn't get to in time."

"All of them?" Maria asked. Straub looked at Maria directly, sizing her up.

"You know about the List then," Straub said, and Andy's skin crawled at the implication; here Straub was talking freely about one of the biggest government secrets in the world, something she would have died to avoid before . . . before.

There was only one reason why Straub would so casually do such a thing now.

"Maria, I take it," Straub continued, smiling sadly. "Tell me; do you take antidepressants?"

"What?"

"Humour me."

". . . yes."

"Have you meditated for any extended periods of your life?"

"I used to be able to do it for over an hour."

"Hmm." Straub nodded. "I think you—all of us—might be very, very lucky indeed, Miss Constance."

"Do you know the name Ruth Wicker?" Maria asked, stepping forward a little. "My sister-in-law . . . was she on GALE?"

"Ruth Wicker," Straub continued. "I assume she . . ."

"The Empty Men took her," Maria said.

"I'm very sorry."

"Thank you."

"I memorised nearly all of the people on LION and GALE," Straub replied. "They weren't huge brackets, obviously, like CROW and TIN, but I could never quite get them all like I could with DIGGS. She may have been on there. I'll get someone here to check. Did she get her immune booster for the Panama Flu?"

"I don't know," Maria said. "It doesn't sound like the kind of thing she'd do."

"Did she volunteer for the Be Prepared appeal?"

"No," Maria said. "I didn't either."

"That's alright," Straub said. "You're here now. As it was, we couldn't contact everyone who was on GALE anyway; there was only so much time to get all the people we could with the communications we had."

"But the Empty Men noticed me, and I'm not GALE." Maria said.

"Field reports indicate they did that with nearly all Stone Sensitives," Straub replied, look out to sea and nodding to herself, sniffing back her tears, starting to steady herself now. "They got close to people and checked them somehow. They were drawn to some more than others, even if they weren't GALE. I understand their touch was very unpleasant."

"At Ladybower," Maria said softly, "when the Empty Men came back, when I was briefly there ... they felt like they were searching for three or four people ... but it was only one, wasn't it? Andy." She looked at Andy and Paul now, her circuit. "Your circuit was so strong ... that they felt all of us, one feeling like three..."

Andy nodded, shifting uncomfortably. Paul changed the subject.

"Maria's been boosted since then," Paul said, "Brigadier, she's stronger than Sophie *Warrender*. A lot stronger." Both of Straub's eyebrows raised.

"He's right," Andy admitted. "She's something else."

"Hmm," Straub said. "Very interesting ... and more evidence for the antidepressant theory."

"How so?" Maria asked. Straub pointed at her.

"Maria Constance. LION. All the frills I just mentioned can apparently bump people across by as much as one whole bracket, so you're GALE at best ... and you lived. You did more than live;

you hid yourself and others. How long have you been on antidepressants?"

"Since the First Arrival, but how did you know which bracket I'm in?" Maria asked. "I never had my—"

"You were listed as one of the first up close and personal encounters with Caementum," Straub said. "And you ended up in hospital. Did you honestly think we weren't going to take some samples?" Straub wagged a finger. "If you hadn't disappeared afterwards in all the chaos, we would have been *very* interested in you."

"It . . . it turned its head to look at me," Maria whispered. "The Stone Man. In the First Arrival."

Straub nodded, and then cleared her throat. She paused for a moment, looking at the ground.

"Alright," she said, finally. "To business. You probably understand what the situation is, but perhaps I'd best brief you on what we know, so that . . ." She cleared her throat again. "I need to be clear, and you will no doubt need some time to process what I'm about to tell you before we move on to the next stage." She paused, and shrugged slightly, taking a deep breath. "And even *that* is contingent on Eric Hatton arriving and being able to produce the goods, as they say, so we have at least until then, if he arrives at all."

A faint *pop* sounded in Andy's head. All four of them staggered slightly.

"What happened?" Straub asked, concerned.

Andy looked at the other three. Their eyes were wide.

"I think something just happened in Coventry," he said. "I think . . ."

"Something's arrived," Maria said. She suddenly stepped forward and went to slap her hand onto the Barrier. Paul grabbed her wrist.

"Wait," he said calmly.

"I'll tell you what I told him," Maria said quietly, equally calm. She gestured to Andy with her head. "We're a team now, and we listen to each other." She gestured at the Barrier. "Eric talked to me fine when he touched this thing outside Coventry, right? And we've only had problems when we've tried to use their signals long distance, without training wheels, when we've, I don't know, *hacked in* to their signal or whatever, to communicate with Eric. This is different. *This* is their landline; we only got in trouble when we were using their Wi-Fi. And if it isn't safe, I'll know as soon as I get in there, but something's happened in Coventry and we need to see what it is, don't we? Okay?" She yanked her hand free. "And can you all *stop* putting your bloody hands on me!"

"Sorry about the hand, you're right," Paul said, holding up his. "But you misunderstand me. I wasn't trying to stop you from doing it. I was trying to stop you from doing it by *yourself*. Like you said: we're a team now, remember?"

Maria reddened.

"Oh," she said. "*Oh.* Sorry."

"It's okay," Paul said, smiling softly. "Andy? You ready?"

"Yeah," Andy sighed. He didn't *want* to see. He just wanted to lie down. But he felt Sophie's arms around him now. He was *Dispensatori*, like it or not.

Ah bollocks, he thought.

"What are you going to do?" Straub asked, as Andy, Paul and Maria stepped closer to the Barrier.

"They're going to use that thing to see what the deal is," Edgwick said. "Have a look at Coventry. Sight beyond sight, that kind of thing."

"They can do that?" Straub asked, excited. "Is it safe?"

"No."

"And what do you do in all this?"

Edgwick shrugged.

"I take the minutes," he said. "Cheerlead. Look pretty. That kind of thing—"

But then Edgwick's voice vanished from Andy's awareness as the three of them moved into a vision clearer than any they'd seen before.

It was the Barrier, far below them and pixel-defined now. Maria was right; not only was this their landline, it was fibre optic speeds. He could see now—horribly—how the Barrier surrounded the country, a bumpy and uneven oval that covered all of the mainland and even some of the surrounding, smaller islands.

—Maria—are we good—

—(I think so)—(for now at least)—(you drive Andy)—(I'll keep watch)—

He didn't argue, and reluctantly he dove down through the Barrier's surface, shivering in his mind as he passed it, towing Maria and Paul's threads behind him. Underneath, the length and breadth of the darkened mainland was speckled with hundreds of little lights.

—Targets—

—I don't know Paul—maybe only potential as there's so many—maybe not fully Targeted yet—

Andy directed Paul's attention to the few, larger lights here and there, only a handful to his view.

—And I think those are the bubble things—

—*(they are)—(Coventry Andy)—*

Again, Andy didn't argue. The land below them began to zoom in rapidly, and as it did, he spotted a moving light heading north.

—What's that—

There was a pause.

—*(Paul)—(Give me more)—*

Andy felt electricity surge down Maria's thread, felt Paul pushing harder, and then happy relief flowed out of Maria.

—*(it's Eric)—(oh my God)—(he's alive and on his way)—*

—*That's great—but don't try to—*

—*(I won't)—(keep going)—*

Andy continued to fly towards Coventry, the lights surrounding them in the darkness like distant stars, and soon the thrumming mass of the Prism began to loom in the distance.

—*(stop here)—*

Maria's voice in Andy's head sounded strained; her thread was suddenly pained.

*—(if we go any closer I don't think I can keep
us hidden from it)—*

She didn't need to tell him. The Stone Giant's awareness was everywhere. It prickled around him inside whatever space he and the rest of his circuit were currently hanging, with only the blanket of Maria's protection to stop that prickling from becoming a stabbing, crushing vice. The darkness around them pulsed and bubbled now with a bright, powerful red.

—Do you see that, Andy, Maria—

He did. The Stone Giant itself, a hulking red outline from their vantage point, still remained motionless at the base of the Prism. Flanking it on either side were the reasons for the popping sensation they'd all just felt in their heads.

—Yeah—

Two Blue Stone Men stood shoulder to shoulder with the Stone Giant, hunched and waiting to awake. Their birth was complete. The number of Stone Men in the country was now nine.

**—The bubbles—Those two will be going to
them soon—**

Andy's trio watched in horror, as silent as the imposing trio standing before the Prism.

—Are we done—

That was enough. Straub swum back into view, partially obscured by a tumbling but flat waterfall of light. Andy blinked a few times and looked at Maria and Paul.

"Good job," he said, forcing a smile. It was brief.

"My God," Straub gasped. "You saw Coventry? Remote viewing?"

"Yep."

"... what did you see?"

"Two new Blues," Paul said, solemnly. "We think a Blue harvested this chap Eric's friend just outside of Coventry, then immediately appeared back at the Pri—at the anomaly, and used it to make new ones."

"They've sped it up, Brigadier," Andy said. "I think this is going to escalate quickly."

"But Eric's on his way," Maria added quickly. "I think ... I think he's in a plane or something."

"Hatton's definitely alive?" Straub asked, her eyes widening.

"Eric *Hatton*, then? Yes."

Straub's shoulders dropped just a little.

"Thank God," she breathed. "Without Hatton, we wouldn't even have ..." She shook her head, clearing the cobwebs. "Alright," Straub said. "Alright." She took a few paces backwards, and then steepled her fingers together in front of her mouth. She looked lost for a moment, and the sight of *that* scared Andy beyond measure. "Alright," she said again, and nodded. She looked up at the four people other side of the Barrier. "We'll do a quick briefing and I'll tell you all the information we have."

"A debriefing?" Andy asked, his denial in full swing. "Isn't there anyone else you need to bring here—"

The pain in Straub's eyes silenced him.

"My team is only me, the people you see behind me," she said, "and a few soldiers at the base." The gestured at the scientists behind her who were busily discussing something that they were examining on a trolley-mounted computer. "These people here. That's it."

Andy put his hands over his mouth. Straub waved her hand limply towards the ground. "You should all sit down," she said. "I have to start by confirming the bad news." She suddenly sniffed, and coughed, and when she continued speaking, she did so while looking down. Before today, Andy didn't think he had ever seen her do that.

"And the bad news has never been worse than this," Straub said. "Ever."

Chapter Twenty-One

Very Bad News and Another Stupid Plan to Deal with It

***

Colin's helicopter gently began to descend on the long stretch of road that led up to the Skye Bridge. The craft had been a lot smaller than Eric had expected, a little twin-seater: when Colin Renwick had told him he was a charter pilot, Eric had expected some kind of corporate six-seater affair. The pilot hadn't said much on the journey, or, to Eric's surprise, asked any questions. Colin was about Eric's build, and a little older, with thin black hair that was turning prematurely grey and a paunch that was coming in right on time, but his demeanour was almost like that of an distressed dog that had been left alone at home. His children were up north, he was divorced, and he just wanted to get to his kids. That had been pretty much all Eric had been able to get out of the man. Eric had given up trying to make conversation after a little while. He'd have expected Colin to be constantly saying things like *what the hell is going on man, what do you think they're doing, where should I go*, but there was none of that. Only a hundred-yard stare through the chopper's windscreen and a jaw clenched so hard Eric thought it might burst through the sides of the pilot's face. He was, perhaps, the single most focused person that Eric had ever met.

Despite everything, to his amazement, Eric had almost enjoyed the ride, for the portion of it he'd been awake at least. He'd never been in a helicopter before. Apart from the nerves he'd felt during take-off—and the landing that he'd just experienced—it had been almost blissful to sit and just float after the forty-eight hours he'd just had. After he'd given up trying to get Colin to talk, Eric's screaming, traumatised brain had mercifully, finally given up too and he'd drifted off into a light doze, the headphones and mic combo that Colin had given him to wear deadening the worst of the noise from the blades above. He'd warned Colin to be on the lookout for any strange movement in the sky ahead. As they'd finally approached the Isle of Skye, Colin easily spotted the Barrier in the distance: its movement distorted the reddening sky and gave it away.

The Barrier had indeed gone as far as the edge of the country then. Eric didn't even want to think about that. It was a concept far too rich with awful possibility.

Rubbing the sleep from his eyes, he felt around with his feet for the new rucksack of supplies that Esther had given him. Food, painkillers, water, a sleeping bag, and a five-year-old roadmap. It was better than nothing, and if he could get to the facility on Skye then he could get washed. He was grateful for the coat and plain grey T-shirt Esther had given him, too; apparently they belonged to her ex-husband. Both were a little on the large side, but they would do.

The helicopter's runners touched the concrete and Eric turned in his seat to face Colin and say his goodbyes and thank-yous. To his complete lack of surprise, Colin was still staring through the windscreen . . . but Eric thought there was fresh fear in his eyes, too.

"Thanks for this, Colin," Eric said into the headset mic. "Seriously. I can't even begin to tell you how much you've helped me. I'll never forget it."

Colin slowly pointed through the glass.

"Look at that thing," Colin's voice said inside Eric's headset. "They've cut us off from everywhere. Haven't they?"

"Maybe," Eric said. "I'm going to try and find out."

Colin finally turned his head Eric's way, considering him for a moment, and then he nodded at the door to Eric's left.

"When you get out," he said, "keep your head low and keep going until you're well clear of the blades."

"Okay. Colin . . . I have to ask you just once to reconsider, as you could be extremely—"

"I understand you asking," Colin said, "but my answer is still no. I'm going to my kids. Please don't ask me again."

"Okay. Okay. Thanks again, Colin. Good luck."

"You too, Eric."

Eric thought for a moment Colin would offer his hand but was glad when he didn't. He couldn't take another jolt today. He gave the pilot a smile and turned away, but paused, thinking of Aiden.

Aiden and Aaron.

He turned back to Colin.

"What are their names?" he asked. "Your kids?"

"Melanie and Cathy," he said. "They're ten and eleven."

"Did they ever get headaches during the Arrivals?" he asked. "Visions?"

Colin eyeballed him for a moment.

"I didn't put them forward for the Be Prepared appeal," he said. "I didn't want them having to be involved in that shit. They were way too young then and they're still too young now."

"I wouldn't either," Eric said. "But if they were Stone Sensitive then they might be, you know ... okay." He pointed at the Barrier.

Colin blinked a few times and his stoic expression nearly, *finally* gave way ... but it didn't. He spoke, though.

"You think?"

"From what I've seen they have a lot better chance than if they *weren't* Stone Sensitive, yes." He didn't add *why* they would still be alive; he suddenly pictured two little girls, eventually trapped inside two prisons made of light, Colin hysterical and helpless nearby. Aiden's face came back to him too. Half asleep, he'd almost forgotten the trapped little boy and his mother in that farmhouse. Almost, but never completely.

He'd promised.

"Thanks again, Colin," he said, and did as he was instructed, dashing away from the aircraft, bent at the waist. As he heard the blades speed up and felt the downward thrust of displaced air, Eric turned and waved at the helicopter as it disappeared into the sky. He didn't imagine Colin would wave back, but Eric felt a deep and profound sense of gratitude as he watched the aircraft leave. He watched until it became a speck in the dusky sky above, and then turned to face the road towards the bridge, the hills of Skye lying high and dark beyond. Grassland stretched away either side of the road to his left and right, where it ended at the water. From here—and he couldn't even begin to consider the alternative—he couldn't tell where exactly the Barrier came down; it looked very close to the mainland. Was the Barrier far enough out to allow him to follow the directions he'd been given? He didn't know.

After the time he'd had recently, surely God wouldn't be cruel enough to allow him to come this far, only to discover that he still couldn't get where he needed to go?

There was only one way for him to find out. He headed towards the bridge.

***

As he drew closer to the mainland end of the Skye bridge, Eric saw that, apparently, God *was* a bastard after all.

He had a funny sense of déjà vu as he approached; the Barrier's edge, a road, and a cluster of military vehicles and personnel. Nearby were some portable floodlights, turned off at the moment, but soon they would be needed; the last of the light was rapidly disappearing from the sky.

The difference was that, this time, there were four people waiting on *his* side of the Barrier.

One of them might be Maria Constance.

The thought was thrilling, even if he reminded himself that it wasn't magic at work here; Maria Constance was a mere human, a Stone Sensitive who, until the Arrivals began, would have been an ordinary person living an ordinary life. She perhaps didn't even have any more insight than any of the other Stone Sensitives. But she was powerful enough to counter the Stone Men to some degree, and that alone created a picture in Eric's mind of a shining saviour. Foolish, he knew, but it felt that way all the same.

The four people were seated on the ground. Three of them were wearing some kind of matching polo shirt uniform, giving them the appearance of just having finished work in an appliance chain store. One of them was dressed in regular civilian clothes and had a much smaller build than the other three, with long curly hair. Eric's heart leapt a little at the sight; could that be her? It sank again as he took in their posture; sitting slumped forward. They all looked defeated. One of them had his hand on his forehead and Maria, if it was her, looked as if she was hugging her knees. Already this didn't look like the strikeback against the Stone Men that Eric had been hoping for.

The light, visual-contact jolt suddenly passed between himself and the four of them—even more faint at this range—and the group turned as one to look in his direction. Awkwardly, Eric raised a hand as he walked across the lonely bridge. He could see someone in military uniform standing on the outer side of the Barrier, flanked by two people in white coats and with a few other soldiers standing nearby. The person was short—*shit*, was that . . . ?

It was.

Straub again.

Eric lowered his hand and continued walking.

By the time he was close enough to be heard without raising his voice, the woman he hoped was Maria had stood. The screeching in his head was loud again, louder than ever here in fact, but he'd become a lot better at blocking it out. He could keep it as a steady background noise right now anyway; the sound had morphed into some sort of base-level signal, containing no significant communication for him to pick out.

"Eric," she said, looking unsteady on her feet. Her voice was quiet. Stunned, even. "You made it."

I have, he thought. *Like I promised Harry*, and in that moment he noted that he'd actually kept a promise. He looked from Maria to the Barrier and hoped that maybe here was the beginning of him keeping his latest one.

"Maria," he said, smiling sadly. Once he was close enough, he knew it was her without question. "I ... I can't believe you're here." Maria just nodded, and her smile faded.

"I'm really glad you're alive," she said. "But ... uh ..."

Eric looked at the Barrier, and Straub standing just beyond it.

"Mr Hatton," Straub said, equally quietly. "I'm very impressed. You've done remarkably well to get here so—"

"Save it," Eric said.

"I'm sorry about your friend," Straub said quietly.

The image of Harry briefly flashed across Eric's mind like a slap. Straub had executed his sister, she'd said, the worst crime against his family ... but for the first time, having now seen the alternative, Eric wondered if Straub hadn't actually done Theresa a very big—

Then his jaw hit the floor.

All the way here, he'd been so busy thinking about getting to the great Maria Constance that he'd forgotten all about who she'd said was with her. That alone was insane; sitting on the ground was a man whom Eric had thought about the same way most people think about the Loch Ness monster.

"Andy ..." he said, raising a shaking finger. "Andy Pointer. Oh my *God*."

Andy Pointer, sitting on the ground, just nodded gently and held up a hand.

"Hi," he said.

Eric, starstruck despite the impossible Barrier shining in the air nearby—he'd already seen it that day, and here in front of Eric was someone on an Elvis's Ghost-level of mythology with the Stone Conspiracy crowd—now found he could only stand there with his mouth working. No complicated words would come, so instead he said:

"Hi."

Then he saw the big man sitting to Andy's left. and leapt about a foot backwards.

"You!" he gasped. "I saw you! In my head, during the Big Power Cut! You . . . you were pinned against a wall, in the air! You were screaming!"

Andy Pointer and the big man exchanged a glance.

"What's this now?" Pointer asked.

"Permutatio Protocol day," the big man said quietly, shrugging.

"Oh, oh, of course." Pointer turned back to Eric. "You *saw* that?"

"In my head," Eric said, pointing at his skull like an idiot.

"Hello," the big man said to Eric, raising a finger. "I'm Paul."

Eric was stunned. He'd seen visions of faces before but the one of Paul was its own legend; so many people in the forums had described the exact same image Eric had seen, right down to describing the walls inside the room where Paul had been pinned. Seeing him now, sitting here . . .

The only person Eric had zero connection to was the even larger man nearby. Whereas Paul was big like a barrel, perhaps a little soft as if he'd lost some weight, this other man was big like a wrestler. He looked solid, powerful, and his bright red moustache topped off the look of . . . well, a soldier. Had to be military.

"Hello," Eric said. The man nodded solemnly before looking at Straub.

"Are you going to tell him?" the soldier asked her . . . but Andy Pointer was looking at Eric curiously.

"Have we met?" Andy Pointer asked.

"Uh . . . no," Eric stammered. *Get it together man*, he thought. *You're making a bad impression.* Andy considered Eric, squinting.

"I feel like we have," he said. "I recognise your, y'know . . . *Stone vibe,* or whatever. Paul, do you . . . ?"

"Yeah," Paul said, looking concerned. "Yeah. Very familiar."

"Oh," Eric said, "I don't think we've met, no."

"You have a brother I might know or something?" Andy said.

"Okay, everyone—" Straub said quickly, interrupting.

"No," Eric said to Andy Pointer, colour draining from his face. He looked at Straub, who stared right back.

"Tell him," the redheaded soldier repeated.

"You'd better sit—" she began.

"I'm pretty sure I already know what you're about to say," Eric said. "I have eyes. I saw the Barrier move. What it does." They were big words for Straub's benefit; the truth was he didn't *want* it confirmed. He hadn't looked at the roads and streets below as he and Colin flew. He couldn't bring himself to.

"I understand," Straub said. "But you weren't here for the brief I gave these four, and I need to make sure you're all on the same page. Please, sit—"

"I'm not doing anything you tell me to do," Eric said. "But spit out whatever you have to say." Maria forced a sympathetic, solemn smile in Eric's direction; it was pity for what he was about to have confirmed, and it chilled Eric's bones. Maria quietly returned to the other four on the ground, and sat. The lab-coated man to Straub's right—a young but stressed-looking fellow— tapped the Brigadier on the shoulder.

"Brigadier," he said in a cracked voice, "do you want me to . . . ?"

"No, I have it," she replied. "Thank you. Mr Hatton . . . Eric—"

"Mr Hatton is fine," Eric said.

"Very well. Based on our list alone, there are only five hundred and thirty-nine people that are in the Stone Sensitive category, i.e. TIN and above. That number could be considerably higher, as that's only the people we have on the registry, and our people projected that number to be anywhere from one to two thousand out of the UK's total population. Based on what Maria, Paul, and Andy here have told Straub—the little lights and the bubbles in their visions—we believe those are TIN, LION, and DIGGS people."

"What about the other category? GALE?"

"You're looking at the very last one, we think," Straub said, pointing at Andy Pointer. To Eric's surprise, Pointer's hands swayed into the air at this, forming weakly-pointing finger guns. He 'fired' them as he smirked bitterly at the ground. "All the existing data suggests the Empty Men were successful in their attempts to carry out a purge of all the people on GALE, and we don't have any reason to believe that anyone in that bracket could stop themselves from being taken. If Maria here—LION—hadn't been boosted by *Paul* here, and present for the Empty Men's second visit to Project Ouroboros, Andy wouldn't be here either."

"Wait, boosted, what does—"

A horrible, heavy feeling began to drop into Eric's stomach. He looked at the people seated on the ground; all of them had lowered their heads again except for Maria. She was watching Eric closely.

"You're still not telling him," the soldier-type said. "Tell him."

Straub took a deep breath.

"I really think you should sit—"

"*Say it.*"

"Everyone else," Straub said, "everyone on CROW—would have been killed by contact with this Barrier. The Barrier that now seems to have expanded outwards across the entire mainland of the United Kingdom."

Eric stared at the Barrier. A glowing wall of death, and it covered the country.

"As best we can tell," Straub said slowly, "outside of those five hundred and thirty-nine to two thousand people—give or take—everyone else on the United Kingdom mainland is dead."

It wasn't a surprise, but the inarguable confirmation nearly took him off his feet.

"You . . ."

His right leg buckled, and he fell backwards onto his bottom. The large rucksack on his back stopped him from falling any further backward. Maria started to move towards him.

"Give him a second," Paul said quietly. "He needs to hear it."

Straub continued talking. He struggled to attach meaning to the words.

Everyone was dead. Everyone was *dead.*

"The early signs appear to be," Straub said, "that I am the highest-ranking surviving member of the British Army, and that the Minister for Education is now the highest ranking surviving member of the government, but we can't contact him or anyone else electronically." She was standing a little straighter now as she spoke, the autopilot nature of a briefing helping her through it. "We don't know for certain how many soldiers we have left inside the Barrier due to the rapidly-worsening comms issues, but the List tells us it would be a handful at best and we have almost no way of contacting them. Outside of the Barrier we have only a fraction of our total forces, including those here at the Chisel. We received broken communications from the beginning of the Fifth Arrival that appeared to tell us that many of our overseas military personnel are inbound, as well as those of our allies, but we can't confirm that. It appears air transport inside the Barrier below a certain height is feasible—"

"How ... many people are ... dead," Eric mumbled. He needed to rubber stamp it in his mind. "What are the numbers. How many have they killed."

Straub cleared her throat before continuing.

"Over sixty-six million people, Eric," she said. "The United Kingdom has, to all intents and purposes, fallen."

There was silence then. The wind blew gently, and the constant wash of the sea was soothing. Inside Eric's head, the screaming of the Stone Men's threads continued alongside the babbling rattle of his horrified thoughts.

"Take a few minutes," Straub said. "You have no idea how sorry I am to be telling you this. But time ... time is also of the essence." She sniffed in air sharply through her nose. "Eric, Paul here is some kind of battery for Stone Sensitives. We've never quite been able to find out how or why, but he is. If what you told me about being able to partially open these energy fields is true, then frankly you're our last hope, if you'll pardon the cliché. We're going to get you boosted and we going to see if you can't punch a hole in this thing."

Eric didn't answer. He continued to sit where he was, blinking at the Barrier in front of him, imagining it sweeping through Manchester, London, Birmingham, on to *Altrincham*, *Worcester*, the resulting red clouds spreading through the streets like a rolling wave before drifting to earth—

"I know you're in shock," Straub continued, stepping closer, "But we need you, *we need you*, and *now*. The Stone Men are already restarting their process, and it's already a *lot* more efficient. They're making more of themselves. If they get everyone in this country, that means a *legion* of them, and *that* means not only are the two thousand people left in this country doomed, but their numbers will easily be enough to spread off this island and onto the continents."

Eric finally focused his eyes back on Straub.

"... what?" he asked.

"I think that before," she replied, "we were a side project. Now—perhaps after how we handled the first Arrivals—we have become their full-time focus." She pointed at Andy, Paul and Maria. All of them were looking at the floor now. "And if you can't get these people through the Barrier," she continued. "Then there's nothing we can do about it."

"But..." Eric said. His voice came out as a wheeze. "What *can* we even do against ..." He looked up into the sky and stopped speaking.

"About two miles from here, Eric," Straub said, pointing behind her, "there's a crater."

"Here we go," Edgwick muttered darkly, shaking his head. He lay back on the concrete and covered his face with his forearm.

"The crater," Straub continued, "is about sixty feet deep and thirty feet wide. We filled it with lead, poured and set as a protective measure. We always had the lead ready to go from day one. As soon as the Fifth Arrival began, we poured it."

Eric was away with the Barrier again, shaking his head slowly.

"Eric," Straub said. "Inside it is the Stone Man. The original. *Caementum.*"

Eric's head came back down. He stared at Straub.

"It was destroyed," he said. "You idiots destroyed it when you test-fired the Chisel device—"

"No," Straub said. "Andy and Paul here shut it down. They stopped it walking. It's been completely dormant ever since, at least in terms of circuits and movement, even if it's still giving off a lot of energy that we don't really understand. Eric, there was an Arrival event at our facility in Sheffield and the Stone Man was supposed to be flown away from it, to Greenland, as per the established protocol. Long story short: flying it away from Paul severed its weakened connection and the resulting release of energy ... well, that was the Big Power Cut you mentioned. Unfortunately, it also fried the helicopter transporting it, which crashed here."

"Here," Andy said bitterly, "*not* Greenland." Straub ignored him.

"There was always *concern*," she continued, "about how much the Caeterus—the Stone Men's overseers, if you will—knew of what Paul and Andy knew. Initially, it was agreed amongst our scientific advisors to keep its actual location secret from the pair of them, but once we decided it was prudent to get these two back to work with the Stone Man, they were brought up to speed *as soon as possible*," Straub finished, aiming this at Andy, who scowled ... but then Straub shook her head. "My apologies," she said. "Now isn't the time for pettiness. It's ... it's been a long day."

Eric saw Andy suddenly look up, horrified.

"Your husband ..." he said to Straub, who quickly shook her head.

"Not ... now," she said quietly. "Not now."

"Laura ..." Andy said. "Oh God. I'm ... I'm so sorry ..."

Eric watched Straub cough and then attempt to compose herself. *My God*, he thought. *What is this woman made of?*

"We—" she began, and coughed again, covering her face with her palm. Someone switched on the nearby floodlights and Eric had to shield his eyes until they adjusted to the sudden brightness. "We staged a chemical spill here," Straub continued, her voice lightly wheezing, "and declared that section of the island a disaster area. Andy and Paul have been trying to work here—with our volunteers—ever since, or rather until we poured the lead the moment the recent Arrival began. They were trying to help us find another Watchmaker to communicate with it. Without one, we couldn't even begin to try ... but now we have Maria here."

Eric didn't know for certain what a *Watchmaker* was, but he got the gist: Maria was a connector of some kind.

"We think we know why the Empty Men targeted GALE people," Straub said. "That's the only good news here. It makes me think the plan we have is going to work." Andy made a little pained noise at this and shook his head slightly. "The people on GALE were the only people who could 'flash in' to the Stone Men," Straub said, ignoring Andy, "and Andy here is the last one, as I say. Fortunately for us, he was the by far the best at it. Combined with Sophie and Paul, he did something that whatever is running the Stone Men didn't expect. I think without the anomaly of Paul we never would have been able to do it, but Andy stopped the Stone Man. It was only very brief, but he *controlled* it."

Andy sat up, realising something.

"... could the Empty Men have come ... *because* of me?" he asked. "Because of what we did? They came to take out the people like me who could ..."

"We'll most likely never know," Straub said. "Maybe they normally come as part of the process? To make sure the threats are all taken out before the next stage begins? It sounds likely."

"But Paul and I could be cut off—"

"From following the signals to Targets, yes. But with a Maria Constance or a Sophie Warrender around, it seems like you can make your *own* connections. We don't know why it took so long for the Prism to arrive; maybe it was always coming? Maybe it was a new tactic after we found a way to keep their lynchpin in place? Again, we don't know. Regardless: the *Prism*, as you call it, has apparently turned a harvesting process that once took months—from the point of harvest and disappearance to returning with reinforcements—into one that takes *minutes*. The Prism looks to be made out of the exact same stone-looking alien substance Caementum is made from. Indestructible." Straub made her left hand into a fist and held it out in front of her, her wrist turned inwards. "But how do you cut a diamond?" she asked.

She raised her right fist and touched its knuckles to her left, rubbing them gently together. "With another diamond," she finished.

Eric got it.

"You mean . . . you want to use the Stone Man . . . ?"

"Paul was dying at the Project," Straub said. "We thought it was because he was boosting the volunteers, but that wasn't the main reason. He was dying *because the Stone Man* was dying, and it was draining Paul of all of he had, or at least taking it and storing it. What was left inside Caementum after it crashed has been slowly bleeding out of it for the last year, and whatever internal defences it has will be weaker than ever. But now Paul is fresh, and Maria is here too. A year ago, even with a worn-out Paul and a less powerful Watchmaker, we managed to control the Stone Man enough to stop it."

Straub looked at Maria.

"We really want to know what we can do with *her*." Maria opened her mouth to protest at being talked about as if she wasn't there . . . but then just nodded.

"Wait . . ." Eric asked, staring at Straub in disbelief. She was hard to see, cast into shadow by the floodlights behind her. "You want to wake it up?"

Straub's words came to him from her now-featureless black outline. For the first time, Eric heard barely restrained emotion in Straub's shaking voice. She was speaking through gritted teeth.

"I want you to open this Barrier, Eric," she said, "and I want *these* three, if they can, to take the Stone Man all the way to Coventry. Then you're going to smash that fucking monstrosity that has parked itself on Ground Zero. You're going to free everyone left alive under the Barrier and put things back on the months-long Stone generation timescale that will buy us, and the rest of the world, some time to plan our next move. But first things first: yes, Eric. I want them to wake the Stone Man."

Her arm came up and pointed the way Eric just came, back over the Skye Bridge.

"And then I want them to *drive* it."

TO BE CONTINUED IN
THE STONE MAN, BOOK FOUR:
MARCH OF THE STONE MEN

Author's Afterword

This is going to be a short afterword for once because, even more so than after THE EMPTY MEN, I can't say too much as we head into the finale (which, as readers of YOU SEE THE MONSTER and it's afterword know, is called MARCH OF THE STONE MEN: THE STONE MAN, BOOK FOUR) without potentially spoiling things or showing you behind the curtain before the story is concluded. So this one will simply be some thank-yous, a little bit of news, and then the usual public begging letter for you-know-what.

Firstly, thanks go to Jeff Hughes for writing to me a few years ago with the numbers for what turned into Paul's rant to Straub about how many Arrivals it would take for the world to end. It was so good that I had to use it at some point, and halfway through writing this book I realised that Project Orobouros would be the perfect place. I asked his permission to use it here and he graciously agreed. Thanks Jeff.

Thanks again to my editor, the great Sam Boyce, whose input was essential, as was her patience and begrudging acceptance of how I mark up my documents. Big thanks also to Barnett Brettler for giving his two cents again and reading, I think, about three different versions of this book, unpaid. Emma Carter was again extremely understanding in her explanation of genetic research to an idiot, and if I wrote anything here that flies in the face of the human genome then that is entirely due to my error, not hers. I also apologise for any mild liberties that I may have taken with the landscape of the UK. Thanks to Kristin Nelson and Ryan Lewis as well as the team at Audible UK.

And a big thank you to the readers who took the time to write a review on Amazon. You didn't blow the reveal of Andy's return, as requested. You did me proud. Smithereens: they'll surprise ya. Usually when you let your guard down for just a second, and especially if they're hunting in packs. If you enjoyed this book, please leave a star rating on Amazon and Goodreads and help spread the word. Come on. Ah, come *on.*

So: news.

The response to both THE EMPTY MEN and my non-Caementum-related YOU SEE THE MONSTER (available now, folks) have been really gratifying and I give a large part of the credit for that to working with an editor for the first time in my career, namely Bad News Boyce herself. I actually feel so strongly about it that I find myself looking at TSM1 and wishing that it could have the full edit that a then-even-more unknown writer couldn't afford; no changes to the plot or structure, but a tightening of the prose and a cutting of the fat. This leads me to the announcement that 2022 (should be. Should be. I have a great track record with these things) will see the release of both the text and audiobook versions of *THE STONE MAN: THE STONE MAN, BOOK ONE, **SPECIAL EDITION.***

Here's what that's all about. There's nearly ten years between the book you've just finished reading and the book that started it all. I've had to do a lot of learning in public, and I want any new readers that discover my work to see it in the best possible light. Don't worry; I won't be replacing or removing the original version, but I thought maybe it might be nice to release a separate, freshly-edited Special Edition of TSG either between now and MOTSM (or perhaps a same-day release with the fourth book in order to make it more of an event, I don't know yet). *Ah, but Smitherd*, I hear you think (I can hear you think), *why the hell would I want to buy a book I've already read? An edit alone wouldn't be enough to make it worthwhile for me to revisit it, you piece of shit. You make me want to put sticks in your eyes.*

Yeah? Take those sticks and whittle them into toys for children instead because TSM: TSM, B1, SE (christ!) will have not one but at least six lengthy deleted scenes from the series. These are:

—A cut chapter featuring what happened on board the plane that crashed in THE EMPTY MEN.

—The dramatic original beginning from THE EMPTY MEN featuring a present-day Maria, her work colleague, and the Barrier turning up to commence the Fourth (actually Fifth) Arrival.

—The original at-home meeting of Maria and Linda, including the return of David the government spook and a monkey (I'm not kidding about the monkey).

—Eric's violent encounter with another Barrier survivor on his way out of Coventry.

—The original, longer and uncut scenes from the helicopter journey, seen from Paul's perspective featuring lots of nice interaction between Paul and Andy.

—And the originally-published-and-then-removed scene from THE STONE MAN where Andy wrongs his brief host, Sean, in the worst way.

Sound good? If it does, why not join the *Luke Smitherd Spam-Free Book Release Mailing List* over at lukesmitherd.com to be alerted when that weighty tome goes on sale. And as always, if you'd like a Smithereen Title so that the airport know to send you to the lane marked INTENSE INTERNAL SCRUTINY, just drop me a line, and your name could be in the Acknowledgements section of the next book just like those of the people who had nothing better to do that are presented here.

I'm really, really looking forward to writing Book Four and I hope to have it out for summer 2022. It's easily going to be the most action-packed book of the series; shit is about to go down and no mistake. As for the book you've just finished reading, I experienced a genuinely warm feeling as I wrote about Paul and Andy again, as well as figuring out the new dynamic of these two changed men as years-long friends; it really did write itself. *Dispensatori* proved to be worryingly easy to conjure up again (perhaps partly because, in my head, he never went away, and was just waiting to be called up from the bench). It's the first time I've ever revisited a lead character (same with Eric and Maria here) and I enjoyed it very much. Sincere thanks to you for coming back for more of his adventures along with, Paul, Maria, Eric, and of course poor Linda and Harry. It made me sad to kill off Linda, but I feel like a *real* arsehole for doing away with Harry.

It might have stung some of you; I'm sorry for that, and I liked him a lot. So did Eric. I think that, when he finally gets out of his funk, he's going to be looking for revenge.

But first they have to wake the Stone Man.

Stay hungry, folks.

Luke Smitherd

January 23rd 2022

Heathrow Airport

Insta: @lukesmitherdyall

Twitter @lukesmitherd

Facebook: Luke Smitherd Book Stuff

*Before we sign off for a little while, here's the opening chapter from my novel **YOU SEE THE MONSTER**, available now in all formats!*

You See The Monster

Chapter One: 2002

***

Sam sits in a café. His coffee is now cold, but the taste was disappointing long before that. He wouldn't have chosen this place to meet. Melissa did.

The clientele says everything Sam needs to know about the establishment, in that there are no other customers present; the only other people there are staff. There's a middle-aged, scruffy-looking gentleman sitting behind the counter reading a paper. There's a woman somewhere, possibly his wife, who wanders in and out occasionally from the back room, saying nothing. There's a large mirror on the wall to the right of the counter, presumably mounted in an attempt to make the place look bigger. It doesn't work, perhaps because the edges of the glass have been plastered over the years with now-faded stickers. The floor is tiled, the walls are tiled, and sounds from a tinny radio echo unpleasantly off both ageing yet impervious surfaces. Sam possesses one out of those two qualities.

Melissa is late—very late—hence the cold coffee, and even though Sam expected that, he's worried that he's already angry.

This was always going to be a difficult conversation, but going in with a hot head certainly won't help. He'd told Leslie to stay at home. It took a three-hour argument to get her to listen. Sam has a decades-long history of saying *yes dear* to his wife, but this is one issue on which he is adamant: Melissa has hurt Leslie enough, and she wasn't going to be present for this. Sam realises he's gripping the handle of his cup way too tight. As long as she doesn't bring that piece of shit with her. Even Melissa wouldn't be that difficult, surely? She knows not to wave a red rag like—

The café door pings as it opens. Sam looks up and for a second thinks that Melissa has no-showed and *oh she wouldn't*, sent the piece of shit by himself . . . but Sam sees he's wrong. The man walking in is long-faced, like the idiot, and unkempt, like the piece of shit, but he's too tall, too stocky, and too well dressed: a full suit and tie job, shoes clean and shiny. In his late thirties, perhaps. Sam notices details like this. He's police, after all. It's 10:27. Sam's brain goes into processes so automatic he doesn't even consciously know they're happening:

Too early for lunch, but anyhow he eats at nice places. A salesman, maybe, needing a coffee to keep him going—

Sam's eyes go back to the door.

"Hello," he hears the man behind the counter say, a slight sigh in his voice as if two customers in the room at once constitutes an early rush. The newcomer mumbles something in response. "Sorry?" the man behind the counter repeats.

"Just a . . . can of coke please." The suited man is audible this time.

"Right." Again, a slight sigh. Some people are never happy. Sam looks at his watch again. Doesn't Melissa realise this is her last chance? He hears a chair scrape out as the newcomer sits down, followed by a faint rustling of paper. Sam's eyes move in that direction of their own accord; the man has pulled a folded piece of yellow-looking paper out of his pocket and is now staring at it intensely. Even though his mind is elsewhere, some instinct in Sam keeps his eyes on what the man is doing. He fumbles with the outer corner of the paper, eyes dark and serious, fingers lightly playing with it . . . and then he slowly tears the very corner off.

He keeps the torn-off piece in his hand, looking between it and the paper still held in his opposite grip. The piece he's torn off is tiny, slightly bigger than a postage stamp. It's mildly weird behaviour, but Sam's bad-guy radar isn't going off. In fact, this fellow barely seems to register in his awareness at all, for some reason. It's almost as if the reason Sam keeps looking at him is to remind himself that the man is still even there.

The door pings again and Sam jumps a little in his seat, but quickly comes back to himself as he sees it's Melissa. He mentally winces as he spots two things: she's skinnier than ever, and she's brought the piece of shit with her. Sam's immediate anger switches to a sudden, deep sadness as he sees a faint smile appear on Melissa's face. She saw Sam's expression as the piece of shit walked in. Sam realises this and understands exactly how the conversation will end. He did the right thing not letting Leslie come.

Sam stands up. Melissa reaches the table, her grey jeans, black cardigan and T-shirt creased and unkempt-looking. The POS stands behind her, shifty as ever, gaze darting anywhere around the room except at Sam. Sam still doesn't know how old this man is. Thirty? Thirty-five? Melissa won't tell him and, despite all his contacts and skills, Sam hasn't been able to find out. *Jake's off-grid*, Melissa had proudly parroted, clearly believing that the piece of shit is some kind of shaman, and not a waster from Binley. That said, the off-grid thing may be why Sam can't even get a surname. Leslie wouldn't let him have them tailed. She's always been too soft, too damn *coddling*, and Melissa realised it from the time she was three. Sam knew he was to blame too; if he'd worked less, hadn't always been chasing those promotions, he could have been there to balance it out. By the time he'd realised how bad things had become, so bad that even his weapons-grade denial couldn't curb the truth anymore—when Melissa took the family car for a spin at sixteen, drunk behind the wheel—it was too late. Now she's about to throw her life away with this scumbag.

"Mel," Sam says, trying to keep his voice steady. "I asked for this to be just you and me." He doesn't look at the POS. Melissa makes the face he's seen far too much of in recent years; the one she's *always* ready to pull. She's always waiting for somebody to say something, it seems.

"And I told you, Dad, that Jake is part of my life now and you have to *accept* that," she says, deliberately loudly of course, so the guy behind the counter and the suited man look their way. The latter looks away quickly, eyes back on his folded and yellowed paper—Sam notices he has another torn-off piece between his thumb and forefinger, the previous one now discarded on the table. "I'm eighteen." Melissa lowers her voice, much to Sam's amazement. "I'm an adult now. *You can't tell me what to do.* I don't live under 'your roof' anymore. So if I want to bring Jake, I will. You're the one who wanted this meet-and-greet." Eighteen. And shacked up with a weirdo old enough to be her dad.

It takes everything Sam has not to snatch the ashtray from the table and bludgeon Jake over the head with it until he's a bleeding mess on the floor, but he manages to keep at least *that* instinct in check. Other internal safety measures are falling away with terrible speed, however, and although Sam feels this, he is powerless to stop it.

"Maybe I should, uh, go," Jake mumbles, both his hands in his jacket pockets. "This is a family thing, and—"

"No, she's right," Sam says, suddenly wanting Jake to stay. If that's the way Melissa wants to play, Sam can fucking well play it. "I'd actually like to ask you some questions, Jake. I was going to ask Melissa, but, seeing as you're here—"

Leslie would be losing it at him right now. Another good reason why she wasn't here.

"Don't you fucking dare," Melissa hisses, leaning forward. "You aren't at work. You aren't *questioning* him."

"Didn't say I was, I said I'd like to ask questions, there's a difference—"

"What? What about? What do you suddenly want to know about Jake? You've never asked anything before." Super defensive. Melissa always was a terrible liar, despite a staggering amount of practice.

Sam's heart breaks. He hadn't wanted to believe the worst, the final straw, but Melissa's classic *what, what* told him everything he needed. This was it. He couldn't let her hurt Leslie anymore. They'd failed their daughter in the worst way, but it was Melissa who had banged in the final nails. Like she'd said herself: she was an adult now.

"You know what about," Sam says, and as he sniffs back tears he sees Melissa's screwed-up bulldog expression soften, *just for a moment*, and in there is the little girl he'd delighted with a surprise trip to Center Parcs when she was six. Then the gate falls again and Adult Melissa is fully behind the wheel. The liar. The thief.

"Grandma's necklaces."

"What *about* Grandma's necklaces?"

It's utterly unconvincing. With that sentence Sam feels something profound break off inside him and begin to float away. It leaves a hole that will never fully heal over. Shrink a little— maybe even a lot over the years—but never reconstruct.

"Was it for you?" Sam says, addressing the piece of shit as a flood of sadness automatically switches to anger, as so often with men. "Did you put her up to it? How much did you even *get* for them—"

"Dad!"

"I'm talking to him—"

"I'm gonna go," the POS says, face flushed, already abandoning his girlfriend, of course. "You guys, uh, you—"

"Dad, what the fuck do you think you—"

"Hey," says the man behind the counter, finally waking up, "can you take this outside, I have customers here!" Sam isn't listening, he's already rounding the table, heading after the piece of shit, flushed now himself, not thinking, but of course he really knows *exactly* what he's doing. Sam's always-on-the-details eye notices that the suited man still hasn't moved, although even more of the paper has now been torn away and . . . is he *crying?*—

Sam's hand grabs the piece of shit's retreating shoulder and Melissa screams. Part of Sam knows this will destroy any remaining hope of a reconciliation with his daughter, but perhaps that's exactly why he's doing it. Rubber-stamping the moment. This was the one thing he'd told himself *must not happen* if Jake turned up, and here he was deciding to—

The POS spins round and slaps Sam's hand off him, shoving Sam away as he does, an action that gives Sam's thick fist the instinctive excuse it's so very hungry for. Sam isn't a big man at 5'9", but he's always had big hands, ones he knew how to use once upon a time. His muscle memory is good, it seems; all the anger, the hurt, and of course the thing that's really behind it all—the knowledge that he let this happen to Melissa and how she's become completely alien to him—shoots down Sam's arm and empties beautifully into Jake's nose. *Smack.*

Jake, Melissa, and the man behind the counter all cry out at the impact—Melissa's is a screech so high Sam almost expects the windows to shatter—and Melissa barges past to get to her boyfriend. Jake's already getting up, a shaking backwards lurch intended to get him as far away from Sam as possible, but the red mist is already leaving Sam's brain and he's realizing just what he's done. It was out of his control, it had just taken him over—

No. He knew what he was doing.

"Fuck you!" Melissa yells, bundling Jake towards the door as Sam opens his fists, holding them out to her stupidly. *"Fuck you! You aren't my dad! You aren't my dad!"*

Sam opens his mouth to say *Melissa, wait . . .* and then doesn't say a word. He just stands there, a storm blowing in his brain that blocks out all thoughts. His pulse beats, hard, and he falls back against the nearest table. His hands are shaking. He watches through the fogged-up windows of the café as Melissa and Jake hurry down the street.

Leslie is going to . . . Sam thinks. *She'll . . .*

But how *will* Leslie react? She must have known this was going to happen, or something like it. They both did.

He looks up towards the suited man and now it's Sam's turn to scream.

The suited man is no longer sitting in the chair. There's the detritus he's left on the table, but that isn't what Sam's looking at, even as he hears the man behind the counter make a strangled sound, repeating *ahhk ... ahhk ... ahhk.* He hears movement as the woman comes out from the back once more.

"What the hell—*OH MY GOD! OH MY GOD!*"

Tables screech as they are flung aside. Sam dives sideways on autopilot, trying to get to a chair that he can swing even as his mind curls up into a ball and gibbers in terror. His big hands grasp two of the nearest chair's legs and he spins round, barely able to hold it, but the attacker has already darted straight to its target: the couple behind the counter.

"*RUN KELLY, RU—*" the man bellows, but it's already too late. The attack is so *fast*, his throat's torn open before he can even finish his sentence. Blood sprays across the room as the man is flung aside and though Sam's legs are telling him to take the man's advice he tries to get to the counter, raising his weapon high, a man wading through water as he attempts to get around the cluster of overturned tables and chairs between him and the woman. She makes a critical mistake, moving out towards Sam— automatically seeking protection, perhaps?—and not towards the back room. Her screams of dismay for her murdered partner— and terror for herself—hit a pitch even higher than Melissa's earlier shriek and Sam knows it's too late. It's a cry of agony as she's torn from crotch to sternum. Bellowing, Sam throws the chair. It misses wildly, shattering the mirror by the counter, and unless Sam can get to another one *right away* he's dead, the speed of the attacker is insane, he probably only has a second or two—

Sam clutches another chair and jerks up with a cry—*AH!*— ready to swing for dear life, thinking only of Leslie now, but he sees he's now alone in the café. The only sound is the tinny, now blood-spattered radio playing away to itself, and Sam's I'm-going-to-start-working-out-this-year breathing. He jumps backwards, eyes frantically sweeping the floor; the attacker's down under the tables!

The attacker is not.

The back room, an exit! While he was looking around for a chair—

He hesitates, light-headed. Spots dance before his eyes. Something shoots down his arm. Wait, is this—

It is. It's really happening. His heart finally rebels after too many steak dinners with a nice red; he drops to one knee as the chair he's holding clatters to the floor. He grunts, trying to stay conscious, fumbling his phone from his pocket. If he doesn't get someone out to him, he's going to die. No one will ever know what the hell happened here. *Leslie* will never know—

"Emergency, which service?"

At that moment, his brain catches up. *Well bloody hell,* it says, like a drunk wandering in after the fight scene. *What on earth did I miss?*

It's not possible. It's just not.

With that, as Sam grunts out the name of the café, holding on—quite literally—for dear life, he's already making a decision, even if he doesn't consciously know it: *all this didn't happen.* He'll give the description of the suited man and how the couple at the counter were butchered, but he'll leave out certain elements. If someone were to know the truth and ask him why he chose this approach, he'd maybe tell them his family had just been shattered, that it was too much to deal with. Or that he had his eyes on promotion and didn't want anything on his record that might jeopardize that. Good, reasonable explanations.

The truth would be that Sam is simply scared out of his mind and attempting to file the unspeakable away is the only option available to his psyche.

He wouldn't be alone in such thinking. Things have been this way for a very long time after all, and thus mutually beneficial for all   parties   involved.

The story continues in YOU SEE THE MONSTER, the Audible USA hit, available in Kindle, paperback and audiobook formats NOW!

YOU SEE THE MONSTER

The sound hits Guy in some low, forgotten part of his psyche - a part of him that understands the truth about shadows. The part of him that knows the deep, dark truth behind fairy stories and myths.

Guy is about to finish writing his breakthrough online article. He overheard the story by chance in a pub and it's guaranteed to go viral - all he needs to do is persuade the World's Unluckiest Man to talk to him. His best friend Larry's quest for killer clickbait material has led him to a recently appeared shanty town in Glasgow, where he finds some kind of urban voodoo cult. Ex-cop Sam has already come face-to-face with the terrifying force behind both these phenomena, but he's been trying to put it out of his mind.

When Larry is killed in inexplicably gruesome circumstances, Guy knows he's also a target. The evidence of malevolent power is suddenly proliferating - but why now? Together, Sam and Guy enter a shadow world of ancient monsters and modern curses, in a battle to figure out the rules of the game and bring them to the light before it's far too late.

From the best-selling author of the *Stone Man* series, *You See the Monster* is for fans of contemporary horror books at their most darkly inventive: a chilling, high-concept fable for our times.

Also by Luke Smitherd:
WEIRD. DARK.
PRAISE FOR *WEIRD. DARK.*:

"WEIRD and DARK, yes, but more importantly . . . exciting and imaginative. Whether you've read his novels and are already a fan or these short stories are your first introduction to Smitherd's work, you'll be blown away by the abundance of ideas that can be expressed in a small number of pages." - Ain't It Cool News.com

Luke Smitherd is bringing his unique brand of strange storytelling once again, delivered here in an omnibus edition that collects four of his weirdest and darkest tales:

MY NAME IS MISTER GRIEF: what if you could get rid of your pain immediately? What price would you be prepared to pay?

HOLD ON UNTIL YOUR FINGERS BREAK: a hangover, a forgotten night out, old men screaming in the street, and a mystery with a terrible, terrible answer . . .

THE MAN ON TABLE TEN: he has a story to tell you. One that he has kept secret for decades. But now, the man on table ten can take no more, and the knowledge - as well as the burden - is now yours.

EXCLUSIVE story, THE CRASH: if you put a dent in someone's car, the consequences can be far greater - and more strange - than you expect.

Available in both paperback and Kindle formats on Amazon and as an audiobook on Audible.

Also By Luke Smitherd:
A HEAD FULL OF KNIVES

Martin Hogan is being watched all the time. He just doesn't know it yet. It started a long time ago too, even before his wife died. Before he started walking every day.

Before the walks became an attempt to find a release from the whirlwind that his brain has become. He never walks alone, of course, although his 18-month old son and his faithful dog, Scoffer, aren't the greatest conversationalists.
Then the walks become longer. Then the *other* dog starts showing up. The big white one, with the funny looking head. The one that sits and watches Martin and his family as they walk away.

All over the world, the first attacks begin. The Brotherhood of the Raid make their existence known; a leaderless group who randomly and inexplicably assault both strangers and loved ones without explanation.

Martin and the surviving members of his family are about to find that these events are connected. Caught at the center of the world as it changes beyond recognition, Martin will be faced with a series of impossible choices ... but how can an ordinary and broken man figure out the unthinkable? What can he possibly do with a head full of knives?

Luke Smitherd (author of the Amazon bestseller THE STONE MAN and IN THE DARKNESS, THAT'S WHERE I'LL KNOW YOU) asks you once again to consider what you would do in his unusual and original novel. A HEAD FULL OF KNIVES is a supernatural mystery that will not only change the way you look at your pets forever, but will force you to decide the fate of the world when it lies in your hands.

Available in both paperback and Kindle formats on Amazon and as an audiobook on Audible

Also By Luke Smitherd:
How to be a Vigilante: A Diary

In the late 1990s, a laptop was found in a service station just outside of Manchester. It contained a digital journal entitled 'TO THE FINDER: OPEN NOW TO CHANGE YOUR LIFE!' Now, for the first time, that infamous diary is being published in its entirety.

It's 1998. The Internet age is still in its infancy. Google has just been founded.
Eighteen-year-old supermarket shelf-stacker Nigel Carmelite has decided that he's going to become a vigilante.

There are a few problems: how is he going to even find crime to fight on the streets of Derbyshire? How will he create a superhero costume - and an arsenal of crime-fighting weaponry - on a shoestring budget? And will his history of blackouts and crippling social inadequacy affect his chances?

This is Nigel's account of his journey; part diary, part deluded self-help manual, tragically comic and slowly descending into what is arguably Luke Smitherd's darkest and most violent novel.

What do you believe in? And more importantly . . .should you?

Available in both paperback and Kindle formats on Amazon and as an audiobook on Audible.

Current list of Smithereens with Titles

Emil: King of the Macedonian Smithereens; Neil Novita: Chief Smithereen of Brooklyn; Jay McTyier: Derby City Smithereen; Ashfaq Jilani: Nawab of the South East London Smithereens; Jason Jones: Archduke of lower Alabama; Betty Morgan: President of Massachusetts Smithereens; Malinda Quartel Qoupe: Queen of the Sandbox (Saudi Arabia); Marty Brastow: Grand Poobah of the LA Smithereens; John Osmond: Captain Toronto; Nita Jester Franz: Goddess of the Olympian Smithereens; Angie Hackett: Keeper of Du; Colleen Cassidy: The Tax Queen Smithereen; Jo Cranford: The Cajun Queen Smithereen; Gary Johnayak: Captain of the Yellow Smithereen; Matt Bryant: the High Lord Dominator of South Southeast San Jose; Rich Gill: Chief Executive Smithereen - Plymouth Branch; Sheryl: Shish the Completely Sane Cat Lady of Silver Lake; Charlie Gold: Smithereen In Chief Of Barnet; Gord Parlee: Prime Transcendent Smithereen, Vancouver Island Division; Erik Hundstad: King Smithereen of Norway(a greedy title but I've allowed it this once); Sarah Hirst: Official Smithereen Knitter of Nottingham; Christine Jones: Molehunter Smithereen Extraordinaire, Marcie Carole Spencer: Princess Smithereen of Elmet, Angela Wallis: Chief Smithereen of Strathblanefield, Melissa Weinberger: Cali Girl Smithereen, Maria Batista: Honorable One and Only Marchioness Smithereen of Her House, Bash Badawi: Lead Smithereen of Tampa, Fl, Bully: Chief Smithereen of Special Stone Masonry Projects, Mani: Colonel Smithereen of London, Drewboy of the Millwall Smithereens, Empress Smithereen of Ushaw Moor, Cate1965: Queen Smithereen of her kitchen, Amy Harrison: High Priestess Smithereen of Providence County (RI), and Neil Stephens: Head of the Woolwellian Sheep Herding Smithereens, Chief Retired British Smithereen Living in Canada, L and M Smith - Lord Smithereen of Gray Court, SC, Jude, Lady Smithereen of Wellesbourne, Joan, the Completely Inappropriate Grandma of Spring Hill, Vaughan Harris - Archbishop of Badass, Rebekah Jones Viceroy Smithereen of Weedon Bec, Avon Perry - Duchess of Heartbreak and Woe, Dawnie, Lady cock knocker of whangarei land, Renee - Caffeinated Queen of the Texas Desert, Carly - Desk Speaker Fake Plant Monitor AirPods Glass of Vimto, John Bate - Infringeur Smithereen of Blackpool, Stephen Stewart - Smithereen of Outer Space, DWFG "Abbess of the Craggy Island Smithereen High Order, Dave Carver - Chief Smithereen of Big Orange Country, Drucilla Buckley - Queen Mawmaw Smithereen, Adele - Mistress of her house and all within it (even the cat) Spanish chapter, David Coykendall – Twixton - A Necessary Evil, Tracey Galloway-Lindsey - Joffers the bastard a spaceworm in the Shire Smithereen, and Jameson Skaife - Smithereen Caped Captain of Chicago and Pablo Starscraper - Purple Lord of Dorchester

Printed in Great Britain
by Amazon

13155511R00284